DAISY LANE

DAISY LANE

Pamela Grandstaff

Books by Pamela Grandstaff:

Rose Hill Mystery Series:

Rose Hill

Morning Glory Circle

Iris Avenue

Peony Street

Daisy Lane

Lilac Avenue

Hollyhock Ridge

Sunflower Street

Viola Avenue

Pumpkin Ridge

Copyright © 2012 Pamela Grandstaff
All rights reserved
ISBN-10: 1480049557
EAN-13: 978-1480049550

For My Mother

CHAPTER ONE – FRIDAY

He knew he was dying. There was not much time left. The pain in his chest was worse now, arriving with the smallest exertion. The bus on which he was riding pulled into a small parking lot in front of a closed fast food restaurant and wheezed to a stop. He hoped he would be able to stand. After watching him struggle, a kind man across the aisle helped him. The kind man said something that of course Nino could not understand, but he nodded and said, "Grazia."

He grasped a small parcel, the one he had kept safe on his flight over the ocean and during the long journey from Newark, New Jersey. His great-great-grandson, who had helped him get his passport, had written out instructions in English for the airline representative, a cab driver, and the bus terminal personnel, so that everyone would know his great-great-grandfather did not understand English; so they could help him find a cab, find the bus terminal, and then find the right bus.

"Rose Hill," the old man said, over and over. His great-great-grandson had made him practice it. "I want to take the bus to Rose Hill, West Virginia. Please help me."

Everyone at home in Alghero who heard about this trip warned him about the thieves and murderers who loved nothing more than to rob and kill vulnerable old foreigners foolish enough to travel alone to America. Fortunately, he had been blessed with assistance from kind people every step of the way; proof, he believed, that God meant for him to make the trip to Rose Hill, to fulfill a promise made as a young man. Now he was finally here, and he was dying.

The bus driver looked concerned, but Nino smiled and waved him off. As the bus departed in a cloud of diesel fumes, he sat down in the bus shelter to rest, to catch his breath, and look around. Out of habit he patted his jacket

1

pocket and realized his wallet and passport must have fallen out. All he had left were his bus ticket and her letter.

'What do I need with all that now?' he thought to himself. 'Soon none of it will matter.'

He looked around at the town he had left so many years before. Of course, it was much changed, after 70 years anywhere would be, but some things remained the same. The bar named "The Rose and Thorn" was still there on the corner of Rose Hill Avenue and Peony Street. On paydays, he and his fellow countrymen had lifted many glasses of strong red wine in there. The building's facade had not changed at all, just aged. It was not open now, at four in the morning, or he would have gone in and purchased a drink to warm his bones.

It was so cold he could see his breath, the white vapor rising and dissipating in the crisp air. After the stuffy warmth of the bus, it was a shock to be so cold. He wished he had a cigarette; even after forty years he still missed them every day. He knew if he didn't get moving soon his joints would seize up. He held his cane in one hand and from the other the parcel dangled from the string tied around it. The effort it took to stand caused pain so sharp in his chest it took his breath away. For the first time, it also traveled down his arm. He knew what that meant. He was so close. Luckily it was all downhill from here.

He crossed Rose Hill Avenue, and when he reached the corner next to the bar, he could see the hulking brick buildings of the glassworks at the end of the street, down by the river. He kept that building as his focus as he slowly made his way down the hill. The houses were dark, smoke curled out of chimneys; a dog barked and the sound echoed off the hills across the river.

His great-great-grandson had done the research, so he knew she was still alive. The child had a romantic soul, much like his own. When they said goodbye at the airport, the young man had cried, knowing this farewell was the last one.

He knew she would have changed, as had he. She probably would not recognize him, but he hoped she would remember. Even if she rejected him, even if she didn't remember who he was, he would have kept his word. He had returned to her.

At the bottom of the hill, he could hear the low roar of the river, and the sharp wind off the water smelled just like it had so many years before. Memories assailed him, things he hadn't thought of in many decades. Bittersweet didn't begin to describe it. Heartbreaking did.

At the bottom of the hill, he turned right and stepped off the pavement onto a narrow gravel road. It was a challenge to keep his balance on the uneven, rutted path. There were no streetlights here, only the light from a full moon just about to disappear behind the hills to the west.

Out of the darkness, the shape of the house began to emerge, even larger than he remembered, and his memory was generous. His legs began to fail him. It seemed to take an hour to walk the last twenty feet.

When he reached the walkway to the front of the house, he could see in the moonlight that it had fallen into disrepair. The paint was peeling, and a few of the windows were boarded up. Surely she could not live in such a place, could not have fallen on such hard times.

It had once been the grandest house he had ever seen, although he had only been inside it once, on the day he left Rose Hill, ostensibly never to return. The iron gate protested with a screech as he opened it, and he noticed tall grass growing up through the cracks of the broken concrete path that led up to the stairs. There were maybe ten steps; there may as well have been a hundred.

He made it halfway up the stairs before the pain in his chest became so crushing he cried out. As he fell, he dropped his cane and his parcel. The steps were stone; he could feel every sharp edge as his body met them as a dead weight. He came to rest on his side but rolled over onto his back. The pain was so intense he became nauseated and

3

dizzy. He closed his eyes and braced himself for death. Then, to his amazement, the pain eased to a dull ache. He opened his eyes.

Upon the hillside, he could see streetlights and porch lights shining along with the many stars in the sky. The moon was behind the house in front of which he lay, so he could no longer see it. He wished he had thought to look at it one last time; just one more beautiful thing he had taken for granted and would never see again. Had he thought to say goodbye to the ocean, the blue sky, the sun? He had not.

He would miss so many things: birdsong before the sun rose, the dappled white, green and gold of sunlight falling through leaves, a blue sky so bright it hurt his eyes, the firm dirt beneath his feet, the buzzing of bees in the orchard, a cool evening breeze after a long day of work, babies overcome with laughter, a woman's sigh of contentment, an old song sung with friends, the smell of lemons, a sweet, juicy peach, a smiling dog. If these things did not exist elsewhere, how could it be called heaven?

There were footsteps in the house, the porch light came on, and the front door opened. He heard a young woman's voice, afraid, and then she was there, where he could see her long dark hair falling like a curtain on either side of her small face. A child's face. She spoke so kindly to him, but of course, he could not understand a word.

"Rose Hill," he said. "Please help me."

His blood had slowed in his veins, was no longer bringing warmth to his exposed skin; soon he would be as cold as the stone beneath him.

She touched his face, and the kindness that flowed out of her fingertips warmed his cheek. She talked in low, soothing tones.

'At least,' he thought, 'I was not alone. I had kind people to guide me clear up to the end.'

"Grazia," he said to the girl.

His body felt so heavy; he understood he would have to leave it behind. What had he come for? There was something he had meant to do before he went.

The young girl was holding his hand. She would not understand him, but he told her anyway:

"Tell Mary I came back for her. I kept my promise. Tell her I always thought of her. I never stopped loving her."

The pain disappeared. He looked out toward the gate and saw his mother and father waiting there. His mother reached out to him, said, "Come with us, Nino. Where have you been? We have waited so long to see you."

They looked just as they had the day he left Italy to come to America and work with his uncle in the glassworks. Behind them a crowd had gathered, family and friends who had all passed away over the years, leaving him alone with memories no one else could share.

It was surprisingly easy to leave behind the worn-out shell lying on the stairs as he went to the gate to join his family. It felt as if he were merely shrugging off a heavy coat.

"Tell us," his mother said. "How is everyone in Alghero? Did the baby get over her cold? Is Carlo going to marry that puta or go to school? How is little Salvatore? We are so proud of him; so smart, that child, so good to his mother and father."

It seemed to be bright daytime, and they were back home on the farm in the countryside outside Alghero, walking into the orchard across the road, where tables were set up for a family picnic under the trees. His uncles played music on a concertina and guitar. His grandmother greeted him warmly and offered him Lemoncelo, which she knew was his favorite. There was a feast on the table, made from recipes his grandmother had refused to divulge before she died. He was suddenly famished and looked forward to putting away large portions of everything.

There was his wife, Elizabetta, who had died in childbirth, holding the daughter they had lost in an influenza epidemic. She held out his daughter, the one he had grieved over for so many years, and he took her in his arms. The child grasped his ears and said, "Papa" in a delighted way. He kissed the child on the cheeks, over and over.

Every good old dog he had ever buried swarmed around his legs, begging for attention. Oh, to see them all again, those he was sure were lost forever, and not to have landed in the fiery hell his priest had predicted. This was heaven. This was all he could have hoped for.

"Tell us how everyone is," his great-grandmother said, after kissing him on both cheeks. "Is Carlo really going to marry that hussy?"

He looked down at his strong arms and hands holding his daughter; his body now that of a young man. He had forgotten what it was like to feel so well, with vast reservoirs of strength and energy. Vitality was once again pulsing through his veins, returning his desire to embrace, to kiss, to reach out and connect with his family.

"I have so much to tell you," he said, "but you had better feed me first."

"You always did have the strongest appetite," Elizabetta said with a knowing smile, as he grabbed her around the waist and squeezed her. "For everything."

The old man was speaking a language Grace could not understand, except for "Rose Hill" and the name "Mary." Then he no longer seemed aware of her presence as he looked out toward the road as if seeing someone Grace could not see. He smiled and seemed glad to see whoever it was.

They had no phone to use to call for help. Grace knew if she woke her grandfather he would only be angry that some stranger had the gall to land on their front porch and go out of his head. He would speak cruelly to the man and refuse to go to a neighbor for help; that would be seeking charity. Plus this would all be Grace's fault somehow, just like it always was.

The man's voice grew softer; his words became whispery and inaudible. She knew she must hurry.

Grace considered which neighbor she should go to and settled on Cal Fischer, who was a volunteer fireman when he wasn't working at the power plant. His wife was always kind to Grace, and their dog liked her. They lived at the other end of Lotus Avenue, across from the train depot.

"I'll be right back," she said to the man, and let go of his limp hand.

She hurried down the steps, across the path, and out to the lane, where the gravel-covered dirt track led to Lotus Avenue. From there she could see Ed Harrison's truck, with her schoolmate Tommy throwing papers from the back. Ed waved to her and Grace waved wildly back. She didn't shout for fear that her grandfather would hear. She ran toward the truck as Ed stopped and Tommy jumped down from the back.

Ed used his cell phone to call the EMS while Tommy ran back to the porch with her.

"Be quiet," she told him, "or my grandfather will hear."

She didn't look for his reaction to this command; she didn't want to see it.

Tommy took off his jacket and laid it over the man's chest. The man was murmuring but not saying anything intelligible. Grace sat down on the steps next to him and took his hand in hers.

"Help is on the way," she told him. "Someone is coming."

"Who is he?" Tommy whispered.

Grace shook her head and shrugged.

"I think he might be speaking Italian," she said.

The man turned his head and looked at Grace. His eyes seemed to clear with awareness of where he was and what was happening.

7

"Sto morendo," he said. "Io non ho paura di andare."

"What's he saying?" Tommy asked.

"I don't know," said Grace, "but he sounds like Matt Delvecchio's father."

Grace was looking into the old man's brown eyes, so she was surprised when they were fiercely alive one second, and in the next simply were not. Whatever animating force had lived behind those eyes had gone; whether to arrive somewhere else or merely to dissipate in the air like smoke from a chimney, Grace could only wonder. Grace's grandmother would have said his soul had gone to heaven or hell, depending upon the manner in which the man lived. On this subject Grace was undecided. There was Edgar to consider, who seemed to be neither here nor there, wherever there was. Blasphemous thoughts, she knew, best kept to herself.

The disappearance of life from the man's eyes was followed by a long, gurgling intake of breath, an expulsion of air from the now unoccupied space, and then his chest did not rise again. Grace felt so sorry for the man, dying with strangers around him, that she gave his limp hand one more sympathetic squeeze before she lay it down on his still chest.

"He's dead," Grace said to Tommy, who was crouched on the steps just below her.

His eyes were wide as he looked from the man to Grace and back again.

"Are you sure?" he asked.

Grace heard the siren and cursed inwardly, which was the only safe way to do it.

"You should go," Grace said. "My grandpa will be out here any minute, and he won't like you being here."

"I'm staying," Tommy said, frowning at her. "Your grandpa doesn't scare me."

"He should," Grace said.

The front screen door hit the outer wall of the porch with a bang that sounded like a gunshot. Tommy, startled, tipped over backward and tumbled down the cement stairs to land on the walkway, just as Ed came in through the gate. Ed helped him up and dusted him off.

"What in tarnation is going on out here?" Grace's grandfather roared. "What have you done now, Grace?"

Grace scooted away from the dead man.

"He's dead," she said, without looking at her grandfather. "He walked up here, fell down, and died."

Ed came forward.

"I called the EMS," Ed said. "They're on the way."

"Who in the blazes is it?" Grandpa demanded. "Grace? Do you know this man?"

Grace shook her head, still looking at the steps in front of her rather than meet his gaze. Eye contact would be considered a challenge to his authority, an insult to his superiority.

"No, sir," she said. "I heard a noise, so I came outside."

"How'd you two get involved?" Grandpa demanded of Ed.

Ed came up the stairs, checked the man for a pulse, and then stood between the body and Grace. Grace looked up at him, willed him with her eyes not to betray what she had done. Ed looked at her thoughtfully and then at her grandfather.

"I saw him walk out this way, so I followed him," he said. "It seemed suspicious to me. Neighbors have to look out for each other."

"Hmph," her grandfather said, which meant he believed it even if he didn't like it.

Ed looked down at Grace and winked.

The EMS arrived and Graced backed up onto the porch. She inched her way into the far corner, where she stood in the shadow of the overgrown hedge.

"Get him out of here," her grandfather said to the EMS workers. "He's nothing to do with me and mine."

Police Chief Scott Gordon arrived and conferred with Ed before addressing Grace's grandfather.

"No one you know?" the police chief asked her grandfather.

"No!" bellowed Grace's grandfather. "Probably some tramp, looking for a handout. Now that this country's gone to hell in a handbasket they'll come creeping, along with the drug dealers and prostitutes. I have to keep my gun loaded and one eye open, so I don't get murdered in my sleep."

He held up his shotgun, and Grace was impressed at how quickly Scott leaped to the top of the stairs and helped Grandpa lower the gun.

"No need for that," Scott said. "Let's just stay out of the way and let these people do their jobs."

"You can't come onto my property and tell me to do a dad-gum thing," Grandpa said. "I know my rights."

Grace's grandfather, Jacob Branduff, was tall and gaunt, with a scraggly long beard and wisps of white hair floating up from his balding head. His old-fashioned glasses might have made him look like a skinny Saint Nick, but his demeanor prevented anyone from making that mistake more than once. He had on his nightshirt and overalls, his swollen feet stuck in tattered slippers. His feet were so swollen he couldn't wear any of his shoes. When he didn't have on his slippers, he had on ancient gumboots.

"There's no need for that, Mr. Branduff," Scott said to him, in a calm, reasonable voice. "As soon as they can get him off your porch they'll leave you in peace."

The EMTs lifted the man's body onto a gurney, secured it with straps, and carried it down the stairs.

"That's done then, so you all get on out of here," Grandpa said. "All of you."

"I need to ask Grace some questions," Scott said.

"You'll do no such thing," Grandpa said. "Grace! Dad-blasted girl. Where are you? Get yourself in the house and stay there. Do as I tell you."

Grace skittered around behind him and slid in through the doorway.

"I can do it now or later," Scott said, "but it will have to be done."

"If you bring a warrant down here, you can take her to jail," Jacob said. "Lock her up and throw away the key, for all I care. It'll save me her room and board. Otherwise, leave us alone."

Grandpa went in the house, slammed both doors behind him and yelled, "Grace! Fix me some coffee!"

Scott left the porch and met Ed and Tommy in the lane, where the EMTs were just closing the doors to the ambulance.

"No ID on him," one of the EMTs said. "Just these."

He handed Scott a bus ticket and a folded piece of paper so old it was soft and coming apart at the folds. Scott wanted to have gloves on when he examined it, so he dropped it into a plastic bag and put it in the squad car.

"I've never seen the man before," Ed said to Scott.

"Grace said he sounded like Matt Delvecchio's dad," Tommy said. "He might be Italian."

"I'll call the bus company," Scott said. "What are the chances I'll be able to talk to Grace, do you think?"

"Slim to none," Ed said.

"Her grandpa is mean," Tommy said. "Since her grandma died Grace is not allowed to do anything but go to school and work in the greenhouse."

"Isn't she a friend of Charlotte's?" Scott asked. "I used to see her over at Ava's B&B all the time."

"Not since Charlotte's dad came back," Tommy said. "After that Grace wasn't allowed to go over there anymore."

"That's been over three years, now," Ed said. "Poor girl."

"Charlotte doesn't want to be friends with Grace anymore, anyway," Tommy said. "She has new friends now."

11

Scott noted Tommy's heartbroken expression. It looked like Grace was not the only friend Charlotte had discarded. Scott had observed that Charlotte Fitzpatrick's recent change in attitude and appearance had developed when she started at the Pendleton Consolidated High School this past fall. He and Ed exchanged looks but no more was said about that.

"Does Grace have any other family members?" Scott asked.

"Grace's grandmother died two years ago," Ed said, "from cancer."

"Grace's mom killed herself back when we were in grade school," Tommy said. "She was kind of crazy. She came to school in her nightgown once and tried to take Grace out of class, but the teacher wouldn't let her. Grace's grandma had to come and get her."

"I seem to remember her mother's official cause of death was an accidental overdose. There was some talk of mental illness, but their church didn't believe in medical treatment for anything," Ed said. "She might have been self-medicating."

"It's handy having a newspaper editor as a friend," Scott said. "How long ago did her mother die?"

"Must be five, six years ago," Ed said.

"Jacob Branduff would not be anyone's first choice to be a young girl's guardian," Scott said. "It might be time to have a social worker look in."

"Whoever does should wear a bulletproof vest," Ed said.

CHAPTER TWO – SATURDAY

On Saturday at noon, someone knocked on the door. It was a sound so rarely heard that it made Grace's heart race. Outside on the porch stood a woman whose house her grandmother used to clean. She was one of those who was never pleased and did not mind insisting that an old woman who walked with a stoop, whose hands were gnarled with arthritis, scrub her floors by hand rather than mop them from a standing position.

Although Mrs. Larson was a tall, strapping woman with strong features, she dressed as if she were petite and girlish. She wore her mousy brown hair in a playful ponytail with a bow, had on a twinset and pearls with her man-sized capris, and a tiny tailored handbag hung over her arm. Her choice of clothing was so mismatched to her physique that Grace felt a stab of pity for her.

The woman was looking around with an expression of disgust until she saw Grace. Then she fixed a big, insincere smile on her face.

"Hello," Mrs. Larson said. "You and your grandfather weren't on the list for a hunger mission dinner, but we had one extra, so we thought you might enjoy it."

Grace was not fooled by the concerned look on her face. Her mouth may have been smiling, but her eyes were still mean. She was holding a basket that Grace knew held all the elements of a traditional Sunday dinner. She could smell salty ham and yeasty rolls. Mrs. Larson kept looking around Grace, trying to see inside the house.

"Thank you," Grace said, firmly holding the screen door open only six inches. "But it would be better if the food went to someone who needed it. We've got plenty to eat."

"Are you sure?" Mrs. Larson said. "It will only go to waste if you and your grandfather don't take it."

"I'm sure someone up Possum Holler could use it," Grace said.

"Well, I'm not so sure of that," Mrs. Larson said. "If you ask me, they're living high on the welfare hog out there. I wouldn't step one foot up that holler if my life depended upon it. Some meth addict would probably kill me for my pocketbook."

There, finally, was the facial expression that matched the mean eyes; Grace was gratified to see it. Mrs. Larson then had trouble changing it back to concern. Grace decided vicious disapproval must be the woman's dominant expression and any other was hard to maintain for very long.

"It's a shame about this house," the older woman said, with a look of contempt. "When my mother was a young girl, it was the Rodefeffer's home; one of the finest in town."

Grace knew better than to reply. With someone like Mrs. Larson no matter what you said it would be wrong somehow.

"I'm surprised it wasn't condemned after the flood," Mrs. Larson said.

Grace just looked at her, willing her expression to be vacant and stupid.

"Well," Mrs. Larson sniffed. "If you really won't accept it, I guess I'll be going."

"Thanks," Grace said.

Grace closed the screen door and locked it with the hook and eye. She was just about to close the interior door when Mrs. Larson spoke.

"We're all concerned about you, Grace," she said. "We're praying for you."

Grace couldn't suppress her shudder.

"Good-bye," Grace said.

"God bless you," Mrs. Larson said, but her back was already turned as Grace shut the interior door.

"Who was it?" her grandfather said as she returned to the kitchen.

14

"A church lady delivering dinners to the poor," Grace said and took her seat at the table. "I told her we didn't need it."

There was an iron skillet, blackened with age, sitting on the table between them, with two biscuits left of the four she'd prepared. Grandpa was buttering his with margarine from a purloined fast food container, the bright yellow grease clinging to his beard.

"Hah!" he said, his mouth full of food. "Makes them feel better, I guess, to feed poor people three days per year and then spit on them the other 362."

Grace took a bite of her own canned biscuit, a recent past-sell-date bargain from the IGA, and tried not to think about the delicious smells that had emanated from the basket Mrs. Larson had offered.

"It was Mrs. Larson," she said. "Grandma used to clean her house."

"One of the worst of the bunch," her grandfather said. "Her father was a falling down drunk but to hear her tell it, he was a saint in human raiment."

"Her son goes to my school," Grace said.

"A chip off the old block, I'd wager," Grandpa said. "Best you stay away from that lot. Too good for the likes of us."

From somewhere upstairs a door slammed, and a cold breeze blew down the hall and through the kitchen.

"Edgar hates strangers comin' around," Grandpa said.

After breakfast Grace did the washing up while Grandpa worked in the greenhouses. He had sold many dozens of tulips, daffodils, and lilies around Easter time, and now he was selling roses, peonies, and irises. There were no signs out front advertising his business, but still, business owners and local people came down to the greenhouse to make their purchases. He also sold flowers at the IGA in town, and in the farmer's market during the summer.

Grace pulled on a sweater and went out the back door, pausing outside the entrance to the second greenhouse only long enough to call out, "I'm going," before pulling an old red wagon out of the bushes and up to the first greenhouse. There she loaded tall zinc buckets full of cellophane-wrapped flowers into the wagon, wedging them together between the wooden guard rails on each side. When Grace was a small child, her grandmother used to pull her to the grocery store in the same wagon. Grace remembered the safe, happy feeling she had being pulled back home amongst the paper grocery bags. It had been her job to hold the carton of eggs so they did not break.

As she passed by the front of their house, she looked up and tried to imagine it the way Mrs. Larson had described it. As far back as Grace could remember the white paint on the trim had been pealing, the mortar between the bricks had been crumbling, and the whole building was sagging in the middle. The 100-year-old Victorian had three stories and an attic, plus multiple gables, porches, and turrets; that would take a lot of paint.

'And a lot of money,' she thought to herself.

Grace Branduff had lived in the house, seated on the bank of the Little Bear River, her whole fifteen years. Before they died, her mother and grandmother had lived there too. Her Aunt Lucy had run off as a teenager. Her father, whom she had never met, lived in another state, with a family of his own.

Just down the street was the old Rodefeffer Glassworks, with only the railroad tracks between it and the river. The Rodefeffers had built the huge Victorian house when there were very few other homes in the town. The Eldridges, who derived their fortune from timber and coal, had also built Eldridge College, and their mansion was high on the hill on Morning Glory Avenue.

For many decades the Eldridges and Rodefeffers were competing scions in what was briefly a boomtown. The glassworks closed after the proliferation of cheap, imported glass took over the American market in the mid-twentieth century, and the Eldridges sold their mine interests after a series of horrific safety violations resulted in the deaths of fifty-two miners. After that, the Rodefeffers moved up to Morning Glory Avenue to live alongside the Eldridges.

Recently Grace had heard a rumor that someone had purchased the glassworks and was going to turn it into a bicycle factory. Some people were excited about the prospect of new jobs. Grace didn't get excited about rumors. She rarely got excited about anything. In her experience, the optimistic combination of enthusiasm and hope was a bet that rarely paid off.

The smoothest route to the IGA lay down Lotus Avenue and up Pine Mountain Road. Grace used the street instead of the sidewalks, bunched up as they were by the tree roots growing beneath them and deep caved-in places from mine subsidence.

Just as she started to turn uphill, she saw a small child running down the narrow alley next to the brick wall surrounding Eldridge College, a dirt track called Daisy Lane. The child left the alley where it ended and continued on downhill toward the river, followed by a pack of barking dogs.

Grace hitched the front wheels of the wagon over the curb and took off at a run.

"Hey!" she yelled. "Stop!"

Her heart was pumping blood so hard her head hurt by the time she reached the alley. As she flew down over the wet grass of the hill that sloped toward the river, she slid and almost lost her balance. When she righted herself and looked up, the boy had disappeared.

"Oh no," she gasped, her lungs heaving.

He couldn't have reached the fast-moving water that quickly, could he?

The dogs were in a stand-off beneath a gnarled and twisted sycamore tree that had been half uprooted by a flood three years before. As a consequence of this upheaval, the limbs on one side were low enough for a small child to clamber up into the tree, which is exactly what the small boy had done. With relief, Grace saw his bare feet dangling from the limb he now clung to.

A Siberian husky and a border collie had their backs to the tree, fending off a pack of three mangy-looking strays. Grace grabbed a rotting limb off the ground and advanced on the strays, hollering and swinging. When they turned, snarling and snapping, the other two took advantage of their divided attention and attacked from the rear. Two injured strays yelped and took off down the river bank toward the rail trail. The third one bared its teeth at Grace and advanced on her.

The husky took a run and lunged at the dog, rolling it over while the border collie stood his ground beneath the tree, guarding the child. Grace sidled around and then backed downhill toward the tree as she watched the two fighting dogs. The skinny stray didn't have the strength to fend off the well-fed, muscular husky, and without his buddies to back him up, he soon found himself pinned by the neck to the ground, helplessly flailing his legs.

"Are you okay?" Grace asked the child as she got close enough to the tree to see him.

She was afraid to get too close because the fur on border collie's spine was standing on end, and he was still licking his bared teeth in the direction of the fight. He was also making an anxious moaning sound punctuated by short barks. The child had his legs wrapped around a twisted limb, his bare feet and ankles scratched and bleeding from clambering up over the peeling bark of the tree. His eyes were wide, and his face was flushed, but he seemed more excited than scared.

"Me Sammy," he said. "Me bweedin' but me not hurt."

From somewhere uphill, a man whistled and yelled, "Jax, leave it!"

Grace looked up to see a man loping awkwardly down Daisy Lane. Jax gave the stray one last shake before he let go. The wounded dog took off after his buddies down the rail trail.

The border collie made as if to chase the stray but the man yelled, "Wally, down!" and the dog immediately lay down beneath the tree.

"Him's me's daddy," Sammy said. "Him's name's Sam."

Sam slowed his stilted, running walk and finally stood, a few yards away at the end of the alley. He put his hands on his knees and bent over to catch his breath.

"The grass is wet," Grace called to him. "Be careful."

Sam came down the wet hill sideways, grimacing as he did so.

"Daddy!" yelled Sammy as he clambered back down the tree and ran to him. "Them's dogs fighted Jax and Wally! Me went up the tree; me bweedin but me not hurt!"

Sam swung his son up into his arms and walked slowly toward Grace. She could tell by the wince that shot across his expression, the pronounced limp, and the sweat that ran down his face that he was in pain but trying not to show it.

The dogs danced around Sam as he reached Grace.

"I saw it happening," he said, "but I couldn't get to him in time."

Grace saw the anguished pain in the father's eyes before he looked away, blinking rapidly to gain control of his emotions. She didn't know what to say. She felt tongue-tied in the presence of so much feeling, so much love.

"You's the flower lady," Sammy said to her. "You's gots a wagon like me's."

Sam stuck out his hand.

"I've seen you around town, but I don't think we've been formally introduced. I'm Sam Campbell, and this is my high-blood-pressure-inducing son, Sammy."

When Grace shook his hand, she could feel it trembling. Sam was still sweating profusely, and it seemed to be an effort for him to stand upright and hold his son. He swayed a bit and reached out to steady himself against the branch Sammy had been clinging to.

"I'm Grace Branduff," she said. "My grandfather owns Branduff's Greenhouse."

She wanted to reach out and take the child from his arms, to give the man some relief, but she was afraid to be so forward.

Impulsively, she said, "Sammy, would you like to help me deliver my flowers to the IGA? You could help me pull the wagon."

"Yes, yes!" Sammy said and wiggled down out of his father's arms.

To Grace's surprise, Sammy grabbed her hand, looked up at her and said, "Me do it! C'mon!"

"What can I do to help you?" she asked Sam.

He laughed a short, humorless laugh and eased himself down to the base of the tree so that his back was against it. His face turned pale as he adjusted his legs, so they stretched out before him.

"Just look after Sammy," he said. "I'll call my wife to come pick me up."

It was then that she noticed the knees of his jeans were stained dark with moisture, and she wondered if it was sweat or blood. Where his ankles should have been metal rods were connected to prosthesis inside his hiking boots. Grace felt herself staring, trying to figure out how much of his legs were mechanical, and quickly looked up.

"I can stay with you if you like," Grace said, "just until she gets here."

Sam shook his head.

"I'll be alright," he said. "If you'll wait with Sammy at the IGA, Hannah and I will pick him up."

"I won't take my eyes off of him," Grace said. "I promise."

"I saw you," Sam said. "That was crazy; you could have been mauled to death."

"I didn't stop to think," Grace said. "I just wanted to help."

"I believe you," Sam said. "I think he'll be in good hands until we can pick him up."

"C'mon!" Sammy said as he pulled Grace's hand. "No talking!"

"What if those dogs come back?" Grace said.

Sam pulled up his work shirt so Grace could see a gun in a holster strapped to one side of his chest.

"I'll be fine," he said.

Grace shook her head, thinking, 'Men and their guns.'

"All right," she told Sammy. "Let's go."

Grace looked back as they reached the top of the wet, grass-covered bank and stepped onto Daisy Lane. Sam was talking on his cell phone. She hated to leave him but somehow thought he would be more comfortable alone. He obviously didn't want Sammy to see how badly he was hurt.

Sammy was determined to pull the wagon all by himself, but Grace convinced him to help her do it instead. The two dogs, now looking more like harmless house pets than two deadly killers, kept running up ahead and then waiting, all the while keeping a 360-degree watch for further trouble.

"Those dogs are like your bodyguards," she told Sammy.

"Them's my friends," Sammy said. "Them's like me."

21

"They love you," Grace said. "There's a big difference."

"Why?" Sammy asked, in that way that a young child will persist in doing.

"Someone who just likes you would feel sorry for you if something bad happened, but they would never risk their lives for you. Jax and Wally fought those dogs because they love you; they were saving your life."

"Like superheroes?" Sammy said.

"Exactly," Grace said.

"Me likes superheroes," Sammy said, and then seemed to think about this.

Matt Delvecchio, the owner of the IGA, gave Sammy and Grace both a box of juice to drink while they waited for Sammy's mother. When she finally arrived, driving an old pickup truck with Sam in the passenger seat, Sammy waved and said, "That's my Hannah," to Grace. "Her's a superhero, too. Her loves me mostest best."

Hannah got out and walked around the truck to where they sat on the loading dock. Grace jumped down and then helped Sammy get down.

Sam rolled the truck window down and said, "Grace, this is my wife, Hannah; Hannah, this is Grace."

Hannah wore work boots with slouchy socks, khaki shorts, and a faded Little Bear Books sweatshirt. The woman was not much taller than Grace, and Grace was tiny for her age. A dark blonde ponytail stuck out from the back of her baseball cap, and she wore no makeup on her plain face. To Grace's surprise, Hannah walked up and grabbed her in a tight hug. The woman's body felt hard and wiry, and her hug almost knocked the breath out of Grace. When Hannah let go, she had tears in her eyes, which she quickly blinked away.

"Thank you, Grace," she said. "Just when I think Sammy has run through all nine of his lives he survives another day due to a good egg like you. You must think I'm an awful mother, losing track of him like that. I swear he's part husky and part hobo; he just likes to roam."

"I think Jax and Wally wouldn't let anything happen to him," Grace said.

"Time to go," Hannah told Sammy, but he hugged Grace's legs and refused to let go.

"But her loves me!" he protested. "Her's my superhero!"

Grace laughed, feeling embarrassed, as Hannah pried her son loose.

"Me bweeded but me okay," he told his mother. "Me fighted the bad dogs and me winned!"

"Oh Sammy, you're gonna be the death of me," Hannah told him as she hugged him tightly. "Your grandmother probably thinks you're still in her TV room watching cartoons."

"Her's in a nap," Sammy said. "Her's gots a headache."

"Come up to the farm," Sam said to Grace. "Anytime; you're always welcome."

"Thanks," Grace said as he rolled his window back up.

"Wow," Hannah said to Grace. "You really made an impression. He doesn't invite just anybody."

The two dogs had already hopped up into the back of the truck as if eagerly anticipating a ride. As the family drove away, Grace found she was sorry to see them leave. It was unusual for her to feel attached to anyone, but there for a few moments, she had felt almost like she was part of their little family.

"How fun it would be to have Sammy as a little brother,' she thought.

Grocery store owner Matt Delvecchio opened the back door to the loading dock just moments after she rang the bell as if he were standing there waiting.

"Exciting morning, Gracie?" he said.

He was a tall, jovial man with dark curly hair shot with gray. He wore wire-rimmed glasses and a too-short tie with his short-sleeved shirt. He was one of the kindest people Grace knew and the only person who called her "Gracie."

"These sure are some beauties," he said, as she unloaded the zinc vases into a grocery cart. "Hold on a sec, and I'll get your money."

Grace waited outside the back door until Matt returned with an envelope full of cash.

"The weeks before and after Easter were really good," he said. "Almost as good as Valentine's Day."

"Thank you," said Grace, as she stuck the envelope in her back pocket without opening it, and turned to go.

"Hey, Gracie," Matt said. "I've got some dented cans and open box items I was just about to toss if you want them."

Grace smiled to herself as she turned around. Matt was always saving things for her, and she suspected he dropped a few things on her behalf as well. He handed her a bag full of various cans and packages.

"Thanks, Matt," she said.

"As soon as you turn sixteen you're coming to work here, right?" he asked. "You've got a birthday coming up."

"I know," Grace said. "If Grandpa will let me."

"Don't you go working for anyone else," he called out as she left. "Remember, I have first dibs."

Grace smiled and waved to him.

Taking the wagon back down Pine Mountain Road didn't require pulling; it was more holding on tightly to keep it from barreling down the hill into the barriers at the edge of the Little Bear River. At the intersection of Iris Avenue and Pine Mountain Road, she met Tommy, who was riding his bicycle. He stopped, hopped off, and walked next to her.

"Scott found out the old man's name," he said. "He called the bus company. It was Nino something, and he was from Italy. You were right about that."

"Did Scott find out why he was here?" Grace asked.

"No," Tommy said. "He's still trying to find his family so he can let them know he died."

"Did they say why he died?"

"Heart attack," Tommy said. "It's kind of like a mystery, don't you think?"

"Yeah," Grace said. "I hope they figure it out."

"We could, like, investigate it ourselves," Tommy said. "Do you want to?"

"What could we do that they couldn't?" Grace said.

"Scott probably doesn't have time to do research," he said. "We could look up stuff on the Internet, maybe find his family."

"You know I don't have a computer," Grace said.

"We could use Ed's," Tommy said. "Or go up to the library and use theirs."

"I don't think I should get involved," Grace said.

"You mean your grandpa wouldn't like it," Tommy said.

Grace nodded.

"He wouldn't have to know," Tommy said. "We could use the library's computer today and the computer lab at school during lunch."

Grace looked at him to see if he was serious. This was a big commitment.

"We could do it that way," she said. "If you really want to."

"Awesome!" Tommy said. "Meet me up at the funeral home after dinner, and we'll go up to the library."

"If I can," Grace said.

Tommy hopped back on his bike, and said, "See ya later."

He had to stand up to pump the pedals hard enough to ascend the steep grade of Pine Mountain Road.

When Grace got home, she pulled the wagon around the side of the house and took the cash envelope into the second greenhouse. Her grandfather opened the envelope, took out a twenty-dollar bill and handed it to Grace. He seemed neither pleased nor displeased at the number of twenties that were left in the envelope.

"Matt said it was a good week," Grace said.

"You want more money?" he said. "Is that what you're trying to say?"

"No, sir," Grace said.

"Well, keep your tongue in your head," he said. "No one cares what you think."

"I turn sixteen next week," Grace said. "Matt offered me a job."

"No," her grandfather said. "I won't have you consorting with tourists and college students. I know how the world is and you're better off out of it than in it."

"I just thought it would be nice to have the extra money," she said.

"For alcohol and drugs, you mean," he said. "You are your mother's child."

"I need some clothes," Grace said. "Some shoes."

She looked down at her sneakers, which cramped her toes and had a hole in the sole that kept her socks perpetually soggy. The laces had broken and been re-tied so many times that there were more knots than string.

"If anyone deserves new shoes it's me," Grandpa said. "Who does all the work that keeps a roof over your head and food on the table? I'm not paying for you to dress up like a whore and get yourself in trouble."

"I don't want to do that," Grace said. "I want to save money for college."

"College?" he said. "Talk about a useless waste of money."

"But I think ..." Grace said before he cut her off.

"What did I just tell you about saying what you're thinking?" he said. "I forbid it, and that's all that needs to be said."

Grace took the wagon around the back of the house and stowed it under the steps. She carried the bag of groceries into the cold house, through the kitchen into the pantry, where she could unpack it without Grandpa watching her. In the bag were dented cans of vegetables and soups, open boxes of soda crackers, rice, oatmeal, and macaroni. Tucked away at the bottom of the box were six instant cocoa packets which were neither dented nor opened. Matt always included a treat, which she hid in a drawer under some tattered dish towels. If it weren't for Matt's contributions, Grace didn't know how she could feed herself and her grandfather on the twenty dollar weekly budget he allotted.

Grace got started on her Saturday chores, which included sweeping and mopping the rooms on the first floor. Grandpa only allowed hot water for baths on Sundays, so she had to boil the water to get it hot enough to clean. The sharp-smelling mixture of borax powder, vinegar, and baking soda reminded Grace of her grandmother, who had taught her everything she knew about housekeeping. The best part about cleaning was the feeling of hot water on her hands. The worst part was waiting for Grandpa to find fault with everything she did.

By lunchtime, the kitchen floor was dry so that she could make a meal for her grandfather. He never commented on what she cooked, only noisily ate whatever was provided after a long, verbal prostration to God that he wasn't worthy of the crumbs under His table. Meanwhile, Grace hovered in the doorway to the pantry in case he wanted more, which he rarely did. Afterward, he left his dishes on the table and returned to his work without a word of thanks.

Grace waited until he returned to the greenhouses before she ate her lunch. She knew from health class that she needed protein to grow, and because she had a vested interest in not always being the smallest person in her class, Grace ate a lot of peanut butter. She heated up some milk from the small cartons she had dug out of the trash cans behind the school cafeteria and made a cup of cocoa. As she sipped the warm liquid, Grace felt deep gratitude toward Matt Delvecchio for the hot chocolate; it filled her not only with physical warmth but a gratifying feeling of well-being. Not for the first time she wished Matt was her father. She liked how he called her "Gracie." She liked that he thought of her when she wasn't around and saved things for her.

After lunch Grace tidied the bedrooms and then washed her and her grandfather's clothing in an old washing machine that sat next to the sink in the kitchen. Grace filled the washtub halfway up with cold water and then added boiling water from the pan on the stove so that the Borax would have a shot at actually cleaning the mud off her grandfather's clothes. The washing cycle made the machine chug and rock. The dirty rinse water emptied through a long black hose into the deep enameled kitchen sink, causing a cloud of steam to rise in the chilly air and fog the windows.

Grace toured the second and third floors, but there was nothing to do but a bit of sweeping; since no one used those empty rooms, they were never very dirty. Grace heard some baby birds chirping in a nest under the eaves at the back of a second-floor bedroom. She hoped Grandpa, being a bit deaf, would not hear it and feel compelled to evict the feathered squatters.

Due to his bad arthritis, Grandpa didn't come upstairs, so it was one place Grace could go and feel a small sense of privacy. In warmer months it was a good place to read and do homework; with windows open on either side of the house a cool breeze off the river flowed through the rooms. That same "breeze" was currently rattling the wavy glass window panes and seeping in around their frames in a steady cold draft.

'Someday,' Grace thought, 'I will live in a house that is warm in the winter and cool in the summer, with as much hot water as I like whenever I like."

As she swept, she daydreamed about working for Matt Delvecchio and living in one of the apartments on Iris Avenue, where many Eldridge College students lived. She had imagined her apartment so many times that it seemed like a real place she actually visited. In this imaginary haven, she had a brown and black-striped kitten named "Tiger" who curled up in her lap and purred as she sat in a deep, cushy reading chair. Beside her on an end table was a reading lamp, a plate of cookies and a big mug of hot cocoa. Nowhere in this dream did her grandfather appear. There was only blissful, peaceful silence. This was her idea of heaven.

Her reverie was interrupted by the bang of the front door being flung open and her grandfather yelling, "Grace! Come down here this instant."

Grace's heart pounded as she dropped her broom and hurried to the head of the stairs.

"What in tarnation is this?" he bellowed.

In his hands, he held a small box tied with twine.

"I don't know," she said. "I've never seen it before."

"It was hidden in the bushes next to the front porch," he said. "Is this a gift from some boy? Is it from that paperboy you had over here?"

"It's not mine," she said as she came down the stairs. "I don't know where it came from."

"We'll just see about that," he said, glaring at her. "I know how these things start. Your mother and your aunt started the same way; sneaking around, meeting boys, hiding things."

He used his pen knife to cut the twine and tore off the brown paper wrap. Underneath was an expensive looking gift box, and inside was a glass swan. It was iridescent and sparkled in the sunlight streaming through the kitchen windows.

Grace's grandpa made a funny noise in his throat as if he were choking on something. His face became pale, and Grace was worried he was having one of his light-headed spells.

"Are you alright?' she asked. "Do you want to sit down?'

29

"There's nothing wrong with me," he said. "Mind your own business."

"It's beautiful," Grace said.

Grandpa thrust it at her and Grace took it.

"Get that out of my sight," he said. "If I ever see it again I'll smash it with a hammer."

"I wonder where it came from," she said. "It didn't get spoiled by the weather so it couldn't have been out there long. Do you think that old man dropped it when he fell?"

"Curiosity killed the cat," he said, pointing a finger at her. "Don't go putting your nose in where it doesn't belong, or somebody is liable to cut it off."

Grandpa stomped back outside, saying, "Clean up this mess," meaning the mud he had just tracked in on his gumboots.

Grace put the glass swan back in its box and hid it an old tin potato chip container in which she kept her savings. She kept the tin on top of the Hoosier cabinet in the butler's pantry. Over the five years since her grandmother had died, she had saved more than two hundred dollars out of the change left over from her grocery money, squirreled away a dollar or fifty cents at a time. She had spent this money a dozen different ways in her imagination, but generally, she thought of it as her rainy day fund, which was what her grandmother had called her stash kept in the same place. Her grandmother had used it to pay for things that her grandfather deemed too expensive; things like notebooks, pens, and other school supplies, new underwear and shoes.

As she mopped up the muddy boot prints in the front parlor, she thought about the gift the old man must have dropped. He must have been bringing it to Mary. After she was through cleaning, she dug out one of her school notebooks from her backpack and turned to the back, where she had written her notes about this morning. She had considered mailing the notes to Scott or giving them to Tommy to take to Ed. Instead, she now thought of them as the basis of their investigation into Nino's life.

She had written, phonetically, as many of the words he had said that she could remember, along with the names. Maybe she could ask Matt Delvecchio for help. His father Sal spoke Italian, and maybe he could help translate. Grace liked Sal, who was small and wrinkled, had twinkly eyes, smelled like black licorice, and called her "Bambina."

She was looking forward to spending lunches in the computer lab with Tommy rather than doing her homework in the library with the nerds, or outside in the cold air with the emos and Goths, or with the sleepy, friendly potheads who gathered under the football field bleachers. These socially peripheral outcasts were nice enough to her, but she didn't belong with them. She and Tommy, whom Charlotte had recently discarded for her new rich, popular friends, represented a club with membership requirements so specific they were the only two kids at school who qualified. They had barely spoken since the previous fall; now it seemed like they might be friends again.

Grace took out her homework, which she had to finish today as she was not allowed to do any work on Sunday, the Lord's day of rest, according to her grandfather. For English class this month the assignment was *Jane Eyre*, which Grace had read but not liked. How, she wondered, could anyone be attracted to Edward Rochester, a man with such a grandpa-like temperament who also turned out to be hiding a crazy wife? Grace had had enough experience with both domineering bullies and crazy women in her short life to have developed an aversion to both, even in great literature. Grace thought Jane should have thanked her lucky stars she escaped, and then looked for another governess job somewhere, working for sane people. Grace couldn't understand why, when Jane finally inherited enough money to take care of herself, she had gone back to find this cranky man.

Grace had already read next month's assignment, Emma, which she also thought was depressing. Emma Woodhouse, whom her English teacher almost swooned

31

over, seemed like a spoiled, selfish snob to her, someone who could easily cast aside her friends when it became obvious they were from very different stations in life. It was fine for Emma to toy with Harriet's life as long as the less fortunate woman didn't presume equality or claim entitlement to the man Emma deemed a more appropriate match for herself. Grace admired Mr. Knightly and felt he was too good for Emma.

In class, Grace would keep these opinions to herself, of course, and instead obediently parrot the interpretations and opinions that would constitute correct answers on the test. Privately Grace believed that although the clothing and manners may have changed, the class prejudices and sexist attitudes of these classic books were still well-established, even in the small town of Rose Hill, even in the twenty-first century.

Underneath her school assignments was the book she really wanted to read, also from the school library. It was the second book in the *His Dark Materials* trilogy by Phillip Pullman, titled *The Subtle Knife*. She had read the first book in the series, *The Golden Compass*, the previous week. Grace considered these the best books she had ever read, and she had read a lot of books.

The protagonist Lyra stayed with her long after she closed the cover. At night she dreamed about huge polar bear protectors. She longed for a small furry companion called a daemon who would always be with her and from whom she couldn't bear to be parted. Lyra was someone she could relate to; a cast-off child at the mercy of grownups, a young girl who had to rely on her own wits to survive. Lyra was brave; reading her story made Grace feel brave. Grace had heard that books could do this for a person; this was the first time she had experienced it for herself.

So immersed was she in her book that she only remembered the wet laundry when she heard her grandfather walking up the back stairs. Heart pounding, she tossed the book toward her backpack and raced to the kitchen, where she hurriedly took out the damp clothes, flung them in a basket, and ran to the back hallway to hang them on the clothesline strung there. She heard him open the door to the screened porch and then kick off his rubber boots. She was pinning the last damp shirt as he opened the door to the back hallway from the screened porch. She tried to seem unhurried as if she had not been behind schedule at all, but he could not be fooled.

"Had your nose stuck in a book I suppose," he said.

"Yes, sir," she said, "for school."

"I hate to think what they're teaching you up there that you feel entitled to sass me and defy my wishes."

Grace knew better than to argue that she never sassed him or defied his wishes; his saying so was just like the awful glue traps he set for the mice in the cellar.

"As soon as you're sixteen you'll leave school and take over some of my work," he said. "I could use the help, and you can finally earn your keep. One of these days I'll be too crippled to do any work, and you'll have to take care of me. That's what children do."

Grace felt as if her heart had stopped. It had never occurred to her that he would take her out of school or that she would be stuck here forever. Tears stung her eyes; she blinked hard to keep them from falling.

"I suppose you want to stay in school," he said.

"I do," she said, her voice cracking.

"Well, don't go to pieces," he said. "I'll let you finish out this year."

So horrified was she by what he had envisioned for her that she couldn't speak.

"You go on and see to supper," he said. "Call me when it's ready."

Luckily, after supper, he took no more notice of her, only paid a visit to the bathroom and then retired to his room to listen to the evening news on his radio. As soon as his bedroom door closed Grace fled to the pantry off the kitchen and crouched down at the very back, in the corner.

Her grandmother's apron hung nearby, and she wadded it up against her face and cried into it, smothering the sound. It still smelled like her grandmother, a mixture of cleaning products and medicated powder.

It was her grandmother who had planted the seed in Grace's mind that she could escape as soon as she graduated from high school. At eighteen, her grandmother had told her, Grace would be free to do as she pleased. This point in the future had been a beacon of hope. With one short declaration, her grandfather had snuffed out that light. What was the point in going on, she thought, in trying to learn or do anything, when she would just end up an over-pruned sapling damaged beyond repair by stunted growth?

A dark thought entered her head, and she allowed herself to consider it. It overwhelmed her with sadness, but at the same time, it seemed like it might offer relief. If she were lucky, she might be able to be with her grandmother; if she were not, she might end up wherever it was her mother had gone, which was probably not a pleasant place. She thought of the blissful look on Nino's face as he spoke to whomever it was who had arrived to escort him into death. She imagined her grandmother coming for her, hugging her, telling her everything would be alright.

'How would I do it?' she wondered.

'What would Lyra do?'

The thought popped into her head seemingly without her producing it.

'What would Lyra do?'

She wiped her eyes and blew her nose while she considered this. She wished she had a giant polar bear to protect her, a small furry friend to devotedly love her, a compass that told her the truth about every situation, and a boy named Will to team up with.

She thought of Tommy. They were not close friends; he had always just been the boy who had a big unrequited crush on her ex-friend Charlotte, her friend since kindergarten. The two of them had been more like satellites revolving around the same planet than friends. Could he be her Will? It was dangerous to trust anyone, but maybe if she was brave like Lyra, she could find a way out of her predicament.

'If I'm desperate enough to kill myself,' she reasoned, 'I'm desperate enough to try to change things instead.'

Grace left her dark thoughts behind her in the pantry with her grandmother's apron. They would still be there where she could find them later, but first, she would be brave and try to save herself.

CHAPTER THREE – SUNDAY

Scott entered Little Bear Books and scanned the room for Maggie. He caught sight of her red curly hair and felt butterflies in his stomach; he'd fallen in love with her a long time ago, but she still had this effect on him. She was helping a child pick out books from a stack on the floor. Scott thought the little girl was probably around seven years old, and Maggie was sitting cross-legged on the floor next to her, her long curly hair draped back over her shoulders. Maggie's facial expression was soft and kind. A twinkly smile played about her eyes and lips. The little girl's expression as she looked up into Maggie's face was wide-eyed and earnest.

'She's not as fierce as she'd like everyone to think,' he thought to himself. 'Look how good she is with children.'

This reminded Scott that he would never be able to give Maggie children, which transformed the scene into something a little more bittersweet. Never totally convinced of her commitment to their renewed relationship, he was always looking for the thing that would derail it. They hadn't talked about this particular issue, but then Scott wasn't looking for ways to rock their leaky boat.

Although he had once been married to someone else and Maggie had lived with a good friend of his, there had always been a special place in his heart for Maggie Fitzpatrick. She may have a red-hot temper and way of speaking her mind that continually got her in hot water, but her passion for life and her love of family and friends reflected her better nature. He had known for several years that she was the only one for him; it had taken her a lot longer to come around to this particular point of view.

Three years earlier he had issued an ultimatum that she rejected, and they had been estranged until recently. A

36

few weeks earlier, when Scott's mother lay dying of cancer, it was Maggie he wanted by his side. One night, in desperation and pain, he had called her, and to his amazement and relief, she came running. They hadn't discussed it or made any public declarations, but they hadn't spent one night apart since then.

In a haze of grief for the first week after his mother died, Scott had clung to Maggie like a drowning man to a lifeboat. She and her large extended family had taken care of all the details surrounding the funeral and burial. Surrounded by Fitzpatricks, Scott had allowed himself to be borne along like a leaf on a river.

All that was left to do was clean out his mother's house, which Scott insisted he had to do himself, yet every time he went there he turned around and left. Maggie, who argued with people like others breathed, had been patient, kind, and compassionate throughout. Scott, who had not thought it possible that he could love Maggie any more than he already did, was convinced anew that she was the best woman in the world and the only one for him.

The mother of the little girl Maggie was conversing with retrieved her and thanked Maggie. As Maggie caught sight of Scott she at first smiled sweetly, then scowled and stuck out her tongue. Scott laughed.

"My mother said to tell you she missed you at church," she said as she approached.

"I went," Scott said. "I just couldn't go inside."

"You didn't miss much," Maggie said. "Hannah came but had to leave when Sammy started screaming for her from the nursery. Big surprise."

"Maybe next week," he said.

"What are you up to today?"

"I'm trying to find out who the old guy was who died on the Branduff's front porch," he said. "No identification on him. All I have is a bus ticket to go by and an old letter. His name was Nino Vincenzo, he spoke Italian, and his trip originated in Sardinia, Italy."

"Paid for with a credit card?"

"Cash," Scott said.

"Sounds like he didn't want anyone to know who he was."

"The Italian Embassy is less than interested in helping," Scott said. "The FBI says unless he committed a crime they are not interested."

"Call Congressman Green or Senator Bayard," Maggie said. "This is an election year; they should be happy to help as long as it gets in the paper."

"Cynic," Scott said.

"Realist," Maggie said.

"Putting it in the paper is a good idea," Scott said. "I'll talk to Ed about writing about it in The *Sentinel*."

"For all five people who read it."

"He also writes for the Pendleton paper," Scott said. "Plus his ex-wife is somebody important on the all-news channel now."

"Eve the Aggrieved," Maggie said. "Did she ever divorce him?"

"No," Scott said. "We don't talk about that."

"Of course not," Maggie said. "Feelings are like cooties to you boys."

"I would love to talk to you about my feelings," Scott said.

"Do we have to?" Maggie said.

"See?" Scott said. "You're allergic to cooties, yourself."

"Spoke Italian, huh?" she said.

"Changing the subject, huh?" he said.

"You may want to talk to Sal Delvecchio," Maggie said. "His father came over here more than a hundred years ago. Sal might remember the name if it was one of the Italian families who immigrated to Rose Hill in order to work."

"Good idea," Scott said.

"I've got to get going," Maggie said. "I have homework."

"What class is this?"

"American Poets of the early 20th Century," she said.

"All the passions, loves, beauties, and delights of the earth," Scott said.

"You just quoted Walt Whitman," Maggie said. "Who are you?"

"I keep telling you I have depths to my soul that you have not yet plumbed," Scott said. "I'm not just a pretty face."

"What's the rest of it?" she said.

"That's all I remember," Scott said. "My mother said it was a dirty poem and called Miss Phipps to complain about it."

"I bet Miss Phipps gave her an ear full."

"She did, but she also suggested I tackle Shakespeare instead."

"Do you remember any of his poetry?"

"I only had to memorize one poem to recite," Scott said. "So I picked the shortest one I could find. Sonnet 116."

"Go ahead," Maggie said. "I'm waiting."

A staff member interrupted their conversation to ask Maggie a question, so Scott took this as his opportunity to leave.

"Gotta run," he said. "See ya later."

"I will have that sonnet," Maggie called out after him. "So you better practice."

Scott walked down Rose Hill Avenue and crossed the street to the Bee Hive Hair Salon, where Maggie's cousin, Claire Fitzpatrick, was working. Recently retired from her globe-hopping career as the private hair stylist to a famous Hollywood actress, she had returned home to help her mother, Delia, care for her father, Ian, who was suffering from the effects of several small strokes.

When he entered the Bee Hive, he found Claire was alone, sitting in the hydraulic chair with her feet up on the counter, reading a tabloid magazine while listening to loud music. Scott turned down the volume on her stereo in order to get her attention.

"Hey, Scott," she said, putting her feet back on the floor. "Need a haircut?"

"Who is that singing?" he asked her.

"Patty Griffin," she said. "Like it?"

"She has a beautiful voice," he said. "Yes, I do like it. Have you seen her in concert?"

"Yep," she said. "She's one of my touchstones. I can always remember where I was and what I was doing when each of her albums was released. This song reminds me of a film shoot in Paris where I finally decided to quit my job. It only took me six more years to do it, but still ... what do you like to listen to?"

"I don't know," he shrugged. "I listen to whatever Patrick's playing in the Thorn, or country music on the radio in the squad car, but that's about it."

"I love the old bluegrass and Irish fiddle music, too," Claire said. "But there's so much good stuff out there. Listening to new music makes me feel like the best might still be ahead of me, you know?"

"I will listen to anything you recommend," Scott said.

"I'll put together a playlist for you. Remember when we used to make mix-tapes? Now every piece of music I own is on my phone," Claire said. "Come over here and let me shampoo you."

Once seated in the shampoo chair, Scott surrendered his head to Claire's magical massaging fingers. He closed his eyes and listened to her quietly sing along with the music. It was very relaxing. He felt warm and cozy here, and her fingers were making firm circles on his scalp. His mind wandered.

"Scott," Claire said and woke him up.

"Sorry," Scott said as he sat up. "I'm working way too many hours right now."

"I heard some man died down at Branduff's'," Claire said.

Scott walked over to the hydraulic chair, sat down, and Claire unfurled a silky cape around his neck and shoulders. He gave her all the background on the case and mentioned he wanted Ed to put an article in one of the papers.

"Did Ed tell you we're running together every morning?" she asked him.

"He said you run three miles and he runs one mile and then has heart palpitations."

"He's coming along," Claire said. "Those two dogs of his need the exercise. Hank sticks with Ed, but Lucida could easily run six miles."

"Maggie's been trying to get me to walk with her," Scott said. "I just haven't."

"Things still good there?" Claire asked.

"Yes, at least I think so," Scott said. "Has Maggie talked to you about it?"

"Not much," Claire said. "There were those rumors about you and me, you know."

"Sorry about that," Scott said. "And for anything I did to start them."

"A kiss and a hug between friends is nothing," Claire said. "Don't think twice about it. Everyone knows you and Maggie belong together. It just took her awhile to realize it."

"Gabe may have disappeared," Scott said, "but they didn't find a body; he could come back."

"He won't come within a hundred miles of Rose Hill," Claire said. "Besides, Maggie made it clear to him that she did not want him back."

"I should never have given her that ultimatum."

"Nope," Claire said. "But it all worked out in the end."

"I hope so," Scott said. "I'm afraid if I propose she'll kick me out on my rear."

"I wouldn't just yet," Claire said. "No hurry, though, right?"

"It's hard not to want more," Scott said.

"My advice is just to take your time, enjoy being together, and be thankful for what you have," Claire said.

"She's so fierce on the outside," Scott said. "But she's got the biggest heart."

"I know," Claire said. "Just don't let that get around."

"Why is she like that, do you think?"

"Well, you know her mother, Bonnie," Claire said. "But you didn't know Bonnie's mother-in-law, Grandma Rose. She was hateful. Bonnie and Rose couldn't stand each other but worked side-by-side in the bakery every day for years. Maggie grew up right there in the middle of those two; it was probably just self-defense."

"Do you think Maggie wants kids?" Scott said.

"Oh, I think Maggie could be happy either way," Claire said softly.

"I don't know if you know it ..." Scott started to say, but Claire put a hand on his shoulder.

"I know," she said. "Don't let that stop you. Maggie loves you, and you're together now. Just let that be enough."

"I hope it is," Scott said.

After dinner Grace told her grandfather she had to go to the library to use their computer. He grumbled but allowed it on the condition that she was home before dark. Seeing that dark came around 9:00 p.m. these days, Grace had plenty of time to do some research with Tommy.

After an interior debate and with major trepidation, she decided to take her notes about the man who died to Scott at the police station. The deputy on duty said Scott was not in so Grace gave her notes to him.

Grace left the station and crossed the street to meet up with Tommy at the corner of Rose Hill Avenue and Peony Street. He had his bike with him, and he pushed it up the hill as they walked together. Up ahead, sitting on the wall outside the Rose Hill Community Center, were three women who turned and watched them approach. Grace recognized the tall red-headed one, who was Maggie Fitzpatrick, and the little blondish-brown-headed one, who was Sammy's mother Hannah Campbell, but not the tall, thin one with long dark hair. They all waved.

Tommy took one hand off his bicycle to wave back at them, and as he did so the front tire of his bike rolled into the sewer drain next to the curb in the street. When he attempted to pull the bike out, it became entangled in his jacket and backpack, which had fallen off the shoulder. He fell over, tangled up and flailing.

Maggie rolled her eyes and shook her head, Hannah laughed out loud and pointed, but the dark-haired one jumped up and came running to assist, saying, "Are you okay?" Grace immediately decided she liked this one best.

As the dark-haired lady and Grace helped untangle Tommy from his bike and backpack, Grace got a closer look at the woman. She had deep blue eyes and shiny long dark hair and was dressed and made up like someone in the fashion magazines Grace looked through at the library. She wore high-heeled boots with her skinny black jeans and a short black trench coat over a black turtleneck. Grace had studied enough fashion magazines to know her clothes were probably as expensive as they looked. She smiled at Grace and caught her staring. Grace looked away, embarrassed.

"Introduce me to your friend," the woman said to Tommy, who was now on his feet and brushing off his coat.

His face was flushed with embarrassment, but he smiled at her in a friendly way.

"This is Grace," Tommy said to the woman, who stuck out her hand to shake Grace's.

"I'm Claire Fitzpatrick," she said. "My family owns the Rose and Thorn."

Grace had never been in the bar, but you couldn't miss it; it was right on the corner of Peony Street and the west side of Rose Hill Avenue. They played loud fiddle music in there that Grace kind of liked. Late at night, if it was just about to rain, she could hear it as she lay in bed. Grace also knew Tommy's mother had worked there before she went away.

"Are you related to them?" Grace asked, subtly gesturing up the hill at Maggie and Hannah, not wanting to be rude enough to point.

The sharp wind was blowing Maggie's wild red mane all around her face, and she was struggling to control it. She finally twisted it around and shoved it down in the back of her coat. Maggie's hair reminded Grace of Lyra's daemon in the *His Dark Materials* trilogy, acting like an unruly daemon she was fond of yet aggravated by.

"Maggie, Hannah, and I are all cousins," Claire said. "Our fathers are brothers."

"She just moved back here," Tommy said about Claire to Grace, and then to Claire, "Grace and I've known each other since kindergarten."

"Where do you live, Miss Grace?" Claire asked.

Grace said, "Down by the river," and looked away, not wanting to see the reaction she usually got.

"So we're neighbors," Claire said. "It's nice to meet you."

When Grace looked back at Claire, she was smiling in a sincerely friendly way. Grace smiled in response, mumbled, "Thanks," and then was embarrassed. The woman would probably think she didn't have any manners.

"Where are you headed?" Claire asked Tommy.

"Up to the library to do homework," Tommy said.

"Tell Ed I want to run in the morning after breakfast," Claire said. "Tell him I said to stretch beforehand or I'm going to leave him in the dust."

Tommy said he would. He and Grace continued on up the hill to where Maggie and Hannah sat on the wall. Hannah jumped off the wall and then up onto Tommy's back, pretending to attack him. Tommy grinned as he dropped his bicycle and backpack, grabbed Hannah's legs, and took off with her, running around the lawn outside the community center. Hannah was screaming, Tommy was laughing, and Grace smiled in spite of her determination not to. It looked like fun.

"Hey," Maggie said to Grace. "Doesn't your grandfather have the greenhouses down by the river?"

Grace's smile folded back up inside of her as she nodded, not meeting Maggie's eyes.

"He's had some really beautiful flowers this year," Maggie said.

"You did not spend money on flowers," Claire said. "As cheap as you are?"

"I didn't say I bought them," Maggie said. "Looking is free."

"Well, I bought a pot of tulips for my mother, and they're gorgeous," Claire said.

"Thanks," Grace said, but her eyes were on Tommy and Hannah.

"Don't mind Hannah," Claire said. "Tommy's like one of the family."

"I know," Grace said. "I don't mind."

"I don't think I've ever seen you in my store," Maggie said.

"I don't buy books," Grace said, feeling uncomfortable.

"I never did, either, when I was growing up," Maggie said. "I was a library girl."

"Me too," Grace said.

Maggie asked Grace about what she was reading and seemed sincerely interested. As they talked, Grace covertly studied her. Grace had never been this close to Maggie before, having only seen her from a distance. Grace's peers referred to the bookstore owner as a bad-tempered person who didn't put up with any foolishness in her store, so Grace was a little intimidated by her reputation as well as her great

45

height. Up close, though, she didn't seem hateful, and her eyes weren't mean at all.

She had the same bright blue eyes as her cousin Claire, but with pale gold eyelashes and eyebrows. Also unlike Claire, every inch of Maggie's pale skin was covered with little auburn freckles. Maggie was not what her grandpa would call "dolled up" like Claire, but she was pretty nonetheless, in a more fresh-air and soap-clean way. As they talked about books Grace revised her first impression of Maggie; she was nicer than she seemed.

"I loved *His Dark Materials*," Maggie said. "He's allegedly working on a fourth, you know."

"I didn't know that," Grace said.

"What else have you read?"

"I really liked *Mapp and Lucia*," Grace said. "We read it for English class last semester, and then I read all the other ones on my own."

"Lucia and Georgie are hilarious," Maggie said. "Have you seen the PBS series of the books?"

Grace just shook her head rather than say she didn't have a TV.

"They probably have the videos at the library," Grace said. "Look for them; they're great."

Tommy put Hannah down, and she promptly head-butted him in the stomach. After he recovered from that they hugged, and then Hannah followed him back over to where the rest of them were standing.

"I know you!" Hannah said cheerfully to Grace. "You saved my son from a pack of wild dogs. He's been talking nonstop about you ever since."

"Jax and Wally really did it," Grace said quietly. "I was just there."

"Sam said you were swinging a branch and screaming like a banshee," Hannah said.

"How is Sam?" Grace said.

Hannah winked at Grace, saying, "Grouchy and sore, but that's nothing new."

46

"You need to tag Sammy's ear," Maggie said. "Then you could track him on a GPS."

"He's doing great in daycare during the week," Hannah said. "It's depending on my mother on the weekend that's the problem. I'm on call, and Sam's got a group at the community center. She just can't keep track of him."

"I'd watch him anytime," Claire said. "Just call me."

"Except Saturday is your busiest day," Maggie said. "Just like me."

"Hey, do you babysit?" Hannah asked Grace.

"I haven't done it before," Grace said.

"Piece of cake," Hannah said.

Maggie and Claire both laughed.

"Yeah, right," Maggie said.

"Just never take your eyes off him, not even for a second," Claire said.

"Sure," Grace said. "I'd love to."

"I'll help," Tommy said. "Sammy's a blast."

"Hey, let's go toilet paper someone's house!" Hannah said. "I wanna be a teenager with you guys."

"Nobody does that anymore," Tommy said.

"No?" Hannah said, looking disappointed. "Bummer."

"You guys go on," Claire said, "before we contaminate you with our oldness."

Grace curiously found that she kind of wanted to hang out with them longer. For older ladies, they seemed like a lot of fun.

Once they were out of earshot, Grace said, "They seem nice."

"They're great," Tommy said. "When my mom and I first came here, we lived with Claire's parents, Ian and Delia. They're kind of like my grandparents, except Ian sometimes thinks I'm his son who died a long time ago. He had a stroke, and now his memory's not too good."

"That's sad," Grace said. "There sure are a lot of Fitzpatricks in this town."

"Maggie's mom runs the bakery. Maggie's dad got hurt a long time ago, so he doesn't do anything. Claire's dad was the chief of police before Scott, and Hannah's dad owns the gas station."

"I know who they all are from hanging out at Charlotte's," Grace said. "It must be nice being part of a big family like that."

"Yeah, I guess," Tommy said. "They treat Ed like that, too."

"So he's an orphan like us," Grace said.

"Yep," Tommy said. "We're all just a bunch of strays they picked up."

"What's the story with Grace?" Claire asked as soon as the two of them were out of earshot.

"It's a sad story," Hannah said. "Her mother killed herself, then her grandmother died of breast cancer, and now she lives in that big old house with just that old sourpuss to look after her."

"I was raised by a sourpuss," Maggie said. "I survived it."

"What about her dad?" Claire asked.

"Some kid her mother dated in high school," Hannah said. "The family moved him away, and they were never involved at all, apparently."

"That's sad," Maggie said. "And she's so tiny."

"There's nothing wrong with being small," Hannah said. "I'm fun-sized, myself."

"She's really cute," Claire said. "I'd love to braid her hair."

"She was friends with Charlotte until they went to high school," Hannah said. "Then Charlotte ditched her for the rich kids; ditched her and Tommy, who has the biggest crush on Charlotte. That's probably how those two became friends."

"Where did you get all this information?" Maggie asked.

"Oh, I ask around, you know," Hannah said. "When someone rescues your child from certain death, you kind of want to know more about her."

Hannah told them the story about what had happened.

"Is Sam really okay?" Claire asked with concern.

"He wouldn't show me what he did to his knees," Hannah said. "So I called Doc Machalvie and told on him. Doc came out to the house to look him over, and is making him use his wheelchair for a few days until they heal."

"He must hate that," Maggie said.

"Oh, he's unbearable, alright," Hannah said. "He might have to sleep in the barn until he's back on his feet, so to speak."

"It's a good thing Grace showed up," Maggie said. "Who knows what might've happened."

"Okay, I get it," Hannah said. "I'm a horrible mother. But you guys know Sammy; he is not a normal child. I'm doing the best I can here."

"Sweetie, I couldn't do it," Claire said. "I don't know how you do."

Hannah stuck out her tongue at Maggie, who stuck hers out in return.

"I'd like to improve that kid Grace's life somehow," Hannah said. "Maybe feed her some oatmeal for starters."

"Maybe Tommy and Grace will fall in love," Claire said.

"No," Hannah said. "I don't get that vibe at all, and everyone knows I am the town's preeminent matchmaker."

"That rotten Charlotte," Maggie said. "Who does she think she is?"

"Sounds like she's stuck on herself," Claire said. "And to think she was such a nice little girl."

"Kind of reminds you of her mother, doesn't it?" Hannah said.

49

All three took a moment to make a rude face about Ava Fitzpatrick.

"Grace's better off without Charlotte as a friend," Maggie said. "It's probably better for her to figure out how people can be now rather than later. She's never going to have an easy life."

"You're so cheerful," Hannah said. "The sun shines right out of your butt, doesn't it?"

Maggie pushed Hannah, who fell backward off the wall into the hedges behind it.

"It just rips your heart out, though, doesn't it?" Claire said as she offered Hannah a hand to pull her back out. "You just want to pick her up and give her a hug."

"She'd probably bite you," Maggie said. "That kind you have to tame first."

"Kind of like you," Hannah said, and Claire laughed.

Maggie reached out to push her again, but Hannah evaded her hand.

"Shut up," Maggie said. "Grace and I don't need your affection; we're self-contained units."

"Everyone needs affection," Claire said, watching the two teenagers as they entered the library. "That poor little girl."

Maggie found Scott in his office, staring at his computer screen, his eyebrows drawn together in a fierce scowl.

"Hey, good-lookin'," she said from the doorway.

As Scott looked up his brows relaxed and his face softened. Maggie felt that familiar queasy-pleasant feeling she always got whenever she saw him. It felt either very good or very bad, depending on her current interior emotional weather. Today it felt good.

Scott motioned her over, and she leaned over his shoulder to see what he was looking at. One of her long curls fell over his arm, and he twined it around his finger as he leaned back into her.

"Whatcha doin'?" she said, while she inhaled that warm, clean scent that was unique to Scott Gordon; it was intoxicating or infuriating, dependent upon the aforementioned mood barometer.

"I'm trying to find someone who can help me track down Nino Vincenzo's family in Italy," Scott said. "Alghero is on the northwestern coast of Sardinia, in Italy, but the international operator could not find him in the directory. There are hundreds of Vincenzos listed, which doesn't help, plus now that everyone has cell phones it's not as easy to find people as it once was. I called the Italian Embassy in D.C., and they're supposed to call me back, but the man I talked to didn't sound like he was in any rush to help. I'll be surprised if they call back at all."

"Have you talked to Sal yet?"

"I talked to Antonia outside of church this morning. She said he wasn't feeling well. His heart, I guess."

"He's been dying of heart failure for the past ten years. He'll probably outlive us all."

"She said I could stop by later."

"You could call the police in Alghero and let Sal talk to them."

"That's a good idea," Scott said. "Grace didn't understand most of what he said, but she wrote some of it down, phonetically. There was a letter in his breast pocket from someone named Mary; it's so old, and the paper is so creased and worn you can hardly read it."

"What does it say?"

Scott took out the letter, which he had slid into a cellophane bag. The sheet of writing paper was yellow with age; the beautiful cursive writing faded and blotched.

"Dear Nino," Scott read. "I had a boy, but they took him. I am in, this next part is illegible, and this line says I hope someday you can forgive me. I will always love you, Mary."

"Romantic," Maggie said.

"So whoever Mary was, she wrote in English, and he must have been looking for her."

"In Jacob Branduff's house?" Maggie said. "What was his mother's name?"

"Colleen," Scott said. "Ed looked it up for me. They belonged to a very strict church out on Owl's Branch Road; one of those that doesn't have many members, or want anymore, probably."

"Wrath of God," Maggie said. "I think the name says it all. That church burned down, didn't it?"

"Yep," Scott said. "Back when we were in grade school. They meet in someone's house now, out on Rabbit Run Road. I don't really know anything about it. I'll have to ask Ed."

"I met Grace this afternoon," Maggie said.

"What'd you think?"

Maggie told him the story Hannah told them about Grace trying to rescue Sammy. She also told him what Hannah had found out about her from asking around.

"I like her," Maggie said. "She's smart and seems very mature for her age. She's read books I didn't read until I was an adult."

"She is very smart," Scott said. "All A's on her report card; every one."

"You've been checking up on her?"

"I can't quit thinking about her," Scott said. "If you had heard how awful her grandfather spoke to her, you would have kicked him across the river."

"Do you think he abuses her?"

"Verbally, yes," Scott said. "Ed and I both witnessed that. There was certainly the threat of violence implied in his words, but she didn't have any marks on her that I could see. What did you think?"

"She certainly looks neglected," Maggie said. "Her shoes are falling apart."

"I don't think she gets enough to eat, either," Scott said. "She's so small for her age."

"Are you going to call Children's Protective Services?"

Scott turned around, and Maggie sat back on the edge of his desk.

"The truth about CPS is that they focus their efforts on really young kids," Scott said. "It's not that they don't care about the older kids; it's just that they don't have the resources to do both."

"So unless she's being molested or beaten ..."

"It's not the way it should be," Scott said. "But that's the way it is."

"What can you do?"

"Take an interest," he said, "which I have. Keep an eye on her; on her grandfather. His health is not good. Doc Machalvie can't tell me anything about the grandfather because it would violate his HIPAA rights; he did say he's never seen Grace in his office, and that she probably hasn't been to a doctor if she hasn't been to see him. They don't have a car."

"She would have to have had vaccinations in order to go to school," Maggie said.

"She could get those for free when the county sends their mobile health clinic to town," Scott said. "Matt Delvecchio said her grandmother cleaned the dentist's office in order to pay for her dental work."

"So when her grandmother was alive she had better care."

"Doc said her grandmother probably would have lived had she had a medical intervention before the breast cancer spread. By the time she had symptoms, it was too late."

"Why can't the richest country in this world take better care of its poor people?" Maggie said. "We pride ourselves on all the wrong things."

"You're preaching to the choir," Scott said. "Proverbs 19:17: 'He who is gracious to a poor man lends to the Lord, and He will repay him for his good deed.'"

"I keep hoping this religious zeal of yours is just a phase," Maggie said. "When you talk like that it worries me."

Scott smiled, saying, "I mostly do it just to bug you."

"I'm relieved to hear it," Maggie said. "Maybe I can lend Grace some books or movies."

"Books, maybe," Scott said. "They have no phone or television."

"Oh, crap," Maggie said. "And there I was recommending a mini-series for her to watch."

"Can you imagine how much money it takes to heat that big ole house?"

"They probably only live in a couple rooms."

"From the outside, it's practically falling down," he said. "I haven't seen inside."

"She'd be too embarrassed to let you in, probably," Maggie said. "You want me to snoop around?"

"If you can do it without her finding out," Scott said. "I don't want to invade her privacy or freak her out, but I have this feeling she's in danger. I can't explain it; it's a gut thing. I feel like I need to protect her from something bad that's about to happen."

"That's sweet," Maggie said, "and I can see why; she had that same effect on us. We all want to adopt her, braid her hair, and feed her something."

"I talked to Ava about her, and she has a whole different opinion," he said. "She said Charlotte felt sorry for Grace but had to drop her because she was such a negative influence."

"Charlotte is a spoiled chip off the smug old block," Maggie said. "How could you live Grace's life and not be depressed? Instead of abandoning her, they could have tried to help her. I thought Ava loved collecting orphans."

"But Grace isn't an orphan."

"Plus Grace is smart," Maggie said. "She probably saw right through her. Ava only collects blindly devoted followers."

"Let's not talk about Ava," Scott said. "We'll just argue."

"Of course," Maggie said. "Because I'll be honest and you'll defend her."

Scott shrugged.

"What happened with her and you?" Maggie asked. "Am I allowed to ask?"

"I love you, and she loves Patrick," he said.

"Hmmm," Maggie said. "I wondered."

"C'mere," Scott said. "Let me prove it to you."

"Nope," Maggie said. "I gotta go. What can I do to help Grace?"

"Ask around but not in a way that will get back to her," Scott said.

"What's Ed say?"

"That she's a nice, quiet girl who Tommy is not in love with, and she's got nice manners for someone being raised by such a grouchy bear."

"I was raised by a grouchy bear," Maggie said. "I survived it."

"Speaking of said bear," Scott said. "How about we get your mother to hire Grace at the bakery? She'd be the perfect person to keep an eye on her."

"Are you crazy?" Maggie said. "Have you met my mother?"

"She kept you out of trouble throughout your teenage years."

"That's true," Maggie said. "I didn't have a thought she couldn't read and then reprimand me for. All that oppression turned me into a rebellious mess later, though. Don't forget that part."

"I think you turned out really well," Scott said and stood up.

"Don't you start that," Maggie said. "We're in your place of employment."

Scott took her in his arms and hugged her.

"I love you," he said.

She pinched him.

"Ow," he said, but he was smiling as he rubbed his arm.

"What'd I tell you about that?" she said.

"Can I come over later?" he said.

Maggie felt herself flush from head to toe at the thought of it.

"Okay," she said and pushed him away. "Bring a pizza for dinner, and we'll watch a movie."

"Or something," he said, but she was already walking away.

"Bye," she said.

"Or something!" he called out to her, but she ignored him.

Maggie walked down the alley behind Rose Hill Avenue to the back door of her family's bakery, where her mother was rolling out croissant dough in the kitchen. Bonnie Fitzpatrick had snow-white curly hair, piercing blue eyes and permanent frown lines etched into the skin between her eyebrows and around her lips.

"What are you still doing here?" Maggie asked her.

"Hello to you, too, daughter," Bonnie said. "Your Aunt Alice has gone down with one of her migraines, and we have a special order for the Baptist church this evening."

Maggie washed her hands before she was asked to, donned an apron, and took over for her mother.

"What's going on?" Bonnie asked as she opened the back door to let some cool air into the stuffy bakery kitchen.

"Nothing," Maggie said

Maggie added little bits of cold butter to the top of the dough before she folded it and rolled it flat.

"You don't put a toe in here unless I call," Bonnie said. "What's wrong?"

Maggie deliberately took her time to answer, but Bonnie stubbornly refused to prod her further.

"Add more butter," her mother said instead.

"I need information," Maggie finally said, heaving the long rolling pin into the air. It was a piece of wood the length of a baseball bat, tapered slightly at each end.

"About?" Bonnie said as she closed the door.

The older woman eased her plump bottom up onto a high wooden stool and eyed her daughter suspiciously.

"Grace Branduff," Maggie said. "Jacob Branduff's granddaughter."

"That old coot," Bonnie said. "His wife died of breast cancer because he was too stingy to pay for a doctor."

"Maybe they couldn't afford a doctor."

"He was offered a pile of money for that old house when Theo Eldridge bought the glassworks," Bonnie said. "Turned him down flat, Jacob did. That family could have lived a whole different life were it not for that selfish man."

"I didn't know that," Maggie said.

She paused to take a breath and stretch her arms backward to relieve the familiar stabbing pain between her shoulder blades.

"Keep rolling," Bonnie said. "You can't let that butter melt."

Maggie did as she was told.

"I didn't know Colleen Branduff that well," Bonnie said. "She was one to keep herself to herself. Those two daughters of hers were as wild as the weeds along the highway. One got herself in the family way in high school, and the boy's parents moved him away. The other one ran off, and I don't know where to or what she's doing."

"What about Grace?"

"She used to come in here with Charlotte; just a quiet little girl with good manners. She hasn't been in any trouble that I've heard of. Ava doesn't like her, but I don't pay any mind to what Ava thinks of people. She'll soon have her hands full with our Charlotte. She was in here the other day, face plastered in makeup, heels so high she could barely walk; couldn't take her eyes off her cell phone."

"Could you use Grace working here?" Maggie asked her mother.

"She's just a speck of a thing, about the size of Hannah at that age," Bonnie said. "To tell you the truth I don't think she could do the heavy work. She looks malnourished."

"You could certainly remedy that," Maggie said.

"Best not to get involved," Bonnie said. "Jacob Branduff is a mean old coot. I'd walk three blocks out of my way not to have to give him the time of day."

"You heard she found an old man dying on their porch this morning."

"Some foreigner," Bonnie said. "Nothing to do with us."

"Now, what would Jesus say?" Maggie said.

Bonnie took a dishtowel and flicked her daughter on the backside.

"Don't you preach to me about Jesus," Bonnie said. "Lightning will strike your tongue."

"What've I done now?"

"Plenty," Bonnie said. "You can't tell me the chief of police isn't sneaking up your backstairs every night and then away before dawn."

"He comes up the front stairs and doesn't leave until after breakfast," Maggie said. "And there's no sneaking involved. What would be the point in this town?"

"You should be ashamed," Bonnie said. "I raised you better than that."

"And you and Dad are such great role models for marital happiness?"

"Only a fool thinks marriage will make a woman happy," Bonnie said.

"Exactly my point," Maggie said. "So why do it?"

"It's what the Lord wants us to do," Bonnie said. "Cleave unto each other. Be fruitful and multiply."

"Well, we may eventually get married, but Scott and I aren't having any children."

"What?" Bonnie demanded, and Maggie cringed, knowing what was coming. "What do you mean you and Scott aren't having any children? I know you're not a spring chicken, but it's not too late. Mrs. Deacon had Pip when she was 40."

"And look how he turned out," Maggie said.

"Why are you so determined to break my heart?" Bonnie asked. "You know how badly I want grandchildren. Your brother Sean's not likely to give me any and Lord knows how Patrick's avoided it, but so far he has."

"You have Brian's children."

"I want *you* to have children," Bonnie said. "I want *your* grandchildren; it's only natural. What have you got against children?"

Maggie stopped rolling the dough, turned, and looked her mother straight in the eye.

"Scott can't give me children," Maggie said. "Do you understand what I'm saying?"

"Oh," Bonnie said, and Maggie could see her mother's brain recalculating like she was the GPS for Maggie's life.

Maggie knew her mother well enough to know her thought processes. Bonnie adored Scott and had wanted nothing more than for Maggie to marry him. She was so close to getting what she wanted, but if they couldn't give her grandchildren, did she still want it?

"Well," Bonnie finally said. "They just grow up and break your heart. You're probably better off."

Maggie smiled, shook her head, and turned back to her task. That was about as good of a reaction as she could hope for.

"You could adopt," Bonnie said.

"No," Maggie said. "Just, no."

Sal Delvecchio was dressed in a running suit and thick-heeled, bright white athletic shoes, but Scott knew for a fact that he never did any exercise. A lifetime smoker, Sal had emphysema and heart failure. The slightest exertion caused him to have coughing fits. He wheezed as he talked.

"Grace's notes, they are not so good," Sal said. "Antonia had the idea to read them out loud to me, and it sounds as if he was saying he knew death was coming but he was not afraid. Italians on the north end of Sardinia have a much different dialect than my Sicilian family. Still, I think this is what he was saying."

"Does the name mean anything to you?"

"There was a Vincenzo who was a glass blower back when my father was the head glass blower," Sal said. "He was famous for making hand-blown glass animals. Many young men would come over from Italy, Romania, Czechoslovakia, and Germany, and eventually bring over their entire families. There were so many different languages spoken in Rose Hill at that time that the city employed an interpreter who spoke seven languages."

"Was that only because of the glassworks?"

"No, no," Sal said. "There was also the timber industry, coal-into-coke processing, as well as the glassworks; that's why my family came here."

"How would I find out if Nino worked at Rodefeffer's?"

"They have all the records down at the museum," Sal said. "If he worked there, he will be listed there."

"Museum," said Sal's wife as she entered the room. "How they can call that tiny shack a museum is beyond me."

Sal was referring to a small house on the corner of Rose Hill Avenue and Daisy Lane, next to Eldridge College, which contained a large collection of Rodefeffer Glass and all the records pertaining to the business.

60

"Knox created that museum and made it a nonprofit just so he could apply for grant money," Sal said. "That man is always looking for ways to get his hands on some money, and he doesn't care how he gets it."

In comparison to her tiny husband, Antonia Delvecchio was an Amazon of a woman, with a lush hourglass figure and a passing resemblance to Sophia Loren that she played to the hilt. Although she had lived in Rose Hill for most of her life, she had made no attempts to assimilate and still spoke with a heavy accent.

"That man is no good," she said. "I would not cross the road to spit on him if he were on fire."

Sal cackled gleefully, which turned into an awful cough as Scott accepted the hot coffee Antonia offered. They both waited until he had recovered to resume their conversation.

"Maybe Mamie will remember him," Scott said.

"Mamie worked in the office at the glassworks after the war started and all the men went into the service," Sal said. "She did the payroll, so she may remember him."

"That woman is crazy in the head," Antonia said. "She is the richest woman in town and dresses in rags."

"Not like my beauty," Sal said, caught her hand, brought it up to his mouth and kissed it.

She smiled, pleased, but pulled it away, saying, "Sal, we have company."

Antonia smoothed her skirt and patted her hair as she left, swaying languidly as she walked. Sal watched her all the way out of the room and then turned to Scott.

"There were richer and better-looking men chasing her, but she chose me," he said, shaking his head. "I ask myself every day what I did to deserve such good luck, and I still don't know. But you know what? Whatever it is, I'll take it!"

Scott thanked the man and told him not to get up, he would see himself out. He was headed to the door when he heard Antonia say, "Scott."

She came with him to the door and wrapped a sweater around her shoulders.

"Come," she said. "I will walk with you outside."

She walked down the front stairs of their large Georgian brick home and out to the long, curving driveway. The view from their front yard encompassed all of Rose Hill, from the manicured campus of Eldridge College down to the Little Bear River, where the hulking glassworks building sat.

"They've sold it," Antonia said, gesturing at the glassworks.

"I heard," Scott said, but he was looking at Grace's house, the lower floors hidden behind overgrown hedges and tall, waving pines, with just the tall Victorian turrets and peaked roofs visible above the treetops.

"I was so sorry about your mother's passing," Antonia said, putting a warm hand on his upper arm.

Her eyes were filled with compassion and sympathy, and Scott felt his throat close as if he might cry. He cleared it instead and looked away.

"Thank you," he said. "It was very quick."

"My Sal," she said, as her own eyes filled with tears. "My Sal is not going to be with us much longer, I fear."

"He seems like he's doing well," Scott said, knowing as he said it that it was the same kind of lie people told him about his mother as if false hope ever helped anyone face anything horrible and heartbreaking.

"Dr. Machalvie says if he gets any kind of infection, even just a little cold, he may die."

"I'm so sorry," Scott said. "He's such a good man."

"He is," Antonia said. "He is the best of men; that is why I chose him."

There was a challenge in her eyes as if someone might disagree with her on this point.

"You were both lucky," Scott said.

Antonia blinked her tears back and smiled.

"Oh no," she said. "I was the lucky one. I know that."

Scott drove down Morning Glory Avenue to Pine Mountain Road and then turned right toward downtown. At Rose Hill Avenue he turned left and drove two blocks toward the end of the street, which ended at the gates of Eldridge College. He turned left onto Daisy Lane and parked outside the small cottage with a big sign outside that said, "The Rodefeffer Glass Museum and Gift Shop."

There were no other cars parked in the lot next to the alley. The tiny Gothic style cottage had been restored and painted so that it looked very much like an oversized playhouse for children. Scott was not quite six feet tall but still had to duck as he entered through the front door. Inside, the place smelled musty; dust tickled his nose so that he felt he might sneeze.

A weak voice called from the back, "Hello?"

Scott replied and waited for the proprietress to make her way to the front room. Meanwhile, he looked around at the gift shop, which was filled top to bottom with shelves full of blown glass items. Small glass animals, vases, plates, cups, and assorted other hand-blown pieces were crowded onto clear glass shelves with seemingly no rhyme or reason to their placement. Everything was covered with a thick layer of dust.

Shuffling footsteps soon produced the museum manager, an ancient woman named Lavinia Bonecutter, who had run the museum for as long as Scott could remember. She had worked for the Rodefeffer family for many years, and this position was created for her when she could no longer cook or clean for the family. She was hard of hearing, so Scott shouted who he was.

"What's that?" she said.

"It's Scott Gordon, Miss Bonecutter," he yelled. "I came to ask a question about the glassworks."

"We don't have a public restroom," she said, "on account of the bad condition of the plumbing."

Scott took a deep breath and then changed his mind.

"Never mind," he yelled.

"The bookstore's open until ten on Sunday," she said. "But Maggie won't let you use the toilet unless you buy something."

"I'll just look around," he yelled.

"Thanks for coming in," she called out as she turned and shuffled back into the nether regions of the small house.

Scott left the front room and entered the middle room of the house, which had been created by combining two smaller rooms. Along the walls from floor to ceiling were lighted cases full of beautiful glass objects hand-blown by the artisans at Rodefeffer Glassworks. At intervals, there were black-and-white photos of the artists at work, and exterior shots of all the workers lined up outside the factory on the side steps.

The workers were all sorrowful looking, gaunt and hollow-eyed, wearing ragged clothing. There was also a photograph of the house in which Grace now lived; the one the Rodefeffers had built during the early part of the twentieth century. There were no trees around it back when this photograph was taken. Servants dressed in formal clothes stood lined up on the long front porch, and Scott wondered if the "Mary" Nino was looking for was one of the servants of the house.

In the forefront of the photograph were Gustav Rodefeffer, his wife, and his children. There was a small boy dressed in an uncomfortable looking suit, like a tiny adult's but with short pants. A taller, thin girl with pale curls stood in the very front. She was dressed in a drop-waist sailor dress and boots buttoned up her ankles. She had a huge white bow in her hair and a fierce, bad-tempered scowl on her face.

"That has to be Mamie," Scott said. "I'd know that look anywhere."

There was a later photograph of Mamie which must have been taken just after the start of the Second World War when she worked in an office at Rodefeffer's. She was standing outside the glassworks on the loading dock, next to the train tracks, with what looked like a small coterie of female office workers. She had the same blonde hair, now done up in a forties style with a high roll over her forehead. She wore a jacket with big shoulders that only accentuated her gaunt frame and a pencil skirt and heels that did no favors for her stick-thin legs.

Mamie didn't look as foul-tempered or fierce in this photo; she was looking off to the side and not at the camera, with a curious half smile on her face. The other women looked a little more down-at-the-heels. They all held glass animals in their hands.

Scott continued on around the wall, looking at the glass as well as the old photos on display, but Mamie wasn't featured in any other pictures. When he came to a case full of delicate glass animals, he recognized the bird Mamie had held in her hand in the staff photo. It was a graceful, delicate swan, abstract in execution to the point that it communicated more the essential swan-ness of the species rather than the exact physical attributes of the bird.

This, Scott thought, is what makes something art rather than just a knick-knack. He looked for the coded key that matched the piece, and to his surprise, saw that the artist's name was none other than Nino Vincenzo.

Mamie Rodefeffer's housekeeper answered when Scott rang the doorbell. Mamie's house was a Gothic monstrosity on the end of Morning Glory Avenue that culminated in Morning Glory Circle. The biggest, most elaborate displays of architecture were there: at the southernmost end of the circle was the Edwardian mansion belonging to Gwyneth Eldridge, whose great-grandfather built Eldridge College; the identically styled Eldridge Inn was right across the street from Mamie's house. Mamie's home afforded a beautiful view of Rose Hill City Park, situated between Morning Glory Avenue and Lilac Avenue, south of Pine Mountain Road.

Mamie's housekeeper looked as beleaguered and put-upon as Scott imagined she must always feel.

"Yes?" she said. "What is it?"

"May I speak to Miss Rodefeffer, please?" Scott asked.

"She's taking a nap," the woman said, even though Mamie could clearly be heard screeching at someone to "get me some more tea!"

"Tell her it's police business," Scott said.

"She's watching television," the woman said in a low voice. "She doesn't like to be disturbed when she's watching one of her shows."

"Rose Hill police business often takes place at times which are inconvenient to the citizens we protect," he said. "Nonetheless, I need to speak with her."

"On your head be it," she said, drawing back to let him in. "She ain't gonna like it."

Scott knew his way to the north parlor, where Mamie spent most of her time. Mamie's house smelled like lemon furniture polish and Murphy's oil soap, which is what Scott assumed they used to wash all the beautiful hardwood floors and ornate moldings. Every Persian rug was spotless though worn, and every piece of wood furniture, ornate and delicate, was polished to a deep glowing sheen.

'Money,' thought Scott, as he did every time he was in this house. 'It smells like old money.'

Mamie was sitting in her padded rocker by a roaring gas log fire, watching a Spanish-speaking soap opera on a massive television sitting just five feet away from her. The television was so wide that it served as a room divider, making the part of the room Mamie sat in feel cramped and crowded. On the bookshelf to the left of the fireplace were hundreds of romance novels, stacked and stuffed into every available square inch of space. There were three more paperback books on the end table next to her, with a cup and saucer perched on the top one. Every horizontal surface in the room had books stacked on it, and there were tall, leaning stacks on the floor as well.

It was so hot in the room that Scott felt smothered. Mamie didn't notice him, so engrossed was she in her television show. On the screen, a man and woman were arguing, and then suddenly they embraced in a passionate kiss.

"Hah!" Mamie cackled. "I knew it!"

A commercial came on, and Mamie began unwrapping chocolate candies, throwing the wrappers on the floor as she ate them, one after another. There was a bowl full of the foil-wrapped candy on her lap and what looked like dozens of wrappers on the floor. Scott wondered how many she could eat, as thin as she was.

"Miss Rodefeffer," he said, and she turned, her mouth open and full of chocolate.

"The police!" she shouted. "What have I done?"

"Nothing," Scott said. "I have some questions for you about someone who may have worked for your father."

"Not now," she said, as the commercial ended and the program began again. "My stories are on."

"It's about someone you may have known, Miss Rodefeffer," Scott said. "Someone named Nino Vincenzo."

Mamie started up out of her chair, and the bowl of candy dropped to the carpet, spilling its contents all over the floor.

"Balenchine!" Mamie yelled. "Come here and clean this up!"

Scott made as if to help but she gestured to him to stay back.

"Balenchine!" she yelled. "Get in here before I have this policeman arrest you!"

The woman whom Scott met at the door came in, shoulders drooping and surveyed the mess before getting down on her hands and knees, picking up every piece of candy and all the wrappers, and putting them in the bowl.

Then she slowly pulled herself up. All the while Mamie was scowling and sucking her teeth in a loud way. There was chocolate smeared on her lip, but Scott thought it best not to mention it.

"Balanchine!" Mamie yelled although the woman was only a foot away from her. "Bring us some tea."

"I don't care for any," Scott said. "But thank you."

"More for me, then," Mamie said.

She pulled a giant remote control with oversized buttons out of the depths of the rocker cushions and muted the television.

"Never heard of him," Mamie said, as she adjusted her layers of cardigans and skirts around her skinny legs. "You're wasting my time."

"In the picture down at the museum you were holding the swan he made," Scott said. "I saw a swan just like it in the case there with his name as the artist."

"My father employed hundreds of foreigners," Mamie said. "I don't remember any of their names. They all looked alike to me. Couldn't understand a word they said."

"Nino Vincenzo," Scott said. "He made the swan you held in the photo."

"I don't remember," Mamie insisted, but her face was reddening as she said it. "It was a long time ago. I'm an old lady who deserves to be left in peace."

"He was looking for someone named Mary," Scott said. "His sweetheart, maybe. Could that have been one of the women who worked in your house?"

"I don't know a thing about it," Mamie said. "When was this?"

"Yesterday," Scott said. "He got off a bus, walked down to the Branduff's house, and asked for Mary."

"Ask him yourself, then," Mamie said. "Why don't you ask Mr. Vincenzo who Mary was?"

"He died," Scott said. "He passed away before we could find out."

"Nothing to do with me," Mamie said, although she was visibly upset.

Balanchine came in with a steaming teapot and seemed taken aback. She looked with concern at Scott and then back at her employer.

"Everything okay, Miss Rodefeffer?"

"I'd be fine if everyone would just leave me alone," Mamie said. "Leave the tea and go."

Balanchine poured the tea and then left the room, giving Scott a disapproving look as she went.

"I'm sorry to bother you," Scott said. "I haven't been able to get hold of Mr. Vincenzo's family, and I was hoping you might remember something about him."

"Nothing to do with my family," Mamie said.

Mamie wiped her eyes with a tissue she kept pushed up the sleeve of her cardigan. She noisily blew her nose and cleared her throat.

"Miss Rodefeffer," Scott started to say, but Mamie interrupted him by turning the television sound back on with a click of the remote.

"See yourself out," she yelled.

She picked up a teacup and saucer, and it rattled in her hand. She set it back down rather abruptly. She glared at Scott, her eyes magnified behind the thick lenses of her glasses.

"Are you hard of hearing as well as stupid?" she asked him. "See yourself out, I said."

"Mamie," Scott said. "You know you can count on me to be discreet."

She turned on him with fury, her face flushed so scarlet he feared she might have a stroke.

"Leave now, and I won't have you fired for the impertinence of calling me by my Christian name," she said. "The mayor is an old family friend on whom I will not hesitate to call for assistance if you harass me any further."

"I apologize, Miss Rodefeffer," he said. "Thank you for your time."

Mamie didn't respond, but she did turn up the volume on the television.

Scott went into the central hall and noticed that the lights were on in the dining room. He looked down the hall for any sign of the housekeeper, and seeing none, he walked softly into the room. All around the elaborately decorated formal room, there were ornate, gilt-covered Victorian display cases with dozens of pieces of Rodefeffer glass inside. He didn't discover any delicate swans among them.

Grandpa had got up at 6:00 a.m. that morning. Grace fed him breakfast before he left the house. Because he did not believe in working on Sunday, he did all the prep work for Sunday morning on Saturday. All he had to do then on the Sabbath was sit out by the greenhouse and wait for everyone to pick up their orders. He didn't accept payment on Sundays, and he didn't lift a finger to help his customers carry anything, either. He took his Bible very seriously.

The deacon's wife showed up at 7:00 a.m. to pick up the flowers for the Owl's Branch Baptist Church. At 7:30 a.m. Sister Mary Margrethe came for Sacred Heart's flowers. At 8:00 a.m. one of the ladies on the altar rota appeared to collect the flowers for the United Methodist Church. At 8:30 a.m. the rector's wife picked up the order for the Episcopal Church.

Grandpa spent the rest of the morning reading his Bible. After lunch, he went to his room to take a nap that Grace knew would last until suppertime. Grandpa's Sunday naps were a respite for him which Grace also enjoyed. Five hours with which to do anything she pleased out from under the watchful eye of her grandfather was a luxury.

Stretched out on an ancient wooden folding lounge chair on the second-floor porch, Grace soaked up the afternoon sunlight while she finished the second book in her series.

Late in the afternoon, from her vantage point on the balcony, she saw a long dark car pull up outside the front entrance. Grace hopped up and ran downstairs as quietly as she could. When she reached the door and opened it, an old lady had her hand raised to knock. Grace recognized her as Mamie Rodefeffer, the daughter of the man who had built their house, known for her sharp tongue and tendency to knock over things with the multiple tote bags she usually carried. She was dressed up fancier than she usually was, no tote bags in sight, with a fur arranged around her shoulders that consisted of two dead foxes biting each other's tails. Grace thought it was disgusting looking.

"Hello," Mamie said and smiled in a way that showed she was someone who rarely smiled. "Is your grandfather at home?"

"He's taking a nap," Grace said. "I can't disturb him."

The smile instantly disappeared.

"Are you at least going to invite me in?"

"I'm sorry," Grace said. "I'm not allowed to invite people in."

"This used to be my house," Mamie said in a cross tone. "My father built it for my mother before he brought her over from Berlin in 1908. My brother and I were born in this house."

"I'm sorry," Grace said. "My grandfather doesn't allow me to have visitors."

"It used to be a beautiful house," Mamie said. "It's a pity what he's let happen to it."

"If you could come back later when he's awake," Grace said. "He might let you see it."

"Might let me see my own house," Mamie said. "That's rich."

"I'm sorry," Grace said.

"How old are you, twelve?" Mamie asked, staring at Grace through smudgy cat-eye glasses that magnified her eyes to an unnatural size.

"I'll be sixteen in a week," Grace said.

71

"Starving you, is he?" Mamie said. "No wonder you're a runty little thing. Probably fit as a fiddle, though. Only the strongest survive among the lower classes; like mongrel dogs, all of you."

Grace could only stare at someone so rude.

"I heard someone died on your front steps this weekend," Mamie said.

"Yes ma'am," Grace said. "Nino Vincenzo. He was looking for Mary."

"Lots of foreigners worked for my father," Mamie said. "Nothing to do with me, I'm sure. What did he say exactly?"

"I couldn't understand him," Grace said. "He spoke Italian."

"He asked for Mary, they said."

"He did," Grace said. "And he brought her a glass swan."

"Do you have it?" Mamie said. "I'd like to see it."

Her eyes had taken on a predatory glint that made her face seem even more pinched and cross, and her smile was sly. Still, Grace couldn't imagine what harm it would do to show her the swan, so she retrieved it from the pantry. She carefully took it out of the box and offered it to Mamie.

Mamie's face was transformed when she saw it. The deep frown lines between her brows and around her mouth disappeared, and softness took their place. At that moment, Grace thought she could see the young person Mamie used to be. Grace allowed Mamie to take the swan from her. The old woman held it up to the sunlight and looked through it.

"There's a mark inside," Mamie said, pointing to it with shaking hands. "Just inside there, do you see?"

"It looks like a cursive 'M,'" Grace said.

"Clever girl," Mamie said. "That's exactly what it is."

"That must be for Mary?" Grace asked her. "Did you know her?"

With a glare at Grace, Mamie turned back into the querulous old lady she had been before she saw the swan.

72

"Nonsense," Mamie said. "Nothing to do with me. I just happen to collect these. I'd like to buy it from you."

"It's not mine to sell," Grace said. "It belonged to Nino."

"Well, he's dead, and you could obviously use the money," Mamie said.

She handed the swan to Grace so she could dig in her old-fashioned pocketbook.

Grace put the swan back in the box and backed up to the door.

"It's not for sale," she said.

"Don't be impertinent," Mamie said as she withdrew her checkbook and a gold-plated pen. "I want the swan, and you want money. Name your price."

Grace's broom, which she had left at the top of the stairs to the second floor, fell over and clattered down the stairs.

"What was that?" Mamie said.

"That's just Edgar," Grace said.

Mamie's face turned pale.

"Who did you say that was?"

"Edgar," Grace said. "He's a ghost. He makes a lot of noise, but he wouldn't hurt a fly."

Just then Grace heard her grandfather bellow from his room.

Grace froze, and the look on Mamie's face showed the sound didn't half scare her as well.

"That's my grandfather," Grace said. "Do you want me to get him?"

"No, no," Mamie said as she backed away. "Don't let's bother him when he's just got up from his nap. You come see me up at my house. You know the one? It's the big gray house across from the Eldridge Inn on Morning Glory Circle. You come up there sometime soon, and I'll give you a nice big check for the swan. Don't break it! It's very fragile."

Grace almost laughed at how scared Mamie seemed to be to meet her grandfather. The old woman hobbled down the steps and hurried out to the car, where a man was holding open a door for her. Once she was inside, it backed down the alley all the way to Lotus Avenue.

"Grace!" her grandfather bellowed again. "Damn your hide, where are you?"

Grace took the box with the swan in it to the kitchen and quickly hid it in the pantry as her grandfather came in.

"Who was that?" he demanded. "Who left in that car I heard?"

"Mamie Rodefeffer," Grace said. "She wanted to see you, but I said you were taking a nap."

Her grandfather was uncharacteristically silent, and Grace was taken aback to see his face flush and begin to perspire.

"Are you alright, Grandpa?" she asked.

"Shut your mouth," he said and sat down heavily in one of the kitchen chairs. "Get me some water."

Grace quickly filled a glass from the tap and handed it to him. His hands were trembling as he accepted it and he spilled water down his chest as he drank. When he had one of his spells, Grace stood well away; he tended to lash out. He sat the glass down on the table top so hard she feared it would break.

"What did she tell you?" he said.

"Nothing," Grace said. "She wanted to see you, and I told her she couldn't come in."

"Good," he said. "Don't believe anything that old witch says."

"Why?" Grace said.

"Dagnabit, girl, don't question me!" he bellowed and threw the glass at her.

His aim was wild. Grace ducked, and the glass hit the wall above the window over the kitchen sink. It shattered, and the pieces fell into the sink, onto the counter, and on the floor.

"Don't you ever talk back to me like that again," he said, shaking with rage. "Do you hear me?"

"Yes, sir," Grace said, and swiftly went to the pantry for the broom and dustpan in order to clean up the broken glass.

"Clean that up and fix me some supper," he said, wiping his sweating face with his handkerchief. "And don't say a word while you do it. Not one word."

Grace did as she was told, and kept her tongue in her head.

CHAPTER FOUR – MONDAY

Grace and Tommy were in the hallway, putting away the books from their morning classes in preparation for lunch. Grace saw the lumbering football player known as Jumbo coming down the hallway, slamming locker doors shut and shoving people out of the way as he went. Charlotte walked right behind him, ignoring what he was doing while she texted.

A small boy was kneeling next to his locker and Charlotte just happened to trip as she passed him. Grace could clearly see he hadn't caused her to trip; she just couldn't walk very well in the tall platform shoes she was wearing. Charlotte was embarrassed, and her face flushed bright red.

"Idiot," Charlotte said to the small boy. "Why don't you watch what you're doing?"

The kid stood up, saying, "I didn't do anything," but Jumbo picked him up, walked across the hall with him, and dropped him in a trash barrel. Some people in the hallway laughed. Jumbo let loose a volley of vulgar language just as the Vice Principal rounded the corner.

"Mr. Larson," the Vice Principal said. "Meet me in my office."

To everyone else, he said, "Go to lunch."

Jumbo tried to look tough but his face flushed as he stomped off down the hall with the Vice Principal. Grace helped the boy climb out of the trash can and then fished out his glasses, which had fallen off. He was crying, and she felt sorry for him. Everyone else had turned away, but Grace picked up the books he had dropped and handed them to him.

"Here," she said.

"Thank you," the boy said and wiped his face on his sleeve.

"No problem," Grace said. "We small people have to stick together."

She was rewarded with a smile, and he seemed to recover some of his dignity.

"Jumbo's just an overgrown toddler but with less impulse control," Grace said. "Just remember someday his job will be stirring the poop at the sewage treatment plant."

The boy smiled and said, "What's your name?"

"Grace Branduff," she said. "What's yours?"

His reply was cut off by Tommy loudly confronting Charlotte.

"How can you be with him?" Tommy asked Charlotte, who was already looking over his shoulder for someone more popular to talk to.

"What?" she said with derision, and the look she gave him turned Grace to stone; she wondered if Tommy could survive what was coming.

"How can you be with someone so stupid and mean?" he said. "He could have really hurt that kid; he's three times his size. How is that a fair fight?"

"How could I be with him?" Charlotte said in a shrill voice that drew attention from everyone left in the hallway. "You mean instead of a dirt-poor hick raised by some dumbass con artist? Huh. Why in the world would I want someone who comes from a nice family, who lives in a nice house, instead of someone like you, whose real mother got blown up in a meth lab?"

Tommy looked as if she had swung a baseball bat into his midsection. He turned and fled, leaving his locker open.

"Shame on you," Grace hissed, and Charlotte had the decency to blush. "We've been your friends since kindergarten. Who in the hell do you think you are?"

"Don't you cuss at me, Grace Branduff," Charlotte said. "I go to church. I'm a Christian."

"Some Christian," Grace said. "You lied about him tripping you; you tripped over your own damn feet in those stupid shoes. I saw you do it."

"You two need to get over it and move on," Charlotte said, flipping her hair over her shoulder as she walked away. "We're not friends anymore, and we never will be."

Grace took out Tommy's and her lunch bags, closed and locked both of their lockers, and then paused. Where would he have gone?

Out in the student parking lot, the holler kids were hanging out with their monster trucks, listening to country music. The girls had on jeans and cowboy boots with their hoodies, while the boys wore construction boots and Nascar T-shirts.

"Hey, Grace," one boy said as she approached.

"Hey, Jimmy John," Grace said. "Have you seen Tommy?"

"Naw," he said. "But if you do, tell him we're going mud-boggin' next weekend. You should come too."

"Thanks," Grace said.

Grace circled around the school, past the hip-hop kids with their pants falling down, listening to rap music. She passed the hipster kids with their half-shaved heads and big glasses, listening to obscure music they hoped no one else yet knew about and headed toward the FFA barn. There, some farm kids were tending to cows, sheep, and pigs that would compete and then be auctioned off in the Pine County Fair later that summer. They were dressed similarly to the holler kids and were also listening to country music.

"Hey, Grace," one of the girls said.

She was brushing a huge black cow's shiny coat. It was the biggest cow Grace had ever seen, and the girl was standing on an overturned bucket in order to reach its back.

"Hi, Dreama," Grace said. "Cute cow."

"She's a he," Dreama said. "Stanley is an Angus bull."

"Is he mean?" Grace said, stepping backward.

"Not to me," Dreama said, as she lovingly smoothed his coat. "I bottle fed him from a calf, so he follows me around like a puppy."

"Won't it be hard to give him up?" Grace said.

"It's what happens," Dreama said with a shrug. "I just don't think about that part."

"Have you seen Tommy?"

"He stopped by earlier," Dreama said. "He's writing about Stanley for the school paper. Did you check the journalism lab?"

"No, but I will," Grace said. "See ya."

Tommy was not in the journalism lab, where two girls were debating the merits of state colleges versus private colleges.

"State is so much cheaper," one said.

"But the classes have like two hundred people in them," the other said. "In a small school, you get much more individual attention."

"I'd kind of like to disappear," the first said. "I'm kind of tired of individual attention."

Grace stopped in the girls' bathroom by the back door and was dismayed to see every stall taken. Underneath one stall door, she could see the entwined legs of the lesbian couple who shared the locker on one side of Grace's.

"Lydia? Louise?" she said. "I'm sorry to interrupt, but I really need to pee."

The door swung open to reveal them both texting, not making out as Grace had expected. Neither looked away from her phone as they left the stall and wandered out into the hallway.

Sitting on the toilet, Grace could hear someone throwing up in the stall next door. It made her a little queasy to hear. As she washed her hands afterward, Stacy Rodefeffer left the stall from where the puking sounds had originated. She had long blonde hair, a giant apple-green handbag, and wore a pink velour sweatsuit.

"Sup?" she said in a bored voice.

"Hey, Stacey," Grace said. "Feeling alright?"

"Just peachy," Stacey said.

She took a swig from a small bottle of mouthwash and then spit it in the sink.

Stacey examined her face in the mirror, and then took out a lip pencil, a pot of lip color, and a brush, with which she reapplied her lip makeup. Over in the corner, waiting for her, was Stacey's best friend, Aleesha. She was eating corn chips and texting.

"Hi, Grace," she said, without looking up.

Grace left the school through the back door and walked toward where the pumped up lifters were weight training outside of the gym.

"Hi, Grace," one of them said as she passed.

"Hi Billy," Grace said.

Billy used to be a small skinny kid until the summer before a growth spurt caused him to shoot up to six feet tall. Now he was covered in big round muscles and could barely fit through the doors to the classrooms.

Charlotte and the Beal sisters were sitting at a table on the quad. They quit talking as Grace passed but gave her an up and down look that conveyed their contempt. As soon as she was a few yards past them one of them said, "Nice shoes," and they all burst into peals of mean laughter. Grace's face burned, but she ignored them.

Grace walked out toward the football field. Under the bleachers the emo and Goth kids were hanging out, listening to their gloomy music. A subset of these groups, the witchy-vampire-emo-Goths, had drawn a pentagram in the dirt and were casting spells. They were dressed all in black with pale faces, black kohl-rimmed eyes, and everything that could be pierced had been.

"Hey, Grace," one of the witchy Goth girls called out.

"Hi, Whitney," Grace said. "Whatcha conjuring today?"

"Oh, you know, demons," the girl said. "Evil spirits, that sort of thing."

"Good luck," Grace said. "Have you seen Tommy?"

The girl gestured toward the bleachers.

Further on, the stoners were passing a joint. The smoke blew over Grace's face and caused her to cough. They all chuckled over that.

"Hola Grace," one of the boys said. "Did you know there's like this wild marijuana field out back of Possum Holler, like up on the hill? An old guy used to live there, like, some scientist type guy? He planted it like fifty years ago, and the buds are like as big as your fist."

"No," Grace said. "I didn't know that."

"Well, we're like, going to go up there this weekend? And look for it? You wanna go?"

"No thanks," Grace said. "But good luck. Seen Tommy?"

He pointed to the far side of the field where Tommy was sitting on the top bleacher, looking out at the nearby highway, his face turned away from the field.

"Hey," Grace said when she reached the top and sat down next to him, putting their lunch bags between them. "Talk to me."

"I love her," Tommy said. "How could she do that to me?"

Tears were streaming down his face. Grace felt a stab of sympathy for him along with burning anger for Charlotte, who didn't deserve his devotion.

"I know you do," Grace said. "I'm so sorry."

"It just really hurts," he said. "Like, I have a real pain in my chest. I think my heart is actually being damaged by her."

He wiped his eyes with the end of his T-shirt and sniffed a few times.

"God," he said. "I hate feeling like this. Why is she doing this to me?"

"She's making a huge mistake," Grace said when what she really wanted to say was, "This is what happens when you fall in love with a selfish person who picks popularity over a lifetime of friendship."

"I tried to talk to her the other day, out on the quad," he said. "She gave me this look like I was beneath her and irritating her."

Grace didn't say what she was thinking. Even though he was hurt he wasn't going to listen to a word said against Charlotte. Not yet.

"It's all their fault, Jumbo and the Beals," Tommy said. "They're a terrible influence on her. If she could just see them for how they really are."

They sat in companionable silence for a while. Then Tommy took out his sandwich and took a bite. Grace started on hers.

"Remember that time we sat on the third-floor balcony at your house and threw chestnuts in the river?" he said.

"We threw them, but I don't think any got as far as the river."

"When you went downstairs to get the cards, I kissed her," he said. "I kissed Charlotte, and she kissed me back. She did. It wasn't all on my side."

Grace knew about this because Charlotte told her, had laughed about it. She was just experimenting with kissing, but he thought it meant she loved him.

It had been the beginning of the end, just after school started last fall. Charlotte got her braces off at the end of the summer and was wearing contact lenses. Suddenly all she was interested in was makeup, clothes, and boys. She also made cutting remarks about how Grace and Tommy dressed and acted.

"It's time for us to grow up," Charlotte said to her one day after Grace tried to kid her about how pretentious she was acting. "We aren't kids anymore."

It wasn't much longer before Charlotte was riding to school in an expensive SUV with an older group of girls, and eating lunch at the popular kids' table in the cafeteria. Grace had tried to talk to her about it, but Charlotte said, "My mom says it's totally normal to outgrow your middle school

82

friends. We all mature at different rates and you and Tommy are just maturing more slowly than me."

Grace had said, "You're acting like an idiot, and those people you're hanging out with are a bunch of stupid snobs."

"I wouldn't expect you to understand the social advantages of hanging out with the right people," Charlotte had said, with a disgusted look on her face. "Considering how you've been brought up I doubt you'll ever need to know."

Charlotte had blushed then as if even she knew how awful she was being. That was the last time Grace had talked to Charlotte until today. Tommy had still been trying, and it was heartbreaking to watch him try to draw her attention only to be dismissed with an eye roll and a disparaging comment shared with her new friends. Now that Charlotte had that hulking dumbass for a boyfriend, Grace feared Tommy might get physically hurt.

"He's not worthy of her," Tommy said. "I'm not saying I am, but for sure he's not."

Even now he still had Charlotte up on a pedestal. Grace knew he would forgive any bad behavior on Charlotte's part if she would just throw him a crust of bread like he was a stray dog.

"What does she see in him?" he asked Grace

"He's popular," Grace said. "I think that's all that matters to her now."

"I talked to her mom about it," Tommy said.

Grace cringed. Charlotte's mother Ava was pretty and gracious, but her kindness seemed very calculated to Grace. It was a role she was playing, and not who she really was. Grace was small and quiet, so people often forgot she was in the room; she had seen and heard some things Ava would not want anyone to know about. Ava was still courteous to Grace when she ran into her, but she never said, "Where have you been?" or "When are you coming to dinner?" Charlotte's mother made it obvious she knew what was up and approved.

Grace had seen Charlotte and her new friends hanging out behind the B&B, lounging around at the picnic table and throwing pine cones at the boys who drove down the alley to flirt with them. They were always whispering, shrieking, or texting, their phones permanently attached to their hands.

They talked in text language and made fun of Grace for things only Charlotte could have told them about her. It hurt, but Grace had come to the conclusion that if you don't want to be hurt you just shouldn't care so much.

"Have you heard from your mom?" Grace said.

"She's getting out pretty soon," he said. "She's worried about what people will think. You can see why."

"What do you think?"

"It'll be weird," he said. "She's been gone for three years; things have changed a lot."

"Do you think she and Ed will get back together?"

"I wish they would," Tommy said. "But neither of them thinks so. Mom says, 'That's water under the bridge,' and Ed says, 'I blew my chance when I had it,' so probably not."

"Will you live with Ed or her?"

"I have to live with Ed since he's my legal guardian," Tommy said. "Since mom's not actually related to me she doesn't have any rights. She rescued me from those people and raised me from a baby, so she's the only mom I've ever known. My real grandma didn't see it as rescuing so much as kidnapping and transporting me across state lines. It didn't help that mom stole her daughter's identity."

Tommy's biological parents were killed in a drug-related accident in Florida when he was still an infant. When his biological grandmother found him and discovered his mother was not the Miranda Wilson she had been searching for, she called the FBI. Melissa Wright, which was the real name of the person he considered his mother, was currently serving her sentence at a federal correction facility for women in Florida, where the crime took place. Tommy's

84

grandmother was dying of cancer when she found him; before she died, she let him pick Ed as his guardian, and had left him a small trust fund to use for his college education.

"All that really matters is that you love the person who raised you and she loves you," Grace said. "You're lucky to have that."

"I only saw your mom that time she came to school," Tommy said. "What was she like?"

"I found the papers from where my grandma took her to a court-ordered psychiatric appointment. The official diagnosis was borderline personality with narcissistic disorder," Grace said, "which basically meant she was crazy in general, but mostly crazy about herself. My grandparents didn't believe in giving medication for things like that; things might have turned out differently if they had. They thought she had a demon inside her. Sometimes it seemed like she did."

"Was she mean to you?"

"Whenever my grandma wasn't looking," Grace said. "She blamed me for ruining her life."

"What about your dad?" Tommy asked. "You never talk about him."

Grace shrugged.

"He lives somewhere out in the Midwest," she said. "His parents moved the whole family away after my mom got pregnant in high school. My Aunt Lucy said I looked just like him but I've seen a picture of him and I don't think so."

"Where's your Aunt Lucy?"

"Nobody knows."

"Have you ever thought about contacting your dad?"

"No point, really," she said. "He knows about me, and if he ever wanted to meet me, he knows where I am, right where he left me."

"We could find him online," Tommy said. "Find out what he's like."

"I don't want to know," Grace said. "I don't want him to seem real."

"We're like orphans, you and me, like in The Boxcar Children."

"At least Ed likes you," Grace said. "My grandfather doesn't even pretend to like me."

"We never talk about this stuff," he said. "I'm glad we are now. It makes me feel better."

"I'll never quit being your friend as long as you want to be my friend," Grace impulsively said and was surprised at the tears that came with the promise.

"Me too," Tommy said and hugged her.

Someone seated further down the bleachers whistled at them and made a loud comment, so they parted. It felt awkward afterward but in a good way. They sat in silence as they finished their lunches, and then watched cars on the highway until the bell rang for fifth period.

"Hey, Ed," Maggie said as she entered the office of the weekly newspaper known as the *Rose Hill Sentinel*, which was quartered in a tiny storefront building next to her mother's bakery.

Ed was working on his computer, which had the biggest, thinnest, flat-screen monitor Maggie had ever seen.

"Nice computer," she said. "Is it new?"

Ed pushed back his chair and got up, gesturing to the screen with a flourish.

"I bought it for my website design business," he said. "I say it's for design purposes, but it also helps with my aging eyesight."

"How's that Internet stuff going?" Maggie said, sitting on a stool by the tall worktable. "The Rose Hill website looks great, and it seems like every website linked to it was also designed by you."

Ed went to the back, got two root beers out of the fridge in his kitchenette, and handed one to Maggie before he sat across from her.

"The website design business saved my hide," he said. "Print journalism is not exactly a growth industry, you know."

"You're telling this to a bookstore owner," she replied.

"How's business?" he said.

"The book part of the business is shrinking as fast as the café part is growing," she said. "If it weren't for tourists buying sweatshirts and students buying textbooks, I'd be back working for my mother."

"Wifi," he said. "That's the next logical step."

"Hell no," Maggie said. "I prefer my customers to eat, drink, and then get the hell out. I don't want them to hang out all day."

"Why did you get into the retail business, again?" he asked.

"I know," she said. "What was I thinking? My best customers are exactly the kind of people I hate the most: privileged and demanding, with an oversized sense of entitlement. They just cannot be pleased. The weird thing is the ruder I am to them the more they seem to like it."

"Just be glad you're surviving," Ed said. "I know I said I'd work on a website for you, but lately I seem to have more on my plate than I can cope with."

"Something new?"

"The college wants to hire me to run their online education program," Ed said.

"That's great," Maggie said. "Are you going to do it?"

"I might," he said. "I just don't want to throw in the towel on the Sentinel."

"Can't you do both?"

"Maybe," he said. "Let me run this past you and see what you think: I'm considering offering the Sentinel to the college as an ongoing journalism project for their English students. I'd turn it into a kind of a lab where the college pays for production in return for their students learning how to run a publishing business. I've also been looking into

87

electronic book publishing, and I think it might be the next logical step for the college press. I've talked to several professors who are interested in publishing that way."

"Wow," Maggie said. "That's a lot of change all at once."

"I'd rather change the way I do business than close it and whine ever after about how life isn't fair."

"It actually sounds like a good survival plan," Maggie said. "Maybe I could get some business major interns, myself."

"Worth a try," Ed said. "The advertising barely covers the cost of production for the physical paper, and while the Sentinel website is self-supporting, I'd kind of like to start saving for my eventual nursing home costs."

"I don't even want to think about retirement," Maggie said. "What retirement? I'll have to work until I drop dead."

"Do you think the café and textbook business will be enough to keep you afloat long term?"

"Not if electronic textbooks outsell the paper kind," Maggie said.

"Sorry," Ed said. "I think it's kind of inevitable at this point."

"Remember record stores?" Maggie said, and Ed nodded. "I feel like the owner of a record store pretending MP3s will eventually go away."

"A few record stores still exist, you know," Ed said. "And some people will always love the feeling of an actual paper book in their hands."

"I keep picturing this dystopian future where all books are controlled electronically, and paper books are outlawed," Maggie said. "It makes me want to hoard all the PG Wodehouse I can get my hands on."

"You may want to ease up on reading Cormac McCarthy for a while," Ed said. "You're making the future sound very bleak."

88

"I need paper books," Maggie said. "I look at my bookshelf at home, and I feel comforted. There are all my old friends just waiting for the rainy day when I'll need them again."

"There is something to be said for a book you don't need electricity to read," Ed said. "As often as the power goes out in this town, that's essential."

"I know this is the direction in which things are going," Maggie said. "I can easily envision Little Bear Books becoming 60% café, 35% tourist souvenirs, and 5% books."

"Wifi," Ed said. "I'll help you install it."

"Not yet," Maggie said. "But soon."

"Did Scott tell you about that guy dropping dead on Jacob Branduff's porch?"

"That's actually why I'm here," Maggie said. "Scott's really worried about Grace. I've met her, and she seems like a nice kid. Do you think she's safe living there with Jacob?"

Ed shrugged.

"He's a huge grouch, but I've never seen signs that she's physically abused."

"She's so tiny and skinny," Maggie said.

"It's not a crime to be poor," Ed said. "If it were, most of the people living out Possum Holler would be guilty."

"Child neglect is a crime," she said.

"True," Ed said. "But we don't know that she's being neglected. We're just assuming that from appearances. You'd think Hannah was starving if you'd never seen her eat."

"Scott's really worried," Grace said. "You know him; he wants to save everyone."

"She's a very well-mannered, smart young woman," Ed said. "I don't really know anything more about her."

"Maybe you could ask Tommy to spy a little," Maggie said. "Find out if Scott needs to intervene."

"I can't do that," Ed said. "That's not fair to Grace."

"How else are we going to find out if she needs help?" Maggie said.

"Well, the first thing you could do is ask her," Ed said. "She might just tell you."

"She barely knows me," Maggie said. "It would have to be someone she trusts."

"I think she's pretty isolated," Ed said. "Since Charlotte dumped Tommy and her, I don't know that she has any close friends."

"That's what Matt Delvecchio said, too," Maggie said. "Poor kid."

"All we can do is to offer our help," Ed said. "We can't make her accept it."

"Oh well," Maggie said. "Thanks anyway."

"Glad to help in any way I can," Ed said. "She seems like a nice girl, and Tommy needs a friend."

"That rotten Charlotte," Maggie said. "I know she's my niece, but I'd like to give her a good hard pinch."

"Unrequited love," Ed said. "It happens to everyone."

"Have you heard from Mandy lately?"

"You mean Melissa," Ed said. "Her real name is Melissa."

"That's going to be hard to get used to," Maggie said. "When's she coming home?"

"Soon, I think," Ed said.

"Tommy will be glad to have his mom home," Maggie said. "Whatever we call her."

Grace was darting through a crowd of people clogging the hallway as she made her way to fifth-period study hall. Suddenly, a huge wall of a person blocked her way and would not move. She feinted left, and so did he.

"I play defense," he said in a soft voice, a voice that did not match his giant stature. "I can do this all day."

Grace looked up, way up, and met his kind, brown eyes. His smile was shy and sweet.

"I'm supposed to escort you to the computer lab," he said. "Here's your pass."

Grace took the pass, which was filled out giving her permission to spend her study period in the computer lab.

"How did you get this?" she said. "And why?"

"You did Elvis a favor," he said. "Now he wants to thank you."

"Who's Elvis?" Grace said. "I don't know him. I think you have the wrong person."

"Nope," he said. "You're Grace Branduff, right?"

"Yes," she said. "What's this about?"

He shrugged.

"Nothin' bad," he said. "Elvis is a righteous little dude. You'll like him. We call him 'the fixer.' If you do him a favor, he'll help you fix your problems."

"What did he do for you?"

"He's helping me keep my GPA high enough to play ball," he said. "I gotta get me a scholarship or I ain't going to college. If I don't go to college, I ain't gonna play pro ball."

"He helps you study?"

"Yeah," he said. "Like with flash cards and memory tricks. There's 'a rat' in the middle of the word 'separate?' Did you know that?"

"That's clever," Grace said. "I still think you've got the wrong person."

"I can't make you go," he said. "Well, I guess I could, but listen, you'll be glad you did. C'mon. You'll see."

Grace searched his face but didn't see anything mean or deceptive, not even a brief flash of an ulterior motive.

"Okay," she said.

In the computer lab, Grace was surprised to find the same boy she had helped climb out of the garbage can into which Jumbo had dropped him. The big boy departed with a shy wave, leaving Grace and the small boy alone in the room.

Grace had been in the computer lab many times but had never noticed this boy before. He was seated in the back of the room in what looked like a makeshift command central. There were two flat screens and a laptop on top of the four-foot desk; multiple, neatly tethered bundles of wires ran between these, and two hard drive towers lined up beneath the desk to one side. There were two printers, one of which looked as if it also scanned, copied, and possibly transformed into a weapon.

He was small, even smaller than Grace. He was seated upon four thick foam booster cushions. His feet, which fell several inches short of the floor, rested on top of a hollowed-out hard drive tower resting on its side, like the ribcage of a former trusty steed.

He was dressed like every other twelve-year-old boy Grace knew, in a T-shirt, jeans, and athletic shoes, earbuds dangling around his neck. He needed a haircut. The physics equations he was studying on one screen reflected off his glasses.

"Elvis?" Grace asked. "You wanted to see me?"

"Yes," Elvis said. "Good to see you again."

He removed his glasses and placed them in a protective case he kept nearby. He leaned over and popped open the top of a smaller cooler.

"Juicebox?" he offered.

"Thanks," said Grace, never one to turn down an offer of beneficial calories and nutrients.

"Organic," he said. "No BHA in the plastic. My mother's very particular about that."

"She cares about you," Grace said. "That's nice."

"Care, like love, is too broad of a term," Elvis said. "There's simple sentiment, which just means warm feelings, pleasure in proximity, or hormonal responses easily cultivated and reproduced in high functioning hominids through a system of stimulus and reward. There's maternal love, an innate genetic instinct which seeks to nurture and protect the young in order to ensure the survival of the species. There's pride of ownership or a sense of investiture in a project from which a reasonable assurance of return on investment is expected. There's common decency, a societal pressure whereby a culture's agreed upon religious or philosophical beliefs require adherence to a concern for the well being of one's fellow believer, or at the very least a concerned pity for the nonbeliever and a shared hatred of what is seen as outside or other. There's possessive desire, overt or sublimated carnal lust, calculated self-interest, nepotism, and favor-currying, which are really just forms of barter. The word 'care' can mean so many things."

Grace thought she might like to take out a notebook in which to take notes. There was a long pause while she attempted to process all that he had said and then tried to remember what they were talking about, to begin with.

"Sorry," he said. "I have a tendency to take a subject and download everything I know about it as a form of conversing."

"I don't mind," Grace said. "I've never thought about all the ways you could interpret the word 'care.'"

"I would say my mother's regard for me contains the appropriate amount of warmth," Elvis said. "In fact, I'd wager she has thoroughly researched what approximates the optimum ratio of attachment to the encouragement of independence and very closely walks that line."

"Attachment?" Grace said. "Do you mean love?"

"Love is another word that can mean many things," Elvis said. "A baby monkey raised in a lab will form an attachment to a cloth-covered puppet. Animals attach to whatever feeds them or appears to feed them. Human attachment is more complex. The human child tends to attach to whoever nurtures him or her, even if it's inconsistent or sub-standard in quality."

"I guess you do what you have to in order to survive," Grace said, thinking of her mother.

"Consider platonic love," Elvis said, "which is a devoted friendship."

Grace thought of Charlotte, who did not appreciate her platonic devotion.

"And romantic love," Elvis said. "Which might or might not include friendship but definitely includes making out. Now there are two subjects that philosophers and poets have spent lifetimes studying."

"What about unrequited love," Grace said, thinking of Tommy and Charlotte.

"Sometimes we imagine people have desirable qualities they don't have and form an attachment to this imaginary construct," Elvis said. "You can form attachments based on a perceived relationship with a person when there is actually no relationship at all. One should never underestimate the human ability to jump to a conclusion without a careful examination of the facts. We tend to idealize people and then get disappointed."

"So maybe there never was a real friendship?" Grace said. "Maybe I just imagined there was?"

"Possibly," Elvis said. "I would need more data to determine that."

"I had a crush on a boy who moved away in sixth grade," Grace said. "He was smart and funny. He made people laugh, but he wasn't mean about it. I think if I ever have a boyfriend I want him to be just like that."

"I myself get crushes on girls who are just like my mother–detached, critical, clinical," Elvis said. "But I also like girls who are the exact opposite–affectionate, sweet, sentimental."

"I've never thought about why we get crushes on the people we do," Grace said. "I thought it was something that just happens in a sort of magical way."

"It seems to me to be more of a function of finding someone whose personality disorders mirror our own or our parents'," Elvis said.

"Why would I be attracted to someone who is mean to me?"

"It's a human instinct to form attachments, especially when we feel endangered. Have you heard of Stockholm syndrome? That's when you form an attachment to the person who has kidnapped you as a way to make your situation emotionally tolerable."

"I think it's smarter not to care," Grace said. "That way you're never disappointed."

"It's probably wisest to keep a detached outlook anytime you feel an attachment. That was a humorous play on words. I'm smart and funny, just like that boy you had a crush on in the sixth grade."

"The problem is you can't trust people," Grace said.

"Some attachment is necessary for a person's emotional health," he said. "Maybe you should be choosier about whom you trust."

"It must be terrible being as smart as you are trapped in this school."

"It is," he said. "I can't wait to grow up so people will take me seriously. I also can't wait to meet people more like me, so I don't feel like such a freak. My mom says it will get better eventually."

"She sounds nice," Grace said. "It must be nice to feel wanted."

"She wanted a child. Delete that. She wanted a brilliant, healthy, well-adjusted child, but she couldn't find someone she liked well enough to argue over how to raise the child. So she saved her money and went to a fertility specialist that offered the best raw material. She sought to balance physical ability with a superior health history and a high, but not too high IQ. Not too much of any of the three, mind you, but a balance. No point in being so smart you can't function in the real world, or too sickly to survive world travel. My biological father was a star rugby player at university and is a successful British barrister. As a result, I have excellent hand-and-eye coordination, but I'm not going to Oxford on a sports scholarship."

"You're going to Oxford?"

"That's the plan," Elvis said.

"When?"

"This is my last year of public school," Elvis said. "My mother wanted me to have as normal of a cultural and social experience as was necessary so I would be able to relate to my peers, but how normal could it be for me anywhere, really? Everyone knows I'm a freak, they're just nice to me because I help solve the odd problem here and there."

"That big boy said they call you 'The Fixer.'"

"I know, I started that," he said. "A sense of mystery and bartered acts of benevolence often give one power over weaker minds. Use that power for evil, and you have fascism. Use it for good, and you have the United Nations."

"You're using yours for good, I guess."

"What is a scientist, after all, if not a solver of problems?"

"I don't think anyone can solve my problems," she said. "No offense."

"None taken," he said. "I do love a good challenge, though. I don't have much time left here, and I would like to do something for you before the end of the term."

"Where will you go after this term is over?"

"I'm going to Disney World in June, and then to Harry Potter World in July. It's been arranged I'm to have behind-the-scenes tours at both venues, but my cousins are coming so it will be just for fun as well. While in Coral Gables visiting my aunt's family I plan to study marine mammals and the healing properties of sea vegetation. In September we're moving to Palo Alto, California so I can attend Stanford, where I will obtain degrees in both theoretical physics and existential-phenomenological psychology. After that, it's on to Oxford. I should be tall by then. I may blend in better. My father and mother are both tall, so I should have an accelerated growth spurt at some point."

"Sounds like a fun summer," Grace said.

"All in all it should be a most pleasant summer," Elvis said. "My cousins only have average intelligence, but they're very fun. We'll have water balloon battles and play hide-and-seek. I'm an excellent hider."

"Me too," said Grace. "What will you do after Oxford?"

"It depends," Elvis said, and then noisily sucked the last of his juice out of the box, collapsing it. "I can keep on learning things, apply what I've learned, teach what I've learned, or earn money by inventing things. Or do all of that, of course. It's just a matter of efficient time management and the prudent use of resources."

"What would you like to do?"

"Well, I'd like to meet a nice girl, get married, and have some children," he said. "I think the rest will figure itself out."

"Do you ever wish you were more like other people?" Grace asked.

"I wouldn't know how," Elvis said, "and it would be psychologically self-limiting to pretend."

"Do you worry about disappointing your mother?"

"No," he said. "I know I won't."

"Is she a huggy kind of mother, though?" Grace asked. "You make her sound kind of cold."

"She's appropriately physically affectionate, certainly," he said. "I'm not a robot."

"I'm sorry," Grace said. "I didn't mean to imply that."

"I'm smart," he said. "But I'm still human. My feelings get hurt, and I have bad moods, just like anyone else. I also have the ability to psychoanalyze myself in any one of a dozen ways and work out all my problems myself, in a rational manner. It's a matter of having the right tools and the knowledge of how to most effectively use them. Sometimes I just need more rest or fluids. Hormonal activity is becoming a bit of an issue, of course. It's the age. Anyone, even the smartest person, can be fooled by oxytocin."

"Oxytocin?"

"It's the hormone that increases trust and decreases fear," he said. "It's that feeling you get when someone you are attached to hugs you or you see someone who approximates your ideal of beauty. It can be quite addictive."

Grace thought of the hug she and Tommy had shared in the bleachers. According to Elvis, what she had thought of as a meaningful moment was actually just a chemical change in her brain. It had felt meaningful. Was that just her imagination applying wishful thinking to a biological reaction?

"We don't have much time," he said. "You had better tell me about your problem."

Grace outlined her situation and was surprised at how easy it was to tell this small boy about her grandfather's dire pronouncement, along with her feelings and her deepest fears. His demeanor was of polite, nonjudgmental curiosity and frank interest. She felt as if she were providing him with a new case study for one of his psychology experiments.

When she was through, he continued to peer at her, and gradually she realized he had discontinued seeing her; seemed instead to be looking at some interior screen she could not see. She wondered if her problem looked like a physics exercise.

"I'm going to need some time to work on this," he said finally. "Meanwhile, I'd like to suggest you read a few things."

Grace took out a notebook and pen.

"Maslow's *Hierarchy of Needs*," he said, "and Joseph Campbell's '*The Hero's Journey*.'"

"Anything else?" she asked.

"Any young adult fiction based on the epic journey of an abandoned child," he said. "I'd suggest *Harry Potter*."

CHAPTER FIVE – STILL MONDAY

G race entered the school library between fifth and sixth periods and was surprised to see Jumbo's mother, Mrs. Lawson, taking books off a cart and stacking them on the counter. Grace had no sooner placed her book on the counter than the woman grabbed it up.

"You shouldn't be reading such trash, young lady," Mrs. Lawson said. "It's not good for you."

"Run along, Grace," the librarian said, with a harassed look on her face. "You'll be late for class."

"Where are you taking those books?" Grace asked.

All the Harry Potter books, the *His Dark Materials* books, and several science-fiction books were among those piled up on the front counter.

"Where they belong," Mrs. Lawson said with a smug smile. "To the dumpster."

Grace felt tightness in her chest and wondered if something like this could give a young person a heart attack.

"You can't do that," she said, and hearing the words come out surprised even her.

"Go on to class, Grace," the librarian said. "I'll handle this."

Grace tried to jerk *A Wrinkle in Time* out of Mrs. Lawson's hand, but the woman held on.

"Grace!" Mrs. Lawson said.

"Let go," Grace said.

"Grace, please," the librarian said. "You're not helping."

"But you're not doing a damn thing!" Grace said.

Grace jerked the book out of the woman's hands so hard her arm flew into a stack on the counter, and they all fell on the floor.

"Grace, that's enough," the librarian said.

"No!" Grace yelled at Mrs. Lawson. "You can't do this!"

Grace fell to her knees and was scrabbling through the pile of books on the floor, looking for the third book in the *His Dark Materials* trilogy.

"I had no idea she was mentally deranged," Mrs. Lawson said. "Just like her mother."

Grace stood up in the middle of the library and unleashed a torrent of verbal abuse on Mrs. Lawson that was laced with so much profanity that when she was finished, you could not hear a sound. Students in the hallway outside the library stood frozen in shock. Grace placed a hand over her mouth and looked at the librarian, whose face had turned a livid red.

Mrs. Lawson said, "The apple certainly didn't fall far from the tree," with a look of pure, evil delight on her face.

The Vice Principal escorted Grace into his office and directed her to sit across from him at his desk. He was not that old of a guy and was dressed in what she knew he thought was a young, hip way. Grace thought he was about two years away from looking foolish in that beard and the hipster glasses.

"Grace Branduff," he read off the infamous blue card the librarian had filled out with a trembling hand. "Are you new here?"

"I'm a sophomore," she said. "This is my second year."

"Well, I apologize," he said with an ingratiating smile. "There's just so many of you and so few of us. It's actually good that I don't know you; it means you're never in trouble."

"I am never in trouble," she said.

"So what happened today?"

"There's this book I want to read, and this horrible woman was going to throw it away."

"Really?" he said. "What book is that?"

Grace started to describe the series, but he stopped her.

"I've read those," he said. "They're very good."

Grace felt the tightness in her chest relax.

"Who was going to throw it away?" he asked.

"Jumbo's mother," she said. "Mrs. Lawson thinks that all these really good books are from the devil or something. She's insane."

"Her I know," the vice principal said with a shudder. "Awful woman, just awful."

Grace felt a fondness for the Vice Principal begin to blossom despite his hipster hair.

"Book banning is abhorrent, I agree," he said, "and I think we should nip that bit of busy-body nonsense in the bud right away, but this card says you were disruptive, disrespectful and used offensive language toward Miss Briggs."

"I did," she said. "I'm not sorry about it yet, but I'm sure I will be. As soon as I am, I promise I will apologize."

The Vice Principal smiled at Grace and shook his head.

"Fair enough," he said. "But before the week's over, alright?"

Grace nodded.

"If I look at your file what will it say about your grades?"

"Straight As," she said.

"What groups or clubs do you belong to?"

"None."

"Why's that?"

"My grandfather won't pay for any of that nonsense."

"I see," the Vice Principal said. "Who's your favorite teacher here?"

"I don't really have a favorite," Grace said. "But my English teacher's okay."

"What would she say about you?"

"I never miss an answer on a test, but I won't participate in class discussions."

"Why's that?"

"Speaking up makes you a target; I like to keep a low profile."

"Not exactly keeping a low profile today, were you?" he said. "Is something going on at home?"

Grace laughed out loud and immediately covered her mouth in embarrassment.

"I'm sorry," she said. "I didn't mean to do that."

"Who's your guidance counselor?"

"Mrs. Pike."

"Tough luck," he said. "You'll get no sympathy there. She and Jumbo's mother are best friends."

"Great," she said.

"I tell you what," he said. "I have about a dozen real sociopaths to sort out this afternoon. I'm going to recommend you see this particular school psychologist for three sessions. She's a friend of mine and very good. She can probably help with whatever's going on if you'll be straight with her. Or, you can lie about it and probably get by with that; it's up to you. As far as I'm concerned, you're a smart kid who had a bad day. We're all allowed one of those per year, and you just used up yours. Please don't make me see you again."

"Thank you," Grace said, and rose to leave.

"Grace," he said. "If it's something really bad at home; something you can't live with, please let us help you. No one should have to put up with abuse of any kind."

"Thanks," she said and walked as fast as she could out of the office and through the labyrinthine hallways to her locker. She felt as though everyone knew what had happened and was laughing or pointing at her, but actually, no one said anything.

When she got to the computer lab, Elvis wasn't there, but Tommy was.

"Well," she said, "I burned my school library bridge today."

"I heard," he said. "I think it might actually make you more popular."

"Lucky me," she said. "I have to apologize."

"Just say the words," Tommy said. "You don't have to mean them."

"I'm not sure I can do that anymore," she said.

"Ed says school is just one of the hoops you have to jump through in life, so why make it harder than it already is? Twenty years from now this will seem like such a small part of our lives; he says don't make it more important than it is by screwing up now. We need to take the long view instead of the short view, or something like that."

"I think some kind of lid came off today," Grace said. "I don't know if I can put it back on."

"It wasn't that big of a deal, really," Tommy said. "Don't freak out about it."

"It's not that," she said. "It's more that it was just like something my mom would have done."

"You're not your mom."

"Grandma said Mom's craziness didn't show up until high school. High highs, low lows, and nothing in between, she said; big emotions and big drama all the time. My Aunt Lucy said she was like a hurricane that blew through the halls."

"Everybody gets mad and goes off sometimes," Tommy said. "And you never ever do that, so cut yourself some slack. Somebody died on your porch last weekend."

"I have to go see the school shrink."

"That's just another hoop," he said. "Tell her what she wants to hear and jump through it."

"I wonder what would happen if I told the truth," Grace said. "It would blow their minds."

"It would also be a first class ticket into a group home or foster care," Tommy said. "If it weren't for Ed, that's where I'd be. Look at it this way, we're almost sixteen, and in two years we can do whatever we want. It may be awful now, but it could actually be a lot worse."

Grace reflected on this. She was hungry and cold a lot of the time, and her grandfather certainly didn't like her, but the glass hadn't hit her, and he had never molested her. In a way, she thought, he was the only thing protecting her from all the awful things that could happen to a small teenager with no one to look out for her.

"So I'll apologize to Miss Briggs and tell the shrink I had cramps today."

Tommy blushed.

"Sorry," Grace said.

"Your lid really is off," he said and pushed her shoulder.

The last class of the day was World Cultures. Grace was in her usual seat, waiting for the teacher to come in and start class when a boy she had never seen before came in and took the seat next to her. He was tall, had sort of longish dark hair, big brown eyes fringed with thick lashes, and he reminded Grace of someone, but she couldn't think who. His cheeks were flushed a becoming faint shade of pink, and his lips were naturally rosy, but his complexion was dark rather than fair. He turned and smiled at Grace, and she blushed, embarrassed to be caught staring. All through class Grace didn't hear a thing for looking at the profile of this lovely boy.

He didn't dress like anyone she had ever met. He had on a T-shirt, a V-neck sweater, jeans, and loafers, but they weren't covered in logos or modified with band names or rude messages. He was dressed plainly, but you could tell he had money. His backpack was a minimalistic sling of what looked like soft leather, and his shoes were suede desert boots. He took notes on a plain drugstore-type notebook, but his pen looked like it was made of highly polished burled wood. When he sneaked a look at his phone, Grace could see it was one of the expensive ones.

A few times he looked over and smiled at Grace, and each time Grace felt her face get hot. She could not stop looking at him and realized by the end of class that she hadn't taken one coherent note. After the bell rang, she pretended to rearrange everything in her backpack until he was gone. When she finally left the classroom, the last one to do so, he was waiting outside in the hallway.

"Hi," he said. "I'm Rowan Gallaher. I just started here. It seems silly to start in the last few weeks of term, I know, but my mom was hoping I'd make some friends to hang out with over the summer."

He was smiling, holding out his hand, and Grace was flustered. She had never shaken hands with anyone but a grownup. As she grasped his hand, she felt an electrical current pass between them, and it snapped with a spark. It scared her, and she looked at him in astonishment.

"Static," he said. "Sorry."

"That's okay," Grace said. "Nice to meet you."

"What's your name?" he asked.

Grace and Rowan were standing facing each other against the wall as a steady stream of people hurried past, going to lockers to gather their things before running off to buses, carpools, or various practices for sports and intellectual competitions.

"Grace," she said. "Where are you from?"

"All over," he said. "My dad just took the college president job at Eldridge; before that, we lived in Vermont, and before that, we lived in California."

"So you live in Rose Hill?"

"Yeah," he said. "On Lilac Avenue?"

"I know where that is," she said. "I live down by the river on the other side of town."

"You make that sound like a bad thing."

Grace shrugged.

"Most people think it is," she said. "Are you riding the bus?"

"Do you ride the bus?" he asked.

"Yeah," she said.

"Then I guess I ride your bus, too," he said. "Maybe you could show me where it is."

Grace felt like she was thinking a million things all at once.

"Sure," she said. "I need to put my books away, but I'll meet you out front in five minutes."

"Great," he said, and he smiled at her again. "See you out there."

Grace ran through the halls to her locker, fumbled with the lock, and then flung most of her books inside, trying to remember what she needed at home for homework but not being able to focus on anything. This guy, this new kid, had dropped out of the sky like some care package to a needy, isolated population. He just, like, smiled at her and instantly liked her and now he wanted to ride the bus with her. She had read about that kind of thing happening but never had in a million years thought something like that could happen to her.

Here was somebody who hadn't known her for her whole life, wasn't predisposed to look down on her because of her family history. Grace felt like she had this opportunity she might lose if she didn't do something quickly, be super likable somehow so that when some clique tried to co-opt him, they couldn't turn him against her.

Grace slammed her locker shut just as a group of noisy jocks passed by. She averted her gaze and willed herself to be small as she skirted their group and tried not to run into the water fountain. She slid around a circle of kids eagerly encouraging two boys who were pushing each other but looked like they wanted to cry instead of fight.

Up ahead she saw the creepy-hugger choir teacher lurking in the hallway, and took an alternate route, which paid off in lack of traffic but took her out of her way and cost her time. She zigged and zagged through an impromptu cheerleader practice, and attempted to go past a large girl at the entrance to a back stairwell.

"You can't go in there," the girl said, snapping her gum and eyeing Grace with bored menace.

"I'll miss my bus," Grace said.

"Not my problem," the girl said, leaning across the closed doorway to emphasize its inaccessibility. "My friend and her boyfriend are doing it in there."

Grace groaned and turned around. Now she had to backtrack, through the cheerleaders, and past the creepy-hugger, who said, "Hey! You look like you could use a hug, young lady."

Grace evaded him and flew down the stairs, but tripped over her own feet at the bottom and almost fell. Her backpack wasn't completely closed, and her books flew all across the hall. No one stopped or tried to help, they just kicked and walked over her stuff as she scuttled, stooped and attempted to gather her things.

When a breathless Grace finally shoved open the heavy entryway doors and scanned the crowd, her eyes finally came to rest on the back of Rowan's head. He had on a jacket now, one of those barn jackets worn by people who had never done a day's work in a barn in their lives. She worked her way toward him through the crowd, being jostled and elbowed as she made her way forward. She reached out and touched his shoulder. When he turned, she could see whom he had been talking to; it was Charlotte. He smiled that big generous smile, in direct contrast to the contemptuous glare Charlotte was now giving Grace.

It was then that Grace realized who Rowan reminded her of; it was Charlotte.

They both had dark hair and big brown eyes, rosy, glowing skin and beautiful smiles. Together the two of them looked like prototypes for a new race of beautiful people. They looked like models in an ad for expensive preppy clothing. They looked like the perfect couple.

"Hey, Grace," he said. "Charlotte's offered me a ride home."

He turned to Charlotte and said, "Is there room for Grace?"

"Unfortunately, no," Charlotte said with faux graciousness. "So sorry, Grace. Maybe some other time."

"That's okay," Grace was saying as she backed away, mortified at how hot her face was becoming.

Grace backed into someone, apologized, and then turned. She scanned the crowd and saw Tommy waiting for her outside their bus.

"Gotta go," she said. "Tommy's waiting."

Charlotte was again glaring now that Rowan's back was turned to her. Grace was taken aback by the hatred she saw there. It wasn't enough that Charlotte had betrayed a decade of close friendship and seen to it that she and Tommy were ostracized and ridiculed. Her look seemed to communicate a desire for Grace to disappear, permanently.

Without another look at Rowan, Grace darted through the crowd and made her way to where Tommy was standing.

"Who's that?" Tommy said.

"A new kid," Grace said. "Charlotte's giving him a ride home."

Tommy glared over her shoulder until Grace said, "C'mon Tommy."

Once seated, Grace and Tommy watched through the bus window as Charlotte led Rowan to the SUV that would take him back to Rose Hill. Of course, there was plenty of room, just not for her or Tommy.

A boy passed their seat on the way back through the aisle and dropped something in Grace's lap.

"From The Fixer," the boy said.

Grace unfolded three sheets of paper wrapped around a pre-paid meal card, which could be used to pay for lunch in the cafeteria. The first sheet outlined step-by-step guidelines for filing for the legal emancipation of a minor.

The second sheet was a long suggested reading list. The third was a note.

"Dear Grace," it read. "Please see my phone number below. I would welcome an opportunity to continue our conversation any evening between the hours of eight and ten. I would also be honored to escort you to the Senior Prom, two weeks from this Saturday. My mother will drive; let us know where to pick you up. Best wishes and regards, Elvis."

Maggie was going through invoices at her desk in a small office at the back of the store. It was the quiet time before the evening business picked up, so her bookstore staff was on break. When the bell on the front door jingled, she looked up and saw Grace enter the store. The girl was so tiny and skinny that it didn't surprise Maggie when she thought, "hungry," whenever she looked at her.

But it was more than physical hunger that clung to the girl like a scent; she also seemed desperate for something else, but Maggie wasn't quite sure what that was. She knew from Scott that Grace was from an impoverished background; the granddaughter of a skinflint like Jacob Branduff couldn't be anything other than deprived. Maggie had been raised by a skinflint herself, but she had never wanted for hot food and a warm house to sleep in. Grace looked, for want of a more tactful word, homeless.

"Hi," Maggie said as she approached her. "I met you the other night with my cousins when you and Tommy were going up to the library."

Grace nodded but could hardly make eye contact.

"What can I help you find?" Maggie said, and then, worried she'd pressured the girl, said, "You're welcome to just look around, of course, or hang out if you want."

Grace started to talk, croaked a little and then cleared her throat, blushing. Maggie was an Olympic blusher herself, so she could sympathize, and knew better than to tease her about it. There's nothing a blushing person hates more than to have it pointed out.

"I'm looking for book three in the *His Dark Materials* trilogy," she said.

"Philip Pullman," Maggie said. "I know him well. I love the books but, just like with Harry Potter, I've got a contingent in this town who would like nothing more than to burn me at the stake for selling them. Even though the story is essentially about good versus evil, all they do is fixate on the magical element, which is exactly what makes them so fun to read. Silly, isn't it?"

Grace nodded and followed Maggie back to the young adult section. There Maggie pointed out all her other favorite authors.

"Mary Hodgson Burnett, Bill Cleaver, S.E. Hinton, Madeline L'Engle," Maggie said. "But that's showing my age I guess. There are some new books that are good; lots of them about vampires, obviously, and various dystopian-themed epics. *The Hunger Games* books are very popular."

"I really just want the one book today," Grace said.

"Sure, of course," Maggie said. "I get a little too enthusiastic about my wares. Sorry."

Maggie had all the books in the *His Dark Materials* trilogy in paperback and hardcover, as well as all three in a paperback set encased in a cardboard sleeve. She saw Grace touch the set but then draw her hand back as if she didn't dare look at the price.

"For the price of the one hardcover you could get the whole set," Maggie said impulsively, deciding to make that true even if it were not.

Maggie, who was raised to pinch a penny until it screamed, who loathed to mark anything down, was surprised at how badly she wanted to give Grace any book she wanted, all the books she wanted, for free. Whatever it was about this girl that had piqued Scott's interest and aroused his protective instincts seemed to have affected her as well.

It wasn't just that Grace was small for her age and dressed in what were basically worn out, ill-fitting clothing and holey shoes. It was the sense that the young girl seemed to long for things that she didn't think she was entitled to. Maggie could remember very well what that felt like. As a child, she wore second-hand clothes purchased at church bazaars and would not have dared to ask her mother for a popular brand of athletic shoes. When her mother bought her something new, it was for church or was chosen to last a very long time. The teenage Maggie had borrowed her books from the library and only received a new book on her birthday or at Christmas.

In her job, Maggie was also used to waiting on spoiled children (and adults) who felt entitled to everything, were impatient to have it, and didn't appreciate it once they got it. Grace's lack of pretention and grateful attitude were like a breath of fresh air.

"It's a good deal," Maggie said.

"Really?" Grace said. "I would love to have all three."

She took the book set from the shelf and cradled it in one arm while she searched her pocket with the other hand.

She drew out a wad of crumpled bills and asked, "How much is it?"

"Fifteen dollars," Maggie said and was relieved to see Grace's face light up.

"I can do that," she said.

Maggie rang her up at the register and put the books down inside a small, handled shopping bags she reserved for only her most special customers.

"It just fits," Grace said.

Maggie also put in several paper bookmarks and some coupons for treats from the coffee bar.

"Hey," Maggie said. "Would you like something from the coffee bar? I usually throw away the morning stuff about this time, and it's a shame to let it go to waste."

"Sure," Grace said. "I mean if you were going to throw it away anyway."

"Go get a seat and I'll join you," Maggie said.

Maggie went to the coffee bar side and said quietly to her barista, "Put this on my tab."

She filled a to-go bag with pastries out of the display case and made an extra large hot chocolate. This she covered with a lid and took everything to where Grace sat, lovingly admiring her book set.

"Here you go," Maggie said and sat down at the table.

"Really? All this?" Grace said.

"Every day," Maggie said. "Show up here about this time, and I'll give you whatever we're about to toss."

"Wow, thanks," Grace said. "This is delicious."

Grace looked around the store and swung her feet like a child as she ate a large blueberry muffin and sipped cocoa.

"Your store is so nice," she said. "You must love it here."

"Well, some days I can't see the forest for the invoices," Maggie said, "But it suits me. I can't imagine doing anything else. Are you looking for a part-time job?"

"I'll be sixteen next week," Grace said. "I promised Mr. Delvecchio I'd go to work for him at the IGA every day after school, but my grandfather wants me to quit school and work in the greenhouse."

"Oh, Grace, no," Maggie said, and then, "I'm sorry; that's really none of my business, is it?"

Grace's eyes filled, and she blinked them hard as she avoided Maggie's gaze.

"Yeah, well, I'm not exactly thrilled about it, either," she said.

"I don't know what to say," Maggie said. "I hope he'll reconsider and let you stay in school."

"He won't," Grace said.

"Even if he makes you quit school," Maggie said, "when you're eighteen you can get your GED and then go on to college. Lots of people do that."

"Can't get a scholarship with a GED, though," Grace said.

"I bet you could find some way," Maggie said. "I got a scholarship to go back to school last year, and I'm as old as dirt."

"You're not that old," Grace said. "Where do you go?"

"Right down the street to Eldridge College," Maggie said.

"Wow," Grace said. "Isn't that pretty expensive?"

"Oh, it's horribly expensive," Maggie said. "I got a grant as a returning student. There are all kinds of grants, scholarships, and loans you can get. Don't you worry about the money; just keep your grades up. When the time comes, I bet you will find a way to pay for it."

"Maybe," Grace said, but she did look cheered up. "Thanks, Maggie."

Grace gathered her things and stood up.

"You're most welcome, Grace," Maggie said. "Come back anytime, even just to visit. And remember what I said about the food. I throw away an obscene amount of it every day about this time. You're welcome to whatever you want."

Maggie walked her to the door and waved to her as she left. When she turned around, her café staff was standing together at the counter, staring at her, open-mouthed.

"Who are you and what have you done with our boss?" the barista said.

"I for one would like to welcome our new alien overlord," said a clerk.

"Oh, shut up," Maggie said. "Get back to work."

"It's still her," the cashier said.

When Grace got home, she was in such a great mood that it took her a few moments to sense the oppressive mood in the house. Her grandfather was waiting for her in the kitchen. He had the tin on the table with her money spread out by denomination. His face was dark red.

"Embezzlement," he said. "That's what they call it in the secular world. I call it thievery, plain and simple."

Grace hid her backpack behind her back as she hung her head, but the movement wasn't lost on her grandfather.

"Give it to me," he said. "Let's see what kind of devilry you've got hidden in there."

Grace's heart sank as she held out the backpack, thinking of the delicious food and her precious books. She couldn't look as he unzipped it and unpacked the contents. His sharp intake of breath brought terrified tears to her eyes; they dripped down her face, and she did nothing to catch them. She willed herself to be small, so small she disappeared.

"The devil has a foothold in your soul, granddaughter," he said. "I see the evidence here. Stealing from me in order to purchase wicked books and rich foods. This was exactly how your mother and your aunt started. What do you think happens to children who let the devil take their souls in exchange for such sin?"

Grace knew better than to answer.

He threw a box of wooden kitchen matches at her. It bounced off her jaw and fell to the floor. She didn't dare touch the place where it had hit her, which stung.

"I want you to go outside and build a fire in the burn barrel," he said. "Go."

Grace turned and walked quickly outside. She knew what was coming and there was nothing she could do to stop it; she could only silently obey. The tears continued to fall as she threw the smaller pieces of dried kindling in the burn barrel, lit them with a kitchen match, and slowly added larger pieces of brush until it blazed.

'This is my life,' she thought to herself. 'This is how it always has been, and this is how it will always be, as long as he is in charge of me.'

As the heat from the rising flames drove her back, she could feel a similar heat growing in her chest. She willed it to go away, to stay tamped down, but it would not be controlled. The fire inside her felt as wild and dangerous as the one blazing two feet in front of her.

'I can't do this anymore,' she thought, and deep inside she felt something open that she knew could not be closed. 'I am not going to do this anymore.'

Her grandfather came out of the house holding her book set. She raised her eyes to him as he took out each book and dropped it in the burn barrel, one at a time. The flames leaped up as they consumed the paper. She tried to look away, to look back down and found that she couldn't. He tossed in the case for the trilogy and then turned to her with hatred and contempt in his expression.

"That's what I think of your devil books, witch," he said.

Where she usually felt an overwhelming force that compelled her to stay silent and small, Grace now felt an even stronger force that compelled her to be big and say what was in her heart.

"I'm not a witch," she said. "There's nothing wrong with me. It's you who's crazy, just like Mom was."

He struck her across the face with the back of his hand; something of which she knew he was capable but had been sure would never happen; if she were careful enough, obedient, a good little girl. Her cheek stung and her eyes watered. She remembered this pain from her childhood when it was her mother doing the slapping. At first, she felt the same sadness as when her mother hurt her, but then anger rose up out of the place where the lid had come off and filled her up until she was boiling over. Hot white rage filled her chest; there was a roaring sound in her ears. She wanted to shove him, to hurt him.

"I should drown you in the river," he said. "Thou shalt not suffer a witch to live."

"I hate you," she said. "I wish you were dead."

His face turned purple; he was sweating and blinking fast, just like he did before a dizzy spell. She resisted the urge to push him over, which she was confident she was angry enough to do.

"Witch," he said. "Harlot."

"I'm leaving," she said. "And you can't stop me."

"Get your things and get out," he said, his hoarse voice trembling. "If I see you on my property again, I'll shoot you."

He was so angry he was gasping for breath. She thought then that he was perfectly capable of killing her, but she couldn't help herself, she wanted the last word. Just this once.

"You killed my mother and my Grandmother," Grace said, "but you won't kill me."

She ducked as he swung a second time. Then she ran.

Once inside the house, she locked the back and front doors so he couldn't get in to get his gun, but he didn't follow her. She hurriedly shoved some clothes and books into her backpack and stuffed the cash from the rainy day fund into her pocket. From the pantry, she took the boxed up swan and her grandmother's apron off the hook. She was afraid to go out the back way to retrieve her bicycle for fear he would kill her with an ax. Instead, she went to the front door, but just as she was sliding back the deadbolt, someone leaped onto the front porch and started pounding on the door.

Police Chief Scott Gordon had driven slowly down Daisy Lane until he reached the bottom of the hill, where a little over three years ago he had almost lost his life in a flash flood. Pulled along by a wild, swirling current of icy water in the dead of night, he had tried to cling to the high brick walls surrounding Eldridge College, only to be battered and scraped as he was tossed like debris down toward where the wall ended in the swollen, raging river, where he was sure to drown. At almost the last moment volunteer firefighter Cal Fischer had shown a searchlight upon him and thrown him a line. His rescue had seemed miraculous at the time, when facing death, all he could think of was how sad he was that he'd never see Maggie Fitzpatrick again.

That flood had destroyed several houses on Lotus Avenue and damaged most of the others, which were condemned and torn down soon after. After the water receded, only the Glassworks, the depot, and the old Rodefeffer house had been left relatively unharmed, a testament to the strong stuff from which they were built.

Most of the Rodefeffer house was hidden behind a wall of shrubbery allowed to grow up past the second story level, with only a narrow walkway left between the alley and the iron gate that led to the front walkway. Scott had to duck to go through it. The iron gate's hinges seemed to protest with a screeching groan.

The front yard was so overgrown it was impenetrable, and weeds grew up between each paving stone of the crumbling walkway. The porch bore the most evidence of the damage the flood left in its wake. There were pieces of plywood nailed down over the many missing floorboards. Scott was not sure it was safe to walk on. Most of the wooden porch railing was missing, but the iron railing along the concrete stairs was still intact. There was no sign of where Nino had lay dying, and Scott wondered again how a man so ill could have made it all the way from the bus stop on Rose Hill Avenue to this porch, and why.

No one had answered his knock, so he backtracked to the lane and walked around the side of the house, where the grass had been replaced with a wide gravel path between two long greenhouses and the side of the house. A decrepit bike was resting against a thick rhododendron that grew high up the side of the house.

Out back, Scott could see smoke pouring from a roaring fire in the burn barrel. Scott found a sputtering water hose connected to a spigot on the outside of the house.

The hose was stretched out through an open greenhouse door; Scott followed it. Inside the greenhouse, long sheets of plywood on top of sawhorses were covered with rack after rack of seedlings planted in trays. As he advanced toward the back of the humid room, the plants were taller, and at the very back a profusion of gloriously colored, fragrant flowers were in different stages of bloom.

Scott didn't see Mr. Branduff until he was almost to the back of the greenhouse. The old man was on the other side of the center aisle of plywood racks, laying face down on the gravel floor. Scott scooted under the plywood and emerged in the aisle behind him, where he picked up and set aside the hose that had created a large mud puddle all around the tall man. He knew before he felt for the pulse that it would not be there. No one but a dead man could lie that still.

Scott radioed for the EMT, even though he knew there was no chance of resuscitation. Scott's next thought was of Grace; where was she? He wanted to get to her before she heard the siren, and before she came out and was surprised by the body. He hurried around to the front of the house and bound up the steps to the porch. He pounded on the door, calling out, "Grace!"

"Grace," he began as she opened the door, wild-eyed with fear.

"Your grandfather ..." he said and gestured toward the greenhouse.

He watched her eyes widen even further as she took in his facial expression.

She pushed passed him and ran down the steps just as the sirens started. Scott tried to catch her, but she was amazingly quick on her feet. He finally caught up with her at her grandfather's side, where she knelt in the puddle and struggled to roll him over. He didn't have the heart to stop her, so he helped her. The man's eyes were open. His expression was blank, and for that Scott was grateful; he'd seen much, much worse. Grace held her ear to his soaking wet flannel shirt. To Scott's amazement, she started prepping him for CPR, tilting his head back and searching his mouth with her fingers for obstructions.

"Grace," Scott said, and reached out, but she batted his hand away.

She pinched his nostrils shut and covered his mouth with her own. When she sat back up, her face was covered with the mud and gravel that had been stuck to his face. She straddled him and started chest compressions.

"Grace, honey," Scott said. "It's too late."

"Help me!" she gasped through the tears that were streaming down her face.

Scott crawled around her and did chest compressions until the first EMT that arrived told him to stop. Grace had to be bodily removed, and after a short struggle, she collapsed into a sobbing heap, crying so desperately that she gagged and choked. Scott had never seen someone so upset. She was wild with grief.

The second EMT calmly took the garden hose and doused Grace with it. Grace gasped. Scott grabbed the hose out of the woman's hand and threw it down; he turned on her, saying, "What in the hell do you think you're doing?"

She shook her head, pointed at Scott, and said, "You need to get out of the way and let me do my job. It was either that or a slap; which would you have preferred?"

Grace, who seemed to have lost her breath from the shock of the water, took a ragged gasping breath and began coughing.

Scott picked up Grace and carried her violently trembling body back to the house and up the stairs, in through the front door. It was colder in the house than outside. He made his way through a tangle of stiff clothes hung up to dry on a clothesline strung the length of the back hallway. There he found the bathroom and flipped on the light. He set Grace on the floor of the cold room, went to the tub, and turned the hot water tap, but nothing came out.

Grace was huddled in a knot, trembling violently and crying, but no longer in a way that scared him.

"There's no hot water," Scott said to her.

"It's Monday," she said, without taking her hands from her face.

Scott went to the hot water tank in the corner of the room and felt it; it was hot. He followed the line to where it connected to the tub and found the connection was turned off. He turned the knob and this time when he opened the spigot hot water flowed into the deep tub. Steam filled the room as he rooted around a linen cabinet for a clean towel, appalled at how ragged and threadbare they all were. On the sink, he found a cake of old-fashioned strong-smelling soap like his grandmother had used when he was small.

Grace's teeth were chattering, but she was calming down.

"You get in the tub and get warmed up," Scott said. "I'm going to turn up the furnace."

When Grace didn't move, he said in a stern voice, "Grace, did you hear me?"

Grace nodded and stood up with his help. Once he was sure, she was steady on her feet he left the bathroom, saying, "I'll get you some dry clothes."

In the hallway, Scott found the furnace thermostat. It was taped with old, gummy black electrical tape so that it could not be turned up past 55 degrees.

"Son of a bitch," Scott muttered as he ripped off the tape and turned up the heat. The furnace kicked on and immediately a blast of hot air filled the hallway from the floor vent, billowing out the clothing that hung above it.

Scott went from room to room until he found Grace's small bedroom. The stack of threadbare quilts on top of the sagging, rusted iron bedstead broke his heart. Her clothes were neatly folded in an old chest of drawers. He hastily assembled the warmest-looking pieces he could find and lay them on the floor outside the bathroom.

"I put some clothes out here for you," he called through the door. "I'll be in the kitchen."

Scott went to the kitchen and began opening and closing cupboards, finding very little food. The refrigerator was empty except for several small cartons of milk like those given out in school cafeterias. There were also about a dozen small plastic container os creamer like those found in restaurants. In the pantry, there was a can of coffee, an almost empty jar of peanut butter, some stale bread, some damaged packages of pasta and oatmeal, and several dented cans of soup.

"I knew it," he said. "Ah, Grace."

He knew the next logical step was to call Children's Protective Services and let them take over. Instead, he pulled out his cell phone and called Maggie.

When Maggie arrived, Grace was dressed and sitting at the kitchen table drinking some hot chocolate. Her long dark hair was wet and tangled down her back, and her face was raw from crying, but her dark eyes were sharp and wary. Maggie could tell that whatever emotions had overcome the girl, she was back in possession of herself.

Scott had been near to hysterical himself when he called; Scott, who was the calmest head in every storm. Maggie hadn't even put on her coat, had just run out of the store, jumped in her Jeep, and drove like a maniac down Daisy Lane and then Lotus Avenue. She pulled up behind the ambulance, nodded to the paramedics, deliberately averted her eyes from the large, still form on the gurney, and went around the back of the house where Scott had directed her to go.

Maggie Fitzpatrick had been raised in a home with very little money, where everything was a little shabby but scrubbed clean. Even so, she was shocked when she entered the house and saw the conditions in which Grace lived.

The long-term effects of poverty covered the inside of Grace's house like the thick dust and cobwebs that clung to every surface the small girl could not reach with a broom. It was hot as the blazes, though, and Maggie was relieved about that.

In the kitchen, Scott's face was ashen, and it was all she could do not to hug him and reassure him. Obviously, it was this young woman who was the object of his concern; it was she who needed a hug. Maggie was not the hugging kind, though. She wondered why Scott hadn't called her Aunt Delia, who would have gathered the girl up in her arms and instantly made everything seem better.

"Hi, Grace," Maggie said. "I hear you're having a really crappy day."

Grace smiled wanly.

"Sorry," Scott said, shaking his head. "Grace, this is Maggie, she's ..."

"Grace and I have met. I'm a good friend of Scott's," Maggie said. "I can vouch for him; you're safe with him."

Scott sputtered, "Grace knows she's safe with me."

"I think it's good to hear, anyway," Maggie said, not taking her eyes off Grace's. "When you're a girl, you have to be on your guard."

Grace nodded so subtly that Maggie wondered if Scott even saw it.

Maggie sat down at the kitchen table and gestured to Scott to do the same.

He was too restless, though, she could tell, and shook his head.

"So what's happened?" Maggie asked. "I saw the ambulance outside."

"That was Grace's grandfather," Scott said.

"I think Grace can probably speak for herself," Maggie said, and then rolled her eyes at Grace, who responded with another flicker of a smile.

"What happened?" she asked Grace.

"His heart was bad," Grace said, in a soft voice. "He doesn't like to go to the doctor, and he won't take any medicine."

"My dad's stubborn like that," Maggie said. "Except he takes more medicine than he should and drinks too much on top of that."

"Grandpa doesn't drink," Grace said. "He didn't, I mean."

"Is there anyone we can call?" Maggie said.

"I already asked that," Scott said.

Maggie ignored him.

"My Aunt Lucy," Grace said. "But I don't know where she is."

"I've called the state police to see if they'll help track her down," Scott said. "They're putting the word out."

"Scott can't leave you here alone," Maggie said, now understanding why he had called.

"I'll be fine," Grace said.

"I'm sure you can take care of yourself," Maggie said. "Unfortunately, Chief Gordon here is what you might call a stickler for the L.A.W. and also something of a professional Boy Scout. When a minor is involved in a situation like this, he's supposed to call C.P.S. They'll want to stick you in a foster home until Aunt Lucy can be found."

Grace's eyes widened and then darted like a trapped animal's.

"He's not going to do that," Maggie reassured her. "You may not believe this, but my family has connections. We go to church with a lady who works for C.P.S., and the local circuit court judge will do anything for my mother's cinnamon rolls. Scott will get the paperwork started, and meanwhile, I would be glad to stay with you or have you stay with me until they find your aunt."

Grace put her face down on her crossed arms and cried.

Scott got a call and left the house to take it.

Maggie didn't know quite what to say to Grace, so she just let her cry. When she finally raised her head back up, Maggie handed her a threadbare dish towel. Grace dried her face and blew her nose. Maggie was embarrassed at how poorly prepared she was to deal with the child's grief and tried to think of something to say.

"Did you know that if you can get someone at Eldridge to vouch for you, you can use the college library?"

"Really?" Grace said, wiping her eyes.

"Do you get good grades?" Maggie asked. "I bet you do; you seem smart."

Grace nodded.

"I know a professor over there, and I'll get it fixed up for you."

"Thanks," Grace said. "That would be awesome."

"So," Maggie said. "Are we having our slumber party here or at my place?"

"I'd rather stay here if you don't mind," Grace said.

"No problem," Maggie said. "I'll call my cousins Hannah and Claire to come over and entertain us."

Scott came back in, and Maggie told him her plan.

"I don't know if that's a good idea," Scott said. "Grace has been through a lot."

"You run along now," Maggie said to Scott. "Grace and I can take it from here."

"I could stay," Scott said.

"Thanks," Maggie said. "But not only do you need to get started on Grace's paperwork, but you're also still on duty. I'm sure some heinous crime is being committed somewhere in Rose Hill. This is such a hotbed of illicit activities nowadays."

"Don't pick up any bad habits from the Fitzpatrick girls," Scott said to Grace, and then kissed Maggie on the forehead in a very un-policeman-like way.

Maggie could sense he wanted to touch Grace, to reassure her somehow, but she grabbed his hand before he gave in to the impulse. The young girl seemed so raw and vulnerable; Maggie wanted to build a wall around her and top it with barbed wire.

"Get out of here, already," Maggie said. "Can't you take a hint?"

Scott smiled ruefully and squeezed Maggie's hand before he left, saying to Grace, "I'll check on you tomorrow. You girls call if you need me."

Maggie excused herself and walked out to the back porch with him. As soon as the door was closed, she said, "Is there something else I should know? Has she been hurt in some way besides her grandfather dying?"

Scott's looked to be on the verge of tears.

"Her cheek," he said. "Did you notice that?"

"Looks like he slapped her," Maggie said.

"She says it was the first time he hit her."

"My mom slapped me a few times when I was growing up," Maggie said. "I know it's hard to believe because I've grown up to be such a proper lady, but I used to be something of a smart ass. All those old coots think that kind of thing is perfectly fine if it will save your soul. It's horrible, but she'll recover."

"I know that," he said.

"Then why are you so freaked out?"

"Look at the way she's been forced to live," he said

He gestured at the house and then struggled for more words.

"Take it easy there, partner," Maggie said. "I know you were raised a sheltered, middle-class child, but plenty of people grow up poor, and there's no shame in it."

"Were you only allowed to have hot water on Sundays?" he asked her, his nostrils flaring. "Were you not allowed to raise the thermostat past the point where pipes don't freeze? There's no food in that house except milk she's probably stolen from school and dented cans of soup."

"Calm down," Maggie said. "You're overreacting; you'll give the poor girl a complex."

"In my town," he said. "This has been going on in my town."

"There it is," she said. "There's the pit of the thing. You cannot save everyone, Superman."

"I'm going to save her," he said. "I mean it, Maggie. This one is not going to fall through the cracks."

"Such drama," Maggie said, taking him in her arms. "You're so sexy when you're fired up about injustice."

He hugged her tight and then didn't let go when she did.

"We can't turn our backs on her," Scott said. "We have to step in and do whatever we have to do to protect Grace."

"Hey," she said. "Do you think that just maybe you might be overreacting a tiny little bit?"

"Her grandmother was around the same age as my mom," Scott said. "My sister's twins are just a little younger than Grace."

"And it's only been three weeks since you lost your mom," Maggie said. "I know it's hard."

"This is not about my mom," he said.

"It's not your fault your mom died," Maggie said.

"I should've made her go to the doctor sooner," he said.

"Stop it," Maggie said. "If rescuing orphans is going to make you feel better, then I'm on board. Let's do it. Project Grace begins tonight. Just please stop blaming yourself for every bad thing that happens."

"I'll work on finding her sister."

"Good, you go do that," Maggie said. "Maybe she'll be a wonderful person."

Scott looked dubious.

"You don't think it's likely."

"She's let Grace live like this," he said.

"We won't know until you find her," Maggie said. "Get out of here. Go. Start the paperwork so we can be in charge here."

"I love you," he said.

"Woe be to you, then," Maggie said. "But if you insist, I'm not going to stand in your way."

"Thank you," Scott said.

"No problem," Maggie said. "She seems like a nice kid."

Maggie returned to the kitchen, where Grace was combing out her long tangled hair.

"Wait'll Claire gets over here," Maggie said, pressing a speed dial number on her cell phone. "She'll be all over that mane of yours."

An hour later there was a hot pepperoni pizza on the kitchen table and Grace, her hair neatly French-braided, was sipping a strong, fizzy cola. It all tasted delicious, and she was ravenous. She wisely did not gorge herself for fear it would all come back up, but she did eat two smallish pieces of pizza.

Grace had gladly let Maggie take over; she seemed like the type of person who could control outcomes, who could sort things out. Grace was too tired to think, let alone make a plan. Maggie seemed so confident and sensible, plus she didn't fawn all over her or talk to her like a child. She didn't seem shocked by the house like Scott had been. Maggie's eyes were by turns flinty and curious, but never mean, and certainly not mean toward Grace.

It felt like she was dreaming; occasionally she would think about her grandpa in the greenhouse and panic would fill her chest, making it hard to breathe, but mostly she felt swept along by events as if it would do no good to resist. While she drifted in and out of alternating feelings of panic and sadness, the three women chattered and bustled around her house like it was the most normal thing in the world to be doing. It distracted her; she liked it.

The three could not have been more different in both looks and temperament. Maggie was tall and curvy, with wild red curly hair, blue eyes, and pale freckled skin. She was the imposing, bossy one of the group. Her cousin Hannah, mother of Sammy, was almost as small as Grace. She had hazel eyes and a prominent nose. She needled Maggie in a way that showed they were not just cousins but long-time friends, and their banter made Grace feel relaxed and warm inside. Hannah brought two pizzas and had eaten one all by herself. Now she was trying to talk Maggie into going to her mother's bakery to get a dozen donuts.

Claire was tall and thin with long dark hair and startling blue eyes. She had used a blow dryer on Grace's hair and then French-braided it in a way Grace had seen in one of the fashion magazines at the library. She talked about the reality shows she watched and the gossip websites she visited; Grace, who didn't have a TV and only limited access to computers, didn't understand any of it, but she loved being included as if she did.

Claire had brought playing cards, tarot cards, and poker chips, but the three cousins ended up sitting and talking amongst themselves, occasionally including Grace, but mostly catching up with one another. In extremely un-normal circumstances, it made Grace feel normal in a way she never had before; she couldn't explain it any better than that.

"When's Sean moving back?" Claire asked, and then to Grace, "That's Maggie's brother."

"In a week," Maggie said. "He's going to stay with Mom and Dad until his apartment's ready."

To Grace, Maggie said, "My brother's going to live in the second apartment over the bookstore. He's having it renovated."

"Who's doing the work now that Pip's in jail?" Claire asked and then to Grace, "That's my ex-husband."

"He's hired a contractor from Morgantown," Maggie said. "That won't endear him to any local people."

"Sean's a lawyer," Hannah told Grace, "but not the murder case kind; he worked for a bank."

"He did legal business for the bank," Maggie said. "Now he's going to teach at Pine County Community College and practice family law here in town."

"Which means wills and divorces," Hannah said.

"He's gorgeous," Claire said. "I mean, movie star gorgeous."

Maggie rolled her eyes.

"You only say that because you look just like him," Maggie said to Claire.

"Are you implying I'm not gorgeous?" Claire said. "Did you hear that, Grace? I think she's disparaging my appearance."

Grace just let their camaraderie wash over her, like the tub full of hot water she had soaked in this afternoon. She had once watched the Wizard of Oz at Charlotte's house. She felt a little like Dorothy after the tornado, when she opened the door of her house in Munchkin Land; suddenly her world was painted in bright, vibrant colors. Not one of the women could pass for Glenda, but they all seemed like good witches. This made her think of her grandfather's accusation. She pictured his livid face. She pictured his dead face. She felt her eyelids droop and her head nod.

"Grace, wake up," Claire said. "I want you to settle an argument. Am I or am I not what you would consider a beautiful woman? I mean, maybe not in Hollywood terms, but here, in Rose Hill."

"In Rose Hill, you could be Elizabeth motherflippin' Taylor," Hannah said. "That's nothing to brag about."

"Somehow your curse word substitutions are almost more obscene," Claire said.

"I've got a three-year-old and a filthy mouth," Hannah said. "I'm doing the best I can."

"I think Grace had better go to bed," Maggie said. "She's probably worn out."

"Thank you for all the food, and ..." Grace hesitated, "and everything."

All three women were silent for the first time since they arrived. They were giving her such warm, compassionate looks that her vision blurred and she felt her lip tremble.

"C'mon," Maggie said. "You need a nap."

"But I didn't finish my homework," Grace protested.

"No school for you tomorrow," Maggie said. "And don't worry, I'll call the school and work it out so you can get your schoolwork."

"So maternal," Hannah said. "Listen to her, Claire."

"You," Maggie said to Hannah. "You shut up."

"That's just like something your own mother would say," Hannah said, and then quickly moved aside as Maggie reached out to pinch her.

Grace felt so lethargic that she allowed Maggie to tuck her into bed under the mountain of quilts. As her head hit the pillow, she felt herself fall immediately asleep. She may have imagined it, but it felt like Maggie kissed her forehead.

"Get some sleep," Maggie said. "I won't let anything bad happen, and I'll be here when you wake up."

"Oh my God," Maggie said in a low voice when she returned to the kitchen. "That kid is going to rip the heart right out of my chest."

"She's so lovely and sweet," Claire said. "Poor thing."

"What's going to happen to her?" Hannah said.

"Scott's looking for her Aunt Lucy, whoever the hell that is," Maggie said. "He didn't want to call C.P.S. until he has his ducks in a row."

"Don't let Ava get her sticky mitts on her," Claire said. "You know how she likes to collect stray children."

"She only likes redheaded boy orphans fathered by her former husband," Hannah said. "But you never know."

"My dear sister-in-law is going to get involved over my dead body," Maggie said. "Don't you worry about that."

"How are you going to take care of her, though?" Claire said. "What with the store and your classes?"

"You two are going to help me," Maggie said.

"Of course we are," Hannah said. "I'll be in charge of comic books, pranks, and substitute curse words."

"I'm in," Claire said. "And you know if my mother gets one look at her she'll be feeding her night and day."

"Okay," Maggie said. "Let's work out a schedule."

Scott ended the call to his contact at C.P.S. and looked up the number for Judge Feinman.

"I've got no problems with your plan," Judge Feinman said. "I would prefer it, however, if you had a doctor look her over this evening or tomorrow, just to cover our bases. Call Kay down at city hall; she's a licensed foster parent, although she says she isn't doing it anymore."

"I'll call her," Scott said.

"Don't be afraid to wake me up if you need me," the judge said. "I'm up several times a night anyway with this damn prostate."

Scott called Doc Machalvie next.

"I heard," Doc said. "Bring her over to the house tonight, and we'll look after her while you make arrangements. Kay has fostered children in the past, and I'm sure she would keep Grace in the short term. Now that she's campaigning for mayor she may not want anything long term. She can stay overnight here if Kay needs time to prepare."

"Now that Jacob's dead, can we discuss the family's medical records?"

"A person's rights under HIPPA end at death," Doc said. "So I can tell you that her grandfather was a ticking time bomb. I'm only surprised he lasted this long. Her grandmother would probably be here today if she'd received the minimum of basic health care. Her mother was a very troubled young woman who may have committed suicide.

I'm looking forward to helping you improve Grace's lot in life, and I'll see you two later."

Scott hung up and started back to work on the C.P.S. paperwork. When his deputy, Skip, said someone was there to see him, he was surprised to see the mayor's secretary, Kay Templeton.

"Hello, Scott," Kay said. "I heard about Jacob Branduff. If you need someone short term, I'll be glad to have Grace at my house."

"I was going to call you," Scott said. "Doc thought that maybe your campaign would keep you from doing it."

"I had no plans to foster any more children," she said. "This last one broke my heart, and I just couldn't face that again. What's Grace like?"

"Really sweet, very smart," Scott said. "She's never been in a bit of trouble. She's special, Kay. We've got to make sure she doesn't get lost in all this."

"I'm glad to help," she said. "Just for a little while, though."

"Doc's going to keep her tonight, so if you could be ready tomorrow ..."

"I'm game," Kay said. "Doc said there's an aunt that may turn up."

"Ran away as a teenager," he said. "The odds are against her being a good guardian."

"Well, I'll get her room ready," Kay said. "Bring her anytime."

"Thanks," Scott said. "I'll feel good about having her under your roof."

"Where is she now?" Kay said.

"Maggie, Hannah, and Claire are over at her house," he said. "I'm going to pick her up and take her to Doc's house for the night."

"Then she's in good hands tonight," Kay said. "Call me tomorrow; keep me updated."

"How's the campaign?" he said.

"It's awkward for them," Kay said. "I've worked for Peg and Stuart for the past twenty years. I know where all the bodies are buried so they can't play dirty. It's been fun watching them try to maneuver outside of their wheelhouse."

Scott shook his head.

"You've got my vote," he said. "I think you'll win by a landslide."

Doc Machalvie and his wife, Doris, lived up on Magnolia Avenue, in a big brick house that smelled like apple pie inside. All the rooms were spotless and furnished with polished antiques. Doc was much taller and larger than his brother Stuart, the mayor, and only resembled him vaguely. Doris was a large soft woman with a kind voice and snow white hair.

Doc led Grace to the kitchen and had her sit on the kitchen table while he rolled up his sleeves and washed his hands. He took her temperature and looked into her eyes, ears, and mouth. He felt the glands on each side of her throat. He took her pulse and pinched the skin on her arm above her elbow.

"I see someone hit you on the face," he said. "Was that a regular thing?"

"No," Grace said. "It was the first time."

"Did your grandfather ever touch you inappropriately?" he asked.

"No," Grace said. "He never touched me; he didn't like me."

"I don't think your grandfather liked anybody," he said. "Especially himself."

Grace didn't know what to say in response to that. She had never thought of her grandfather liking or disliking himself.

"Anything else I need to know?" Doc asked her. "Are you sexually active, that sort of thing?"

"No, sir," Grace said, a little taken aback.

"You're sound as a bell," he pronounced, and then patted her on the head. "You just need a few more meals than you've been getting."

"I'm smaller than everybody else in my class," Grace said.

"You're just a late bloomer," Doc said. "I'm not worried about it so neither should you be. Have you started menstruating yet?"

Grace shook her head, embarrassed.

"That's probably because you don't have enough body fat," Doc said. "Do your breasts hurt?"

"Sometimes," Grace said.

"That's normal. You'll have periods before long, I'll wager," Doc said. "I'm sure I have a pamphlet somewhere I can give you, or you could just talk to my wife. More likely she'll talk the most, but she's also a good listener."

"Thanks," Grace said. "Did you know my grandmother?"

"Your grandmother was a lovely woman. Unfortunately, your grandfather was a cantankerous old fart," Doc said. "I don't imagine he knew the first thing about caring for a child, and I'm sure he was hard to live with. If I were you, I wouldn't take to heart anything he ever said to you. You're on your own now and can make your life what you please. You'll always remember the things he said, just don't make the mistake of believing he knew you well enough to make a sound judgment of your character. I think you're going to do just fine."

Grace thanked him again. She thought she might already love him.

After the exam was over, Mrs. Machalvie made scrambled eggs and toast and poured a big glass of milk for Grace.

"You'll feel better after you eat," she said.

Doc, the chief, and Doris went to the front room to call Mrs. Briggs at C.P.S. Grace ate in small bites and chewed everything up really well so she wouldn't get sick. After she ate, she needed to go to the bathroom, but she didn't know where it was, so she pushed open the swinging door to the kitchen and went to look for it.

Chief Gordon, Doc, and Doris were in the living room talking about her and hadn't heard her enter the hallway. She tiptoed closer to the doorway and listened.

"She's not a stray cat," Doc was saying. "She's a person with her own preferences; we have to take that into account."

"I know she's not a stray cat, Sean," Doris said. "But this is a critical time in that young woman's life, and she needs protection; she needs guidance. If she gets put into the foster care system, she may get a wonderful family or she may get something much, much worse."

"There is an aunt," Chief Gordon said. "We just haven't been able to locate her."

"What I've heard about that one doesn't lead me to believe she'd be a good parent," Doris said. "This is a situation we've all known about for years, and yet no one has stepped in to do anything to help. Now the worst has happened, and we cannot just stand by and let her disappear. God has sent this girl to us, and we must help her. 'Send me, use me,' we tell the Lord, and now we are being called upon, all of us. What do we go to church for if we then turn our backs on a child in need?"

"I appreciate your intentions," Doc said. "I just don't want you to forget that she is, for all intents and purposes, a young adult. We have to respect her wishes."

"To a certain extent," Doris said. "But she is way too young to make a fully informed decision on her own behalf."

"Grace has been taking care of herself for a very long time," Chief Gordon said. "I'm sure she knows how much is at stake."

"Obviously she needs several days of rest," Doris said. "But a young mind needs to stay busy, or it can turn on itself. Can we collect her schoolwork and have her do it here?"

"Let's ask Grace what she wants to do, sweetheart," Doc said.

Grace scooted back into the kitchen, so she was seated when they returned.

"Thank you for supper," she told Doris, who hugged her.

The grownups all sat down at the table.

"Grace," Scott said. "You've had a great shock. I think you should take the rest of the week off from school."

"I'm okay," Grace said.

"You have my word that I'll make sure nothing bad happens to you," Scott said. "I'm going to make sure you live in a safe place with people who will take good care of you."

"We'd like to take care of you," Doris said. "We'd like to offer you a safe place to stay."

"That's charity," Grace said. "My grandpa was against it."

"Your grandpa had a right to make that decision only for himself," Doris said. "But you must weigh the benefits against the cost. You're nearly sixteen years old without a high school diploma. You're at a crossroads in your life. You could make things very hard for yourself out of pride, and miss out on opportunities for a better life. If you allow people to help you, on the other hand, you'll be able to finish high school and go on to college. Then you will have the tools you need to take good care of yourself. You need protection and a safe place to live; we can give you that. You don't have to be grateful; that's not why we help people. If you feel some sort of debt will be incurred then repay it when you're an adult. Repay it by helping someone else. That's what Christians are supposed to do for each other."

Grace couldn't speak for the lump in her throat.

"That was a very eloquent speech," Doc said. "And I agree with every word. Let's let Grace think about it."

"I'm going to go, but I'll be back to pick you up in the morning," Chief Gordon said to Grace. "I'll tell your principal not to expect you tomorrow. Call me if you need me."

Doris left to show Scott out.

Doc filled a kettle with water and put it on the stove.

"Do you eat much protein?" he asked her.

Grace was taken aback by the question.

"Peanut butter," she said. "Bologna. Hot dogs."

"You're a bit malnourished," he said. "I think if we fed you half of a cow you might grow six inches."

Grace laughed.

"That's good to hear," Doc said.

CHAPTER SIX – TUESDAY

When Chief Gordon arrived to pick up Grace in the morning, Doris was feeding her oatmeal.

"I promised her half a cow," Doc said from behind his newspaper.

"Oatmeal has a lot of protein in it," Doris told Grace. "Plus it sticks to your ribs."

"You look better," Scott said as he sat down.

"A good night's sleep will do that for you," Doris said. "She slept like a log."

"She snores," Doc said.

"Sean!" Doris said and flicked his newspaper with a tea towel.

"Grace, Grace, Grace," Doc said, raising his paper back up. "What are we going to do about Grace? That's what the whole town will be talking about today."

"If it's okay with you, Grace, Claire and her mother are going to take you to Machalvies to make funeral arrangements," Scott said. "Then I'll take you home to get your things, and we'll go to our friend Kay's house to talk about staying with her. I think you'll like her."

"Kay Templeton is a wonderful person," Doris said. "But if you would prefer to come back here, you are most certainly welcome."

Grace thanked Doris and carried her dishes to the sink.

"We'll see you soon," Doris said. "Meanwhile, if you need anything you just let us know."

"Judge Feinman wants to be in on whatever decision is made," Scott said. "I'll let you know what her schedule is as soon as I know it."

"Sounds like you're in good hands," Doc said, as he folded up his newspaper. "Don't worry too much if you can help it; that's my two cents."

138

Grace came around the table and kissed the old man's cheek.

"Thank you," she said after she did it.

"You won't get around me that way," he said, but he was smiling.

Doris wasn't about to be left out, and she gave Grace a big, tight hug before she left the house.

It was cold out, and Grace shivered. Chief Gordon was not dressed in his uniform, and he was driving his own pickup truck. He shrugged off his outermost jacket and handed it to her.

"Here," he said. "We'll go get yours later."

Grace put on the warm jacket, which smelled like his laundry detergent.

"Aren't you working today?" she asked him.

"I start nights today," he said. "I should be home sleeping but I never can that first day."

"Chief Gordon," Grace said. "I really appreciate all that you're doing for me."

"I think after all we've been through together you should call me Scott," he said. "I'd like us to be friends, Grace. Appropriate friends, I mean, with the appropriate boundaries, of course, and only if you want to. I don't mean anything weird by that."

"I'm not worried about you," Grace said, with a serious face, but then she smiled out the window so he wouldn't see.

Claire and Delia were waiting outside Machalvie's Funeral Home. Claire's mother was tall and thin like Claire but dressed much more casually in a cardigan, jeans, and tennis shoes. Claire, on the other hand, looked like she had just stepped out of a fashion magazine. Her hair was wound up in a deliberately messy chignon on the back of her head, and her makeup accentuated her startling blue eyes and neatly arched dark brows.

"Here she is," Scott said, and introduced Grace to Delia.

Grace stuck out her hand to shake Delia's, but the woman said, "In our family, we hug," and embraced her, patted her back. She smelled like a pretty perfume, and her hug was so comforting it made Grace tear up.

Scott left, and they all waved.

"I like your hair," Grace said to Claire.

"I can do the same to yours if you like," Claire said.

"Plenty of time for that later," Delia said. "Let's get this over with."

"Peg Machalvie is the owner of this funeral home," Claire said. "She's a little ..."

"Eccentric," Delia said.

"To put it mildly," Claire said.

"If you want us to, we can take care of everything for you," Delia said.

"We're good at that," Claire said. "Just try and stop us."

"What I meant was, if you need help making any of these decisions we would be glad to help," Delia said. "Of course it's all up to you."

"But I can't pay for this," Grace said.

"The state pays for a basic funeral," Delia said. "And the United Methodist Church has a fund to help out with anything not covered."

"I'm not a member there," Grace said. "I don't go to church."

"Doesn't matter," Delia said. "That fund's for everyone in Rose Hill."

Delia rang the doorbell at the back door, and eventually, someone answered.

Grace had seen Peg Machalvie before, and it would be hard to forget her once you had.

Her hair was darker than black, if that were possible, and teased out into a high and wide hairdo that was sprayed so stiff it did not move. Her face was very pale so that the heavy, dark eye makeup and blood red lipstick she wore made her look like one of the Goths at school. She was skinny, but her breasts stuck way out up high on her chest, like an undulating tray for her chunky jewelry. The top of her red pantsuit was cut very low so that Grace could see the lacy black of her bra. Her nails were long and painted blood red to match her lips. Her face was motionless, and after she looked Grace up and down once, she never looked directly at her again.

"Come on in," she said, in a tone that conveyed how unwelcome they actually were.

She led them down a long hallway to an office, where her desk chair was covered in faux leopard skin, and the walls were decorated with multiple large, canvas photos of herself, her husband, and their two sons. There were only two chairs on the other side of her desk, so Delia and Grace sat down while Claire stood in the doorway, her arms crossed.

Peg opened a folder and picked up a pen that was covered with fake rhinestones.

"We have the body," Peg said. "I'm assuming this will be a state-funded burial."

"To start with," Delia said. "Our church is taking care of any extras."

"I figured as much," Peg said. "Burial or cremation?"

Grace thought of the big fire in the burn barrel, of grandpa throwing her books in one at a time. 'I ought to burn you,' he had said. She heard his voice so clearly in her head that she felt like everyone else should have heard it, too.

Grace felt a pain in her stomach, bent forward, and Delia grasped her hand.

"Do you want us to do this for you?" she asked.

Grace nodded.

"Claire," Delia said. "Why don't you take Grace outside to get some air and I'll help Peg make the arrangements."

Grace felt like she couldn't get out of the building fast enough. As soon as she felt the fresh air on her face, she ran to the nearest shrubbery and threw up her breakfast. Claire held her hair back and gave her a tissue afterward. Then they sat on the stoop behind the funeral home. Grace slowly rocked back and forth, her arms crossed over her stomach, her head bent. She didn't want to think anything. She wanted her mind to stay blank. The rocking helped.

"I was in Spain when my grandfather died," Claire said. "I didn't come home for the funeral. I've always regretted that."

"What was Spain like?"

"Beautiful, hot, far away from home," Claire said.

"What were you doing there?"

"I worked for a movie star," Claire said. "Sloan Merryweather. Do you know who that is?"

Grace shook her head.

"Lucky you," Claire said. "She was in a movie that was being filmed there. I would have been in breach of my contract if I had come home for the funeral. I cared a lot about contracts back then; more than about my family, apparently. I traveled all over the world for that job, and I hardly ever came home."

"You're here now," Grace said. "Why did you come back?"

"My dad has dementia," Claire said. "He's had a lot of little strokes, and it makes him confused. After I quit my job, I came home for a visit and realized how much my parents needed me. That was about a month ago, and it looks like I'm here to stay."

"Do you miss your job?"

"Not as much as I thought I would," Claire said.

"Your clothes are so pretty," Grace said. "You don't look like someone who lives here."

"Thanks," Claire said. "My first week back I gained five pounds from eating everything smothered in gravy. After that, I had a serious talk with myself and started running. I'm willing to live here, but I refuse to revert to type."

"Be in the world but not of it," Grace said. "That's something my grandpa used to say."

"He was pretty religious?"

"When my grandma was alive, they went to church every Sunday. After she died, the preacher at the church said that God gave her cancer to punish her for how sinful her daughters were. After that, Grandpa never went back."

"That's awful," Claire said.

"I think church people are the worst," Grace said.

"They're just like everybody else," Claire said. "Some are good, and some are bad. I know some good church people. My mom, for instance."

"She is nice," Grace said.

Delia came out then and rolled her eyes at Claire.

"That woman," she said, but did not finish.

"You feeling better?" she said to Grace.

Grace nodded.

"Well, don't you worry about a thing," Delia said. "We'll take care of all the arrangements and bring you to the funeral when it's time."

"Thank you," Grace said.

"Where are you going to be staying?" Claire asked.

"With someone named Kay," Grace said.

"She's wonderful," Delia said. "One of our dearest friends."

"Plus she's running against Peg for mayor," Claire said. "And we're going to make sure she wins."

At his office, Scott searched online for a glass swan like Nino's and found a dealer in New Jersey who had one for sale. The amount he wanted for it surprised Scott. He decided to call the man just to get more information.

"They're rare," the man said. "That's why they're so valuable. When the artist left Rodefeffer Glassworks in the

143

early forties, he went back to Italy, fought in the war, and then went to work for Murano in Venice. He never made another swan that I know of. The ones that are left are all so old and delicate they break easily; not too many left."

"Do you know any collectors of this particular piece?" Scott asked.

"There's one crazy old cat from the Rodefeffer family who I call whenever I get my hands on one," he said. "She has a funny first name; if you don't mind to hold, I'll look it up."

"Not at all," Scott said, thinking "one crazy old cat" perfectly described Mamie.

"Here it is," the man said. "Mary Margaret Rodefeffer's the name."

"Did you call her about the one you have now?"

"Sure did," the man said. "Problem is the check she sent me bounced, so unless I get a cashier's check, she's not getting her hands on it."

"How many would you say she's purchased from you in the past?"

"Close to a hundred," he said. "She must have the biggest Rodefeffer swan collection of any person I know. I started this business on a bidding site back when online shopping first got popular, back in 1995. I did so well I started my own website, and now I just sell direct. Mrs. Rodefeffer was one of my first customers. It was her nephew who did the purchasing for her up until the bounced check. The credit card receipts say Richard Rodefeffer."

Scott thanked the man and wrote up the notes from this call. It was gratifying to find out Mamie was obsessed with Nino's swans, despite her protestations, and interesting that her nephew, Richard, known as "Trick," used to help her buy them. He would have to pay Trick a visit and see what he had to say about it.

Trick was in his real estate office playing "Angry Birds" on his tablet, an open bottle of beer on the desk beside him.

"Hey, Kemosabe," he said. "What can I do ya for?"

"I just wanted to touch base with you," Scott said. "I visited Mamie yesterday and got her all riled up. I didn't mean to, but she was pretty mad when I left."

"That old biddy stays riled up," Trick said. "I wouldn't worry too much. She's always throwing things at me. Luckily her aim's not that good."

"I was asking her about the swans she collects," Scott said. "I came across one the other day and found out it was made by your family's glassworks back in the day. Worth quite a lot, apparently."

"Oh, yeah," he said. "She's crazy about those swans. Must have dozens of them; keeps them all in a glass case in her bedroom. I used to order them online for her until she kept forgetting to pay me back."

"Any idea why she's so keen on those in particular?"

"Says her father commissioned them for her," he said. "I guess he told her she was an ugly duckling who would one day turn into a swan. I can vouch for the ugly part but the swan period must have been brief if it occurred at all."

"That would explain it," Scott said. "Well, if you see her tell her I'm sorry I bothered her."

"Don't worry about it," Trick said. "Aunt Mamie was born in a bad mood."

But Scott did have reason to worry about it, as he soon found out after he was called to Mayor Stuart Machalvie's office.

When he greeted the mayor's secretary, Kay, in the outer office, she warned him, "Mamie called him. She's upset about your visit."

When Scott entered his office, Stuart was shredding documents from a tall stack on his desk.

"You have a secretary who can do that," Scott said.

145

"Some things are too important to be delegated," Stuart said. "Now that Kay's running against Peg I'm a little more circumspect in my assignments."

"Peg worried?"

"We all are," Stuart said, lowering his voice. "Kay's a fine person. She's also a competent city manager, but when it comes to the fine art of negotiation and diplomacy, she lacks what I like to call seasoning."

"May the best woman win," Scott said, to which Stuart just grunted.

"I guess Mamie called," Scott said.

"Why'd you have to go get that old hen all stirred up?" Stuart asked him. "What was that about?"

"I'm trying to find out who this man was who died on Jacob Branduff's front porch last weekend. He has a tie to her family."

"From now on," Stuart said. "I would appreciate it if you would give me a heads-up before you call on her for any reason. She's getting on in years, and Knox says she's starting to lose some of her faculties. Just between us, Knox is taking steps to be officially appointed her guardian. Very sad, but a time comes for us all, as they say."

"I didn't know that," Scott said. "That would account for her not remembering who this man was."

"No doubt," Stuart said. "While you're here, I've got something else I want to talk to you about. I understand you've taken an interest in Grace Branduff."

"Just trying to make sure she gets situated in a safe place," Scott said. "We're still looking for the aunt, and social services notified her biological father of her situation."

"Has the will been found?"

"Not yet," Scott said. "After I leave here, I'm taking Grace back over to the house to look for it."

"Too bad about the property," Stuart said. "That house was once a showplace, you know; might be hard for her to unload it in this economy."

146

"I wouldn't know," Scott said.

After Scott shut the door to Stuart's office, Kay followed him outside.

"How's the little girl?" she asked.

"As well as can be expected," Scott said. "She's had a tough life, and now it looks like she's completely alone in the world."

"I'm glad to take her in," Kay said. "Just temporarily, you understand."

"I understand," Scott said. "I was planning to bring her over tonight if that's okay."

"My most recent foster just ended, and I had decided not to do another one anytime soon. So this is just a temporary measure. I want that to be clear."

"It is," Scott said. "I'll call C.P.S. and tell them."

"I've already called," Kay said. "I know everyone down there and got the judge's approval, too. That may expedite things."

"She'll certainly be in safe hands," Scott said.

"Jacob Branduff was a horrible old man," Kay said. "Some say he worked his wife to death. It can't have been easy to be raised by someone like that."

"She seems remarkably stable for someone who's been through what she has," Scott said.

"I've had some experience with teenagers," Kay said. "Don't be surprised if she acts out or blows up over something quite small."

"Grace isn't like that," Scott said. "She's just a sweet young girl."

"Just don't be surprised when it happens," Kay said. "Put anyone in a pressure cooker situation long enough, and they'll eventually explode. Add to that all the teenage hormones and any bullying at school, and you've got yourself a bomb waiting to go off."

Scott shook his head.

"I'm just telling you," Kay said. "Don't expect too much from her. She's only human."

Scott picked up Grace from Machalvie's Funeral Home and took her back to her house.

"Sorry I couldn't do that with you," Scott said. "My mom died a few weeks ago, and it's just ..."

"It's okay," Grace said. "I'm sorry about your mom."

"She was sick for a long time, and I didn't know it," he said. "If I had known, I would have made her go to the doctor."

Grace thought about her grandma, to whom doctors were not an option because of the religion she was raised in and the mean, stingy man she married.

She dreaded going back to her house to look through her grandfather's things, but she knew she had to. She doubted there was anything of value, but she guessed the house would be hers to sell, and she needed the will to prove that.

When they arrived at her house, Grace said, "I need to water the plants in the greenhouse. I forgot about them."

"Tommy and Ed are doing it," Scott said. "I hope you don't mind that I asked them. They come this way early in the morning when they deliver papers, so they're going to water everything then."

"That's nice of them," Grace said. "I really didn't want to go back in there."

"Are you sure you're up to this?" he asked her.

She nodded.

Scott took her key and opened the back door. The house was still warm from where he had turned up the heat the day before.

"Do you want me to help?" he asked her.

She shook her head.

Just then Scott's radio came to life and Skip informed him that there was an emergency at Owl's Branch Baptist Church. Someone had reported a break-in.

"I have to go," Scott told Grace. "Do you want me to have Maggie come over and hang out with you?"

"I'll be okay," Grace said. "It may take me a while anyway."

"I'll lock the door behind me," Scott said. "If it seems like I'll be a long time I'll call Maggie and have her come down."

After Scott left, Grace took a deep breath and opened the door to her grandfather's room. The increase in the heat made the smell of him ten times stronger, so her eyes watered and she gagged. She covered her nose and mouth with her T-shirt and opened the window. Big gusts of cool air billowed through the dusty curtains and helped disperse the foul odor. She leaned out the window to take a deep breath and was surprised to see the mayor standing on the stone path, looking back at her.

"Hello there, young lady," he said. "I thought I would pay my respects. Do you mind if I come in?"

Grace did not want to let Mayor Machalvie into the house, so she let herself out the back door and met him on the back stairs.

"All alone?" he said.

"Scott will be right back," she said.

"Called out on an emergency, was he?" Stuart said. "That could take some time. Maybe I better come in and keep you company."

"Maggie's coming over," Grace said. "She'll be here any minute."

"Ah, well, I didn't foresee that," Stuart said. "I'll make this quick, then. I'd like to buy this property, Grace, as soon as the estate is settled. I'm prepared to give you a large deposit to hold it. I know you could use the money, and that way you won't have to worry about meeting any expenses. The house is in pretty bad shape, you know, Grace, and you'd be required to do so many things to it before you could sell it; things that will cost a lot of money. I just don't see how you could afford the liability insurance or the utilities on your own. The property's not worth much but for the land. I'd be willing to give you $50,000.00 for it, with $10,000.00 down to hold it until the estate settles."

"I don't know," Grace said. "I don't even know if it's mine to sell."

"Well, you think about it," Stuart said. "And be careful; don't let anybody try to trick you into doing anything else with it. In fact, let's just keep this deal between you and me, and when you find the will you bring it to me. I'll be glad to steer you through any legal matters you might come up against."

Grace didn't know what to say, so she just said, "Okay."

"Good, good, good," Stuart said. "Now you take care, ya hear?"

He winked at her and left. Grace went back inside and locked the door behind her. The mayor had seemed very kind and helpful, but there had been something in his eyes she didn't like; something that had laughed at her in a mean way. Fifty thousand dollars sounded like a fortune, though.

Scott walked around the outside of the Owl's Branch Baptist Church but didn't see any evidence of a break-in. He checked in with the nearest neighbors, but they said they hadn't seen anything suspicious. He drove out to the pastor's house, and he said he hadn't called the station. Together they returned to the church and looked in every room; all seemed well.

Scott called the station to question Skip, and he said it had been an anonymous caller. Scott thought about this as he drove back toward town over the winding roads that connected Owl's Branch to Pine Mountain Road. By the time he got to Pine Mountain, he had a strong enough cell signal to make a call.

"Mayor's office," Kay said.

"Is Stuart there?" Scott asked her. "It's Scott."

"No," Kay said. "He left a little while ago; I'm not sure where he went."

Scott told her his suspicions.

"You're probably right," Kay said. "I know for a fact he wants the property; he was talking to Trick about it earlier today. It wouldn't surprise me a bit if he pulled something like that to get Grace alone."

"It's going to take me twenty minutes to get there," Scott said. "Could I ask you a favor?"

"I'm leaving right now," Kay said. "I'll be there in two minutes."

Grace searched her grandfather's room top to bottom, but she didn't find the will. While she searched, she heard noises from upstairs as Edgar made his daily mischief. She wondered if Edgar would be lonely in the house with no one to hear him act out. Lonelier, she thought. It must be awful to still be someone but not be able to be seen or communicate. She hoped her grandfather went straight to wherever it was people went and did not stop back by to visit.

Grace looked everywhere she could think of where something might be hidden on the first floor. Meanwhile, Edgar opened and closed doors, made footstep noises on the attic stairs, and turned the lights on and off.

"You're awfully busy today, Edgar," she called up the stairs. "Where did grandfather hide the will?"

It was very quiet for a few moments, and then the door to the stairs that led from the second floor to the third floor creaked as it slowly swung open. Grace climbed the stairs to the second floor and heard Edgar's footsteps on the third floor. Then she heard the door from the third floor to the attic stairs open. Grace climbed to the third floor and paused at the top of the stairs. She could hear the baby birds cheeping in their nest below, and a tapping noise in the attic. Grace climbed the stairs into the attic and saw that one of

151

the windows was not secured. The tapping had been the sound of it rattling in its frame.

It was cold in the attic. Grandma's dress form was there, dusty and stained, but there were no old trunks full of clothes or antiques that could be sold. Anything that was worth anything had been sold before Grace was even born. Her mother and aunt used to come up here and smoke out the open window. When Grace was little, she sometimes brought her dolls up here to play, far away from the shouting and crying that often could be heard on the floors below.

Grace walked to the windows on the front of the house, firmly secured the one that was loose, and then looked out over the field across the alley, the trailer park, and the backs of the businesses on Rose Hill Avenue. The mayor was out back of the city building, standing in the parking lot, talking to Trick Rodefeffer, who was sitting in his orange Corvette. The mayor was gesturing with his cigar towards her house. Grace thought about his offer. She could take that money and run away, make a life for herself somewhere else.

The door at the bottom of the steps slammed shut and startled her.

Grace turned, saying, "Oh, Edgar," but then stopped when she spotted something. She would have to be standing exactly where she was and turn exactly as she had in order to see it. There was a space between the two-by-fours that framed the dormer area in which she stood. At the top of the window, where the wall met the dormer, the frame made a ledge. On that ledge was a cigar box, covered in thick dust.

The will was in it. It also had her grandparents' marriage certificate and birth certificates for everyone in the family. On hers, where the name of her father should have been printed, it said "unknown." She knew she shouldn't be surprised, but seeing legal proof seemed to confirm the horrible word with which some children had teased her as a child.

She read through the will, which wasn't very long. Her grandfather had bequeathed all his worldly goods to his wife, and if she pre-deceased him, to his living children and then their children.

She unfolded the next thick sheaf of papers, and a photograph fell out. She recognized the subjects as her great-grandparents. The photo had been taken when they were very young, standing outside this house, holding an infant. The house was beautiful, but their faces were grim. She had often wondered how they managed to purchase such a grand house, but her grandmother had told her to mind her own business. The papers folded around this photograph were the deed to the property. She put the deed aside and took out the last folded paper in the box. It was a letter written fifty-seven years ago, from a bank in Pittsburgh. This she did understand; it just didn't make any sense.

She heard someone knock on the front door. Grace put the papers back in the cigar box, stuck it under her arm, and ran down three flights of stairs to answer it. To her dismay, she saw it was Mrs. Larson. Grace opened the front door but did not unlatch the screen door.

"Grace?" Mrs. Larson said. "Are you home alone?"

"Scott had to leave, but he'll be back soon," Grace said.

"You should refer to him as Chief Gordon, dear," Mrs. Larson said. "I don't hold with children using the first names of adults; it's such bad manners. Bless your heart, you just never had anyone to teach you those things, did you?"

Grace could feel hot rage fill her chest, just like it had the day she cursed out Mrs. Larson for removing her beloved books from the library. This time she held her tongue but found it only built up the pressure in her body until she thought she might burst.

"Aren't you going to invite me in?"

"I'm sorry," Grace said. "Scott ... Chief Gordon told me not to let anyone in."

"I hardly think that would include me ..." Mrs. Larson said.

Her fake smile had worn off, and her pinched lips now matched her mean eyes.

Grace was trying to think of a nice way to ask "What do you want?" but everything she considered saying she knew would make Mrs. Larson mad. So she said nothing.

"I had hoped you would come to me in person to apologize for your ugly outburst," Mrs. Larson said. "I was disappointed when I didn't even receive a call."

"My grandfather died," Grace said. "I've been sort of busy on account of that."

"Well, I know that, of course," Mrs. Larson said. "I'm not insensitive to the fact that you have suffered a loss. I don't know why you would accuse me of such a thing."

"Accuse you of what?" came a voice from the stairway behind Mrs. Larson. "I didn't hear Grace accuse you of anything."

Mrs. Larson whirled around, having been startled by the sudden appearance of a woman on the stairs. Grace knew this woman from seeing her around town but didn't know her name. She worked at city hall and was always pleasant when Grace passed her in the hallway on her way to pay the garbage/sewage bill. It was hard for Grace to tell how old she was because she was generously padded and had a chubby, pretty face devoid of wrinkles.

"Kay!" Mrs. Larson said. "I didn't hear you. It might have been nicer manners to announce yourself rather than sneak up on a person."

"There's nothing wrong with my manners," Kay said. She winked at Grace as she came up to the front door. "Sorry I can't say the same for you."

"I don't know what you could possibly mean," Mrs. Larson said. "If anyone needs a lesson in manners, it's this young lady. You should have heard her language in the school library the other day. I was shocked. Shocked, I tell you! Such language."

"I heard you were gathering up books to burn," Kay said. "I would have swung you by your hair if it had been me. Don't you have anything better to do than meddle in things that are none of your business?"

"If you think you'll get elected mayor by talking to your constituents like that, you've got another think coming," Mrs. Larson said. "I for one will lead the campaign against you, and I have a lot of influence in this town."

"If I needed people like you to get elected I wouldn't bother running," Kay said. "Be sure and tell that to all your important friends."

"Well, I never," Mrs. Larson said. "I'm not going to stand here listening to you talk to me like that."

Having said that she stomped off the porch, down the steps and out to her car.

"Are you okay, Grace," Kay asked. "My name's Kay Templeton; I'm a friend of Scott's."

Her kind words matched her kind face and eyes.

"I'm okay," Grace said.

"Scott sent me to check on you," Kay said. "Was the mayor here earlier?"

Grace nodded.

"Well, don't you listen to anything that rotten rascal says, and don't you fall for any of his lies."

"He wants to buy the house," Grace said.

"Sure he does," Kay said. "You probably didn't know this, honey, but this property has something called 'mineral rights' that go with it. That means you have the rights to all the resources underneath it, including natural gas and coal. Not many people have those rights anymore, and they're very valuable."

Grace unlatched the screen door and pushed it open.

"Come in," she said.

Kay followed her to the kitchen, where Grace had left the cigar box and documents on the kitchen table.

"I found the will," Grace said. "There's also a letter from a bank I don't understand."

"Do you want me to look at it?" Kay asked.

Grace handed the letter to Kay, who sat down at the table. She put on the half glasses that hung on a brightly beaded necklace and frowned as she read.

"It sounds like your grandfather's been contacted a number of times about some financial matter but hasn't responded to their letters," Kay said. "I can't tell from this letter what it's about, but this bank is still in business. There's a number you can call. They might not be able to talk to you about whatever it is unless you prove you're his next of kin. You'll need the death certificate. What you're also going to need is an attorney to help you with the estate."

"Estate?"

"Yes, honey," Kay said, removing her glasses. "This house and any other assets your grandfather had are all part of his estate now that he's passed. Unless he appointed an executor, you'll have to get an attorney's help to probate the will. That just means to make sure your grandfather's wishes are honored, and the right people inherit his assets."

Grace handed her the will. Back on went the glasses and Kay read through it.

"It's not complicated," Kay said. "It shouldn't take a long time to process if there are no contestants. That means no one challenges the terms of the will."

"How can I pay for an attorney?" Grace said.

"We'll figure something out," Kay said. "Right now we just need to put all this in a safe place."

Grace shrugged.

"Most people use safety deposit boxes at the bank for this kind of thing," Kay said. "Unfortunately, our bank is run by Knox Rodefeffer, whom I wouldn't trust as far as I could throw him. Maggie has a safe at her store. How about we ask her to keep this in there until we figure out our next steps?"

Grace searched Kay's face but could not find one tiny bit of false cheer or meanness. She was so relieved to hear that someone else was willing to help her. Between the Fitzpatrick cousins, Doc Machalvie and his wife, plus Scott and Kay, somehow everything felt less overwhelming.

"Okay," she said.

"I'm a foster parent," Kay said. "Did Scott mention that to you?"

"He said I would go to your house tonight," Grace said.

"And you're very welcome," Kay said. "It was just such short notice that I haven't had time to get ready."

"I'm sorry," Grace said.

"Oh, honey, no need to be sorry," Kay said. "I'm apologizing to you for not having everything just perfect for you."

"I don't need anything special," Grace said.

"I've got a campaign committee meeting to go to here in a little while, so how about we go to Maggie's and then later Scott can bring you to my house? I hate to run you around town like that, but it's the best I can do; it's too late to cancel the meeting, and it would look pretty bad to stand them up."

"I don't mind," Grace said.

Kay helped her gather up her few clothes, schoolwork, and the legal documents. As they were about to go out the front door, there was a loud bang upstairs. Kay's hand flew to her chest as she gasped.

"What in the world was that?" she asked.

"That's just Edgar slamming the door to the attic," Grace said. "He's a ghost."

"I don't think I could live in a house where that kind of thing happened on a regular basis," Kay said.

"He doesn't hurt anybody," Grace said. "He's just lonely."

Kay gave Grace an odd look but quickly smiled.

"Do me a favor," she said. "Don't invite Edgar to stay over at my house."

Grace smiled.

"Don't worry," she said. "I won't."

Kay's house was a tiny cottage on Lilac Avenue, across from the Community Center. There were flowers planted in white window boxes beneath window sills, which were painted a cheerful apple green in contrast to the white clapboard exterior of the house. An old metal glider painted a bright shade of pink shared the front porch with a generous rocking chair painted turquoise. There was a colorful flag declaring, "Spring has Sprung!" flying from one column and various wind chimes and party lights strung along the porch ceiling. On the front door was a knocker in the shape of a bug-eyed green frog.

Kay answered the door.

"Come in, come in," she said and gave Grace a genuinely friendly smile that extended to her twinkly blue eyes.

Her house smelled like cookies baking. Grace and Scott entered the front room, which was decorated in the same whimsical way but was not as cluttered as the front porch had been. There were faded pastel colored quilts folded on the end of a slip-covered sofa, and a chubby upholstered reading chair with a crocheted granny-square throw draped over the back.

Everything was homey, colorful and cheerful, just like Kay. She was dressed in a hot pink sweater, faded jeans, and had multiple strands of colorful beads around her neck. Her earrings were brightly colored to match her necklace. Her fingernails were painted pink to match her lipstick, and her light brown hair floated around her head in a fluffy bob haircut. On her feet, she wore floral-patterned tennis shoes with pink ribbons for laces.

"Come into the kitchen," she said. "I've just baked some chocolate chip cookies, and it's warmer in there. I may have to cover up my peonies tonight; the weatherman says it may frost."

The kitchen was tiny with a booth built into a small alcove at one end. Grace and Scott sat on either side of this. There were white shutters at the windows, and all the cabinets were white to match. All the accessories were bright red, and the leatherette of the booth was red as well. The curtains were red-and-white gingham, and the floor was black-and-white linoleum squares. There was a salt-and-pepper shaker collection in a built-in corner china cabinet. The pair on the Formica tabletop was a chubby chef with a black mustache, wearing a poufy hat, holding a rolling pin marked "pepper," and the salt shaker was meant to look like a big bag of flour.

Grace's mouth watered as Kay set a plate piled high with cookies on the center of the table. Kay gave Grace a tall glass of milk and the chief a large mug of coffee. She pulled up a stool to the end of the table and seated herself there, along with a cup of caramel-colored tea. It smelled like flowers.

"Thanks for having Grace on such short notice," Scott said.

He drew the paperwork out of its folder and handed it to her, but Kay merely set it behind her on the kitchen counter and focused on Grace.

"I'm glad to have you here, Grace," she said. "I had decided not to foster anyone for awhile, but I stay on the books for emergencies, as a favor to Judge Feinman. I'm sure we'll get along fine."

"Grace has an aunt whom we're trying to find," Scott said. "She's going to take a few days off from school, but they will send her work home."

"I'm not sure what we'll do during the day," Kay said. "I work from eight to four, but you're welcome to come along to city hall with me. I think it's important for you to not be alone."

"Hannah, Claire, and Maggie are going to help out," Scott said.

"That will be much more fun than city hall," Kay said. "I'd rather hang out with those ornery girls any old day. They've been thick as thieves since birth. Always laughing, always up to something, but you never ever saw one without the others. When Claire moved back last month, I said to her mother, 'Now the whole gang's back together.' "

The cookies were delicious, warm and melty, crunchy and sweet. The milk was ice cold and full of fat. Grace thought she could feel the nutrients feeding her hungry cells as she drank.

"We brought her things," Scott said. "I guess Stuart was nosing around trying to get his bid in already."

Grace was interested to see Kay's blue eyes turn steely.

"You leave the mayor to me," she said. "I'll jerk a knot in his tail."

"How's the campaign going?" Scott asked her. "It must feel odd to be running against your boss's wife."

"Stuart has been as gracious as can be," Kay said. "Almost too gracious, if you know what I mean. He doesn't take me seriously yet, but he will. Ed's taken a poll that's going to surprise some people when the Sentinel comes out on Sunday."

"I heard," Scott said. "You know I can't overtly campaign for you, but everyone knows I support you and Maggie can certainly help."

"You know, Scott, I have no doubt I can win this race," Kay said. "And deep down I think Stuart knows it too. My only concern is what will happen when Peg realizes it."

"She's not exactly America's Sweetheart," Scott said. "And there is so much at stake."

"That's just it," Kay said. "Rose Hill is at a dangerous juncture right now. We could easily be seduced into overdevelopment and become a town full of non-resident home-owners. There has to be a balance between protecting our longtime residents and making the most of our resources."

"If anyone can do that, it's you," Scott said. "Everyone knows you've been running the town while Stuart and Peg wheel and deal for their own benefit. They just need to know you have the residents' best interests at heart."

"You can't please everyone," Kay said. "Unfortunately, there's no sweet spot between preventing any progress and allowing a complete transformation. All I can do is to remind everyone what happened on Lotus Avenue."

This piqued Grace's interest.

"What happened on Lotus Avenue?" she asked.

"When the flood washed away most of the homes on Lotus Avenue, the mayor pulled some strings with the insurance companies so the city could purchase the properties from the residents at a very low cost. He then invited developers to bid on the condemned properties and went with the highest bidder."

"With kickbacks to Stuart, no doubt," Scott said.

"Most likely," Kay said.

"What are kickbacks?" Grace asked.

"Stuart may have rigged it so one particular company won the bid, and in return, he may have received a secret payment or a favor done in return," Scott said.

"It's illegal," Kay said. "Not that something like the law's ever stopped Stuart and Peg."

"So what's wrong with the condos?" Grace asked.

"The developer didn't take into account our ancient sewage system or the demands on the local electrical plant. The previous homes were heated by coal or gas and had one bathroom a piece. In these condos, there are two and a half bathrooms plus a hot tub in every unit, and electric central heat and air; consequently, there has been nothing but problems. Plus most of the people who lived on Lotus Avenue had to leave town; with the pittance they got from the city they couldn't afford to repurchase here."

"The condos have turned into student housing and vacation rentals," Scott said. "I could keep a squad car parked down there 24-7 and still not be able to deal with all the trouble we have."

"It used to be the college students were confined to campus housing and the apartment buildings downtown," Kay said. "Now outsiders are buying up houses all over town and turning them into multiple rental residences, all because Stuart's allowed the zoning laws to be changed. Rose Hill is no longer the quiet, peaceful community we grew up in."

"We can still turn it around," Scott said. "It's not too late."

Kay sighed and shook her head.

"It will never go back to being what it was ten years ago," she said. "But we can keep it from becoming worse."

"The Baltimore and Detroit drug trades have now moved into this area," Scott said. "The feds have set up a permanent surveillance detail at the bus station in Pendleton. We are an unclaimed territory since Mrs. Wells died."

Grace didn't know who Mrs. Wells was, but she didn't want to keep piping up with constant questions, so she stayed quiet.

"I can get you an extra deputy if we pass the new business tax," Kay said.

"Will previously existing business owners be exempt?"

"That's my plan," she said. "If we could have stopped Stuart and Peg giving new business owners tax breaks in return for kickbacks, we could have already had several new officers."

"Any chance we can make that tax retroactive?"

"That would kick up a mighty stink," Kay said. "I'd like to make this transition as peaceful as I possibly can."

"So they'll just get away with it all, again."

"Politics is about compromise," Kay said, "whether we like it or not."

"I know," Scott said. "I hate it, but I can't deny it."

"Meanwhile, we're boring Miss Grace to tears," Kay said.

"I'm not bored," Grace said. "I like hearing the truth." Kay laughed out loud.

"Then we're going to get along just fine," she said.

"Kay will never sugar-coat anything for you," Scott said.

"Life is tough, and we have to watch out for each other," Kay said. "We're all in this together."

After Scott left, Kay showed Grace to a small, snug bedroom at the back of the house. It had a tiny half bath attached to it. The white iron bed was made up with a blue and white pinwheel quilt and a fluffy comforter folded at the end. The pillow slips and sheets were white cotton with pink and yellow embroidered flowers on the edges.

"You make yourself at home," Kay said. "Let me know if there's anything you need. I'm going to fill out your paperwork and then see about getting your homework delivered."

Grace felt like a dusty piece of coal in this spotless dollhouse of a bedroom. She lowered her backpack full of belongings onto the floor and slipped off her shoes. In the bathroom, she ran warm water over her hands and arms until it was too hot to bear. It felt wonderful, and she longed to immerse herself in it. As if reading her mind, Kay knocked at the entrance to the bedroom and said, "The tub's down the hall here on the right; why don't you take a long hot bath? I bet it will help you sleep."

Kay set a white terry cloth robe and a thick terry towel on the bed and then left the room.

Down the hall, Grace filled the tub with steaming water until it began running out the overflow drain. She lay back and immersed her head, luxuriating in the feeling of hot water surrounding her. It was heavenly.

'People don't know,' she thought. 'They just don't know how good they've got it.'

Kay had some pretty-smelling coconut and vanilla bath gel, shampoo, and conditioner. Grace used a generous amount of each and then had to take a short shower just to get it all rinsed off.

As she combed out her long tangled hair, she looked around the small bathroom. Kay's whole house was decorated to reflect her cheerful, playful attitude. Here there were watercolors of the elephant couple Babar and Celeste, and there were silly mermaid light sconces on either side of the medicine cabinet. Grace cleaned up behind herself and hung the towel over the towel bar before she went back to her bedroom. In the hall, she could hear someone talking to Kay in the kitchen. She paused. It was a man's voice.

Grace tiptoed up to the end of the hallway and hoped a squeaky floorboard wouldn't give away her presence.

"Let's be honest," Stuart Machalvie said. "They want to back a winning horse, and they've got deep pockets. It's in everyone's best interests to bring this off without any scandal or uncomfortable questions. There's bound to be some mud slinging, people expect that sort of thing; I just think it would be wise of us to realize we are all on the same side, ultimately, and make arrangements for who will be mayor ahead of the election."

"And Peg would withdraw? Just like that? How would she save face?"

"Peg's thinking of expanding the family business," he said. "She will say she has too much respect for Rose Hill to shortchange it due to familial obligations."

"How can she expand? Where to?"

"We're going to relocate the whole operation," Stuart said. "Everything's in the very preliminary stages right now, but we have plans to purchase several acres. We'll build a new funeral home, crematorium, and a really stunning burial complex. Peg's anxious to get going and this election is frankly just one more headache she doesn't need."

"Where is this property?" Kay asked, and Grace could hear the suspicion in her tone.

"Oh," Stuart said. "We're considering several locations."

"Like the Branduff place," she said.

"Too small by far," Stuart said. "No, I'm not interested in that worthless piece of property."

"I see," Kay said.

"Whattaya say?" Stuart said. "Do we have a deal?"

"If Peg wants to withdraw, I'm fine with that," Kay said. "With no one standing against me, I don't need anyone's campaign donations."

"You're missing the whole point, Kay," Stuart said. "I have deals in place, and I want to make sure that everything will play out just as it's supposed to. I'm not going to meddle in the town business; you know I could care less about that. I just want my projects to go forward without any unnecessary complications."

"The bicycle factory," Kay said. "That man should not have any special tax exemptions."

"He's restoring a historic property and creating economic development," Stuart said. "The renovations are being done by a 501 (c) 3 with federal funds. They're a nonprofit; you can't tax them. They will own the building and rent it to him."

"I can, and I will tax his manufacturing and event business," Kay said. "That man makes millions running those bike races."

"He'll be employing local people and giving them health benefits," Stuart said. "You have to give business owners some incentive to settle here."

"The wind farm people," Kay said. "I know Congressman Green is beholden to them, and Senator Bayard is backing the protected land set-asides, but that first unit is way too close to Rose Hill. We will all see it, hear it, and it will endanger the migrating Canada Geese."

"That's a done deal, Kay," Stuart said. "You know that as well as I do."

"I heard the Marcellus Shale people were in town," Kay said. "A sudden influx of transient workers would ruin this community, not to mention what the process might do to the water supply. You and I both know there is so much mine subsidence underneath this town that the slightest pressure from fracking might sink the whole town. I won't support it."

"Not going to happen," Stuart said. "There are no mineral rights available anywhere near here."

"Is that so?" Kay said. "Interesting."

"You've got a suspicious mind," Stuart said. "All I want is what's best for Rose Hill."

"What else?" Kay said. "I know you and the Rodefeffers are still working on the Eldridge Point project with Gwyneth Eldridge."

"Waiting on the same protected land set-asides," Stuart said. "It's just a matter of a small, discreet piece of legislation and the glacial movement of the state bureaucracy."

"The property taxes will come back to Rose Hill?"

"In a tiered plan," Stuart said, "After the initial investment is recovered."

"You mean after our city retirement account funds are either recovered or lost."

"All legal and above board," he said. "The town council voted."

"You won't control the town council after this election," Kay said. "I've seen to that."

"Kay, my dear, why so hostile? I keep telling you, we're on the same side. I'm not going to interfere in the town business as long as you don't interfere with my business."

"I'm not going to give you a blanket approval in return for Peg's withdrawal," Kay said. "I can win without it, and I certainly can govern without your support."

"Think about it," Stuart said. "Wouldn't it be easier for everyone if we all just cooperated?"

"No," Kay said. "Tell Peg to bring it. I'm not afraid of her."

"You're a stubborn woman," he said, and Grace could hear him push his chair back and get up from the table. "No one knows that better than I do. But you're also smart and practical. Think of what you could do for Rose Hill using my connections, my clout. Bottom line, here's what's on the table: two more police officers, a new street cleaner, a grid boost from the wind farm, and a sewage plant upgrade."

"In return for?"

"Blanks to be filled in at a later time."

"No," Kay said. "That was your way, but it will not be my way."

"We'll talk again."

"Of course we will," Kay said. "I'll see you at work tomorrow."

Grace scurried down the hall to the small bedroom and hurriedly put on her threadbare flannel nightgown. She was towel-drying her hair when Kay knocked on her bedroom door.

"Come in," Grace said.

Kay came in and sat on the end of the bed.

"I wanted to have a talk with you before you spend your first night," Kay said. "I think it's a good idea to get the ground rules set; make sure everyone's expectations are clear."

"All right," Grace said and sat down on the other end of the bed.

Grace's heart was beating fast, and she felt like she was in trouble for something. Had she not cleaned up the bathroom well enough? Had Kay caught her eavesdropping in the hallway?

"I've had lovely experiences fostering children, and I've also had my heart broken," Kay said. "In fact, I recently fostered a young lady with marvelous potential, but fulfilling potential depends upon hard work and self-discipline, and she just couldn't resist temptation. That experience was so traumatic I've decided not to do another long-term placement."

"What did she do?" Grace asked.

"Drugs, alcohol, sneaking out, sneaking boys in; you name it, and she did it."

"I won't do any of that," Grace said.

"Oh, sweetheart," Kay said. "You seem like a nice girl, and I hear you have excellent grades, but I also understand from your guidance counselor that there was some sort of outburst earlier this week and that you were verbally abusive to staff members. Was this about Mrs. Lawson taking the books out of the library?"

Grace explained to Kay what had happened, about the book and Jumbo's mother.

"That woman is a menace," Kay said, "but I shouldn't have been so rude to her this afternoon; I didn't set a very good example. The world is full of those people, Grace. You and I have to rise above their behavior and not jeopardize what we want in the long term for what satisfies a fit of pique in the short term. We've got to pick our battles, and frankly, avoid as many as possible."

"I'm a good kid," Grace said. "I promise. I won't cause you any trouble."

"Here's the thing, Grace. I'm running for mayor this year. It's been a dream of mine for many years, and this is my chance. I can't afford any scandal, and more than that, I can't afford to have any distractions. This is going to take every ounce of my energy, all of my time, and it's the worst possible moment for me to take you on in addition to everything else. It's not fair to you, either. You need someone's full attention and support, and I wouldn't be able to give you that."

"I've never had anyone's full attention or support," Grace said. "I'm not sure I would like it. I can take care of myself. All I need is a safe place to live until I can graduate. I won't be any trouble, and I might even be able to help."

"I couldn't ask you to work on the campaign," Kay said. "I wouldn't."

"It would look good to foster an orphan, though, wouldn't it?" Grace said. "Think about it. The newspaper could say you took in a homeless child or something like that."

Kay looked taken aback and then laughed long and hard.

"Oh, Grace, you are precious," she finally said. "And worse, it's true. That would make me look good."

"Don't decide right now," Grace said. "Please. Give it a few days. It may work out fine."

"I don't know," Kay said. "You're certainly not like any other fifteen-year-old girl I've ever met. The timing just could not be worse."

"Life's like that," Grace said. "We've all got to look out for each other."

"Very good," Kay said. "Using my own words against me. Okay, here's what we'll do. We'll get through this week. They may find your aunt, after all."

"If she's not in jail, she'll be dead," Grace said.

"Oh, honey," Kay said and scooted over to give Grace a quick, warm hug. "I'm sorry. I just can't make you any promises."

"At least you're honest," Grace said.

Grace lay in bed that night, enjoying the feeling of the crisp cotton sheets against her skin and the soft bed beneath her tired bones. She was warm, her belly was full, and she knew it was a safe place to sleep.

'Don't get used to it,' the voice in her head said.

It was the same voice from the cupboard the day she considered ending it all.

'I'm going to save myself,' she told it.

169

Maggie woke up as she felt Scott get up. She lay still and quiet until she heard the bathroom door shut, and then she crept out of bed. She walked along the side of the hall so the old floorboards would not creak; she stopped outside the bathroom door and listened. Inside she could hear the unmistakable sound of a man weeping. Her heart hurt in her chest. She raised her hand to knock, as she had every night since he came home with her on the night his mother died, and just as she had on all of those nights, she let her hand drop without knocking.

What more could she say or do to ease his pain? She argued with herself every night and always came to the same decision: if he needed privacy to grieve she would give it to him. Back in her bedroom, she turned away so that he would not know she was awake when he came back to bed.

CHAPTER SEVEN – WEDNESDAY

G race woke up to hear Claire and Kay talking in the front room.

"That was so kind of you," Kay said.

"Well, I knew she probably didn't have anything to wear, and I was shopping anyway," Claire said. "I hope they fit."

Grace walked into the kitchen to find Claire holding open a shopping bag for Kay to look into.

"Good morning, Grace," Kay said. "How are you feeling?"

"Okay," Grace said.

"I brought you some clothes for the funeral," Claire said. "I hope you don't mind."

"I don't mind," Grace said, accepting the shopping bag Claire offered. "Thank you."

"Why don't you get showered, and then try on your new clothes," Kay said. "That way if they don't fit we have time to find something else."

Back in her bedroom after her shower, Grace put on the new clothes. She had read about people being transformed by clothing, but this was a new sensation for her. She looked in the mirror and saw a new person. It may only have been a dark navy blue sweater set and slim skirt with matching low heels, but suddenly she felt like someone who didn't need to hide or feel ashamed. At the same time, she felt like an imposter, pretending to be someone she wasn't, someone who mattered. It was a mixture of feeling reckless and exhilarated, but also a little scared.

When she went to the front room, Claire clapped her hands together.

"Oh, honey," Kay said. "You look so much older in those clothes; like a proper young lady."

"You look really nice," Claire said. "I thought you might let me do your hair."

Grace sat obediently on a kitchen stool while Claire dried, braided, and wound her hair into an intricately woven knot at the base of her neck. She seemed anxious as Grace looked at the back of her head by using two hand mirrors.

"I hope you like it," Claire said. "Maggie let me practice it on her last night, but it's much more suited to your hair texture."

"I like it," Grace said. "I feel like Cinderella but for a funeral, not a ball."

"We'll all be there," Claire said. "You won't be alone."

Kay brought in a short strand of pearls and draped them around Grace's neck.

"These were my mother's," she said. "I was never dainty enough to wear them."

Grace felt the smooth, cool weight of the pearls and said, "I'll be really careful with them."

"I know you will," Kay said.

"We better get going," Claire said.

Kay led them into the funeral home by the side entrance.

"The better to avoid Peg and her crew," she said.

Grace had only been to a funeral twice before, for her mother and then her grandmother, and the room hadn't changed much. Folding chairs faced a closed coffin on a stand at the front. There were large vases of flowers, mostly white lilies, none of which were from her grandfather's greenhouse because he refused to do business with Peg Machalvie, whom he had called, "a whore of Babylon." Grace thought Peg seemed more like an actress in a play, made up to look better from far away than up close.

Kay directed Grace and Claire to sit on the chairs directly in front of the casket, and then she went to, as she put it, "Attend to business."

"I hate funerals," Claire said.

172

"This is only my third," Grace said. "My grandmother went to lots of funerals. She said it was out of respect for the dead person and the family. I don't think anyone will come out of respect for my grandfather."

"You'll be surprised then," Claire said. "Most of the folks in this town come to funerals because they're curious and some just because they want to eat for free at the reception afterward."

"There's supposed to be a reception after this?" Grace asked. "I didn't do anything about that."

"My mom took care of it," Claire said. "Don't worry about it."

"But how will I pay for that?" Grace asked.

"The IWS takes care of it," Claire said.

"What's the IWS?"

"It's the Interdenominational Women's Society," she said. "They're ladies from all the different places of worship in and around Rose Hill. They get together every Tuesday night out at the Owl Branch Baptist Church and make crafts. Then twice a year they sell their crafts in a big bazaar at the Community Center, and all the proceeds go to their favorite charities. One of those is a fund for funeral receptions."

"Grandpa would hate that," Grace said. "We weren't allowed to accept charity."

"Look at it this way: accepting their help is actually a gift you're giving them," Claire said. "It allows the IWS ladies to feel good about helping people."

"I never thought of it that way," Grace said.

"They get a big kick out of organizing and putting on these receptions," Claire said. "They're very competitive about their cooking. The food is delicious."

Grace heard the low murmur of conversation in the outer room and tensed up, but Claire squeezed her hand.

"Just smile sadly, shake hands, and say, 'thank you for coming.'" Claire whispered. "After anything they say about your grandfather, no matter how rude, just say, 'Thank you, he will be missed.'"

173

Grace was surprised at how many people showed up. She estimated she knew fifty percent of them by name, another forty percent by sight, and then there was a mysterious ten percent she didn't think she'd ever seen before.

They all said the same things with very little variation: "I'm so sorry for your loss," "He's in a better place," and "Your grandmother would be so proud of you."

She was taken aback by the number of people who cried when they talked to her. She figured it was because funerals made them feel sad about their own losses, or they pitied her, left all alone in the big bad world. It would surprise them to know, Grace thought, that this was the first time she didn't feel so all alone, what with the Fitzpatricks, Doc, Deloris, Kay, and Scott all looking out for her.

Maggie came with her mother and sat right behind Grace. She looked like she wanted to say something, but she didn't, just gave Grace a very concerned look and sighed deeply instead. They were joined by Hannah and Sam, Ed and Tommy, and Hannah's father.

"Where's your mom?" Claire asked Hannah.

"Headache," Hannah said and rolled her eyes.

Hannah put a hand on Grace's shoulder and squeezed it.

"Hang in there, kiddo," she whispered in her ear. "This part won't last long, and lucky for you it won't be pouring rain at the cemetery. The best part is there's some really good food at the shindig they hold after that. You're the bereaved, so people will bring you anything you want. Make sure you get some of Erma Bertowski's pierogies but stay away from Ida Langenfelter's cabbage rolls. They give me killer indigestion, and I can eat anything. If you see any coconut cupcakes, grab one; those are my favorite, and they go fast."

"Who's keeping Sammy?" Grace asked her.

"He's in a secure location," Hannah said.

"He's with my mom," Claire said.

174

Scott came in and sat down next to Grace.

"How are you holding up?" he said.

His face was so kind Grace thought she might cry.

"I'm okay," she said and pressed her eyelids together a few times until the tears receded.

He squeezed her hands, which lay clenched in her lap, said, "I'll be right behind you," and then went back to sit next to Maggie.

Doc and Deloris came in, and both hugged her. They sat further down the front row. Kay came back and sat on the other side of Grace. Peg Machalvie came in and stood front and center, decked out in one of her tight, black outfits and stiletto high heels. Her overpowering perfume wafted out over the crowd like tear gas, and Grace heard Scott cough.

Peg supervised her two sons, Hugh and Lucas, as they opened the top section of the coffin. She then gestured to Grace to come forward, and Grace froze.

"I'll go with you," Kay said and took her arm.

They rose from their seats, took a few steps forward, and then climbed two more steps to the platform on which a long pedestal held her grandfather's coffin. The coffin was made of oak, and the lining was dark gold silk. Her grandfather's face looked unnaturally pink, and when Grace looked up, she could see a pink-colored light shining down on his face, while all the other lights were regular white. His neatly trimmed beard was no longer stained yellow but had been bleached white. She could see they had put makeup on him, and she thought how much he would hate that.

He had on a grey suit she had never seen before, along with a bright white shirt and blue tie that looked new, that still had the folding creases in them. His face was relaxed and peaceful looking, so he didn't look at all like himself. Her grandfather's face had been deeply lined, and he always, always had a scowl on his face. This man looked like Santa Claus.

Grace thought to herself that maybe this version of her grandfather had been inside him all along. Maybe if he had had nicer parents or an easier life, it would have been this man who raised her. He looked like someone you could hug.

A tug from Kay indicated they could return to their seats. Grace looked out over the crowd assembled and was taken aback at how many people were there. She felt instantly self-conscious that they were all looking at her. She realized with a feeling of dismay that she would never again be invisible in this town. A few rows back, Tommy sat next to Ed, looking uncomfortable in a suit jacket that was too big for him and a tie that was on crooked. He smiled at her and waved. She smiled back before she sat down.

Just then there was a ruckus in the outer vestibule, and Mamie Rodefeffer came in. Dressed in her dead foxes and a black woolen dress coat, she was scowling and swinging her cane as if to ward off anyone who might try to stop her, although no one did. She went straight up to the casket, put her hand on Grace's grandpa's chest, and said something so quietly that Grace could not hear. When she turned around, it surprised Grace to see tears in the old woman's eyes. She came forward off the platform, missed a step, almost fell, but was saved when Claire leaped forward and grabbed her arm, steadying her.

In return, Mamie gave Claire a contemptuous look and said, "Let go of me, young woman. I'm perfectly capable of looking after myself."

Mamie came forward and stood in front of Grace, looked down at her through her thick glasses and said, "You're better off, you know. He was just as mean as his mother, maybe worse."

Grace was speechless.

Kay said, "Mamie, really, this is not the time or the place for one of your tactless remarks."

"You hush up," Mamie said to Kay. "This is between this young lady here and me."

176

To Grace, she then said, "Remember what I told you; you come up and see me."

With a contemptuous look that took in the whole room, she turned on her heel and, waving her cane, lurched out of the room.

"Don't mind her," Kay said. "She's very eccentric."

The service was a blur to her. A young minister from the United Methodist Church said nice things about a man he had never met, and certainly not someone familiar to Grace. He quoted the Bible, said there was a lesson in this for everyone, and then told a bible story about the death of Moses.

During all of it, Grace kept thinking about what Elvis had said about attachment. He had mentioned an attachment you could form with your kidnapper as an emotional defense mechanism, and Grace guessed that was the closest thing she felt to love for her grandfather. She was glad he was gone in the sense that he would no longer be in charge of her, and she wouldn't have to endure any further abuse, but now that she was free of her sad situation she kind of missed it. It hadn't been good, but it had been familiar, it had been hers. Now everything seemed out of her control, and she didn't know what would happen next.

Recorded organ music played from speakers in the ceiling as they closed the lid of her grandfather's coffin. Scott, Ed, Patrick, Sam, and some other men she did not know surrounded the casket, and at Peg's direction, picked it up. They carried it through the side door where Hugh and Lucas were holding the doors open. Kay directed Grace to stand and go back out the side door she had come in. As she approached, Hugh and Lucas looked Grace up and down in a way that made her feel uneasy. She didn't like it.

Claire said, "I'll see you up there."

Kay and Grace got into a long black car with leather upholstery, quite the nicest car Grace had ever been in. The minister got in with them and during the ride asked Grace where she went to school, what grade she was in, and what subjects did she like. She couldn't concentrate on answering for thinking about the next part, the burying part. It was the worst part, to her mind, and something she thought no one should have to see. After a few short answers, the minister eventually quit asking her questions, and they rode out Possum Holler in silence.

As they turned right, through the entrance to Rose Hill Cemetery, Grace thought about all the people buried there and imagined their ghosts gossiping about the new ghost about to join them. She wondered if Edgar would be lonely in the big house without them, or if he hung out here with friends when he wasn't at home. Where would he go if the house was torn down? Grace was not afraid of Edgar but she hoped he wouldn't follow her to Kay's.

As she had when her mother and grandmother were buried, she wondered where her grandfather had gone. Was he in the heaven he thought no one was good enough to get into or in the fiery pit where he was sure everyone was eventually headed? He would be irritated if he saw all the people he had verbally consigned to the bad place waiting for him. He would shake his head and sigh, forever condemned to put up with all the people he hated, for eternity. That would be hell for him.

Wherever it was, would he meet Nino there? Maybe Nino would say, "Hello, you might not remember me, but I died on your front porch. That was my glass swan you found."

Would her grandmother be there, and her mother? Would they be the same people, or somehow better, nicer people? Would her mother be sane?

Or was there nothing, no place, and no one, just a coffin covered in dirt and a vacant space where there once was a person? That thought made Grace shiver and feel hollow inside. She was reminded of the dark thoughts she'd had in the cupboard that day. How could she ever have thought she'd be better off to run toward this awful place? It would be better to fight against it for as long as she was able. She looked up at the bright blue sky. She wouldn't be able to see that if she died.

Grandpa was to be buried next to Grandma, with Grace's mother on the other side; just as in life, Grandma stayed in the middle to keep the two hotheads apart.

They had a canopy set up, and its flaps were blowing in the sharp wind. Kay put her arm around Grace and said, "I should have got you a coat."

Only a few people came to the graveside, most of them Fitzpatricks. They gathered around her and each would occasionally touch her, as if to remind her they were there. Grace was glad for the company as well as the wind block.

The minister talked some more, quoted the Bible and then said the "ashes to ashes" part, which meant it was almost over. Grace felt light-headed and could feel herself sway. It was the oddest feeling; as if her soul wanted to leave her body and soar away, but just for the briefest moment. She heard Kay say, "Scott!" with quiet urgency and then the next thing she knew she was in the long black car again. Kay was saying, "She probably just needs something to eat."

At the community center, Grace realized she had run out of whatever fortification it was that had brought her to this point. She didn't want to talk to any more people or feel their prying eyes upon her; she didn't want to be the object of so much attention, well-intentioned or not. She wanted, she needed to hide somewhere, sleep if she had to, anything to get away. She was feeling almost panicked but didn't know how to say it. She was having trouble meeting anyone's eyes; she was fighting the urge to flee.

"Hey," said Sam, who had come up so silently in his wheelchair that she hadn't noticed him. "Had enough?"

She nodded, and tears swam in her eyes.

"Come with me," he said.

Grace followed him across the large room and through a hallway, past the cloakroom and bathrooms, and out a side door. Just outside they paused on a porch at the top of cement stairs that led to a sheltered grassy area facing nothing but trees and sky.

"Have a seat," he said. "Here, this is Hannah's."

Sam gave Hannah's jacket to Grace, and she put it on. She let out a long, deep breath she hadn't realized she had been holding and sat down on the top stair.

He offered her some cookies wrapped up in a napkin.

"I stole these from Hannah's plate," he said. "But don't worry, there were plenty left. Her pockets are probably full as well."

Grace took the cookies and nibbled on one.

"You're like me," he said. "There's only so much community support we can take."

"They're all so nice," she said. "I don't want to seem ungrateful."

"Don't worry," Sam said. "I think you've done enough smiling and thanking people for one day. It can get to the point where if one more person looks at you with pity in their eyes you just want to scream."

"Yes," breathed Grace. "Exactly."

"We can talk or just sit here," he said. "Either way suits me."

"How long will you have to stay in that chair?" she asked.

"Until my knees heal up," he said. "If it were up to Hannah, I'd stay in it forever."

"Because she worries," Grace said.

"Yep," he said. "But people have to go and do brave things sometimes, even if they get hurt; even if they die."

"Where do you think people go after they die?" Grace said.

"We won't know until we go," Sam said. "Anything anybody else tells you is just their best guess."

"So you're not, like, religious at all," she said.

"Nope," he said. "I definitely think it's a big mystery, and the truth may be something we can't even imagine, but nothing anyone believes is worth starting a war over."

"Is that what your war was over?"

"Depends on whom you ask," he said. "Some might say it was about who gets to control billions of dollars of oil reserves."

"What do you think?"

"I think it was a combination of a lot of things," Sam said. "I fought because I believed our country's freedom was at stake. I still believe in fighting for that, every time, no questions asked. Other people had different stakes that had nothing to do with that. No matter how honorable a cause is, there's always somebody looking to make a dime off the back end."

"Did you kill people in the war?"

Sam looked at her with a facial expression she couldn't read.

"I'm sorry," she said. "It's none of my business."

"I did," he said. "And I saw plenty of my friends get killed as well. It's an awful, horrible thing to kill a person. It haunts you ever after. But at the moment I wasn't thinking about killing at all. I just wanted to survive, and to protect the soldiers in my unit. The thing is, you see, the people shooting at us were doing the same thing: believing their freedom, their families, and their friends' lives were at stake. You think about that long enough, and it'll drive you crazy."

"Do you still see anyone you were with over there?"

"Not often," Sam said. "Some of the strongest bonds I ever formed were with the people in my unit. I would do anything for them and them for me."

"That's a kind of love, isn't it?" Grace said.

"It is," Sam said.

"And you feel that way about Hannah and Sammy, too."

"Absolutely," Sam said. "But just like me, they both want to go out in the world and have adventures. It killed me not to be able to get to Sammy and protect him from those dogs. I didn't feel like much of a dad that day."

"But Sammy had the dogs to protect him," Grace said. "I think they'd do anything to keep him safe."

"And he had you," Sam said. "I saw you swinging that tree branch. I thought, 'Those dogs are gonna eat her up.' But you held your ground. That takes guts."

"I didn't really know Sammy," Grace said. "I would have done the same for any kid."

"That's exactly what it feels like to fight for your country," Sam said. "There's plenty of people I don't like or agree with, but I would fight for them, regardless."

"I appreciate that you did that," Grace said. "You didn't have to, but you did."

"Same to you, Grace," Sam said. "Same to you."

Scott came through the door behind them and said, "Grace, there's an attorney here representing your father, and he wants to speak with you."

Sam looked at Grace. His gaze was intense, but Grace couldn't read the emotion.

"Go on," he said. "Do what you have to do to survive."

Scott led Grace to a small meeting room, where Kay was sitting across from a large man with abundant gold hair and startling white teeth. When he saw her, he rushed forward to shake her hand. He gripped it so hard it hurt.

"Nice to meet you, Grace," he said. "I'm Ken Sheridan; I've got a law practice in Morgantown. I've never met Mr. Clark, you understand, but he hired me to bring these papers to you. Please have a seat."

"Do you want me to stay?" Scott said.

"Yes," Grace said.

Scott and Grace sat down next to Kay across the table from Mr. Sheridan. He took some papers out of his briefcase and spread them out on the table.

"I know this is a terrible day to be doing this, but he wanted it done right away, just so there was no question, about, you know, what would happen next. This first document is a refusal of any claim to parental rights; the second is basically a hold harmless agreement wherein you relinquish any claims of paternity."

"What's the third one?" Grace said.

"Well, Grace, that's in case you refuse to sign the second document," he said, with a big toothy smile that did not extend to his eyes. "That's an agreement to undergo paternity testing."

"But in the first one he's saying he knows he's my father, but he doesn't want me," Grace said.

"Actually if you read it closely it says he does not believe he is the father. He's disclaiming paternity."

"Then why bring me any documents at all," Grace said. "If he's not my father, then nothing about me is any of his business."

"I'm sure it's hard for you to understand this grownup legal jargon," the man said.

"No," Kay said. "I'd say she understands it perfectly well."

"Basically, here's the situation," Mr. Sheridan said. "Mr. Clark doesn't know if he's your biological father or not, but he has no interest in claiming paternity either way. Either you agree with this by signing the second document, or you will be forced to take a paternity test to prove he is or isn't. If you are his biological issue, you'll have to fight him in court for any remuneration you think you may deserve."

"Hold on just a minute," Scott said.

"No," Grace said. "He's just telling the truth. I appreciate that."

"You should have a lawyer look at those documents," Kay said, "before you sign anything."

Scott said, "Maggie's brother Sean is a lawyer; let's have him look them over and advise you."

"Fine with me," the man said. "Here's my card. Let me know what you decide."

"Will you be talking to my ... to Mr. Clark?" Grace said.

"Well, yes," the man said. "As soon as I leave here."

"Tell him I said thanks for nothing," Grace said. "Tell him I think he's a worthless coward for not doing this in person, and I hope with all my heart that he's not my real father."

Grace cried, the tears streaming down her face. Kay reached over and put an arm around her.

"Listen, kid," the man said. "I don't even know the guy."

"Then maybe you should be more particular what you do for money and for whom," Kay said.

The man rolled his eyes and then sighed as he closed up his briefcase.

"I wish I could pick and choose," he said. "Unfortunately I work for a firm, and when they say go, I go."

"You're just doing what you have to do to survive," Grace said.

The man gave her an odd look.

"I guess you could say that," he said. "By the way, I am sorry for your loss."

"Which one?" Grace said, but the man didn't answer.

After he was gone, Scott said, "If it's okay with you, Grace, I'll ask Maggie to call Sean."

"It's fine," Grace said. "I feel so stupid. When he said he was representing Mr. Clark, I thought my father might want me to come live with him."

"He's an idiot for not wanting you to," Kay said.

"He'd be lucky to have you for a daughter," Scott said. "He just doesn't know it."

Scott's cell phone buzzed and he excused himself to take the call.

"How are you holding up?" Kay said.

"I want to go home and take a nap," Grace said.

Kay gave her such a funny look that Grace said, "What?"

"Do you mean at my house?"

"Yeah, sorry," Grace said. "That's what I meant."

"Don't be sorry," Kay said. "I'm honored you called it home."

"I know you don't want to foster me," Grace said, "but I appreciate you keeping me until I know what happens next."

"Actually," Kay began, but Scott came back in and interrupted, saying, "Grace, I need to talk to you. We've had some news. It's not good."

"What's happened now?" Kay said, and Grace was struck by a certain tone in her voice, one that seemed to convey that all the news related to Grace was bad news, and she had had just about enough. It made Grace want to disappear.

"Just tell me," Grace said.

"It's about your Aunt Lucy," he said. "She died around Christmas time last year, from a drug overdose. She was in Las Vegas."

Grace tried to feel something, but she felt nothing.

"Can we go home now?" she said to Kay. ""I'm so tired."

"I'm so sorry, Grace," Scott said.

"I think Grace has had enough bad news for one day," Kay said. "Let's give her some time to process it all."

"Meanwhile, I'll ask Maggie to call Sean," he said.

Grace found she was all out of thank-yous. She just nodded instead.

Scott found Maggie in the community center kitchen with Claire and Hannah, washing food containers in the big double sink. Maggie was washing, Hannah was rinsing, and Claire was drying.

"Can I talk to you for a minute?" he asked her.

"Maggie and Scott, sitting in a tree," Hannah said. "T.A.L.K.I.N.G."

"So mature," Claire said. "Now you wash."

Maggie and Scott went out through the door to the side porch of the community center.

"What's up?" she asked.

Her hair was pulled up off of her neck, but a few wild curls had escaped. Scott reached up and tucked one behind her ear. Maggie adjusted his tie, which was hanging crooked.

He told her about Grace's father and deceased aunt.

"That poor kid has the worst luck," Maggie said. "What's going to happen now?"

"That's what I wanted to talk to you about," he said. "I know we just got back together, and it's the completely worst time to think about doing this, but I've been thinking I would like us to adopt Grace."

"Adopt her?" Maggie said. "Holy crap, Scott."

"I know, I know," he said. "I just want to make sure nothing bad happens to her."

"But adopting her," Maggie said. "Even if we wanted to would they even let us?"

"I don't know," he said. "I'm not saying we have to get married, I just want us to be her parents."

"Well, I gotta say, I wasn't expecting this," she said. "Have you told Grace about this?"

"No, of course not," Scott said. "She just buried her grandfather. I've been thinking about it, though, and I wanted to see if you would even consider it."

"I don't know what to say," Maggie said. "I'm surprised. I hadn't thought about it myself. She seems content at Kay's."

"She needs two parents," he said. "We could be that, Maggie, think about it. It would probably be the only way we could have a child."

"I know that," Maggie said. "But that doesn't matter to me, not at all. I never had that rabid maternal instinct. I like kids, but I don't need one of my own."

"She's almost grown up," Scott said. "It would mostly just be us protecting her, making sure she makes it to adulthood with the least wear and tear."

"There's a lot more to it than that."

"I know," Scott said. "And I know it's crazy, but I still want to do it."

"Your mom just died," Maggie said. "You probably shouldn't be making any major life decisions while you're still dealing with that."

"I'm doing okay," he said.

"Scott, I live with you," Maggie said. "I know you're not doing okay."

Scott turned and walked to the edge of the porch. He pushed his hair back with one hand and then crossed his arms. Maggie followed and put her arms around him.

"If you want us to adopt Grace, I will consider it," she said. "But only if it's what's best for Grace. We have to consider her feelings in this."

"I will," he said and turned around to face her. "You really would consider it?"

"Heaven help me," Maggie said. "You've turned me into a cootie-covered feeling machine."

"I love you," he said and kissed her.

"I love you, too," she said. "Just don't rush into anything."

"There's a hearing tomorrow," Scott said.

"Great," Maggie said. "That gives me, what? Twelve hours to decide?"

"You're the best," he said. "You're going to be a great mother."

Scott grinned and hopped over the railing onto the lawn.

"Where are you going?" she asked him.

"I thought there might be a pinch coming," he said. "I'm learning to identify the signs."

"I'm going out to Hannah's tonight," Maggie said. "Do you want to come?"

187

"Can't," he said. "I've got to work."

"Are you ready to recite your sonnet?" Maggie asked.

Scott just waved and jogged off in the direction of the squad car.

"Your final grade depends upon it," she called after him.

Grace thought she was so exhausted she could sleep for a week, but as soon as she was back at Kay's house, she lay wide awake in the pretty bed, her mind churning through information. She couldn't settle on any one line of thought but just cycled through impressions and information over and over until her stomach hurt. She wished she could turn off her mind.

Her father didn't want her. She didn't know why she was surprised; he hadn't so much as written to her once in her whole life. When she was younger, on her birthdays, she used to wait for a card, or better, for him to show up with a wonderful wife who wanted nothing more than to take her back to their beautiful home and love her. In the back of her mind, after her grandfather died, she had been hoping he would finally rescue her. Seeing his rejection in black and white destroyed that magical thinking forever.

The door to her room was open, and the conversation Kay was having with the guests in her sitting room was easily heard down the hall. People had descended as soon as Grace and Kay had arrived back at Kay's house, almost as if they had followed them home from the reception.

Grace had been introduced when they came in, but she was so fatigued she hadn't paid too much attention. A large, colorfully dressed, red-headed woman named Delphie and her dark-haired daughter, Denise, who sometimes worked with Claire at the Bee Hive; Maggie and her mother, Bonnie; Claire and her mother, Delia; and some other friend of Kay's.

"I was so hurt," Delia was saying. "It felt as if everything Claire did she was doing to me. Of course, now I realize she was just living her own life and making her own mistakes like we all do. But back then I was so angry because I couldn't make her do what I thought she ought to do. I could see so clearly that she was going down the wrong road, but she just wouldn't listen to me. I was disappointed in her poor judgment, when really, who has the greatest judgment when they're teenagers?"

"Alright," Claire said. "Enough about me and my horrible misdeeds."

"Their brains aren't fully developed yet they think they're geniuses," Maggie's mother, Bonnie, said. "All you can do is your best, and sometimes even that's not good enough. Keep 'em alive and nourished, body and soul. Pray a lot. If you're lucky, they eventually realize they're not as smart as they think they are and come back to you for help."

"You're still waiting, though, aren't you?" Maggie said. "Don't hold your breath."

"I don't think you do them any favors if you present an unrealistic view of the world and their place in it," the unknown woman said. "We're not all special butterflies to whom the world owes anything. I've told Elvis that no matter how hard he works, or how smart he is, someday life will kick his butt. I'm hoping that if I prepare him for it, maybe he will survive it."

Grace's ears pricked up at the mention of Elvis. Could that be his mother? There couldn't be two Elvises in Rose Hill, could there? Grace slipped out of bed and went to the door so she could hear more clearly.

"Sometimes you get lucky," Delphie said. "My Nicky was the perfect baby and such a well-behaved child. He never gave us any trouble growing up, and he still doesn't."

"Because he was a mama's boy," her daughter, Denise, said. "And he still is. Just ask his wife."

"But our Denise," Delphie said. "She came out screaming bloody murder and never stopped. If I said pink, she said purple. If I said braids, she said ponytails. We never could agree on anything."

"Watch this," Denise said. "Give us your thoughts on breastfeeding, Ma."

"He would get all your immunities," Delphie said. "Think about that, Neecy. Give him six months at least."

"See," Denise said. "We still don't agree."

"I breastfed Sammy 'til he bit me," Hannah said. "Bit me and then had the nerve to laugh."

"I breastfed Elvis for a year," his mom said. "He was a very healthy baby."

"Don't even start," Delphie said. "The more you push, the more she pulls. Believe me."

"At least you wouldn't have teething to deal with," Denise said to Maggie.

"Or potty training," Hannah said.

"Or chicken pox," Delia said. "Do children still get chicken pox?"

"If they don't get vaccinated," Elvis's mother said. "Measles, Polio, and whooping cough are all back as well."

"Stupid celebrities," Claire said.

"Grace is already her own person," Maggie said. "She's fifteen years old. How can anybody be a good mother to her if they haven't had any positive experience with that particular relationship?"

"I beg your pardon," Bonnie said. "Are you referring to me?"

"You are a good mother, Aunt Bonnie," Hannah said. "You were the mother of all mothers. While you were chasing Patrick around the yard with a wooden spoon for ditching school, my mother was lying down in a dark room with a headache; one that's lasted thirty-six years."

"Now, Hannah," Delia said. "Your mother loves you; she may not say so, but she does. It's just that your four brothers were born one right after another and it was too much for her. By the time she had you, she was worn out."

"My dad taught me how to be a mom," Hannah said. "He made the lunches and braided the hair; he helped with the homework and kissed the boo-boos. My mother could not be bothered."

"Curtis Fitzpatrick is a saint," Bonnie said. "He's waited on your mother hand and foot for over forty years."

"If it makes you feel any better," Hannah said to Maggie, "I didn't turn out anything like my mother, and if being Sammy's mother isn't too much I don't know what would be. That child brought home three baby moles the other day. He told me their names are Shadrach, Meshach, and Abednego."

"Baptist church daycare, right?" Elvis's mother said. "I remember that Bible story from when I was little."

"Are you letting him keep them?" Delphie asked.

"It'd be cruel not to," Hannah said. "It was one of my cats that ate their mother."

"If I thought there was any chance I'd turn into my mother," Maggie said, "I wouldn't do it."

"I'm in the room," Bonnie said. "I can hear you."

"You can't help it," Denise said. "The truth is I hope Tony Jr.'s a mama's boy just like my brother, and if the next one's like me, I'll probably pull her braids a little too tight, too."

"She was so tender-headed," Delphie said. "And so sensitive; you couldn't say anything to her."

"I was scared of my mother," Maggie said. "I would never want Grace to be scared of me."

"A little fear is not such a bad thing," Bonnie said.

"I hate seeing people make the mistake of being friends with their children instead of being parents," Delphie said. "What they need is someone who's not afraid to be hated for a couple years."

"I always could get around Dad, though," Denise said.

"Your brother is the same with his girls," Delphie said.

191

"Speaking of mama's boys," Hannah said. "You always said you wouldn't marry Scott while his mother was alive and now she's gone."

"You'll fool around and lose him," Bonnie said. "You're lucky he's held on this long."

"I'm not worried about Scott," Maggie said. "He's got some grief to get through first."

"He'd be a good father for Grace," Delia said. "And she'd be good for him."

"He'd be overprotective," Maggie said. "He probably wouldn't let her do anything."

"Just like Ian," Delia said. "He was the worst about saying no to everything."

"I just sneaked and did it anyway," Claire said. "Sorry, Mom."

"I will try not to take that personally," Delia said. "Retroactively."

"What would I do if Grace sneaked and did things anyway?" said Maggie. "Scott would be crushed, and you know my temper."

"You sound like typical parents to me," Delphie said. "You'll be hurt and mad, and then you'll get over it. That's what it's like. You have to forgive them seventy times seven, sometimes all in one day."

"I'll make mistakes," Maggie said. "I just know it."

"You'll screw up and then try harder next time," Elvis's mom said. "And Grace will screw up and try harder the next time as well."

"I don't even know what Scott's views on child-rearing are," Maggie said. "It's never come up."

"I wonder," Claire said, "if you and Scott shouldn't work out being a couple before you try to become parents."

"A married couple," Bonnie said. "In a church by a priest."

"Those two have been a couple for years," Delia said. "Even if they didn't always know it."

"I have thought about that," Maggie said. "It's probably the sensible thing to do to wait, but Grace needs parents now."

"She and Kay are getting along so well," Claire said. "It may be the best thing just to leave her where she is."

"She's certainly welcome to stay," Kay said. "Although it might be nice for her to have younger people to raise her. I'm in bed by nine o'clock most evenings. She'd probably get bored living here."

"You could adopt her yourself, Maggie," Claire said. "You and Scott don't have to rush into marriage just for Grace."

"Bite your tongue, Claire," Bonnie said. "Don't talk like that when we're this close."

"But doesn't she need a father?" Maggie said. "I'll admit my dad was nowhere near the role models Uncle Curtis and Uncle Ian were, but I always knew I had a dad to go to if I needed him."

"He never was one bit of help," Bonnie said. "They were his children when they did right and mine the rest of the time."

"I think a child needs two parents," Denise said. "Whether that's two moms, two dads, or a mom and a dad. It helps split the work, like a tag team."

"I don't think children necessarily need a father," Elvis's mother said. "As long as there are healthy male role models in her life, she will probably be just fine."

"But isn't it exhausting to do it all yourself?" Denise asked her.

"Yes," Elvis's mom said. "Yes, it is. But it's also exhausting to live with someone who is no help, or with whom you don't get along."

"Amen to that, sister," Hannah said. "Sam's a good dad, don't get me wrong, but he doesn't do anywhere near what I do for Sammy. He just doesn't. He was raised that the moms took care of the children while the dads mowed the lawn and watched football."

"Or drank themselves silly every evening," Bonnie said.

"Your father never changed a diaper," Delia said to Claire. "Plus he worked all hours of the day and night. It was sometimes very lonely even with a husband."

"There's no perfect recipe for successfully raising a child," Delphie said. "We all just do the best we can and hope for the best."

"Scott will be heartbroken if this doesn't work out," Maggie said. "And he's still grieving his mother's death so hard."

"Scott can be in her life even if he's not her father," Claire said. "So can you."

"But this is an opportunity for him to be a father," Maggie said.

"Scott can't father children," Delphie said to someone.

"Is this common knowledge?" Maggie asked.

Delphie said, "You know there are no secrets in this town."

"Oh," Elvis's mother said. "I didn't know that."

"The bottom line is Scott wants to do it," Maggie said. "And it's not that I don't want to do it. I'm just scared I'll screw it up."

"You'll be fine," Delia said to her. "We'll all help you."

"Just what Maggie loves," Hannah said. "A whole town telling her what to do."

Grace's mind was reeling; Scott and Maggie wanted to adopt her? Now there was even more information swirling around in her head. She felt tears start to well up and her throat closed a little. Why couldn't everyone just slow down?

Grace finally slept and woke up only when she heard Kay calling her name from the doorway.

"Grace," she said. "Maggie's brother Sean is here. He needs to talk to you."

Grace, who had slept in her clothes, dragged herself out of bed and went down the hall.

"I'm going to run down to city hall for a bit," Kay said. "If you'll call me when you're through, Sean, I'd appreciate it. Grace, be thinking about what you'd like to eat; I need to go to the grocery store, and I'll get anything you want."

Sean Fitzpatrick was tall, with the same dark hair and bright blue eyes as his brother, Patrick, and cousin, Claire. Grace thought he might be the most handsome person she'd ever seen. She was instantly embarrassed about her shabby clothes and messy hair. After the funeral, she had carefully hung up her new clothes and changed back into her regular clothes. Her hair, which Claire had so carefully braided and pinned, had come undone as she slept.

Sean stuck out his hand and shook Grace's, but compared to the other lawyer she had met today his grip was firm but gentle. Her hand didn't feel crushed afterward.

He sat down across from her in the kitchen nook, and took a sip of the coffee Kay must have prepared for him. She'd left a glass of cold milk on the table for Grace along with a plate piled high with leftovers from the funeral reception. Grace sipped the milk but didn't feel like eating.

'That's a first,' she thought. 'All this food and I don't want any of it.'

"I've received a lot of background information on your situation from Scott and Kay," Sean said as he smoothed out the top blank page of a legal pad and raised his pen. "Why don't you tell me what you would like to have happen?"

Grace's mind went blank. What did she want to have happen? Honestly? She wanted to disappear, go somewhere she could be left alone to think.

"I know a lot has happened," Sean said. "You're probably feeling overwhelmed right now. We wanted to get this scheduled quickly so you wouldn't have to go into the larger foster care system, but that puts a lot of pressure on you to decide where you want to be."

"I don't know," Grace said. "I don't know what to say."

"Do you want to pursue a paternity claim against Mr. Clark?"

"No," Grace said. "I know for sure I don't want to do that."

"I looked over the paperwork they sent, and I'm not happy with it," he said. "We'll do our own paperwork and have Mr. Clark sign it."

"Okay," Grace said.

"Doc and Doris Machalvie have expressed a desire for you to live with them," Sean said. "Maggie and Scott would love to have you with them as well. It sounds like a lot of great people care about you, Grace. Either of those placements would be good ones."

He hadn't mentioned Kay, Grace noticed. She thought that must mean Kay did not want her. Grace was so disappointed by this. She loved this little house, and Kay made her feel so safe.

"Does Kay not want me?" she finally asked, fearing the answer.

To her mortification, she felt tears fill her eyes.

"I'm so sorry, I should have said that first," Sean said, reaching out and putting his hand over hers. "I thought that went without saying. Of course, she wants you. She's crazy about you."

Grace couldn't stop the tears from falling. They had started from sadness but now fell from relief.

CHAPTER EIGHT – THURSDAY

At the courthouse, Maggie's brother Sean sat next to Grace at the long table in the conference room; behind them, Scott, Maggie, Kay, Doc and Doris Machalvie sat on hard chairs along the wall. Other than these people there was no one else in the room. The clock on the wall showed 9:00 a.m.

Grace realized she was jiggling her leg up and down and stopped it by crossing her legs. A few moments later she realized she was jiggling her foot the same way. The braids Claire had woven in her hair were pretty, but one particular hair at the nape of her neck was pulled so tight it hurt. She was afraid to reach up and pull on it for fear the whole hairdo would fall apart. She clasped and unclasped her hands in her lap; her palms were sweaty, so she wiped them on the sides of her skirt. The tag in the back of her new shirt was scratchy; her new panties were riding up. She felt like a mess.

"Relax," Sean whispered in her ear. "Judge Feinman is on our side."

Grace nodded, wondering what that meant. Did that mean he would let her decide where she would live or that he would choose what he thought was best for her? She really wanted to live with Kay, whom she felt truly understood her and what she needed (and didn't need); but being a single person, and older, Grace worried it might be a strike against her.

Doc and Doris would be good to her, albeit in a smothering but well-meaning way. Maggie and Scott were nice, and they would probably be good parents, but the situation between them didn't seem that stable to Grace. Besides, Grace wanted to be more to someone than a good deed they were doing just because she was so pitiful.

The door opened, and Judge Feinman came in with the woman who had earlier brought them in the room. The judge didn't have on a long flowing robe; just a business suit. He looked irritated, but when he greeted Grace and shook her hand, he winked.

"Good morning, everyone," Judge Feinman said.

He sat down across from Grace and the woman sat next to him. He then put on his reading glasses and opened a folder that the woman placed before him. After a brief silence, during which he scanned the documents before him, he addressed those assembled.

"We are here today to decide on the fate of Miss Grace Branduff, who is fifteen years of age and without a legal guardian."

He looked up at Grace over the glasses, perched far down on his prominent nose, and said, "You have my deepest sympathies on the death of your grandfather, Grace."

His voice was warm, and his eyes were sincere in their empathy. Grace felt her eyes fill with tears and looked down, blinking hard to drive them back.

"Your aunt, Lucille Branduff, has also recently passed away. It seems Mr. Clark has no interest in pursuing any paternal rights and neither are you interested in establishing paternity. Meanwhile, there are five good people here who know how lucky they would be to have the privilege of raising you."

Judge Feinman scanned the faces of the adults, one by one, nodding as he did so.

"Not a dud in the bunch," he pronounced. "Does anyone here have anything they would like to say before I make my decision?"

Kay jumped right in with, "I have plenty of room in my house and would love to have her. I had put forth my name as a candidate for mayor, but I would be willing to withdraw from the race if necessary."

Grace was startled to hear this declaration. She turned and looked at Kay, but Kay just winked at her and smiled.

"Thank you," Judge Feinman said. "So at Kay's house Grace would have space aplenty and, if necessary, Kay's undivided attention. I would hate to see you withdraw from the race, though, Kay. A change of city administration might be the best thing for Rose Hill. Anyone else?"

Doris Machalvie cleared her throat, and said, "My husband and I would love to have Grace live with us. We would see to it she has everything she needs to grow into a healthy, happy, productive member of the community."

"Well said," Judge Feinman said. "You have anything to add, Doc?"

"I would be proud to call her my own," Doc said, which again brought tears to Grace's eyes.

"I bring this up only because I have to," Judge Feinman said. "You and Doris are not spring chickens, and Grace will need many years of parenting. This is a concern for me."

Doris fretted, but Doc nodded in agreement.

"And what about you, Miss Fitzpatrick?" the Judge said. "I'm not going to vote against you because you can't seem to tie the knot with the Chief, here, but I am a little concerned about how many irons you have in the fire, so to speak. You have the bookstore, plus you are often called upon to work in the Fitzpatrick family's other businesses. I understand you are currently enrolled in Eldridge College as a part-time student and also serve on several church and community committees. All commendable activities, but I don't see how you have time to sleep let alone raise a teenager."

"Scott and I have talked it over," Maggie said, and Grace was surprised to hear her voice tremble a bit. "I'm going to make it plain to my family that Grace is my first priority, and that I need to refrain from working in the evenings so I can be available to her. If I need to, I'll stop taking classes; I want Grace to have as much of my time as she needs."

This was the first Grace had heard of all these sacrifices people were willing to make on her behalf. She had been so focused on her own problems that she hadn't considered what other people would have to give up in order to take care of her. Kay was willing to give up her dream of being mayor and Maggie was willing to give up going to college. She didn't want anyone to lose anything because of her.

"Chief Gordon?" the Judge said. "Do you have anything to add?"

"This is kind of personal," Scott said, "but I'm among friends here so I'll share it. I'm not able to father children; biologically, that is. So this is an opportunity for me to be a father. I can't think of anyone I'd rather be there for, as a father, more than Grace. She's a great kid, and she's going to be an amazing woman. Maggie and I are committed to seeing her through."

Grace couldn't stop the tears that fell. Sean gave her his handkerchief, and Judge Feinman looked at her with compassion.

"This is quite a testament to the belief these people have in you, young lady," he said. "Now I'd like for all of you to excuse Grace and me; we need to take a walk and have a talk."

Grace looked at Sean, and he nodded. She didn't look at anyone as she left the room with the judge. She was so overcome with emotion she thought she might break down if she did. Judge Feinman took Grace down the hall to his office, a room that overlooked Pendleton City Park through large arched windows that were ten feet high. The sky was cloudy, but a few rays of light shone on the worn, oak floor and the massive wooden desk behind which he sat. Grace sat down across from him, looking around at all the books, files, and mementos that were strewn about.

"Please excuse the mess," he said. "Every night my secretary straightens it all out, and every day I undo all her hard work."

Grace smiled.

"You're at a crossroads, Miss Grace," he said. "This is one of those momentous decisions that will set you on a course for the rest of your life. I'm sorry I can't give you more time to decide, but I want to avoid making you a ward of the state if there is an alternative. If you decide today, we can put the machinery in motion, and you'll only have to move once. The sooner your life achieves some sense of normalcy the better."

"I understand," she said.

"You need to be completely honest with me," he said. "You can't worry about people's feelings being hurt or how they'll react if they're not chosen. There are five great people in there, and you would do well with any one of them. The question is where do you think you would do best? Who do you think would give you what you need?"

"Kay," Grace said, without hesitation. "Doc and Doris are so nice, but I would probably wear them out. I think Maggie and Scott need to be married awhile first before they take on a kid. Kay and I get along so well, and I already feel at home in her house. I don't want her to give anything up, though."

"I agree," Judge Feinman said. "I think you've chosen well. I've known Kay Templeton for many years. She has a big heart, but also a backbone made of steel. She'll give you good guidance and a place to call home. I'm glad to see it work out, for the both of you. Since she's already a foster parent that will make the process much easier as well; less paperwork."

Grace smiled and let out a breath she hadn't realized she was holding. She felt a sense of relief she hadn't expected to feel. There was a lightness inside; a sense of looking forward to something good happening. This, she realized, must be what happiness felt like when it was related to people, not books.

There was a knock on the door, and the judge's secretary came in with a note. The judge read it and frowned.

"Stay here," he said to Grace. "There's something I have to attend to, and then we'll give Kay the good news."

Grace relaxed back in her chair and let herself imagine a future with Kay as her mother. Kay would have no problem giving her the boundaries and privacy that she needed, and she'd do her best not to make Kay worry. Would she be Grace Templeton after she was adopted? Grace Templeton. That didn't sound bad at all.

The door opened, and Judge Feinman came back in with Mamie Rodefeffer. Grace was surprised to see her. Judge gestured for Mamie to have a seat next to Grace. Mamie, who was out of breath, dropped heavily into the seat and then wiped her nose with a lace handkerchief. She wasn't carrying her tote bags again today and was even more dressed up than she had been when she came to her house before her grandfather died. She wore a moth-eaten velvet jacket over a wrinkled wool dress, and there was a cameo pinned at her throat.

"I'm going to let Miss Rodefeffer tell you what she just told me," Judge Feinman said. "I'm going to need further proof of her claim, but we have to follow up on this before I can make a ruling."

Grace was bewildered. What could Mamie Rodefeffer possibly say that had anything to do with who adopted her? It must be something about the house, Grace decided, while Mamie caught her breath. She must be trying to claim it still belonged to her family.

"I apologize," Mamie said, still a little breathless, "for waiting so long to come forward. I have kept this secret for 70 years. You probably can't even imagine that number of years, young lady, or what all has happened in that time."

Mamie smiled at Grace, but her eyes seemed to be calculating the effect of her words. Grace nodded, and the judge sat back with his hand to his chin and a troubled brow. Mamie continued.

"You may not believe it to look at me now, but when I was a young woman I was considered quite a catch. It wasn't because I was pretty; I was rich, which is better, don't let anyone tell you it isn't. I was 22 years old; considered an old maid at that time. My father and I could never agree on a suitor, and being stubborn, I just refused to marry anyone, period. Why should I? Just one more man telling me what to do and when to do it, as if I didn't have the brains God gave a goose."

Mamie had worked herself up, and took a moment to calm herself, smoothing her wrinkled dress, and touching her nose with her handkerchief before she continued.

"My father employed many foreigners who were very talented. One young man, in particular, made the most intricate, delicate glass animals you could ever imagine. His work is in museums all over the country. In my collection, I have many of his pieces which are one of a kind. He was an artist, a genius, and a very handsome young man.

"I worked in the payroll office at that time because my father believed that only family members could ensure he wasn't robbed blind. I took my lunches out back on the dock overlooking the railroad tracks, where the shipments of sand would come in, and shipments of glass would go out. This young man went out there to smoke, and we got acquainted.

"I'll gloss over the more scandalous details of our relationship in deference to your age. It's impossible for you to imagine, I'm sure, that this bag of bones before you could have once been young like yourself, and in love with a handsome man who loved her, too. He was the love of my life. I never had another.

"I hid the fact that I was in the family way as long as I could, way past the point where a discreet medical intervention could be made. We had those then, too; I know you're surprised. But we were good Catholics. They sent me away to a woman's home in Pennsylvania where unwanted situations are handled discreetly in exchange for large sums of money. After I delivered the child, I was sent to Europe for a year abroad.

"Romantic fool that I was, I expected him to rescue the child and me. I received a letter instead. I won't share that with you; some things are too painful to be borne more than once. Men, as you will no doubt find out for yourself, love anywhere it is convenient to do so. They are driven by passion; they have no loyalty."

"Miss Rodefeffer," Judge Feinman said.

"The sooner she learns it the better," Mamie said.

"Please, let's just stick to the facts," the judge said.

"A couple who worked for Daddy agreed to raise the child in exchange for the house and a monthly stipend. I had no idea this child was living in the same town as I; I assumed the boy would be adopted out far away. In fact, he was brought up in the same house I was. In the same house you were."

"Grandpa?" Grace said, incredulously.

"Yes," Mamie said. "He came to me when he turned 21, and his adopted father told him the truth. I didn't believe him at first because I was shocked and angry, you see, at being tricked so close to home. He disavowed the Rodefeffer family, and I accepted it."

"His father was Nino?" Grace said. "That man was my great-grandfather?"

"They paid him to go away, you know; after my father died, I hired a detective who found him living in Venice with his family, working in a glass factory there. He married a woman, and they had many children. He's dead now," she said and dabbed at some tears that gathered in her eyes. "Everyone is dead now. Everyone but me."

"Nino," Grace said. "You're talking about the man who came to our house and died."

"Yes," Mamie said. "Haven't you been listening?"

"Nino came for you?" Grace said. "He spoke Italian so I couldn't understand him, but he was asking for Mary. Is your real name Mary?"

"Mary Margaret," Mamie said. "My father liked to call me Mamie, after his mother."

"Have you told Scott?" Grace said. "Scott's been trying to reach his family to let them know he died."

"This is no one's business but my own," Mamie said.

"He must have really loved you," Grace said. "He came back for you."

"Probably looking for money," Mamie said.

The look she gave Grace was filled with contempt.

"He brought you the glass swan," Grace said. "I'll give it to you; it's yours."

"It might be worth something," Mamie said. "You shouldn't be so generous; other people will take advantage."

"But it's yours," Grace said. "He loved you, and he brought it to you."

"He never loved me," Mamie said.

"He must have," Grace said. "He was so sad. His heart was broken; I could tell."

"What could you know about it?" Mamie said sharply. "If he loved me, he wouldn't have waited so long. If he loved me, he would have come back for me, for us. No, mark my word, he was down on his luck and hoping I'd be some sentimental old fool. Or he was after the boy's trust fund."

"There's no trust fund," Grace said. "I would have known about it."

"Oh there's a trust, alright," Mamie said. "Your grandfather was notified of its existence when he turned 21. He may have refused it, but it exists. It's yours now."

Grace felt dizzy with this new information.

"Grace's attorney will have to verify all of this," Judge Feinman said. "Is there a birth certificate?"

"There are two," Mamie said. "The real one and the one my father paid to have made when the Branduffs adopted him."

"Why didn't you do something?" Grace said. "You knew how poor we were; why didn't you help us?"

"My son made it very clear that he didn't want to have anything to do with me or my family's money," Mamie said. "He used very rude, offensive language."

"I don't believe it," Grace said to the judge. "If there had been money, Grandma would still be alive. If Grandpa had money, he would not have let her die."

"My son was a stubborn, angry, horrid little brat," Mamie said. "It must have been Nino's bloodline at fault; no Rodefeffer ever acted like that."

The judge made a little choking noise but seemed to quickly recover.

"You can call the bank in Pittsburgh," Mamie said. "As soon as they get the death certificate, they'll transfer it all to you. Should be several million by now, I reckon. My lawyers can help you get it all sorted."

"Grace has an attorney," the judge said. "He'll look into this for her."

"There would have been statements mailed," Mamie said. "That's how I get them."

"I found a letter," Grace said. "It was with the will."

"There would have been statements that were sent every quarter," Judge Feinman said. "He may have destroyed them."

"Why should this hold up what we're doing today?" Grace asked the judge. "This is just about money."

"You're my heir," Mamie said. "You're my great-granddaughter."

"But you don't want me," Grace said. "You don't even like me."

"You're mine," Mamie said. "I shall decide where you live and with whom you associate."

"Is that true?" Grace asked Judge Feinman.

206

He sighed.

"Pending verification of the claim, we will have to consider any rights Mrs. Rodefeffer might have in regard to you."

"No!" said Grace, jumping out of her chair. "It's all decided. She can't just come in here and change everything."

Mamie stood up, shakily, to her full height, which was considerable. She looked down her nose at Grace through her thick lenses and said, "I can, and I have."

Back at Kay's house, Claire Fitzpatrick descended with baked goods and hugs. Grace couldn't bear to stay in the room with so much sympathy, so she retreated to her bedroom and listened instead.

"Mamie's a crazy old lady," Claire said. "She probably just made the whole thing up."

"She's not fit to raise a child," Kay said. "Anyone in that room would have been a better choice."

"I know it's your decision to make, but I have to say, you two seem to fit," Claire said. "She seems comfortable with you. She trusts you, I can tell."

"I told her I wouldn't lie to her or sugarcoat anything and I won't," Kay said. "I don't want to give her a dark worldview, it's just that there's so much bullshit to watch out for."

"Look at it this way," Claire said. "You're preparing her to be independent and to use her common sense. If you just convince her she's so special that everything must go her way and nothing bad can ever happen, you won't be doing her any favors."

"I don't know," Kay said. "Maybe she would be happier with younger people, like Maggie and Scott. Maybe she needs a father and a mother. I'm worried I'll cheat her out of something. This campaign is taking all my energy, and if Stuart and Peg decide to play dirty, it won't be pretty."

"Bottom line," Claire said. "Do you want to be Grace's mom?"

Kay paused, and Grace realized she was holding her breath.

"Oh, I do," Kay said. "I really do. Whether that's rational or reasonable, I don't care. My grandmother always said what's yours won't pass you by, and I feel like Grace is mine somehow, that she's here with me for a reason."

"Then there's your answer," Claire said.

"Except now we've got Mamie to contend with," Kay said. "She may have money, but I don't mind telling you I've got connections. I'm owed a lot of favors in this county, and I plan to call in all of them. Everyone who knows that crazy old bat knows she's too mean to raise a young girl, and there's no jury in this county who would decide in her favor."

"If you need any money," Claire said, "for attorneys or anything, please let me know. I want to help, and I can afford to."

"Thanks," Kay said. "We're not going to let that mean old lady get our Grace."

Grace could barely keep her eyes open, and besides, she had heard all she needed to hear. With a contented smile, she tiptoed back down the hall and slid into bed. As soon as her head hit the pillow, she was out. It was the most relaxing sleep she had had in days.

Scott sat in the front room of Maggie's apartment, a beer in his hand, staring out the window. He was watching a cloud of starlings dip and swirl in the sky above the Bijou Theater.

"Do you want some lunch?" she asked.

"Thanks, but I'm not hungry."

"Are you sure you're going to be okay?" Maggie said. "I don't have to go out to Hannah's."

"I'm fine," he said.

"You don't seem fine," she said and sat on the arm of his chair.

He pulled her down onto his lap and snuggled her neck, his arms wrapped around her.

"I can't believe Mamie's her great-grandmother," Scott said. "I knew Mamie had something to do with Nino, that he was connected to her family in some way, but I never would have guessed Jacob Branduff was her son."

"Well, he was mean and cold-hearted," Maggie said. "And if you think about it, there was a resemblance. They had the same nose."

"She will ruin Grace's life if we let her," Scott said. "She deserves so much better."

"What did Judge Feinman say?"

"He said he couldn't talk to me about it if he was going to stay involved."

"Are you going to talk to Mamie?"

"It probably won't do any good," Scott said. "I thought I might get Doc to go with me. Maybe the two of us could talk some sense into her. She can't really want to raise a teenager."

"She just wants the money," Maggie said. "Mamie's broke."

"That's just hearsay," Scott said. "We don't know for sure."

"She's let go all of her servants except her driver and housekeeper," Maggie said. "Her checks are bouncing all over town, and my mother recommended I start making her pay cash. That's pretty good evidence."

"I'd like to try reasoning with her first," Scott said. "Even if it's pointless."

"I'm glad you're taking Doc," Maggie said. "At least you'll have a witness."

The phone rang, and Maggie ran down the hall to answer it.

"I can't talk long," Hannah said when she answered. "Sam's got Sammy in the tub, and I'm on deck to read three books, and then rock him in the blue rocking chair while singing three songs. Consecutively, that is. Not all at the same time."

"How'd you bribe him into the bath and a nap?"

"Well, he likes going to daycare now that Aunt Delia is the teacher's aide. I told him that his teacher is going to smell him every morning as he comes in, and if he's stinky, he will have to go to my mother's house, which is a fate worse than bath time."

"This is quite the change from him escaping from daycare every day."

"He loves his Aunt Delia," Hannah said. "Plus this new teacher is awesome. She's young and sparky. No kids of her own, which I think is key. Kids have a way of wearing you down."

Maggie got Hannah caught up on the Grace Branduff situation.

"So you think Scott's obsessed with rescuing her because his mom just died?"

"I don't know. Maybe. It's distracting him from his grieving, so maybe it's a good thing."

"Is it still bad?"

"He doesn't know that I know this, but he gets up in the middle of the night, goes into the bathroom and cries."

"Bless his little heart," Hannah said. "I wanna rock him in the blue rocker and sing him three songs, maybe four."

"I know," Maggie said. "It breaks my heart."

"How long will this go on, do you think?"

"I don't know," Maggie said. "I don't know how long it takes to grieve losing a parent; a long time, probably."

"Maybe he could talk to Father Stephen."

"I'm afraid he'll get even more religious than he already is," Maggie said. "I don't think I could tolerate it."

"Is he still quoting scripture?"

"Like a Baptist deacon," Maggie said.

"Maybe it will pass," Hannah said. "Like Chicken Pox."

"Oh my gosh," Maggie said. "I can hear Sammy howling. What's going on?"

"Getting his hair washed," Hannah said. "I better go. Hey, bring some chips and pretzels with you when you come. Oh, and I ordered four large pizzas; you need to pick those up on the way."

"Anything else?" Maggie asked. "A sheet cake or three?"

"I'll let you know."

As soon as Maggie hung up the phone rang again. It was Kay.

When she hung up and came back down the hallway, she was flushed with anger.

"That was Kay," she said. "Mamie served papers on Kay demanding that Grace be transferred into her custody tonight. She had the state police and her attorneys there. Judge Feinman says there is nothing he can do about it tonight."

As Scott stood up, she could sense the anger build in his body so that he had to clench and unclench his fists in order to contain it.

"She doesn't care anything about that girl," Scott said. "I'm going up there."

"Talk to Doc first," Maggie said. "I know I'm a poor one to suggest this but calm down before you go up there. Have a plan."

"You're right," Scott said. "I'll go over to Doc's."

"Call me at Hannah's when you get done," Maggie said.

"We can't let her get away with this," Scott said.

"I know," Maggie said. "I'll put Hannah on it; she's just devious enough to come up with something."

211

"Sammy's asleep," Hannah said. "After four books and three songs he had the nerve to say he likes the way Claire sings better. Then he rolled over and fell asleep."

"The truth is sometimes hard to hear," Maggie said.

"I can't help it if I have such an amazing natural talent," Claire said.

Hannah flicked condensation off her bottle of beer toward Maggie and Claire, who laughed and ducked. The three were seated on Hannah's front porch, with pizza boxes and snack bags all around them.

"I can't believe Mamie sent the cops to Kay's," Claire said. "Mamie's a crabby old lady, but I didn't think she would drag Grace off kicking and screaming."

"What are you and Scott going to do?" Hannah asked Maggie.

"We still want to adopt her, but you know what Mamie's lawyers will dig up on me," Maggie said. "My ex-boyfriend was an ex-con drug dealer. What judge would let me have custody?"

"I got my start in Hollywood doing hair and makeup in a strip club," Claire said. "None of us have a spotless background."

"I beg your pardon," Hannah said. "You floozies may have skeletons in your closets, but mine only have dirty clothes and dust bunnies in them."

"Would you and Sam consider adopting Grace?" Maggie said. "I wouldn't mind if either you or Claire did."

"Sam and I talked about it," Hannah said. "Ever since she saved Sammy's hide from those feral dogs Sam thinks she's the bee's knees. He said it was up to me. Sammy loves her, and I do like her. She seems like a nice enough kid, and I feel sorry for her, but is that enough of a reason to adopt a whole real live person?"

"It's one thing to talk about saving her and another to talk about raising her," Claire said. "That's a huge commitment."

"What about you?" Maggie said to Claire. "You're the only one of us who can afford the legal battle."

"I have the sordid Hollywood past, remember? Plus she's happy at Kay's," Claire said. "I think she should just settle there."

"Kay's got her hands full with her campaign," Maggie said. "If she wins the election, then she'll have Stuart's and Peg's mess to clean up plus running the town."

"Kay's run this town for years," Hannah said. "You don't really think Stuart or Peg ever lowered themselves to deal with the day-to-day business."

"No, I know that," Maggie said. "I just don't want Grace to be neglected."

"If Mamie has her way, Grace will be living up on Morning Glory Circle in the haunted mansion with only a housekeeper for company," Hannah said.

"Gothic," Maggie said. "That's the architectural style."

"Grim and gruesome," Hannah said. "That's what I call it."

"We don't have to disappear from her life just because someone else adopts her," Claire said. "Kay still thinks we have a fighting chance to stop Mamie. She's going to call in all her favors, and that woman's done favors for many people over the years. In this whole county, there isn't a clerk, secretary, administrator, committee or council member who doesn't owe her something."

"It's the little people who hold the community together and make things work," Maggie said. "Mamie doesn't realize that."

"I bet Mamie's lawyers will have trouble getting things filed with the county," Hannah said. "I bet lots of her paperwork will mysteriously disappear before this thing is over. For my part, I think Mamie might just develop a skunk infestation problem at her house."

"You've talked to Kay," Maggie said to Claire. "Does she really want to adopt Grace?"

"She's crazy about the kid," Claire said. "It surprised her how attached she got so fast. I think Kay always wanted children, it just didn't work out."

"She was in love with Matt Delvecchio when they were teenagers," Hannah said. "I don't think she ever got over him marrying that crazy nut."

"That's so sad," Claire said. "I don't think he and his wife have ever gotten along very well."

"She's mean as a striped snake, as our Grandma Rose used to say," said Maggie.

"Maybe a snake infestation would be better," Hannah said. "Nothing poisonous, mind you but marked like poisonous ones. I seem to remember that corn snakes are like that. I need to get out my reptile book."

"Kay will be a wonderful mom," Maggie said. "Better than me, probably. I guess I wouldn't mind if that's what Grace wants."

"I will give you Sammy plus throw in both dogs," Hannah said. "You'd be an awesome mother."

"Thanks," Maggie said. "I appreciate the offer."

"So we'll support Kay and be there for Grace," Claire said. "Like the three fairy godmothers."

"If we're the three fairy godmothers, who's the bad fairy who'll try to screw it all up?" Hannah asked.

"My default answer is always Ava," Maggie said. "Plus in this case, she's been trash-talking Grace to whoever will listen."

"Sons-of-witches," Hannah said. "Are you kidding me?"

"Really?" Claire said. "Why would Ava do that?"

"Ava's darling daughter Charlotte and Grace had a falling out," Maggie said. "It happened right around the same time Charlotte's snotty brat gene got activated."

"She was always such a nice little girl," Hannah said. "Too bad she realized she was pretty."

"Beautiful," Claire said. "Just like her mother."

"Ava Fitzpatrick, the fairest flower in all of Rose Hill," Maggie said with sarcasm.

"If poison ivy had a flower," Hannah said.

"I guess there were some altercations with Grace at school this week in which Charlotte has not come out smelling like a rose," Maggie said. "She's dating Marigold Lawson's son."

"Jumbo?" Hannah said. "That big jerk? What could Charlotte possibly see in that huge doofus?"

"He's popular, apparently," Maggie said. "Charlotte's been running around with the rich kids at Pine County Consolidated, and little Grace doesn't fit in."

"Thank goodness," Claire said. "I like Grace just the way she is. She's got integrity."

"She's also courageous and brave," Hannah said.

"And has an accurate bullshit detector," Maggie said. "She probably saw right through Ava."

"You just tell me who Ava's been talking to and I'll set them straight," Hannah said. "I am sick and tired of that mother-flippin' hussy getting away with everything just because she's got all the men in this town wrapped around her pinky finger."

"It's Theo Eldridge's money that's bankrolling Charlotte's social success," Maggie said. "Not one of those rich friends of Ava's seems to mind where the money came from."

"Do you think those two really had an affair?" Claire said. "Theo was so icky."

"I can't think of any other reason why he'd leave her millions of dollars," Maggie said. "It broke my brother's heart when that came out."

"Which one?" Hannah said. "She was married to one and cheating on the other."

"Bryan didn't have a heart to break," Maggie said. "But Patrick has never recovered."

"He's sure been crying on some soft shoulders," Hannah said. "I think he goes home from the bar with a different woman every night."

"He's just lonely," Claire said.

"He's lonely, but he doesn't want to settle down with any of them," Maggie said. "I think if Mandy hadn't gone to prison he would be married to her by now."

"It's Melissa now," Hannah said. "And she gets out soon."

"I've missed her," Maggie said. "I bet Ava and Charlotte will turn up their noses at her, too, just like they did to Tommy and Grace."

"I have always wanted to do something about Ava," Hannah said to Maggie. "But you would never let me."

"I think Ava will do herself in," Claire said. "This is a small town, and no one gets away with anything forever."

"I'm thinking of having a talk with her over this Grace thing," Maggie said. "It's not right to pick on someone who's so defenseless."

"Oh, I wouldn't call Grace Branduff defenseless," Claire said. "I think she's a survivor."

"I don't think you'd talk to Ava so much as you'd yell and throw things," Hannah said. "I think we could be sneakier about it but get the point across just as effectively."

"You sound like someone with a plan," Maggie said. "We're intrigued. Tell us more."

"Oh no," Claire said. "Leave me out of it."

"Too late; you were born into this family," Hannah said. "Don't try to deny your God-given mischief-making ability; that's like hiding your light under a bushel. Baby Jesus hates that."

"What an interesting interpretation of scripture," Claire said.

"Just listen," Hannah said. "Here's what we need to do ..."

Grace and Kay were seated in the breakfast nook at Kay's house. For the first time in her life, Grace didn't feel like eating and was picking at her macaroni and cheese.

"Try to eat something," Kay said. "You're going to make yourself sick."

"I don't want to go to their house," Grace said. "Why can't I just stay with you?"

"It may not be for long," Kay said. "Meanwhile, we'll all be working on a plan to get you out of there."

"I keep thinking of all the times we needed money and Grandpa had it," Grace said.

"It had to be a shock to find out Mamie was his biological mother," Kay said. "And then to have her reject him in what no doubt was a very rude manner. It must have made him terribly bitter. I wouldn't give that woman a rat to raise."

"I just don't understand how he could let us live so ... poorly," Grace said.

"Wounded pride can make people do foolish things."

"But he found out about the money when he was twenty-one," Grace said. "That was before he married Grandma. She used to tell me about how cold they were and how little they had to eat after the glassworks closed, before Grandpa got hired on in the mines. When my wisdom teeth had to come out, Grandma cleaned the doctor's office for six months to pay for it. She was too old to do that kind of work. She didn't go to the doctor about her lump because she didn't think she could afford it. She might be alive ..." Grace broke down and couldn't continue.

Kay put her hand on Grace's and squeezed it.

"I don't understand it either," Kay said. "It's a doggone shame is what it is. It's one thing to make that decision for himself, but to put his family through such needless misery when the means to relieve your burden was sitting right there in the bank ... that's worse than stubbornness."

217

"He never liked me," Grace said. "But I thought he loved Grandma. How could he let her go without if he loved her?"

"I'm sure he loved you in his own way," Kay said, but she sounded dubious.

"When I think about what our lives could have been like ..." Grace said.

"It will do no good to torture yourself thinking what if this and what if that; you'll drive yourself mad and it won't change the past," Kay said. "Focus on the future. Think of all the good you can do with that money. Not just for yourself, but for other people. Mamie's not only mean she's stingy; one single dollar in the collection plate every Sunday and never a donation when we need one for the food bank."

"Why does she want me?" Grace said. "She didn't want Grandpa or my mom. Why me?"

"Well, first of all, who wouldn't want you? You're a very special young lady," Kay said. "But I see what you mean. Why now? Why not just leave well enough alone?"

"I don't think it's about wanting me," Grace said. "I think it's about not letting anyone else have me, like I'm just another one-of-a-kind piece of glass for her collection."

Kay was quiet for a few moments, but finally, she just said, "I think you might be right."

Later that afternoon Grace sat on her bed and listened to Kay talk to Doc Machalvie in the kitchen. When the furnace wasn't on, she could easily understand every word.

"When does she have to go?" he asked.

"At 7:00 p.m. for dinner," Kay said. "Mamie's driver is picking her up."

"Scott and I are going to go over there this evening and try to talk some sense into her," Doc said.

"You always seem to know every dirty little secret in this town," Kay was saying. "Did you know about this?"

"I'm just a few years older than Jacob Branduff," he said. "By the time I came back here to practice, Gustav was

218

dead, and Mamie and her brother were living in Europe. I wasn't citified enough to do her doctoring when she moved back to town; she went to someone in Baltimore."

"Jacob's wife was one of the sweetest women I ever met. She had a time with her girls, that's true, but all of that might have been different if Jacob had shared some of that money with her."

"No point in obsessing over what might have been," Doc said. "We have to focus on Grace's future."

"She's only been here a few days, but I feel like when she leaves, I'll miss her so much," Kay said. "It's so nice being needed by someone; being able to help."

"Doris says maybe she'll let us adopt her as grandparents," Doc said.

"Oh, wouldn't that be perfect?" Kay said. "I wouldn't be so sad if you'd do that."

"Scott's so fond of her," Doc said. "Maybe he could be her adopted uncle."

"Do you think Maggie will ever marry that man?" Kay said.

The furnace came on, and Doc left before it clicked off again.

Later that afternoon, while Kay was meeting with her friends at Children's Protective Services, Maggie took Grace home with her to the apartment over the bookstore. Maggie was concerned about how shut down and emotionless Grace seemed. She guessed the events of the past few days had taken their toll, and the girl had retreated inside herself to try to process everything.

"Well, this is my home sweet home," Maggie said, as she stepped inside her front room and stood aside for Grace to enter.

The apartment had a long hallway that led from a sitting room that overlooked Rose Hill Avenue at the front all the way back to a kitchen with a balcony that overlooked the alley and the backyards of the houses on Lilac Avenue at the back. Off the left side of the hallway a sitting room, bedroom, and bathroom lined up one behind the other. Warm sunshine was flooding the front room, and the radiator hissed and rattled, providing warmth against the brisk spring chill that seeped in around the hundred-year-old window panes.

An enormous tabby cat lay curled up on the seat of a large cushy armchair; he had one paw covering his face and his tail curled around him. He opened one eye, focused in on the intruders, closed it again, and then curled himself up even tighter into a black and caramel-colored furry striped ball.

"That's Duke," Maggie said. "He can be crabby until he knows you better so you probably shouldn't pet him; he's got a bad reputation for biting first and asking questions later."

The phone rang, and Maggie said, "I better get that; make yourself at home, and I'll be right back."

Maggie ran down the hall, shedding handbag, coat, and shoes along the way. She answered on the third ring. It was Scott.

"I've just been to see Trick," he said. "He says Mamie's determined to get custody of Grace."

"I'm not going to let her ruin Grace's life," Maggie said, trying to keep her voice down. "Mamie doesn't know who she's dealing with."

"Don't do anything crazy," Scott said. "Let's keep this civilized for Grace's sake."

Maggie shut the door to the hallway so Grace could not hear her.

"We need to reconnoiter with Sean, make a game plan," she said. "He's in Pittsburgh talking to the trust attorney, but he's coming for dinner about six. Can you come?"

"I'll be there," Scott said. "Doc's agreed to go over there with me this evening to talk to Mamie. That way we can check on Grace while we're there."

"That woman," Maggie said, "is not going to get her mitts on our girl."

"I'm not going to let it happen," Scott said.

"I love you," Maggie said. "We're going to win this fight."

"I love you, too," Scott said. "Please don't blow up Mamie's house or let Hannah tase her."

Maggie hung up the phone, feeling the anger that had blossomed in her chest making her heart beat faster, and her face grow hot. She opened the doors to the back balcony and let cold air blow over her, taking deep breaths to calm down before she went back to Grace. She wanted to keep everything calm and low-key so Grace could rest with no further drama.

As soon as she regained her composure, she closed the doors and went back up to the front room, saying, "Sorry about that; are you ready for the grand tour?"

But Grace was lying on her side, asleep on the sofa, her coat and shoes still on, with Duke curled up against her chest. He was purring so loudly Maggie was amazed she could sleep through the loud rumbling. Duke narrowed his eyes at Maggie but then squeezed them shut at her in a contented way.

Maggie draped a quilt over them, left Grace a note, and went downstairs to work.

When Mamie walked through the entrance to the bookstore, with the determined air of someone injured yet superior to all she surveyed, Maggie could not believe her eyes. Her blood seemed to boil in her veins, and the steam flushed her face up to the roots of her flaming hair.

"Uh oh," the barista Benjamin said. He fled to the café side, out of the line of fire.

Mamie strode right up to Maggie, her tattered, faded tote bags swinging, and looked through her dirty cat-eye glasses, down her long humped nose at Maggie.

"I'm not interested in anything you have to say," Mamie said. "I'm here to shop. Although by the look of your shrinking book stock, I have to wonder how you stay in business. I'm sure there's nothing new in the romance section, but I need something to do while I wait for my attorneys to prepare my case. They say it will be like shooting fish in a barrel, and you'll all go broke long before I'm finished ruining you. It will amuse me to put you out of business."

She made as if to go past Maggie but Maggie shot out an arm and barred her way.

"You're banned," she said, and although she kept her voice low, the husky timbre conveyed the dangerous depth of her anger.

"What do you mean?" Mamie demanded. "What did you say?"

"You and I both know there's nothing wrong with your hearing," Maggie said. "You are now officially banned from this store, and you must leave the premises immediately."

"You can't do that," Mamie said. "I'm a paying customer."

"You're a vicious, selfish old hag," Maggie said. "You'd ruin a young girl's life out of spite and greed, even though you don't give a damn about her."

"And I suppose you'd be a better role model, living in sin with the chief of police."

"Get out," Maggie said.

"I won't," Mamie said. "What are you going to do, add the assault and battery of a senior citizen to the list of strikes against you? I dare you. I'll take this place from you, burn it to the ground, and then roast marshmallows over the coals."

"You can act like you have enough money to buy and sell everyone in this town," Maggie said, "but you've underestimated me; that's to my advantage."

Maggie went to the café side of the bookstore, pulled out a chair, and climbed up to stand on it.

"May I have your attention," she said in a loud voice. "That woman over there, the one with the cane, has been banned from this store because she's trying to keep me from adopting an orphan who needs a home. She's doing this because she's a mean-spirited, vindictive person, with no soul or conscience, and not because she wants what's best for the child. She's the richest person in this town yet she never donates a penny to any charity; not so much as a can of beans to the local food bank. She's an unrepentant racist and an elitist, upper-class ninny who for her entire miserable life has terrorized the people of this town with her condescending comments, rude behavior, and constant criticism. I want you to join me in letting her know what we think of cruel, heartless buzzards who hate orphans and the people who love them."

Maggie started booing and one by one every person in the café joined her. Some stood up; some hissed. The volume increased, and tension filled the room like a flammable gas. As soon as the customers and staff on the bookstore side joined in, the noise was deafening. Her face stained pink with anger, Mamie fled from the store, knocking over a rack of newspapers with her tote bags as she went.

Maggie got down off the chair and strode to the wall to the left of the entrance, where the dry-erase board of shame was mounted. Over the years it had been replaced several times to accommodate the growing list of the banned and banished. It was now six feet high by four feet wide, most of its surface covered with names written in block letters two inches high. Maggie took the eraser that was attached to it by a string and erased the top four rows of names (both Eldridge sisters and both Rodefeffer brothers). Then she took a red permanent marker from a pencil cup on the front counter and wrote "Cockamamie Rodefeffer" across the top in block letters four inches high. Her staff, all of them former victims of Mamie's daily abuse, some for many years, applauded and whistled.

Maggie turned around to take a bow, and that's when she saw Grace standing in the doorway of the stairwell to her apartment. Maggie froze in place, horrified to realize that Grace had just witnessed Maggie's hostile attack on her great-grandmother. She was afraid Grace would either be hurt, embarrassed, or both. To Maggie's great relief, Grace smiled and began to clap her hands. Maggie was instantly conscious of being the center of attention, which caused her to blush, which morphed into cross irritation. She told everyone, "Get back to work," and walked over to where Grace stood.

"How much of that did you witness?" she asked her.

"I came in as you got up on the chair," Grace said. "It reminded me of myself in the library earlier this week."

"We probably both need some anger-management training," Maggie said. "I'm not going to lie to you; that's not the first time, and it certainly won't be the last time I do something to embarrass myself in public."

"I thought it was awesome," Grace said. "You did that for me."

Grace had tears in her eyes, and Maggie felt hers fill as well.

"We're not going to let her have you," Maggie said. "She doesn't realize it, but I have a secret weapon that never fails."

"What's that?"

"My family," Maggie said.

By the time all the businesses in Rose Hill closed for the evening, Mamie Rodefeffer had been made to realize that the Fitzpatrick family and their loyal friends had all banded together against her. Her housekeeper, Mrs. Balanchine was turned away from Fitzpatrick's Bakery; Mamie's driver was refused gasoline at Fitzpatrick's Service Station; her attorneys were denied entrance to the Rose and Thorn, and Claire Fitzpatrick called to tell Mamie that all her standing appointments at the Bee Hive Beauty Salon were canceled.

According to local gossip, all of this made Mamie furious, but nothing made her as mad as when she sent Mrs. Balanchine to Little Bear Books to buy some bodice rippers, only to find out the woman was politely but firmly shown the door. Mamie railed at her attorneys, who informed her that the owners of privately-owned businesses had every right to refuse to serve someone who threatened their livelihood.

Mamie called the mayor, who said she should let her nephew, Knox, handle it.

"It's an election year, Mamie," he said. "Peg and I support you in our hearts, but public sentiment will be against you."

All this did was make Mamie dig in her heels even further.

"I'll show them," she said to her attorneys, as reported by her eavesdropping housekeeper. "I'll remind them that I am a Rodefeffer and not to be trifled with."

Her attorneys checked into the Eldridge Inn; they seemed cheerful, according to the desk clerk. They ordered the best rooms and full breakfasts the next morning. All of which was charged to Mamie.

Mamie's dining room was overheated, and it made Grace sleepy. The walls were covered with framed pictures, so many that she could barely see the floral-patterned wallpaper behind them. Mostly they were paintings of birds and flowers, but there were a few of couples in clothing from long ago; a man rowing a boat with a woman holding a parasol, and one of a woman with her head on man's shoulder.

'It's kind of creepy,' Grace thought to herself.

"My mother decorated this room," Mamie said from the doorway, startling Grace, "When I was a young woman."

"When did you move here from our house?"

"They moved while I was away in Europe," Mamie said. "I hope you're not planning to interrogate me at every turn. I told you what happened once, but I don't plan on repeating it."

"Do you have any pictures of Nino?"

"No," Mamie said. "And don't ask again."

With that, she left the doorway and disappeared down the corridor.

Grace wondered what she was supposed to do now. Mamie had directed her to sit there and wait for their dinner guests. Alone with her thoughts, they started churning again. Grace held her hands to either side of her head and pressed, but she couldn't stop her worries and anxieties racing in circles around her brain.

Could Mamie really make the court award guardianship to her? Did the money she had really make that much of a difference? Judge Feinman knew being with Kay was what she wanted; would Mamie's lawyer get him removed from the case due to what he had called undue influence? How could a bakery box of cinnamon rolls be considered bribery?

She felt like Sara Crewe, forced to live with a mean old woman in a creepy old house. In that book, the father miraculously reappeared. Her father had made it clear he had no interest in rescuing her. Scott was forbidden from doing anything, or he would lose his job. Doc meant well, but even he was powerless in the face of Mamie's checkbook. If she waited for some man to rescue her, she might live in this house until she was as old as Mamie.

'What would Lyra do?' thought Grace. 'Probably run away.'

But this was not a book, and she didn't have a huge polar bear to protect her on her journey. She didn't want to leave Rose Hill; she just wanted to leave Mamie's house.

Grace lay her head on her arms on the table in front of her and fell asleep. She dreamed she was traveling with Iorek Byrnison, the fierce warrior prince polar bear enslaved because the villagers had taken away his armor. Iorek turned into Scott, and it seemed Mamie had taken away his badge and his police car.

"I will find them," Grace told Scott in her dream. "I will use the alethiometer and find them for you."

In her dream, the alethiometer was the glass swan, and it led her to a room at the very top of Mamie's house, the very highest attic room. A wizard was sitting on a balcony there that overlooked the entire town of Rose Hill. He was watching everything that was happening below with great amusement.

"Please help me," Grace said.

"Hello, Grace," the wizard said. "I am so glad to see you."

"I'm in terrible trouble," Grace said. "Can you help me?"

The wizard got up and left the balcony, saying, "Let us have tea, and we will discuss it."

Grace began to clean off the table so they could sit and have tea but found people already sitting there.

"Who are you?" she asked a young boy.

"James Trotter," he said.

Grace noticed a grasshopper, a spider, a ladybug, and an earthworm having tea at a small table in front of the boy. They all waved to Grace, and she waved back.

"I'm Sara Crewe," the young girl next to him said.

Her clothes were old-fashioned, and there were dark circles under her eyes.

"Your father is coming for you," Grace said.

"No, he isn't," the young girl said, shaking her head slowly. "He died in the war."

Grace recognized Oliver, dressed in rags, holding his food bowl.

"I want some more," he said.

"The wizard is coming back with some tea," Grace said. "There's bound to be something you can eat."

A plainly dressed woman was sitting at the table, embroidering, and she smiled shyly at Grace.

"Who are you?" Grace asked her.

"Jane Eyre," she said.

"You're going to inherit a fortune, so you don't have to marry anyone," Grace said. "Not the missionary guy or the mean one with the crazy wife."

"I do not know of whom you speak," said Jane.

Ava was there, looking at Grace with contempt.

Ava said, "You're not fit to sit at the table with the wizard."

"He asked me," Grace told her. "I can sit anywhere I want to."

She realized, however, that every chair had someone already sitting in it, and there was no room for her.

A clothed rabbit ran through the room, looking at his pocket watch.

"Don't tell me," Grace said. "You're very late."

"Don't be a smartass," the rabbit said and went down the stairs.

The wizard came back, but he brought a jeweled box instead of tea.

"This is for you," he said to Grace, "because you have been so good for so long."

He opened the box and showed her what was inside. It was full of papers.

"What will these do?" she asked him.

"Give your bear back his armor," he said, smiling. "And bring you home."

Grace woke up to the sound of the dinner guests arriving.

Knox Rodefeffer was a very large man dressed in tight clothes, with rolls of fat under his chin. He seemed sweaty and nervous; his hand when he shook Grace's was clammy. He, like her biological father's lawyer, had unnaturally white teeth. There was also something wrong with his hair; it just didn't look right. When he raised his eyebrows or wrinkled his forehead, it didn't move. Grace wondered if it was a wig. He greeted her briefly, didn't look her in the eye, and then ignored her the rest of the evening as if she were invisible.

Knox's brother Trick was much slimmer, with thinning blonde hair. He looked Grace in the eye with his own red-rimmed ones when he shook her hand, and Grace could smell the alcohol on his breath. His wife, Sandy, trembled when she shook Grace's hand. Her eyes darted here and there and never seemed to settle on anything. She kept touching her hair as if to make sure it was behaving itself.

Grace knew their daughter, Stacey, from Pine County Consolidated. She gave Grace a bored look and said, "Sup?" That was all. She spent the whole dinner texting on her cell phone and pushing her food around to look as if she was eating, but she never took a bite that Grace could see.

The housekeeper, Mrs. Balanchine served dinner, which was pot roast, potatoes, and rolls. Grace thought it was delicious and told her.

Mamie said, "Don't speak to the help, Grace. It's considered lower class to do so."

Mrs. Balanchine winked at Grace and glared at Mamie, but Mamie ignored her.

The dinner conversation was awkward. Knox and his brother talked about business, Sandy fussed over her daughter, and Stacey ignored her mother. Mamie kept trying to get Knox's attention, but he ignored her. Grace enjoyed the good food and hoped it would all be over soon.

After dinner, Sandy said, "You should come spend the night with Stacey one night, Grace. You two girls are cousins, you know."

Sandy nudged Stacey, who huffed as she lay down her cell phone.

"Please come over, Cuz," Stacey said, with a fake smile and an eye roll everyone could plainly see. "We're going to be besties now."

After Trick, Sandy, and Stacey left, Knox and Mamie went across the hall to her sitting room, and nobody seemed to care what Grace did. She had always wanted to be invisible, and in this house, it seemed she was.

Mrs. Balanchine removed all the dishes, and when Grace offered to help, she said, "Oh no, Miss Grace. Your great-grandmother wouldn't hear of it. If you ever need anything, you just let me know."

Grace got up and walked around the dining room, looking at all the knick-knacks and glass that seemed to cover every horizontal surface. She looked at all the glass in the ornate glass cases, but when she tried to open them, she found them locked. She wandered out into the hall, where she could hear Knox arguing with his aunt.

"Boarding schools cost money," he was saying. "Money, may I remind you, that we don't have yet."

"But I don't want her here, underfoot," Mamie said. "Once we get the money, I can pay you back."

"My money is tied up in investments, and in case you haven't noticed, the stock market has taken a turn for the worse. I need her money as much as you do, maybe more. Meredith's hospital isn't cheap, you know."

"Lunatic asylum, you mean," Mamie said. "When does she get out?"

"Never, I hope," Knox said. "It's going to take me years to distance myself from the scandal."

"You never could pick a wife," Mamie said. "Bats in the belfry, all of them."

"There have only been two," Knox replied. "I can't afford another divorce."

"Well, don't arrange another accident," she said. "That didn't work on Anne Marie, and people might get suspicious if Meredith dies."

"Oh, do shut up," Knox said.

"Somebody's got to pay the lawyers," Mamie said. "They want a retainer, and they want it tomorrow."

"I don't have it, and Trick doesn't have it," Knox said. "Can't they give you credit against the trust fund?"

"Only if Grace signs the papers," Mamie said. "With that blasted Irishman as her lawyer, I doubt she will."

"It's too bad you didn't come to me sooner," Knox said. "We might have got our money before the Fitzpatricks got involved."

"There's another problem," Mamie said. "Scott Gordon."

"What?"

"There's something he knows about that I wouldn't want to be spread around."

"What is it?"

"Something I don't want you to know about, either."

"Has he threatened you?" Knox asked. "I'll have him arrested for extortion."

"He hasn't yet," Mamie said.

"That's a chance you'll have to take," Knox said. "There's too much at stake to back out now."

"I'm not backing out," she said. "The attorneys are going to offer him an incentive to withdraw his name as a potential guardian."

"A bribe, you mean."

"Maggie Fitzpatrick is his weakness, and she has quite the history," she said. "He'll do anything to protect her."

"Aunt Mamie, please try to stay out of trouble," Knox said. "Don't go signing anything without me reading it. And for God's sake, stay home. I'm tired of being banned from every business but my own."

"You'll have to speak to the bank board about my mortgage," Mamie said. "Soon as I get the trust funds I'll be able to pay it off and clear all these debts."

"I hope so," Knox said. "It's been mentioned that I have a conflict of interest where you're concerned. It would be much easier on me if you'd just put the deed in my name."

"Much easier for you to rob me," Mamie said.

"I'm leaving," he said. "Try to be nice to the kid. She's saving our family from ruin; it's the least you can do."

Grace hurried back to the dining room as Knox left. After she heard the front door shut, she went to the sitting room and knocked.

"What do you want?" Mamie said.

"I want to talk to you," Grace said.

"Well, I don't want to talk to you," Mamie said. "In my day children were to be seen and not heard; in the future, I'll thank you not to speak unless you're spoken to. Now go have Balenchine show you to your room."

The doorbell rang, and Grace could hear the squidge of Mrs. Balenchine's rubber-soled shoes coming down the hallway to answer the door.

"I'm not staying here," Grace said. "I know you don't care about me; you just want the trust fund."

"Eavesdroppers got their ears boxed in my day," Mamie said. "Don't tempt me."

"Lots of people would be interested to hear you're broke," Grace said. "Don't tempt me."

"How dare you!" Mamie screeched and swung her cane.

It caught Grace by surprise, and she didn't have time to duck. She was lucky the end was covered with a rubber stopper. Otherwise, it would probably would have cut her as it hit the side of her head. Knocked off balance, Grace fell over, and as she did so, she knocked over the glass swan, which Mamie had sitting on the table next to her armchair.

It bounced on the thick rug but then shattered on the stone hearth.

"You horrible child!" Mamie screamed and raised the cane in preparation to swing it down on Grace.

Grace covered her head with her arms and cried out.

"Stop!" said a voice from the doorway. "Mamie!"

Grace peeked out from under her arms to find Scott and Doc Machalvie standing in the doorway to the sitting room with a shocked-looking Mrs. Balanchine right behind them.

Mamie dropped her arm, and the cane fell to the floor. Grace scurried away on her hands and knees, and Scott helped her up. Doc looked at her head above her ear and then glared at Mamie.

"You ought to be ashamed of yourself, Mamie," Doc said. "There's not a court in this land that would give you this child after that display. I'm going to report you for child abuse."

"Get out!" Mamie cried and sank into her armchair. "All of you! Balanchine!"

"We're going," Scott said. "C'mon, Grace."

"I quit," Mrs. Balanchine said. "You're a nasty piece of work, Mamie Rodefeffer. You'll be hearing from my attorney about my back wages."

She untied her apron and flung it on the floor.

"I don't care," Mamie said, in the petulant voice of a little girl. "Get out!"

CHAPTER NINE – FRIDAY

"Scott, you've got to help me," Ava Fitzpatrick said as she rushed into his office the next morning.

Her long dark hair cascaded over her shoulders in shiny waves. Her delicately arched brows were drawn with worry above her big brown eyes, and the rosy pink of her flushed cheeks matched the color of her perfectly shaped mouth.

Scott's heart started thumping, and his palms began sweating. He thought of Maggie, felt guilty, and then silently cursed himself for his weakness. What would he have to do to get rid of this terrible crush?

"Sit down, Ava," Scott said. "Calm down and tell me what's happened."

Ava was blinking fast as if to hold back her tears as she took a seat on the other side of the desk. Scott pushed the box of tissues toward her. She took one and twisted it in her hands. Scott mentally braced himself to resist getting involved in Ava's latest drama.

"Someone has been sending me flowers," she said.

He laughed.

"That doesn't sound too bad," he said. "Most women like to get flowers."

"No, it's not like that," Ava said. "They're coming every hour, and each bouquet is from a different person."

"That's kind of weird," Scott said. "Who are they coming from?"

"Husbands," Ava said. "The husbands of my dearest friends, who are also the fathers of Charlotte's school friends."

"Hmm," Scott said. "That's an awfully expensive prank for someone to pull."

"You know how people love to gossip about me," Ava said, touching each eye with the tissue, although there were no actual tears falling that Scott could detect. "Something

234

like this could ruin not just my reputation but Charlotte's as well."

"No one is going to think you're carrying on with all those husbands," Scott said.

"You don't know these women," Ava said. "If it weren't for the legacy that was left to me, they wouldn't have anything to do with me. One whiff of scandal and they'll not only drop me, but their daughters will shun Charlotte as well."

"Then are they really the kind of friends you care to keep?" Scott said.

"You know how difficult it's been for me," Ava said. "All alone, raising three children while managing the B&B. Bryan and Theo nearly ruined me in this town. It's taken me years to hold my head up in public again. I can't let things from my past hurt Charlotte. These are the people who will help Charlotte get into the right college, find a good job, and meet the man she marries. It does matter, Scott, whether we like it or not."

Scott thought of Grace, and how, according to Ava's philosophy, she was doomed to fail because her parents weren't big fish in this small pond. By this same logic, Grace would never be successful in life because she couldn't afford designer clothing and an expensive car. Hard work and education wouldn't matter, not unless she got filthy rich or attended the most prestigious school. It was a game very few could ultimately win; no matter how rich or important your parents were, there would always be someone richer and more important who could look down on you.

Ava's background wasn't much better than Grace's. She was only accepted by the upper echelons now because she had money, and well, let's face it, he thought, because she was so beautiful. Scott suspected the ladies she was most desperate to impress kept her close just so they could keep an eye on her. If there were a scandal, they would drop her instantly and enjoy doing it. No doubt about it, Ava's reputation was her Achilles heel.

"So who do you think is sabotaging you?" Scott asked.

"I don't know why anyone would do such a thing, Scott," she said. "You know me. I mind my own business and try to help others whenever I can."

"Grace Branduff needs your help right now," he said. "You don't seem very sympathetic to her situation."

"She's not as perfect as you seem to think."

"It's not just me," Scott said. "Maggie, Claire, Hannah, and all the Fitzpatricks are doing everything they can to help her. I'm surprised you don't feel the same way."

"I know her better than you all do," Ava said. "Grace Branduff's one of the most negative people I've ever met. I extended every courtesy to that child, but she never appreciated it. I'm just glad Charlotte had the good sense to drop her before Grace infected her with that bad attitude. Her new friends, the Beal twins, are so outgoing and have such positive attitudes."

"You were an orphan, Ava, before you were adopted," Scott said. "I'm surprised you don't have more compassion for her."

"It's all well and good for Maggie, Hannah, and Claire to help her," Ava said. "They don't have to worry about her sour disposition poisoning their daughters' chances. They're perfectly happy to stay at the same social level they were born into. I have higher aspirations than that for Charlotte, and if that makes me a bad person, then so be it."

"Okay, Ava," Scott said. "We'll just have to agree to disagree. Now, back to your flower problem. Who's mad at you and why?"

"I can't imagine," Ava said, and then she paused.

It was interesting to watch the emotions flit across her beautiful face as Ava realized something. She looked almost amused, then angry, and then determined.

"What?" he asked her.

Ava stood up and smoothed the skirt of her dress.

236

"I think I know who's behind this," she said. "I can take it from here, Scott."

"Ava," he said. "What's going on?"

"Nothing I can't handle," she said.

Scott stopped in at Sunshine Florist and greeted Erma, who was behind the counter assembling a large funeral wreath.

"Hey, Chief," she said. "What's shaking?"

"I'm looking into the curious case of the mysterious flower deliveries," he said as he leaned on the counter. "I know I can count on your discretion."

"Then you don't know me at all," Erma said. "Is this about Ava's flowers?"

"Did she stop by?"

"I'll tell you the same thing I told her," Erma said. "When I got to work today, there was a list of delivery times, names, and more than enough cash to cover the whole operation in an envelope taped to the door. That's all I know."

"Can I see it?"

Erma handed him a creased piece of plain white copy paper with the aforementioned schedule and list of names printed on it.

"Could have come from any computer," he said. "Not really worth the county's time and money to try to get fingerprints from it unless something else happens."

"Something else?" Erma said. "Do you think someone's stalking Ava? I saw a show about that once. It started out harmless enough, but eventually, the man killed a woman."

"No, don't go starting that rumor," he said. "I don't think it's anything more than malicious mischief. But I would like you to keep your eyes open, and your ears tuned in, and let me know if anything else happens. Can I keep this?"

237

"Sure," Erma said. "I don't need it now."

"Kind of an expensive prank, don't you think?"

"I wish more people would use me for their pranks," Erma said. "It made my week, money-wise."

"Any ideas?"

"Oh, I've got lots of ideas," Erma said. "Apparently Ava Fitzpatrick has made one doozy of an enemy. My guess is it's one of the wives."

"Are you making the rest of the deliveries?"

"I had six more to go before Ava stopped them," Erma said. "Suits me. You need some flowers for Maggie? They're paid for."

"You know Maggie," Scott said. "If she found out I gave her Ava's flower rejects, she'd smack me down the nearest rat hole."

"When are you two going to make it legal?"

"As soon as she says yes," Scott said. "I keep asking and hoping one of these days she just might accept."

"Maggie Fitzpatrick is a stubborn fool, in my opinion. No offense."

"None taken."

"Are you gonna stake out my shop, see if someone does the same thing tomorrow?"

"Naw," he said. "You just give me a call if you get another one."

"Will do," Erma said. "Do you think Ava would mind if I took these flowers to the nursing home?"

"No," said Scott, "I don't think she'd mind at all."

"Hey, Scott," she said. "What do you think is going to happen to Jacob Branduff's granddaughter?"

"I don't know," Scott said. "What have you heard?"

"I heard the county took Grace out of Mamie's house, sent her back to Kay's," Erma said. "You care to let me in on the details?"

"Nope," Scott said.

"I also heard Trick was down to the Branduff place with a surveyor, taking measurements."

"Really," Scott said. "Anything else?"

"Between you and me, Mamie hasn't been paying her bills for a while," Erma said. "I think she owes every business in this town."

Hannah came running into Little Bear Books shouting, "Maggie!"

Maggie came out of her office and said, "Shush. Come in here. What's happened?"

Hannah followed Maggie back into the office and closed the door behind them.

"Mission accomplished," Hannah said. "I told you it would work."

"What happened? Did you see her? What did she say?"

"She called me," Hannah said. "And I bet you'll get a call, too, before long. She said she wanted to see if there was anything she could do to help Grace Branduff. She went on and on about what a sweet, precious child she was, and that she would hate if anything bad happened to her."

"You're kidding me," Maggie said. "That fast?"

Maggie's second-in-command, Jeanette, tapped on her window and mouthed the word "phone."

"That'll be Ava," Hannah said.

Maggie picked up the phone and then said, "Oh, hi, Ava."

She listened for a few moments and then said, "Well, I appreciate your call. I don't know that there is anything we can do now except pray and offer our support to Grace. I know she'll appreciate hearing you want to help in any way you can."

Hannah was beside herself. She jumped up and opened the office door as Claire come rushing in the store.

"She called me," Claire started to say when Hannah shushed her, pointing at Maggie on the phone.

"I'll let her know," Maggie said into the phone. "Although I'm sure she'd appreciate hearing it directly from you and Charlotte. Okay, Ava, thank you. Bye."

Maggie hung up.

"You're a frigging genius," Maggie said to Hannah. "I can't believe how well that worked and how fast."

"She's falling all over herself," Claire said. "She's so worried about Grace."

"She doesn't know which one of us did it, but she was smart enough to figure out why," Maggie said. "Hannah, what can I say? I underestimated you."

"I know, I know," Hannah said. "You may read all the hard books, but I'm the secret smarty-pants in this outfit."

"She made that connection pretty fast," Claire said. "I didn't know Ava was that bright."

"Cunning is the word," Maggie said. "Clever and cunning."

"Do you think she'll give Charlotte some marching orders?" Claire said.

"I'd count on it," Maggie said. "Whether or not Charlotte marches, though, remains to be seen."

Grace was surprised to see Ava and Charlotte at Kay's front door. Ava was holding a bouquet of flowers and had on her "greeting B&B guests" smile. Charlotte was looking at her phone and sulking.

"Kay's not here," Grace said. "She had a campaign committee meeting."

"We came to see you, silly," Ava said. "Didn't we, Charlotte?"

"Uh huh," Charlotte said, but a hateful look conveyed her real feelings toward Grace.

Grace felt funny about inviting people into a house that was not her own, so she stepped out onto the porch. The three stood awkwardly until Ava seemed to remember she was holding flowers.

"These are for you," she said. "We wanted you to know we are thinking of you and if there is anything we can do to help, you just let us know."

Grace accepted the flowers and a hug with as little body contact as possible. Ava nudged Charlotte toward Grace, but she just scowled at her mother and went back to her phone.

"Charlotte," Ava prompted. "Wasn't there something you wanted to say?"

Charlotte rolled her eyes and then glared at Grace.

"If you'd like to come over that would be okay."

"We'd love to have you over," Ava said. "For dinner, a sleepover; just come anytime, no need to call. You know you're always welcome."

Grace couldn't think of what to say. It was obvious Ava and Charlotte didn't mean any of the things they were saying, and she couldn't imagine why they felt compelled to say anything. She started to ask that very question and then thought better of it. She was learning that sometimes it's better to just let things unfold and keep her mouth shut.

"Thanks," she finally said, and then just stood there, holding the flowers.

"Well, we'll let you get back to your day," Ava said. "Charlotte?"

Charlotte rolled her eyes.

"If you want to ride to school with us tomorrow, you can."

"No thanks," Grace said. "I promised Tommy I'd help him with his homework on the bus."

"Of course," Ava said. "Well, you keep in touch and let us know when you and Charlotte can get together."

"Thanks," Grace said.

Grace was sure that if Charlotte could have stuck her tongue out at Grace without her mother seeing it, she would have. Instead, she smirked.

Grace went back inside and shut the door.

What just happened? And why?

241

Maggie looked up from her invoices to find Scott standing in the doorway to her office.

"You scared me," she said. "What's going on?"

"Send any flowers lately?" he asked.

Maggie could feel her face flush with shame.

"I'd like to have my attorney present during questioning," she said.

"Was that Hannah's idea?" he asked. "Cause that had the Masked Muttcatcher written all over it."

"At least no one was tased in the commission of the crime," Maggie said.

"There is that," Scott said. "What's your dinner plan?"

"If you recite your sonnet, I'll cook," she said.

"That would be a first," he said.

"I'll have you know that no one has ever perished from eating my cooking, including you."

"What will you cook?"

"Sonnet first or it doesn't matter."

"Right here?"

"No, actually," Maggie said. "You have to recite this sonnet from the top of a chair in my café, while it is open for business."

"No way."

"Then no supper."

"Nope."

"I'll throw in a back rub," she said.

"I'm listening."

"Supper, back rub, and a shared shower," Maggie said. "And you know what that means."

"'Sonnet 116,'" Scott said, "by Shakespeare."

"In the café," she said.

She stood and pushed him out of the doorway, through the bookstore, to the café side of the store.

There, she pulled out a chair and said, "Attention, everyone. Today we have a special guest, Police Chief Scott Gordon. He's going to recite a sonnet that he learned in, which grade?"

"Fifth grade," he said.

"A sonnet he learned in the fifth grade," Maggie said. "Please give him your undivided attention."

Scott stepped up onto the chair and recited:

Let me not to the marriage of true minds
Admit impediments. Love is not love
Which alters when it alteration finds,
Or bends with the remover to remove:
O, no! it is an ever-fixed mark,
That looks on tempests and is never shaken;
It is the star to every wandering bark,
Whose worth's unknown, although his height be
taken.
Love's not Time's fool, though rosy lips and cheeks
Within his bending sickle's compass come;
Love alters not with his brief hours and weeks,
But bears it out even to the edge of doom.
If this be error, and upon me prov'd,
I never writ, nor no man ever lov'd.

Maggie applauded and whistled, and the staff applauded politely, but the students and customers mostly looked at them both as if they were crazy. Maggie offered him her hand to help him down, and he took it, but when he stepped down to the floor, he went further, down on one knee. Maggie inhaled audibly.

"You wouldn't."

"Mary Margaret Fitzpatrick," he said.

"Please don't," Maggie said. "Not in here."

"Would you do me the honor of becoming my wedded wife?"

"You're going to get such a pinch," she said.

"It's worth it," he said. "What's it gonna be?"

"Oh, alright," she said. "Although you'll probably live to regret it."

Scott stood up as the staff and customers applauded. He held out his arms, and she walked into his embrace.

"You are the tempest," he whispered in her ear, "but I will not be shaken."

"I like it," Grace said.

On the way to school she had read the short story Tommy had written for his creative writing class. Now they were walking to their lockers.

"Really?" he said.

"Yes, really," Grace said. "It's very good."

"I was thinking about time travel, you know, like if we ever could do it, would it be controlled by scientists or would it become a business? Like only really rich people could afford to go as tourists to different periods in time."

"I like your idea of having outposts for time travelers to go to," Grace said. "To get oriented and get the right clothes and money before they go out and explore."

"Yeah, and if you worked at one of the outposts it might be really dangerous, or just really boring most of the time, depending on what era you were in."

"I liked the guy who asked every traveler if they had modern cigarettes," Grace said.

"Yeah, but not carbonated drinks because they would explode in the time machine," Tommy said. "You couldn't bring anything volatile like that."

"You've put a lot of thought into it," Grace said. "I think you'll get an A."

"I like creative writing," Tommy said. "I'm wondering if I really want to be a journalist. Ed says newspapers are disappearing, anyway."

"Maybe you could do both," Grace said.

Tommy and Grace parted at their lockers; Tommy off to the computer lab and Grace to the gym. The gym was not somewhere anyone could be invisible, but it was where the food was located this early in the day. Even though she had been fed well recently, old habits were hard to break. As she entered the gym, Grace took the orange offered to her by a girl named Tory from the Christians in Action Club, and to her, "God Bless you, Grace," Grace replied, as she always did, "Thanks for the orange."

In the gym, some kids were playing basketball while others were listening to their music through earbuds attached to various tiny devices. Some were doing homework, gossiping, or sleeping. Grace wove in and out of the crowd, searching for the huge lime green handbag belonging to Stacey Rodefeffer.

Stacey was texting. Her long blonde hair was ironed straight. Her pink sweatpants hung from her pelvic bones, and every rib was clearly outlined under her tiny pink zip-front hoodie. Around her neck were strung several delicate gold necklaces with flashing pendants: her initials, her zodiac sign, and a unicorn. Her shoes were four-inch platform sandals. Her toenails were painted pink to match her fingernails, which also sported tiny rainbows. She flicked her big blue eyes at Grace, nodded, and then moved her purse so Grace could sit down.

"'Sup," she said, but Grace knew she didn't expect an answer.

While Stacey texted, she emitted a series of huffs, "as ifs," and "yeah, rights." Meanwhile, Grace scanned the bleachers until she found Charlotte, sitting with the Beal twins, Sabine and Bianca.

From neighboring Pendleton, where their mother was an attorney and their father a property developer, the Beal twins were the most popular girls in Pine County Consolidated. Smart, cute and athletic, these two perky girls were widely admired and emulated, to the point that local vendors gave them free products in order to promote them to their fellow student body. They shared a white Range Rover, a bright yellow VW Beetle convertible, and their own Pilates studio. Their parents had recently purchased them airfare, hotel room, and tickets to the Olympics for their forthcoming summer birthday.

"Here, Cuz," Stacey said to Grace as she handed her the pink plastic Barbie lunch box from within the vast confines of her lime green bag. "You can have my lunch."

"Thanks," said Grace.

She opened the box and slipped out the note Stacey's mother had left for her daughter. It read, "Love you sweetie, Mommy." Grace handed it to Stacey, who glanced at it, rolled her eyes, and dropped it down between the bleachers. As Grace transferred the turkey sandwich, chips, and cupcake to her own backpack, she sensed someone approaching with the intent to loiter. A quick glance confirmed it was only Stacey's best friend, Aleesha.

You could tell Aleesha wanted so badly to be the redheaded, baby blue track-suited version of Stacey, but she was pear-shaped, couldn't bear to starve herself, and her single mother couldn't afford the accessories. She and Stacey had been best friends since kindergarten, and Grace admired Aleesha's continued loyalty.

"Hey, Grace," she said. "I heard you're Stacey's cousin now. Who's she texting?"

Grace shrugged as she closed her backpack.

"There's the new kid," Aleesha said. "Have you seen him?"

Grace watched as Rowan Gallaher climbed the bleachers to sit next to Charlotte, who beamed under his attention.

Grace just nodded while she peeled her Christian orange.

"His father is the new president at Eldridge. If we can pry Harlot's hands off of him, he'd be a good replacement for Steve."

Steve had been Stacey's boyfriend before his parents had moved him away. His departure had been the catalyst for the eating disorder that fueled Stacey's war against the unfairness of the world in its continued attempts to ruin her life. Grace reflected that it never occurred to Aleesha to want someone new for herself; she was more concerned that Stacey date someone highly desirable.

Aleesha took out her cosmetic bag and applied another layer to her already heavily painted face.

"I don't know why they bothered to start him this week when there are only three more weeks of school," Aleesha said. "Their house is on Lilac, on the park end, and they're planning an addition. His mother doesn't work, but she's all in his father's business all the time. My mom says everyone at Eldridge is excited to get someone who isn't two hundred years old. She said he looks like a hot politician who cheats on his wife, which is probably why the wife keeps a close eye on him."

Grace listened intently while Stacey's wrung her cell phone back and forth in a flurry of texting.

"Charlotte and Jumbo are on the outs," Aleesha said as she used a mirror and the pointy end of a safety pin to separate her black, gummy looking lashes.

"Why's that?" Grace asked.

"He said something gross to Sabine and Bianca's little sister that freaked her out, and now he's banned from the Beallery."

Grace figured Charlotte wouldn't hesitate to drop Jumbo for the Beals, especially now that Rowan was available to replace him.

"Do you think they did it?" Aleesha asked.

"Jumbo and Charlotte?" Grace asked.

"Uh huh," Aleesha said. "She acts like Miss Perfect, but my mom says her mom is an alley cat."

"I wouldn't know," Grace said.

The Charlotte Grace used to know was saving herself for the love of her life. Grace could hardly picture Jumbo

247

fulfilling that role. As far as Charlotte's mother Ava was concerned, Grace had more than once witnessed a pretty passionate embrace between her and the bartender from the Rose and Thorn, who also just happened to be Ava's brother-in-law, Patrick. Scott had hung around the bed and breakfast for a while, but Ava was never into him except to use him for favors. Those were the only men Grace had ever seen with Ava.

"I can't imagine that oaf on top of me," Aleesha said. "He's so disgusting."

The bell rang for homeroom. Stacey sighed and put her phone in her handbag.

"Who were you texting with?" Aleesha asked her.

"My mom," Stacey said. "She wants me to go to this eating disorder camp. I told her I'd probably just learn all new bad habits and get hooked on hard drugs while I'm there."

"Your dad will never make you go."

"I know that," Stacey said. "The problem is I weigh 87 right now, and our deal is 90. If I end this month below 90, the doctor might make me go."

"Fishing weights," Aleesha said. "Hide them in your hair."

"They're on to me," Stacey said. "It's a naked weigh-in at the doctor's office, and they pat me down."

"Why don't you just eat more?" Grace asked her.

Stacey and Aleesha rolled their eyes at each other.

"I heard Aunt Mamie smacked you," Stacey said. "They're all freaking out about it."

"I don't want to live with her," Grace said.

"My dad's trying to get them to put you in our house," Stacey said. "My mom doesn't want you, but I said I didn't mind. I'll make you over, and then you can hang out with us."

"When's that supposed to happen?" Grace asked.

"Tomorrow night," Stacey said. "My mom's going to have a pizza party to welcome you."

"How lame," Aleesha said.

"I know, right?" Stacey said.

"I don't want to live with you," Grace said. "I want to stay where I am."

"I don't think you get to decide," Stacey said.

"You'd be lucky to live there," Aleesha said. "I'd do it in a minute. Their house is awesome."

"See you tomorrow night," Stacey said.

Grace went to homeroom, feeling hostile toward Stacey even though she was grateful for her lunch. Stacey was probably eight inches taller, yet they weighed approximately the same. She couldn't figure out why starvation was the flag that Stacey had chosen to fly over her war with the world. Rationally, she had to know that ultimately she could only win if she died. And what would she have won, really? Control over life and death? We all had that, every moment of every day. Stacey was mad because her boyfriend moved away. So now she was getting back at the world by slowly killing herself? Grace didn't understand it.

A student working in the Vice Principal's office brought a note to get Grace out of biology class to meet with the school psychologist. Aware of every eye in the room upon her, Grace could feel her face flush as she put her books in her backpack and left the room.

The "school psychologist" was actually alternating members of a local group practice who rotated visits every other week. Their temporary office was in a construction trailer in the parking lot. On the way out to the office, Grace was practicing in her head what she would say.

'I had really bad cramps,' she'd say. 'I just had a really bad day. Nothing like this has ever happened before, and it won't happen again.'

The psychologist visiting this day was so young looking Grace thought she was probably fresh out of college.

She wore old-fashioned wire-framed glasses, her hair was long and falling out of a messy bun on her head, and the sleeves of her business suit were rolled up to her elbows. She was small and thin, and Grace thought to herself, 'She looks like the grownup me.'

"Hi. Grace?" the woman asked, and when Grace nodded, she stood up and shook her hand. "I'm Jessica. Have a seat; I'm just reading through your file, and I want to get caught up before we start."

Grace sat down across the desk from the woman and looked around the messy temporary office. She glanced at Jessica, who was chewing on the end of her pen while reading with such concentration that her brows were furrowed. Grace looked out the window. She listened to the small sounds in the room: the clock ticking, machinery noise from outside where construction workers were erecting the permanent building that this function would eventually be transferred to, and the occasional vibration of Jessica's cell phone, which was sitting on the desk.

"Wow, Dude," Jessica said, as looked up from Grace's file. "You've had one hellacious week. How are you doing?"

Her words surprised Grace so much that at first she smiled, but the compassion and kindness in the look Jessica was giving her brought tears to her eyes. Jessica pushed a box of paper tissues toward her and leaned forward on her elbows.

"You're dealing with a lot of issues right now," she said. "Let's talk about it, and see if maybe I can help."

Grace squeezed her eyes shut and willed the tears to recede, but they did not obey. She took a tissue and cried into it. When she finally got hold of herself, she felt wrung out and exhausted. She looked up. Jessica was sitting back in her chair, looking at her with the same compassionate expression.

"I don't think a lot of adults could handle all you're dealing with," Jessica said. "If I can help in any way, I'd like to."

"What could you do?" Grace said.

"I can listen," Jessica said. "Sometimes it's helpful to talk to someone who doesn't have a stake in what's going on. I may be able to teach you some coping techniques that will help, and I could make a written recommendation to the court."

Grace took a deep breath and decided to trust Jessica. She told her everything.

"I want them to leave me with Kay," Grace said at the end of her story. "I would give them all the money in the trust fund if they would just do that."

"It sounds to me like you have lots of good people helping you," Jessica said. "I will be glad to give my recommendation to the judge."

"Thanks," Grace said.

"Meanwhile, though, let's talk about ways you can deal with all this stress you're having," Jessica said. "It's hard enough to handle a bad situation when you're feeling well, but if you're hungry or not getting enough sleep that can make it even harder."

"I'm eating better than I ever have before," Grace said, "and I'm sleeping a lot."

"Tell me, Grace," Jessica said, leaning forward again. "Are you having any thoughts that scare you?"

Grace thought about the day she hid in the pantry and thought about killing herself. Since she'd decided to save herself, she had been clinging to the idea that there was some way in which she could. She hadn't given up yet.

"No," she said. "I think it's going to work out somehow. I don't know how, but I believe it will."

"That's good," Jessica said. "If you ever do have dark and scary thoughts, I hope you'll call me."

She handed Grace a card with her name and the group practice contact information on it.

"Now, let's talk about some things you can do when you're feeling stressed."

When Grace left the trailer a half an hour later, she gripped Jessica's business card like a talisman. She felt as if she had just added another polar bear to her army.

When Grace entered the computer lab, she found Tommy talking to Elvis.

"There are like all these different kinds of aliens," Tommy was saying. "Like some are small grays and some are lizards. They have some deal with the government where they're allowed to experiment on us, trying to make a hybrid between our two species so they can survive in our atmosphere."

"I'd need to see tangible proof of extraterrestrial life before I believed it," Elvis said. "To date there just hasn't been any credible evidence."

"Look on the Internet," Tommy said. "There are pictures and everything."

"I don't believe it," Grace said. "It's science fiction."

"It's no weirder than what religious people believe," Tommy said. "Some big man up in the sky is controlling what happens to us and you have to constantly tell him how great he is and give him money or he'll send you to burn in a never-ending fire? That's not even science fiction. That's crazy."

"What do you think happens after you die?" Grace asked.

"I think we all go back into like a big pot of energy and come back when there's an opening," Tommy said. "Like when someone makes a baby, it's like a job's available, and you can come back and try again."

"Reincarnation is a basic tenant of Buddhism and Hinduism," Elvis said. "Some of the greatest philosophers also believed in it. Plato, for instance."

"Some people have near-death experiences," Tommy said. "Like they die and come back and say they saw a tunnel of light and people they loved who died before them."

"Studies suggest that might be the brain's way of soothing the dying intellect," Elvis said. "An NDE may just be a hallucination, like a dream, that people have due to oxygen deprivation."

"You have any links to that?" Tommy asked.

"Sure, I'll send them to you," Elvis said.

"You ever dream about somebody who died?" Tommy asked.

"No. Why? Have you?" Elvis asked.

"Yeah, like after my real grandmother died; I didn't know her very long, but she was a real nice lady. She had cancer and was really sick, but she had like this great attitude about it. She wasn't afraid to die. She said she was looking forward to seeing what all the fuss was about. She said she would come to me in a dream afterward if I wanted her to."

"And she did?" Grace asked.

"Yeah, but she didn't say anything profound or tell me what happened," Tommy said. "She just hugged me and smiled, like she was real happy. She was with Ed's dog, Goudy, who died a few years ago. She was just, like, walking around with Goudy, like they were good friends. They both just seemed really happy to see me."

"I have these dreams about my grandma where she's in the house somewhere, but I can't find her," Grace said. "In my dream our house is huge, just hundreds of rooms and stairs and hallways and I can hear her, but I can't find her."

"Maybe you should stand still and let her find you," Tommy said.

"I'll try that," Grace said. "You ever realize you're dreaming and try to make stuff happen?"

"Oh yeah," Tommy said. "It's so cool, but then I usually wake up."

"There's a scientific term for that," Elvis said. "It's called lucid dreaming."

"Charlotte used to have nightmares that her father came and tried to steal her brother," Grace said. "She said she was terrified but also jealous that he didn't want to steal her, just her brother."

"I miss her," Tommy said. "I feel like the Charlotte we knew died, and someone else took her place. Somebody took over her body, like possessed her or something."

"Maybe she's an alien hybrid," Elvis said. "That was a joke."

"I guess I was fooling myself," Tommy said. "She was never as great as I thought she was. She must've been secretly horrible all along."

"No, she was great," Grace said. "And she really liked us. I don't know why she changed."

"Do you think she misses us?"

"No," Grace said. "I think she's embarrassed we were ever her friends."

They were both silent for a long moment.

"Did you need something?" Elvis said. "Not that I'm rushing you, I just need to finish these equations I'm working on and send them to the professor at Stanford."

"I gotta go," Tommy said. "Do you want to meet up at the library this evening?"

"Sure," Grace said. "I'll see you up there."

Tommy smiled at her. She felt as see-through as an aquarium, in which he could see all her private feelings and thoughts swimming around; some ugly, some pretty, some spiky, some graceful, and he was okay with all of it. He didn't mind anything. And she didn't mind him seeing it, or seeing him in turn. She wasn't scared of it, she felt relieved to have this, whatever it was. She didn't want to make out with him, so she guessed it was platonic friendship.

"What's up?" Elvis said as soon as Tommy left.

"What do you think happens when people die?" Grace asked. "What did your mom tell you about it?"

"My mother is a scientist," Elvis said. "I'd say my mother's more agnostic than anything. She just doesn't share her doubts with her church friends."

"Would they kick her out of the church?"

"It's dangerous to challenge someone's beliefs about politics or religion," Elvis said. "A human's beliefs are integrated into their sense of identity, like what sports teams they follow or what musical performers they idolize. If you challenge any of those beliefs, it's like you're attacking who they are. Perceived threats trigger the fight-or-flight response, which is the not the ideal physiological or psychological state in which to pursue civil discourse or support rational thinking."

"So what do you believe?" Grace asked.

"Scientific research can only explain what happens on a physiological level," Elvis said. "I know what happens biologically. The physical form, if allowed to decay naturally, nourishes animals, insects, and other living organisms, such as nematodes, bacteria, and fungi, and enriches the soil in which plants grow."

"But what about your soul?" Grace asked. "Where does it go?"

"I'm a scientist," he said. "I need more data."

"Do you and your mom go to church?"

"My mother was raised in the Baptist church," Elvis said. "She still attends even though she doesn't like the sexist politics of the doctrine. It gives her a sense of belonging to a community. Communities are essential to a civilized society."

"Do you believe in God?"

"I don't have enough data yet to make an informed opinion."

"I kind of hope there isn't," Grace said. "People give God credit for the good stuff, but when bad things happen, they always say, 'We don't know God's plan' as if there's a way to look at it that makes sense but we aren't smart enough to see it. If God is powerful enough to create the world but is more interested in which football team wins then I don't have much respect for Him. He should be looking after starving children in Africa, not wasting time on sports."

"There's a compelling argument for intelligent design, but that would eliminate the possibility of favoritism that humans seem to require from their deities," Elvis said. "Maybe it's just easier for people to have a deity to thank or blame because the alternative is that we are all alone here with no one to thank or blame but ourselves."

"What about luck?" Grace said. "Where you're born or who your parents are makes a huge difference."

"Chaos theory allows for every continuum," Elvis said. "Everything is still random."

"My life sucks because of choices my grandparents and my parents made," Grace said.

"But you can choose differently," Elvis said. "Nothing is predetermined."

"It doesn't feel like it," Grace said. "It feels like the world has already made up its mind about me and there's nothing I can do about it."

"Prove the world wrong," Elvis said. "Scientists do that every day."

Grace had a headache as she made her way to English class. Seeing Rowan Gallaher sitting next to Charlotte, their heads together, whispering, did nothing to help. She wanted nothing more than to get this day over with, go back to Kay's and have a nap in the pretty bed.

The teacher was in an especially chipper mood.

"This is one of my favorite exercises," she said. "Today we're going to take turns playing the parts of the characters in Jane Austen's *Emma*. We'll be utilizing improvisational acting techniques. I will assign roles, give you a situation from the book, and you will interact as the characters in the book would act."

A few people groaned.

"C'mon," she said. "It will be fun."

The first students assigned this activity were theater geeks and got into it. The teacher was beside herself with praise. The next students were less enthusiastic and seemed embarrassed to be in front of the class. Then the horrible thing happened.

"Grace, Charlotte," she said. "I'd like you two to go next. Charlotte, you will be Harriet, and Grace, you will be Emma. The scene is the one in which Harriet reveals her hopes to marry Mr. Knightly and Emma is taken aback by Harriet's ambitions to marry a man Emma believes is more suited to herself."

Grace froze in her seat.

"C'mon girls," the teacher said. "We have several of these to get through. Don't dawdle."

Grace turned and looked at Charlotte. Rowan was teasing her, poking her, saying, "Go on Charlotte, do it."

Charlotte's pretty face was flushed red, and she looked at Grace with such contempt that Grace felt her face flush as well. They both got up and moved to the front of the class, but stood as far away from each other as possible. The teacher took Charlotte's arm and pulled her to the middle, then did the same to Grace.

"Alright," she said. "Charlotte, you're Harriet; you start."

"This is so stupid," Charlotte said.

"Then get it over with," the teacher said, "so someone else can do theirs."

Charlotte would not look at Grace; she looked at a point just above her head.

"I want to marry Knightly," she said.

"You're not good enough for him," Grace said. "You're not rich enough or pretty like me."

"She didn't say that in the book," Charlotte said to the teacher.

"That's okay," the teacher said. "You're improvising. Just go with it."

"I should be able to marry anyone I want," Charlotte said. "You're just jealous because he likes me and not you."

257

"You may be pretty on the outside, but you're ugly on the inside," Grace said. "And that's where it counts."

"Says who?" Charlotte said. "Some ugly person, that's who."

"You used to be a good person," Grace said. "Now you're just shallow and stupid. Why is that? Why is it more important to be popular than loyal to your friends?"

"This isn't in the book," Charlotte said to the teacher. "Grace is just insulting me because she's jealous."

"This is meant to be an improvisation," the teacher said. "Keep going."

"Knightly can marry me if he wants to," Harriet said. "I don't want to marry that dirty farmer."

"How can you treat people the way you do and live with yourself?" Grace said. "Don't you feel bad about what you did to me?"

"You're always so negative and depressed all the time," Charlotte said. "I just got sick of hearing about it. I got sick of trying to cheer you up all the time. You're like a bottomless pit of gloom."

"Maybe that's because my life sucks," Grace said. "Maybe that's because my mom killed herself, my grandma died of cancer, and my grandfather hated me. Maybe if you had a heart, you would have understood that, and not abandoned me like everyone else I ever loved."

Grace was crying now. The classroom was so quiet you could hear the teacher talking in the classroom next door.

"I hate you," Charlotte said to Grace. "I wish I'd never met you."

Grace grabbed her backpack and ran out of the classroom. She went to the first-floor girl's bathroom, locked herself in the last stall, and cried until she threw up her Christian orange. She slumped to the floor and leaned against the wall, hugging her backpack. Eventually, her tears stopped falling, and she stopped gasping for air. It was quiet in the bathroom, so quiet that she finally heard someone else breathing in the stall next to hers.

"Who's there?" she asked.

"'Sup," said Stacey.

"What are you doing in here?" Grace said.

"What do you think?" she said.

"What did you eat?"

"Candy bar," Stacey said. "Okay, it was really, like, two candy bars, and they were, like, really big ones."

"Why do you do it?" Grace asked.

"Why do you care?"

"I'm your cousin now, remember?" Grace said. "Really, Stacey, I want to understand."

Stacey was quiet, and Grace just let her words hang there, waiting.

"At first it was just to see if I could do it, you know, be really skinny and hot," Stacey said. "Now it's just, like, food is so gross, you know? I mean, really, how gross is food, if you think about it? There's this voice in my head that tells me how fat and gross I am if I eat. All the time. It won't shut up about it. And I feel really hungry all the time, like, my stomach hurts constantly. Food is all I think about, but then food is so gross, and I hate how I feel when I'm full. It's just so gross. So I throw it up, and the voice shuts up."

"You know it will eventually kill you," Grace said.

"I don't care," Stacey said. "Sometimes I wish I would die."

"You might want to go to that camp," Grace said. "You need help."

"I've been to those camps before," Stacey said. "I learned some new tricks there, like using the fishing weights."

"What about the school psychologist?" Grace said. "Maybe you need to talk about this with someone professional."

"I went to a shrink in Pendleton once," Stacey said. "She didn't like me much."

"Here," Grace said. "Take this."

She reached out under the divider and offered Stacey Jessica's business card.

"This one is really good, and not at all lame," Grace said. "She really helped me, and I bet she could help you."

"Maybe," Stacey said as she took the card. "Why are you so bummed out? When that trust fund starts paying out, you're gonna be rich."

"Just life in general," Grace said.

"I hear ya," Stacey said. "Life sucks."

After Grace entered her next class, the teacher handed her a note directing her to go to the school counselor's office. Grace walked what felt like two miles to the administrative offices, knocked on the door of her grade's counselor, and heard a faint, "Come in."

Ms. Pike was sitting behind her desk with her eyes closed and ear-buds in her ears. She seemed to be doing some deep breathing exercises. Grace didn't know what to do so she sat down in the chair nearest the door and looked around the office.

There were several posters on the walls. One said, "If life gives you lemons make lemonade!" Another said, "Do what you would do if you knew you could not fail." Hanging over her desk was a mobile of butterflies, rainbows, and angels twirling in the breeze from the nearby heat vent. "Carpe Diem" was printed on the oversized mug that sat on her desk; there was a tea bag floating in the steaming liquid.

Ms. Pike had on a sweater with big bright daisies embroidered on it. Her blonde hair was cut in a short shag, and she wore big daisy earrings. She had on a multi-colored necklace on which glasses dangled against her stomach. She was kind of pretty, thought Grace, in the same cheerful way Kay was. Maybe she wouldn't be as bad as the Vice Principal seemed to hint she was.

"I'll be right with you," Ms. Pike said without opening her eyes. "I'm just finishing up a guided visualization."

She started to hum a little bit, and to Grace's amazement, she raised her arms and waved them around her head in wafting, looping motions. Then she reached up toward the ceiling, brought them down on the desktop, and opened her eyes.

"That was refreshing," she said, but then annoyance flitted across her face as soon as she looked at Grace.

"And you are?" she said and squinted.

"Grace Branduff," Grace said.

"Why are you here?"

"The Vice Principal sent me," she said.

Ms. Pike sorted through some files and pieces of notepaper on her desk. She picked up a pink message slip and put her glasses on. She read with a frown and then set the paper back down on the desk. She took a deep breath in through her nose and then blew it out through her mouth. She fixed a kind look on her face that didn't extend to her eyes and smiled. She tilted her head forward so she could look at Grace over her glasses.

"I'm sorry to hear about your father," she said.

"My grandfather," Grace said.

Ms. Pike looked at the paper again and said, "It says here your father just died."

"My father is alive," Grace said. "My grandfather died."

"Oh, well," Ms. Pike said. "Not so terribly sad then. You expect old people to die."

Grace didn't know how to respond to this, so she didn't.

"You teenagers take everything so hard," Ms. Pike said with a sigh. "When you get to be my age, you realize that death is just one more passage in life."

Grace felt like she was expected to agree, so she nodded.

"Well, let's look at your file and see who Miss Grace Branduff is and how she's doing."

She rooted through a filing cabinet drawer until she came up with a file, then sat it on her desk and flipped through it.

"You've done very well on all your state and national tests," Ms. Pike said. "Your grades are excellent. You have an above average intelligence score but just missed getting into the talented and gifted program. There are no behavioral notes on your record. Have you started looking at colleges?"

Grace shook her head.

"You keep these grades up, and you'll be able to get a scholarship. Where are you thinking of going?"

Grace was tongue-tied. On the one hand, she didn't want to share anything with this weird lady, but she had to try to seem normal. She tried to remember what she had heard the girls in the journalism room say about this subject.

"In-state," she said, "because it's cheaper."

"That's true," Ms. Pike said. "Let's sit down again next year and work on those applications."

She shut the file and Grace thought she was just about to get out of the office without any further trouble.

"Tell me about the fight you had with Charlotte Fitzpatrick in English class today," Ms. Pike said, and Grace was startled by both the statement and the sly smirk on the counselor's face. The mask of kindness fell away as Ms. Pike fixed her with a beady eye.

"You didn't think I knew about that, did you?" she said. "I see all and know all, Miss Branduff. Sometimes I wish I didn't, but that's my job. You've had quite a drama-filled week so far. You blew up at the librarian and Mrs. Lawson, you got into an altercation with her son in the hallway, and now a fight in English class with his girlfriend, Charlotte. If this is because of some crush you have on Mr.

Lawson, I have to tell you, you're going about it all the wrong way."

"I don't have a crush on Jumbo," Grace said. "He's gross and a bully."

"Jared Lawson is a fine young Christian athlete and a credit to his family," she said. "I taught him in Sunday School for ten years, so I should know."

"He picks on kids smaller than him," Grace said. "Ask the Vice Principal."

Ms. Pike waved her hand, saying, "That was all a misunderstanding, some horseplay that got out of hand. Elvis has no business being in school here with normal children; he should be in some special school for children with his problems."

"Elvis is smarter than anyone in this school," Grace said. "That's the only problem he has."

"I think, Miss Branduff, that you need to watch the back talk," Ms. Pike said. "I'm beginning to see what the issue is, and why you can't get along with anyone."

"Sorry," Grace said, but it was through clenched teeth.

"So my second theory is that it's Charlotte who is the object of your affection," Ms. Pike said. "You can tell me, Grace. I'm not allowed to judge you."

"I don't have a crush on Charlotte," Grace sputtered.

Ms. Pike looked Grace up and down with a raised eyebrow. Grace suddenly felt self-conscious in her clothes, as Ms. Pike seemed to appraise them and make some judgment that found Grace guilty.

"Girl crushes are perfectly normal in girls much younger then you," she said. "By your age, though, they can tend to mean something much more serious. Have you acted on any of these impulses before?"

"I'm not interested in girls," Grace said. "Not in that way."

"I'm not judging you," Ms. Pike said. "I would just hate to see you go down the wrong path out of curiosity or a lack of adequate parental guidance."

"I'm not gay," Grace said.

"You might not even understand what that word means," Ms. Pike said with condescension.

"I know what it means," Grace said, thinking of the couple who shared the locker next to her, their passionate fights and the subsequent sight of their entwined feet beneath the bathroom stall door after they made up. She'd never thought there was anything wrong with their preference, but she also knew she didn't share it.

"I'm not allowed to say it's a perversion," Ms. Pike said. "I'm not allowed to say that it's the kind of thing that will ruin your life and send you straight to hell. I'm supposed to support diversity; I've had the training. Personally, I find it disgusting, but I'm not allowed to say so."

"But you just did," Grace said.

"Mind your manners," Ms. Pike said. "I can make life very hard for you if I want to."

Grace felt the rage build in her chest and didn't know if she could hold it back. She tried to think what it was Jessica had told her to do. Deep breaths? Something about imagining she was in her happy place? She couldn't think straight. She hated this woman.

"My grandfather died," Grace said. "Even though he didn't like me he was all I had in the world. My mother killed herself because she was crazy. My grandmother died of breast cancer, and my aunt died of a drug overdose. I've got a father who doesn't care if I'm alive or dead so I'm living in a foster home right now while people I don't like are trying to steal my grandfather's money. I don't know what's going to happen next, and it's horrible. Horrible! Do you understand that?"

"There's no need to raise your voice in here, Grace," Ms. Pike said. "This is a safe zone where we can share feelings and work out problems. I hear you, and I can tell you're hurting. It's my job to help you, but I can't do that if all you do is yell and don't listen."

Grace took a deep breath and willed herself to speak calmly and slowly.

"I yelled at Mrs. Lawson because she was throwing away books from the library because that's censorship, which is wrong. I yelled at Jumbo because he was bullying a boy who is much smaller than him. And I yelled at Charlotte because she used to be my best friend, but then she dumped Tommy and me because we aren't rich and popular."

"Are you sexually active with this Tommy?"

"No!" Grace said. "This is not about sex!"

"You're going to have to calm down, Grace. I'm warning you for the last time."

"I'm sorry," Grace said. "I just can't anymore. I just can't."

"What I hear you saying, Grace, is that you're frustrated because you can't control people, and that this is causing you anxiety."

Grace couldn't think of any response to this statement except to scream, which she certainly felt like doing, but knew it wouldn't help.

"I'm supposed to make you take the depression test," Ms. Pike said. "I ask you some questions, and if you score in the depression range, we can get you some medication. Honestly, though, I think this is just a case of negative thinking bringing negative attention. What you need to do is try on a positive attitude for a change. I think you'll find that the more positive you are, the more people will respond positively to you. If you go around thinking bad things will happen, they probably will. If all you think are positive thoughts, then only positive things will happen. Do you understand?"

Grace understood that Ms. Pike was a crackpot, but instead, she just nodded.

"Okay," Ms. Pike said. "If you'll promise to think more positively in the future I won't make you take the depression test. Do you promise?"

Grace nodded and stood up. As she opened the door, Mrs. Pike said, almost under her breath, "Be glad you aren't gay. Lord knows you don't need any more strikes against you."

Grace clenched her teeth and fists as she left the office, but she did not say another thing.

When Grace got home from school, Kay was waiting on the porch for her, holding an official-looking piece of paper.

"What now?" Grace asked.

"It's a court order," Kay said. "You have to go to Trick's house tomorrow."

"Isn't there anything you can do?" Grace said as she dropped her backpack and sank onto the porch steps.

"I've got calls in to everyone I know," Kay said. "Unfortunately, Knox Rodefeffer got Congressman Green's office involved. I guess the president of the United States would have to be a friend of mine in order for me to win this one."

"Did you call Sean?"

"I did," she said. "He's trying to figure out your next move. It might be legal emancipation, but that would take awhile. For now, it looks like you're going to have to do as the court orders."

"I hate those people," Grace said. "Why do I have to be related to them?"

"Luck of the draw," Kay said. "How was school?"

"You don't want to know," Grace said.

"You went back too soon," Kay said. "I wish you could take some more time off."

266

"I know Stacey Rodefeffer," Grace said. "She's completely messed up. Her parents shouldn't be allowed to screw up any more kids."

"Trick is kind of a goofball," Kay said. "But if I had to pick between him and Knox I'd pick Trick every time. His wife, Sandy, has always seemed like a nice person, although she has a lot to put up with being married to Trick. I know they've had trouble with Stacey because of her eating disorder. She almost died last year. Got down to 70 pounds and had to go to a special clinic in Michigan."

"I don't want to go," Grace said. "Why can't I just give them the money to leave me alone?"

"I don't think that's an option," Kay said.

"I really have to go?"

"I'm so sorry, sweet pea," Kay said and put her arm around Grace. "Just remember we are not giving up. We just have to rally our troops and plan our next attack. The best thing you can do is cooperate with the legal process and keep your nose clean."

Grace didn't tell Kay that she got in trouble again at school that day. She wasn't sure she could keep her nose clean. It was getting harder and harder.

"I just want to stay here with you," Grace said, and began to cry.

"I know, honey," Kay said. "And I promise you I will do everything in my power to make that happen."

Daisy Lane by Pamela Grandstaff

CHAPTER TEN – SATURDAY

Stacey's mother, Sandy, opened the door and displayed a big smile that didn't match the resentment in her eyes.

"Welcome to our home," she said, and although her words were almost gleefully cheerful, Grace didn't miss the quick, up-and-down appraisal and a fleeting look of disapproval that followed.

Sandy was dressed just like her daughter in a pink velour tracksuit, and her streaked hair was wound up in a messy knot on the top of her head. Her skin was deeply tanned and lined, and heavy makeup caked in the creases. She wore a tangle of gold chains around her neck, heavy gold rings on every finger and the piercings up the side of her ear were filled with gold stars. Her manicure was French, the long nails squared off at the ends like little bulb trowels.

Sandy instantly replaced her disgusted micro-expression with deliberate beaming of goodwill which felt to Grace like a command: "See how nice I'm being!"

"I hope you'll be happy here," she said. "I'm so looking forward to getting to know you better."

Grace stepped into the large, warm foyer of the mammoth home and was assaulted by the glare of crystal chandelier light bouncing off the gleaming stone, marble, and polished wood. As Sandy led the way down the hall, Grace counted two more chandeliers, all dripping crystals. The kitchen, full of vast expanses of stainless steel and marble, was lit by three additional chandeliers.

"I'll show you to your room later," Sandy said. "First we have a surprise for you."

Sandy paused, then pointed to a doorway and said, "The girls are down there."

After walking down a couple of narrow flights of dimly lit stairs, Grace came to a long hallway with many

268

doors shut along its paneled length. The end of the corridor opened up into a room as big as one of her grandfather's greenhouses and featured a ping pong table, a pool table, a poker table, a vast flat screen TV with deep, plush movie theater style seating, and another large wood, marble, and stainless steel kitchen. A bank of sliding glass doors faced the backyard, where a long pool sparkled in the spotlights hidden in the landscaping.

Aleesha was helping herself to several slices of pizza from one of the four boxes on the counter.

"Hey," she called out when she saw Grace. "I hope you're hungry."

Grace's heart sped up as it always did when there was an opportunity to acquire food, and she had to suppress her immediate thought, which was how best to separate Aleesha from the food's proximity so she could discreetly steal some of it to hide in her backpack for later.

Instead, she calmly picked up a paper plate, and as if this was something that occurred every day, she looked through each box to see what kinds of pizza were available. She did ultimately pick the pizza topped with the most vegetables before choosing a soda that purported to contain real fruit juice and cane sugar as opposed to artificial flavorings, coloring, and high fructose corn syrup. Grace was surprised to see so much beer and wine in the refrigerator. She guessed Stacey's parents were not worried Stacey would be tempted to drink because there were so many calories in alcohol.

She joined Aleesha in front of the huge television, where she was cycling through channels looking for something to watch. She finally settled on a show about several young Caucasian people dressed up in very little clothing, preparing to go out to a nightclub. Their skin was so tan it was orange. The females' globular breasts and the males' exaggerated muscles looked like they had been polished with walnut oil. After watching for a few minutes, Grace discovered the theme of the show seemed to be a constant repetition of catty remarks and reaction shots among the females intermingled with fighting and boasting among the males. She wondered what anthropological observations Elvis would make.

"Where's Stacey?" Grace asked.

"She's still getting ready," Aleesha said. "She can't decide what to wear."

"Is she going somewhere?" Grace asked.

"Her cousins Hugh and Lucas are bringing over some guys they go to college with," Aleesha said. "We'll probably go out with them somewhere. They're nice. You'll like them."

Grace started planning her exit strategy.

"How soon are they coming?" she asked.

"Any time now," Aleesha said.

A few minutes later Grace heard a thundering of footsteps on the stairs followed by male voices in the hall. She recognized Hugh and Lucas, of course, who worked at Machalvie Funeral Home. Their mother and Stacey's mother were sisters, but she couldn't see any resemblance. Sandy and Stacey were both blonde, and Peg Machalvie's hair was as black as a raven's wing. The boys' dark hair was stiff with gel, and they were dressed up just like the young men on the TV show Aleesha was watching, with tight V-neck T-shirts straining over their oily orange muscles. The three boys with them were dressed much the same.

"Hey, Leesh," Hugh said, with a nod in Aleesha's direction.

"Hey," Aleesha said, briefly looking away from the hair-pulling fight on her show.

"This is awesome," one of the boys said. "Have you seen this one? That girl is a mega creeper, and The Abdomination is all, like, you're so done, creeper, you're toast."

The boys went to the kitchen and then returned with boxes of pizza and bottles of beer to the area where Grace and Aleesha sat.

"Where's Stace?" Lucas asked.

"She'll be down in a minute," Aleesha said, not taking her eyes off the television screen.

One of the boys made a rude gesture in her direction, and the others laughed.

"Hey, Leesha," one of them said. "How about taking a walk with me? We'll hunt for snipes."

"No thanks," Aleesha said. "Not interested."

"That's not what you told me last time," he said, and they all laughed.

Aleesha rolled her eyes and shook her head but didn't respond.

So far all the boys had pretended Grace was not there, which suited her just fine. She had shrunk as far back into the corner of her seat as she could, and was warily watching.

"Whatta we gonna do tonight?" Hugh asked Lucas. "I ain't babysittin' teenagers all evening."

"I say we go down to Morgantown and visit Duce and Chaz," Hugh said. "They've got a place in South Park."

"How soon can we leave?"

"Soon as Stacey's ready," Lucas said.

"You guys wanna go?" Hugh asked Aleesha.

"Sure, why not?" Aleesha said.

"What about you?" Lucas asked Grace. "Whatsamatter? Cat got your tongue?"

"No," Grace said. "No thanks."

"C'mon," Lucas said. "Don't be a party pooper. We'll show you a good time, promise."

"She doesn't know what a good time is," Hugh said. "Mom says she's been locked up her whole life."

"Really?" one of the other boys said. "A V-card carrier, then?"

"No doubt," Hugh said. "No doubt in my mind whatsoever. Look at her."

"Looks like a lezzy to me," one said. "You a lezzy, little girl?"

"Collecting V-cards is my specialty," another said.

"I wouldn't mind having a go," the third boy said. "You can hardly find a V-card carrier anywhere these days. Girls are such sluts. Like Leesha."

"Eff you," Aleesha said.

The boys all laughed and mocked Aleesha. Grace was glad for the redirection of their focus. She thought she could probably outrun them if they drank enough. She started assessing her exit opportunities and settled on the sliding glass door to the pool area. If she jumped over the back of her seat, she wouldn't have to pass any of them. She might need to throw something first, to divert their attention. She could feel her adrenalin build as she considered what to throw.

She was saved by Stacey's entrance. Dolled up and smelling like no flower Grace had ever known, with one flick of her long blonde hair Stacey immediately drew all the attention from Grace and Aleesha. Grace watched with interest as the males vied for her attention.

Stacey's glance flicked over Grace with a nod of her head.

"'Sup," she said.

"We're going to Morgantown," Hugh said. "Wanna go?"

"Sure," Stacey said. "Nothing going on around here."

Hugh got out his phone and started texting.

Aleesha stood up and stretched. One of the boys reached out, grabbed her rear end, and although she swatted his hand away, saying, "You guys, stop it," she was smiling a lazy smile and looking sideways at him, from under her lashes.

There was no talk of telling anyone's parents what their plans were, let alone asking permission. Grace knew she wasn't going anywhere, she just didn't know how to make a graceful exit.

"Chaz says come on," Hugh said, looking up from his phone. "He says if Stacey's coming he'll even take a shower."

"It'll take a lot more than a shower," Stacey said, and all the boys laughed like it was the most hilarious thing they had ever heard.

"Go unlock the mudroom door," Stacey commanded Aleesha, who jumped up and left the room.

"My mom locks the doors upstairs at midnight," she told Hugh. "And I don't want her to know I lost my key again."

When Aleesha came back, they left via the sliding glass doors, all jockeying for position near Stacey, and no one even looked back at Grace. It left her with the feeling that no one cared enough to even say goodbye to her. All these years she had wished for nothing more than to be invisible, and for once, she was. Not that she cared what those people thought; those big boys were more than a little repellent and scary. She never in a million years would want to go anywhere with them in a car. Why did she mind so much that they didn't invite her?

She was still wondering that when she heard footsteps on the stairs from the kitchen and men's voices. Her first instinct was to hide, so she did. The mammoth pool table had the perfect hiding place on a broad shelf underneath. She pulled her legs up and knew without a doubt she was undetectable in the darkness.

"They must've just left," Trick said. "I was just talking to Stacey right before she came down."

"I guess if I want to see my boys while they're home from college I'll have to invite your daughter over for dinner," Stuart said.

"Good luck getting her to eat anything," Trick said.

"Well, they've left us some pizza," Stuart said.

"And more importantly, some beer," Trick said

"We can do this down here. Spread the plans out on the pool table, Trick," Knox said. "Is there any sausage and onion left?"

Grace watched the shadowy movements of the men's legs as they gathered around the pool table. She could hear some papers being moved about. She could hear them open beers, move pizza boxes, and in one funny instant, emit a long, loud fart.

"The property extends from the north edge of the glassworks property all the way up both sides of the river, for twenty odd miles in this direction. Several parcels on the Rose Hill side are leased to Tug Napier for his sorghum. As you can see," Trick said, "the majority of the property is across the river to the west. Almost 11,000 acres, none of it leased, zoned, or protected."

"Plus all the mineral rights," Stuart said.

"Yes, sirree," Trick said. "A gold mine."

"Is it enough land to interest the Marcellus Shale people?" Stuart asked.

"More than enough," Knox said.

"Would the trust be willing to sell it?" Stuart asked.

"I don't know yet," Knox said. "I called Jim Barry; he's the officer in charge of the trust. He can't talk to me without her permission. I've got a letter of authorization written up; she just has to sign it."

"Any idea what else is in the trust?"

"Considering it was created almost 75 years ago, I'd wager it's blue-chip stocks and bonds. Jacob Branduff never touched it so you can imagine the compounding interest."

"Any way to find out what the child's worth altogether?" Stuart asked.

Grace realized then that it was she whom they were talking about. She owned land? On both sides of the river?

"All I have is the deed to go by, and that's in the public domain," Trick said. "I wish the old man would've kept a copy of everything in a safety deposit box in Knox's bank. Then we'd have it."

"No account there?" Stuart asked.

"No, he dealt in cash only," Knox said. "I'm sure trust statements came to the post office box but, unfortunately, the postmistress isn't someone who is conducive to bribing. She's not one of your conquests, is she?"

"Quiet, Knox," Trick said. "Sandy has excellent hearing. And no."

"Any chance there's old statements stashed at the house somewhere?"

"Chief Gordon changed all the locks, and there's a steady patrol presence."

"Then the only way we can get our hands on the next statement is if the girl picks it up at the post office and hands it over."

"Unless she's found the statements, she doesn't have a clue what she has," Stuart said. "Just offer to take over her business for her, Knox. You're her uncle, or cousin, or something."

"Unfortunately, Chief Gordon got Sean Fitzpatrick involved before Mamie told us who she was," Knox said. "That makes things more difficult."

"You've got to earn her confidence," Stuart said. "One of you has got to become a sort of fatherly figure to the girl."

"Mamie's wrecked my chances," Knox said. "It'll have to be you, Trick."

"I spoke to Sandy and Stacey," Trick said. "They're doing their part. They aren't happy about having her live with us, of course, but they understand what's at stake."

"I can't have her live with me right now," Knox said. "I'm just not in a position to take her in until Meredith gets out of the hospital. Even then, I'm not sure that would work out."

"I haven't had a chance to talk to my boys," Stuart said. "But I will as soon as possible. If we could get her smitten with one of them that would help."

"You're just hoping one of your boys will knock her up," Knox said. "He'd be the son who laid the golden egg."

They all laughed.

"Now, now, now," Stuart said. "I'm fine with my cut, boys. A rising tide will lift all our boats."

"I'm willing to sell you all the land on the east side of the river," Knox said. "But without the mineral rights."

"Don't need 'em," Stuart said. "All I need is all that precious acreage with access to the interstate."

"Is the new highway confirmed to cross between Pendleton and Rose Hill?"

"Congressman Green's aide showed me the plans," Stuart said. "It will make that particular parcel very valuable. Plenty of room for Peg's business and a strip mall."

"How's the wind farm project coming along?" Knox asked.

"It's a done deal," Stuart said. "Legislators meet next month. It's tacked on to the roads bill."

"How in the world are they getting around the environmentalists?" Knox asked.

"Congressman Green is a genius," Stuart said. "One of his ex-staffers created a nonprofit agency to study the environmental impact of land development on the local ecology. Green got it federally funded, and any favorable finding we need they can get."

"That's going to help us in all our projects," Trick said. "It's like an automatic stamp of approval from the tree huggers."

"We're still purchasing other land elsewhere to be protected in exchange for what we develop," Stuart said. "It's just much less desirable than what we have to work with here."

"And the endangered gray flying squirrels?"

"Succumbed to a mysterious disease," Stuart said. "It was a very sad thing."

All three men laughed, and goose bumps rose up on Grace's arms.

"So what are our next steps?" Stuart asked.

"I need to get my hands on one of those trust statements," Knox said, "and get her to sign that letter of authorization."

"Stacey and Sandy have got to gain her trust," Trick said.

"I'll see what Hugh and Lucas can do," Stuart said.

Stacey's mother called down the stairs that Stuart's phone was ringing.

"Coming," Stuart called back. "I must have left it in the kitchen. It's probably Peg, calling to see if I'm coming to her campaign committee meeting."

"I've got a bank board meeting," Knox said. "I've got to go."

"Just leave all this," Trick said. "I'll come back down later and clean it up."

Grace listened to them talking as they went back down the long hallway and up the stairs to the kitchen. As soon as she was sure they were all upstairs, she crept out from her hiding place and looked at the many documents on the pool table. There were building plans, email print-outs, and official-looking letters. She paused, considering what she should do next.

She hated the way they had talked about her as if she were a weak and stupid child they could manipulate to get what they wanted. To them she wasn't even a person; she was a means to an end. She wanted to ruin their plans. She wanted to show them she wasn't as witless and helpless as they thought she was. She also wanted someone to know what they were up to, to get them in trouble. She gathered all the papers, rolled them into one messy tube, folded it, and shoved it in her backpack.

The sliding glass door made only the quietest swishing sound as she opened it, let herself out, and slid it to a close behind her. Grace ran up the steps to the first-floor level. Through the windows, she could see Knox, Trick and Stuart in the kitchen with Sandy. She ducked down behind the shrubbery, scooted past the windows, and then rounded the corner of the house into the driveway. She hurried across the cul de sac to the Eldridge Inn and down the driveway until she reached the entrance to Rose Hill City Park. She crossed the park, darted between the houses on Lilac Avenue and came out in the alley between Lilac and Rose Hill Avenue.

All the way down the hill she considered whom to take the papers to. Then she remembered there was one person who gave the most excellent advice if only she could find a phone she could use in privacy. Hurrying down Main Street, she saw that the Bee Hive was still open.

"Hey, Grace," Claire said as she entered. "I heard you were going to a slumber party tonight. What happened?"

Claire had a client in her chair and another waiting, so Grace didn't feel free to talk.

"May I use your phone," she asked. "Do you have one in the back?"

"Sure," said Claire, with only a slight suspicious frown. "Go right ahead."

Elvis's mother answered.

"May I tell him who's calling?" she asked after a long hesitation.

"Grace," she said. "A friend from school."

"Certainly!" his mother said. "Hold on just a moment."

There was a muffled sound, as though Elvis's mother was holding the phone against her body while she spoke to her son. Then he was there.

"Good evening, Grace," he said. "How are you?"

"I'm fine," Grace said. "Was this a bad time to call?"

"No girl has ever called me before," Elvis said. "My mother is currently breathing into a brown paper bag, but I'm sure she'll be fine. I, on the other hand, could not be more delighted."

Grace outlined her dilemma and described what she had in her backpack.

"No police or government officials," Elvis said. "They may already be in league with the bad guys or will hand it up to someone who is."

"Okay," Grace said.

"Hmmm," Elvis said. "It needs to be someone with the power to protect the evidence, some sort of immunity from prosecution, perhaps. Someone who won't have to say

278

how they came by it. Tell me, do you know any members of the press?"

"I do," Grace said. "Tommy's guardian is the editor of the *Rose Hill Sentinel*."

"Quaint paper," Elvis said. "My mother takes it purely as a demonstration of her support for the traditional press. She says it has a liberal bias so that might make the editor more sympathetic to your cause."

"Ed Harrison is a good person."

"And by that you mean ..."

"I don't think he'd help them cover it up."

"Good, good," Elvis said. "Take it all to him. You're his source, so he has to protect you. Whatever you do, don't tell anyone else what you've done. You're going to need an alibi. Work on that after you give the goods to Ed."

"An alibi? What for?"

"You stole something very valuable, Grace," Elvis said. "Before long they're going to notice the papers are missing and so are you. As a consequence, you may be a prime suspect. My advice is to copy everything, put the papers back, and then establish yourself somewhere. Understand?"

Grace hung up and punched in Tommy's number.

"Tommy, it's Grace," she said when he answered.

"Hi," he said. "How are you?"

"I'm in trouble," she said. "Is Ed there?"

"He's at the Rose and Thorn," Tommy said. "What's wrong?"

"Can you come over to the Bee Hive?" she asked him. "It's kind of an emergency."

"I'm on my way," he said.

Grace went back out into the salon, where Claire's last customer was paying. Grace waited until the woman went out the door to speak.

"I'm sort of in trouble," Grace said, "and the Rodefeffers might come looking for me."

"Oh my goodness," Claire said. "Let's get these curtains closed."

Claire closed all the curtains and drew the blinds on the front door. As soon as Tommy arrived, she shut and locked the front door.

Grace spread the papers out on the counter for Claire and Tommy to look at. Someone banged on the door, and they all jumped. Turned out it was Hannah. They let her in.

"What's going on?" Hannah said. "You all look guilty. I want in on it, whatever it is."

"Grace was just about to tell us," Claire said. "Listen."

As soon as everyone was filled in, there was a brief silence.

"Holy Hottentots," Hannah said.

"Oh my," Claire said.

Grace said, "I want Ed to put all this in the paper."

"Tommy, you run down to the Thorn and get Ed," Claire said. "Hannah, how can we distract Trick and Sandy so that we can sneak these papers back in after Ed copies them?"

"Leave that to me," Hannah said. "I just need something to eat so I can think."

Claire dug through her purse and then handed Hannah a candy bar.

"Ah, chocolate," Hannah said. "Some of my finest schemes have been fueled by the cocoa bean."

After Ed returned with Tommy, Grace repeated her story again.

As Ed listened and looked at the evidence, his mouth fell open in slow motion. When she was through, he studied her with a fierce look on his face.

"I stole them," she said. "Are you going to turn me in?"

"Heavens no," he said. "I'll make copies while you guys figure out how to get them back into Trick's house."

"I'm on that," Hannah said, licking chocolate off her fingers. "I'm almost there."

"Do I really have to put them back?" Grace said.

"It would be better if you could," he said. "Then they won't know how we got the evidence."

Ed's hands were shaking as he rolled up the papers and put them under his arm. Seeing him nervous made Grace extra nervous. He left by the back door.

"So as far as you know, only Knox, Trick, Stuart, and Sandy were in the house," Hannah said.

"Yes," Grace said. "They thought I went with Stacy and the Machalvie twins to Morgantown."

"Those young girls have no business going barhopping with those rotten Machalvie boys," Claire said. "What are Trick and Sandy thinking?"

"They just want Stacey not to starve herself to death," Grace said. "She can do anything she wants as long as she weighs 90 pounds."

In fifteen minutes Ed came back and handed Hannah the rolled up stash of papers.

"I've got the manager of the printing press in Pendleton on standby to reprint the whole issue," he said. "He feels the same way about Knox and Stuart as we do. I've got to write up the whole thing and lay it out, and there's not much time. Can you take it from here?"

"Never fear!" Hannah said as she put her hands on her hips. "The Masked Mutt Catcher is here!"

Ed left, and Hannah began stuffing the papers back into Grace's backpack.

"Did it seem like they were done with these?" Hannah asked.

"Yeah," Grace said. "Knox and Stuart had meetings to go to, and Trick said he'd clean up later."

"It all depends on whether Trick has gone back downstairs yet or not," Hannah said. "If he hasn't missed them, you can put them back where they were."

"But how can I know?"

Hannah picked up the phone and punched in a number.

"Hi, Sandy," Hannah said. "Is Trick there?"

Grace stared wide-eyed, but Hannah mouthed, "It's okay."

"Hey, Trick," Hannah said into the phone. "How's it going? Good, good. Listen, there's some chick down here at the Rose and Thorn who's shouting your name and threatening to come up to your house. She looks to be about six months knocked up. I thought you might want to come and have a word with her. Sure, no problem. Neighbors have to look out for each other. Have a good evening."

Hannah hung up the phone.

"Now you run back down to the Thorn," she told Tommy. "Tell Patrick I said to stall him. Take Claire's cell phone. Call me when he gets there and when he leaves."

"What are we going to do?" Grace asked.

"You've got to go back up the hill and put these back on Trick's pool table."

"You go with me," Grace begged.

"Of course," Hannah said. "I'm going to distract little old Sandy-kins while you sneak the plans back into the basement."

"What can I do?" Claire said.

"You are command central," Hannah said. "We'll all meet back here when we're through."

"If you're not back in thirty minutes, I'm coming up to Trick's," Claire said, "and I'm bringing Scott."

Hannah's cell phone rang, and after she finished listening, she hung up and said, "Trick's at the Thorn."

Grace's heart beat fast as Hannah drove up Pine Mountain Road.

"I'll knock on the front door and keep Sandy talking while you put the plans back," Hannah said.

"I'm scared," Grace said.

"Don't you worry," Hannah said. "When all else fails, I always zap everybody with my taser and then ask questions later."

When they reached the Rodefeffer's, only Sandy's car was in the driveway. Grace's heart was pounding so hard in her chest she thought surely it could be heard several yards away. She waited until she heard Sandy open the front door.

"Hey, Sandy," Hannah said. "I'm looking for a lost dog, and I wondered if you had seen it."

Over the hedge and along the brightly lit area behind the kitchen, Grace retraced her earlier steps. Down by the pool, the unexpected sudden glare of the security lights scared her, but she ran down the back steps onto the patio and grasped the handle of the same sliding door by which she'd left. It was locked.

She could see inside the basement that no one was there; no one had cleaned up the beer bottles and pizza boxes strewn across the edge of the pool table where she had set them when she stole the papers. There was a good chance Trick hadn't come back down, would not know anything was amiss, and she could leave the papers and get right back out the way she went in. Except she couldn't get in.

Grace tried every window along the back side of the house, but they were all locked. On the south side of the house was a steel door that Grace assumed would also be locked. It wasn't. She remembered then that Aleesha had left that door unlocked for Stacey. Entering the house, she realized she was in the mudroom, and by following a sort of panicked, meandering path she finally reached the game room.

She took the rolled up plans and documents out of her backpack and placed them on the table, sliding beer bottles and pizza boxes back over the edges how she imagined they had been. Just as she was sliding her backpack back over her shoulder, she heard Sandy and Hannah coming down the stairs. She didn't have time to get out by the sliding glass doors; they would surely see her. It was too late to go past them and somehow meander back to the mudroom, even if she could find it.

Desperate, she ducked back under the pool table and tucked her feet up.

"I've meant to bring these things to you for ages," Sandy said. "Since you're here, you might as well take them. Stacey thought she wanted a dog, but it was just too much responsibility for her. She's sensitive, Stacey is, an emotionally delicate girl and that dog was way too needy. So now we have all this stuff we bought for it, and I'd rather donate it than throw it away."

"No problem," Hannah said. "I'll be glad to take them. I'm sure some needy Chihuahua will love a princess bed and rhinestone collar."

"There's some dog food left upstairs in the pantry," Sandy said. "You may as well take that, too."

"Where are Stacey and Grace?" Hannah asked.

"I think they went to Aleesha's house," Sandy said. "Stacey has taken Grace under her wing in the most generous way. She has a big heart, just like me. We were only too glad to take her in, poor thing."

As soon as they mounted the steps back up to the kitchen, Grace slid out from under the pool table and let herself out the sliding glass door. She paused before it locked behind her and then went back inside. She folded a paper towel around two slices of pizza and tucked them into her backpack.

Hannah and Grace reconnoitered at the end of the block and took the long, roundabout way back to the Bee Hive. Claire was sitting in one of the hydraulic chairs with her feet up on the counter, talking to Maggie, who was seated in the other. Tommy was sitting in the shampoo chair, and he jumped up when Grace came in.

"How'd it go?" he said.

"I don't think he'd been back downstairs," Grace said. "I put everything back the way it was."

Tommy grabbed her up in a big hug, and Grace laughed out loud as he swung her around.

284

"Would somebody please tell me what's going on?" Maggie said crossly.

Grace filled Maggie in on what she had witnessed in Trick's basement game room.

"Those rotten eggs," Maggie said. "Those lowdown snakes."

"Motherflippin' sons-of-witches," Hannah said. "Thievin' bass-tarts."

"Finally," Maggie said. "After knowing they were doing this kind of stuff for years and years, and getting away with it, finally we have proof."

"We shouldn't have sent her back up there," Claire said. "Those guys are dangerous."

"Except I'm the goose with the golden trust egg," Grace said. "They wouldn't dare hurt me."

"Unless the Rodefeffers would inherit your trust," Maggie said. "You might be worth more to them dead than alive."

You could have heard a pin drop as everyone digested this.

"We need Sean to draw up a new will," Claire said. "Let's call him now. We need to take steps to protect Grace."

Maggie took out her cell phone and seemed surprised when Claire took it out of her hand.

"Landline," Claire said.

"Oh my goodness," Maggie said. "I can't believe I almost did that."

"What?" Grace asked.

"Scanner Grannies," Hannah said. "There's a whole network of geriatric spies in this town who listen in on cell phone conversations with illegal scanners."

"Really?" Grace said. "Cool!"

"Always remember that," Claire said. "It's great if you want to start a rumor but not so great if you don't."

"Where are you supposed to be staying tonight?" Maggie asked Grace.

"I'm supposed to be at a slumber party at Stacey Rodefeffer's, but Stacey and Aleesha went with the Machalvie boys to Morgantown."

"Sandy must be crazy," Maggie said. "Those poor girls don't stand a chance."

"She doesn't know where they are," Hannah said. "She doesn't have a clue."

"I'll call Scott," Maggie said. "We need to get you back to Kay's without anyone getting arrested."

"Welcome back," Kay said.

Her eyes were full of sympathy and concern. When she reached out to hug her, Grace rushed into her arms. Her embrace felt warm and safe. Grace realized that she had been hugged more in the past week than she had in all the years since her grandmother died. That thought started her crying, and then she found she could not stop.

"Come in here and sit," Kay said while keeping one arm around Grace's shoulder to guide her to the kitchen. "It has been my experience that everything seems better with cookies and milk."

Scott followed them down the hallway, but Kay did not invite him to join them.

"I explained the situation to Judge Feinman," Scott said. "He's going to sign off on a temporary emergency placement order for Grace. Sean will have to file for a hearing this week to extend it."

"I think, Chief Gordon," Kay said over her shoulder, "that Grace needs some quiet time. Why don't you come back in the morning and talk then."

"Is that okay, Grace?" he asked.

Grace could only nod and snuffle. As soon as she was seated in the homey breakfast nook, she put her head down on her arms and wept some more. When she finally sat back up, Kay handed her a box of tissues.

Because Ed had asked her not to, Grace had not told Scott or Kay about the papers she had stolen and then returned. He said they would be safer not knowing and Grace didn't want to do anything that might jeopardize Scott's job or Kay's run for office. As far as Scott and Kay knew, she had merely had a bad experience with the Machalvie boys at Trick's house and then narrowly escaped being taken bar hopping with Stacey.

Grace gestured to the tissue box.

"When I use to be invited to Charlotte's house," Grace said as she wiped her face, "there was a box of these soft tissues in every room. I used to think that when I grew up, I'd have a box of these in every room."

"I feel that way about zippy plastic bags," Kay said. "My mother wouldn't have them in the house; she used waxed paper for everything and put plates on top of bowls instead of plastic wrap. If you looked in that drawer right now, you would see zippy plastic bags in every size. It's almost a sickness; I get a panicky feeling if I'm about to run out. They make me feel like I must be doing all right because I have all these plastic bags. Crazy, isn't it, the things we think?"

The cookies were wonderful, crunchy peanut butter, and the milk was ice cold. Kay was having some of her fragrant tea in an oversized mug. Her face was pale, she had dark circles under her eyes, and looked older tonight. Grace then realized she didn't have any makeup on, was wearing a housecoat and slippers. She must have thought she was peacefully in for the night when Grace arrived.

"Sorry to get dropped on you again," Grace said. "You're probably sick of this."

"That's not true," Kay said. "You haven't been off my mind since you went to Trick's house. I just knew they were going to do something stupid and look what they did. You haven't been here for very long, Grace, but after you left, it was like there was a hole in this house that wasn't there before. You can stay as long as you like. I not only don't mind it, I like you being here. I want you to be here."

Grace was so taken aback by this kindness that the tears again welled up in her eyes.

"We've got to get you settled," Kay said with a deep sigh. "Those awful Rodefeffers shouldn't be allowed to keep a goldfish, let alone a child."

"I guess since I'm one of them they have a right to say what happens to me," Grace said.

"Mamie forfeited that right yesterday," Kay said. "I think Sandy and Trick have both now proved they can't be trusted."

"I probably got Stacey in big trouble tonight," Grace said. "Scott said the state police are going to look for her and Aleesha. I may get every Rodefeffer arrested before this is over."

"Do you mind if I ask what the fight with Mamie was about?"

"We didn't fight," Grace said. "I talked back to her, and she hit me with her cane."

"I have a hunch about Mamie," Kay said. "I wonder if she isn't having money problems."

"I heard her and Knox talking about it," Grace said. "He said he was tired of paying her bills."

"I see," Kay said. "I'm so glad Sean is helping you. You need someone to represent you who has your best interests at heart. I'm sorry to say the Rodefeffers may be your family but you could hardly have done worse."

"I wish there was no one at all," Grace said. "I liked being invisible."

"Ah, to be invisible," Kay said, "I know exactly what you mean. Ever since I was a little girl, I've had a weight problem. It was just how we were in my family, and no matter how many times I dieted I never could seem to keep the weight off. It's not really a mystery; I just love food, and eating makes me feel better, always has. I like feeding people, and I like to cook.

"Anyway, when I was a teenager, and in college, I used to wish I was invisible because people were always making comments: 'You have such a pretty face; it's a shame you can't lose some weight.' Some were well-meaning, and some were mean-spirited, but everyone seemed to think they had a right to let me know their opinion of what I looked like. I always dressed in dark, multiple layers of clothing and I never went swimming or did anything where much skin was exposed. I rarely looked anyone in the eye, and I always made self-disparaging comments because I assumed other people were already thinking them, and I wanted them to know I knew how revolting my appearance was to them."

"You aren't like that now," Grace said, thinking of the colorful outfits and bright lipstick that Kay always wore.

"I used to be a solitary, lonely person," Kay said. "I didn't date much. The men I was attracted to were never attracted to me, and the men who were attracted to me I never liked. I had female friends, but they always seemed to get married and drift away. I was always the third wheel, the odd one out. I had pretty much accepted that as my lot in life until something happened that changed everything."

Grace stayed quiet, interested to hear this story.

"After my mother died, I got very depressed. I went to see a counselor, and she was this wonderful old lady named Henrietta Gustafson. I spent most of the first appointment telling her about my sad, unhappy life. I was telling her that I knew other people judged me and found me wanting when she interrupted me and said, 'What other people think of you is none of your business.' Well, I had to think long and hard about that one, but what she meant was that if I spent all my time worrying about what other people thought of me, I would never be happy.

"I only saw Dr. Gustafson three or four times, but let me tell you it was nothing like how I thought therapy was going to be. There was none of that nodding and asking me how it all made me feel. Every time I would say why I thought I was unhappy she would challenge the belief that I was allowing to oppress me. It wasn't all these other people and circumstances making me unhappy, it was what I believed about myself, and about the world."

"What kinds of things did you believe?"

"That I would never be good enough unless I was perfect in every way; that I couldn't be happy if I weren't married with children; that I couldn't take care of myself; that I shouldn't wear things like red lipstick or silly shoes; or that I shouldn't paint my window sills bright green and my porch swing hot pink. I believed all sorts of silly things, and they formed a sort of moveable prison all around me. What Henrietta showed me was that all I had to do was identify the beliefs that were hurting me and trade them for beliefs that helped me."

"I like your shoes," Grace said. "I love your funny little house."

"And so do I," Kay said. "People still make rude comments about my weight, and they sometimes laugh at my shoes or my house, or tell me my bright lipstick is inappropriate for someone my age. Bad things will continue to happen. I just don't let that stop me from being happy. Being happy is a decision I make every day, and no one can talk me out of it without my permission."

"I'd like to be happy," Grace said.

"What would that look like?" Kay said. "What would that feel like?"

"What do you mean?"

"Imagine happiness," she said. "Where would you be and what would you be doing?"

She told Kay about her imaginary apartment with the reading chair and the striped kitten.

"That's as far as I got," Grace said. "I can't imagine anything more."

"Then there's some homework for you," Kay said, "The kind that will make a real difference in your life. Once you know what it is that will make you happy, every decision you make, every action you take, can be consciously made to bring you closer to it. Then you won't need to be invisible because you'll have confidence in what you're doing and where you're going. You'll be the captain of your own ship."

"My school counselor said I should only think positive thoughts and say positive things. She says if I do that nothing bad will happen to me."

"I know Beverly Pike, and she's an idiot," Kay said. "Ask her if babies in Third World countries get cholera and die because they don't have positive attitudes. She's the kind of imbecile who blames people with cancer for getting sick. There's a lady in my quilting club who's like that, always reminding us to look on the positive side, for goodness sake stay in denial at all costs; pretend everything's wonderful when it's horrible. I call that getting hit with the positive stick. Sometimes, my dear, life is awful, and it doesn't do any good to pretend otherwise."

"You should be a school counselor," Grace said. "You have good sense."

"I'm flattered you say so," Kay said. "Let's hope that means I'll be a good mayor."

"So everything you do as mayor will bring Rose Hill closer to being a happy place?" Grace asked.

"That's an excellent campaign slogan," Kay said. "I'll have to talk to my committee about using it."

Grace yawned deeply.

"Why don't you have a good long, hot soak in the tub?" Kay said. "Then go to bed. We'll talk again in the morning."

After her bath, Grace could barely stay awake long enough to put on her nightgown. She fell into bed with wet hair, but a warm feeling inside.

'Is this what happiness feels like?' was her last thought before she fell asleep.

Grace woke up to a knock on her bedroom window. It was Stacey. Grace pulled the sash up, and Stacey crawled in. Her huge handbag got caught against the frame, and she fell the rest of the way in.

"The police are looking for me," Stacey said. "If anybody asks, I was here with you all evening," Stacey said.

"Nobody's going to believe that," Grace said.

Stacey's clothes were disheveled, and she reeked of alcohol and cigarette smoke.

She tried to stand up, stumbled, and almost fell, laughing.

"I am so effed up," she said.

"Be quiet," Grace said. "You'll wake up Kay."

"Oh, good, a bed," Stacey said and fell into it.

"You can't stay here," Grace said.

"I can and I will, Cuz," Stacey said. "Aleesha's mother has locked her out."

"So where's Aleesha?"

"She's with Hugh and Lucas," she said. "They're going to blow up the newspaper office."

"They're what?!"

"They're at the funeral home making some kind of cocktails that are bombs or something."

"Right now?"

"Yeah," Stacey said. "I'm just so tired, Grace. I need to sleep."

Stacey passed out, and Grace couldn't wake her.

Grace got dressed. As she climbed out the window, she thought about her promise to Kay that she wouldn't do the very thing she was doing.

She ran across the lawn and climbed over the fence. She could see the light on in the funeral home, and Hugh's truck was parked in the lot. She ran over and hid behind it just as the back door of the funeral home opened.

"I wanna come with you," whined Aleesha.

"Go home, Aleesha," Lucas said. "You're underage, and the police are looking for you."

"Can't," she said. "Mom locked me out."

"Then stay here," Hugh said. "But you can't come with us."

"I hate you!" Aleesha screamed.

"Shut up!" Hugh hissed. "Do you want the cops to catch us?"

"Come right back," Aleesha said. "I don't want to stay in there with the dead people."

"We'll be right back," Lucas said, and then to Hugh, "I told you we should have ditched them."

Grace could hear their voices recede as they walked away. She crept around the truck and found Aleesha sitting on the back porch of the funeral home, drunkenly attempting to light a cigarette.

"Hey, Grace," she said when she saw her. "My mom locked me out of the house. Can you believe that? I could totally call social services and report her for that. She could go to jail."

"Where are Hugh and Lucas going?" Grace asked her.

"They're gonna blow up the newspaper office on account of something that newspaper guy is gonna put in the paper," she said. "He called their dad and Stacey's dad about it. I don't know what they did. Something bad, I guess."

"Can I borrow your phone?" Grace said.

"Sure, sure," Aleesha said. "Hey, Grace, can I stay at your house?"

"As soon as I get back," Grace said. "I'll take you to my house."

"You're a good friend," Aleesha said. "Stacey's still my best friend, but sometimes she can be such a beeyotch."

Grace took Stacey's phone and dialed 911.

"This is Grace Branduff," she said when the operator answered. "Hugh and Lucas Machalvie are going to set the *Sentinel* newspaper office on fire. Hurry."

Grace hoped that if the 911 operator didn't take her seriously, all the scanner grannies who were awake and listening would.

She crossed Rose Hill Avenue and ran down Peony Street to where the alley behind the Rose and Thorn began. She could hear the boys walking ahead of her, their shoes scuffling in the gravel. She stayed to the side, in the shadows, and hurried to catch up.

"... idiot tries to hurt our family," Hugh was saying. "We'll teach him a lesson."

"Shut up!" Lucas hissed. "You wanna get caught?"

"You shut up," Hugh said. "I'm tired of you tellin' me what to do."

"If you're so smart then you do it," Lucas said. "Here, take it."

"Which door is it?" Hugh said. "Is it this one?"

"Try the one with the sign that says '*Sentinel*' on it, genius," Lucas said. "I'll break the window, and then you light it. Throw it in as soon as you light it."

"Did you bring a lighter?" Hugh said.

"Yes, you idiot," Lucas said. "Now wait until I break the window."

Grace heard the glass break and knew she had only moments to stop them. She looked around but couldn't see anything with which to defend herself.

"Light it," Lucas said. "Light it and throw it."

"You light it," Hugh said. "I don't wanna blow up."

"Give it to me," Lucas said.

"Dammit, Lucas!" Hugh said. "You got it all over me. You wanna blow me up?"

"Stand over there, then," Lucas said. "Get out of the way! Gah, you are such an idiot."

"Light it then, if you're so brave," Hugh said. "You'll probably blow yourself up."

"I'll show you," Lucas said.

Grace could hear the click of the lighter.

Grace saw a flash of fire and Lucas screamed.

"Lucas!" Hugh yelled. "Are you alright, broh?"

"My hair!" Lucas cried. "I burned my friggin' hair!"

"Did you throw it?"

"No, I didn't throw it, you moron. I caught my friggin' hair on fire, and I dropped the lighter."

Grace could hear a window rattle open in an apartment high above the alley.

"Lucas, Hugh, you boys stop that right now," an older lady's voice said, "or I'm going to call your father."

Another window opened, and another older woman's voice could be heard.

"Letisha, is that you?"

"Yes, Edith," the Letisha said. "Hugh and Lucas Machalvie are down there trying to set the *Sentinel* on fire."

"You boys ought to be ashamed," Edith said. "I'm going to call your mother."

A siren started.

"Let's get out of here," Hugh said.

"What do I do with the bottle?" Lucas hissed, with panic in his voice.

"Drop it!" Hugh said. "Run!"

Grace could hear the glass break as the bottle hit the ground. She flattened herself against the wall and slid down until she was deep in the shadow of the closest dumpster. Hugh and Lucas ran past her back toward the other end of the alley behind the Rose and Thorn.

"Here comes Malcolm," Letisha said. "I called the fire station and told him the Machalvie boys were going to burn down the *Sentinel* office, so he better get over here."

"Those two boys have always been trouble," Edith said.

"Spoiled is what they are," Letisha said. "Peg and Stuart have no one to blame but themselves."

Grace saw the flashing lights of the fire truck come to a stop in front of the newspaper office. She ran toward it. The sirens stopped as she exited the alley and ran straight into the arms of the fire chief, Malcolm Behr.

"Whoa, there, little bit," he said. "What's going on?"

Grace told the fire chief what Hugh and Lucas had done. She led him back down the alley and showed him the broken window and the remains of the bottle. The formaldehyde label could still be seen on one of the bigger pieces, and the hand towel that had been stuffed in the narrow end was embroidered with the logo of Machalvie Funeral Home.

"Those two rocket scientists are lucky they didn't blow themselves up," the fire chief said. "Did you make the 911 call?"

Grace nodded.

"Malcolm," Edith said, from on high. "Is that Grace Branduff with you?"

"The poor thing," Letisha said. "Did you know Mamie Rodefeffer is her great-grandmother?"

"I heard that," Edith said. "I also heard Mamie beat the poor child to within an inch of her life."

"Ladies," Malcolm said. "Did you witness anything in this alley tonight?"

"We saw them," Letisha said. "You need us to come down to the station and pick them out of a line-up?"

"I'll tell Chief Gordon," he said. "If he needs you he'll call you."

"Did you know Scott proposed to Maggie in the bookstore and she finally accepted?" Edith said.

"No!" Latisha said. "I was in Pendleton all day at my sister's. Go inside and call me."

Grace could hear both windows close.

"You've had quite a night," Malcolm said. "You better come with me to the station. I'll call Scott to come and take your statement."

"What about Hugh and Lucas?" she asked. "They're getting away."

"We'll just look for the one with no eyebrows," Malcolm said. "He shouldn't be too hard to find."

296

When Deputy Frank brought Hugh and Lucas in, Lucas's singed eyebrows and hair, along with the strong smell of formaldehyde all over them both, made up the best circumstantial evidence the police could have asked for. They both wailed for their mother, their father, and a lawyer. When Stuart arrived, he pointed a finger at Grace.

"Think long and hard before you accuse my boys, Grace Branduff," he said. "You won't be doing Kay any favors."

"Don't you threaten her," Kay said as she came through the door behind him. "If you have a brain in your head, Stuart Machalvie, you will shut up until your lawyer gets here."

Kay hugged Grace.

"I'm so sorry," Grace cried. "I promised I wouldn't sneak out and I did. Please don't hate me."

"I couldn't hate you," Kay said. "Why in the world didn't you wake me up?"

"I didn't want you to get involved in a scandal," Grace said. "But I couldn't let them burn down the newspaper office."

"That's slander!" Stuart yelled. "I have witnesses!"

"Frank," Scott said. "Please escort Stuart to the holding cell where he can stay with the boys until their lawyer arrives."

"False arrest!" Stuart yelled. "I'll have your job for this!"

Scott rolled his eyes as Stuart left the room.

"Tell me what's happened," Kay said.

Grace looked at Scott.

"All of it, please," Kay said. "And now."

CHAPTER ELEVEN – SUNDAY

Maggie pulled up in front of her mother's house just as Bonnie was walking down the front steps. Bonnie pursed her lips and frowned at Maggie's Jeep, but she did that every Sunday. She also said the same thing she always said as she struggled to climb into the front passenger seat.

"Why can't you drive a normal car? I think you do this just to torture me."

"You didn't mind it when I drove you through a blizzard to the Megamart sale last Thanksgiving."

Bonnie pretended not to hear Maggie's response.

"Is Scott coming to Mass?"

"He was dressed and ready when I left the apartment," Maggie said. "Last Sunday he got as far as the front steps before he bailed out."

"I know he misses his mother," Bonnie said, "but life does go on."

"It reminds him of the funeral," Maggie said. "He's just not ready yet."

"Men are so weak," Bonnie said. "They're lucky we've let them run things as long as we have."

"He hasn't cleaned out her house yet," Maggie said. "I offered to do it for him, but he says he wants to do it himself."

"I'll put a bug in Delia's ear," Bonnie said. "She'll take care of it."

Maggie parked down the street from Sacred Heart Catholic Church. She could see Scott standing out in front, his hands in his pockets, staring up at the façade. Maggie ran around to the other side of the Jeep to help her mother out.

When Bonnie saw Scott, she said, "You leave this to me."

"Don't be mean to him," Maggie said.

298

"I won't hurt his precious feelings," Bonnie said. "You watch."

As they approached Scott, he turned, waved, and walked toward them. Just as he got within arm's reach, Bonnie stumbled, and he leaped forward to catch her, to keep her from falling.

"Here, Bonnie," he said. "Lean on me."

"Are you okay?" Maggie asked.

"I think I've turned my ankle," Bonnie said. "Scott, if you could just help me into the church I think if I sit awhile I'll be okay."

As Scott turned to allow her to lean on his other arm, Bonnie winked at Maggie.

Maggie shook her head and laughed to herself.

"Hey, Bonnie," Scott said. "Did Maggie tell you our big news?"

"Scott," Maggie said, with a warning note in her voice.

Bonnie stopped limping and turned to look at her daughter.

"What is it?" she said. "Is this about Grace?"

"Your darling daughter has finally consented to be my bride," Scott said.

Bonnie's face lit up as she grinned from ear to ear. Then she smacked Scott on the arm and pinched him.

"Ow!" he said. "She pinches even harder than you do."

"That's where I learned it," Maggie said.

"It's about time," Bonnie said to her daughter.

"So glad you're happy," Maggie said in exactly the same cross tone.

Bonnie had completely forgotten her fake limp as she pulled on Scott's arm.

"Hurry," she said. "Let's get Father Stephen to publish the banns before she changes her fool mind."

Grace heard Kay leave for church; she was relieved Kay didn't ask her to go. As soon as the front door closed, Grace got out of bed and took a shower. She was in her room getting dressed when she heard a knock on the front door. Her hair was hanging in wet strings down her back when she answered the door wearing a Little Bear Books sweatshirt Maggie had given her, new jeans from Claire, and new tennis shoes from Kay.

The woman standing on Kay's porch was dressed in a dark suit and low heels. Her dark hair was pulled back in a low, tight bun.

"Hi," she said. "I'm sorry to bother you so early, but I'm on my way to church and thought I'd just stop by. I'd like to speak to Grace Branduff. Is she at home?"

"I'm Grace," Grace said.

The woman raised her eyebrows in surprise.

"There must be some mistake," she said. "The young woman I'm looking for is sixteen years old."

"That's me," Grace said.

"Oh my," the woman said, touching her hand to her chest. "I can't tell you how much it relieves my mind to meet you. I'm Jane Johnson, Elvis's mother. When he told me your age, I was picturing someone much more, well, older looking."

"I called pretty late last night," Grace said. "Sorry about that."

"No problem," Jane said. "Elvis stays up late anyway."

Grace didn't know what to say next, so she said nothing.

"Can I talk to you for a minute?" Ms. Johnson said.

Grace walked outside onto the porch, sat on the porch swing, and Ms. Johnson joined her there.

"I've done my best not to be one of those helicopter mothers," she said, "but I also think it's wise to honor the maternal instinct; I mean, it's there for a reason, right? At first, I was just so glad to know Elvis had a friend to talk to, you know? Not many children his age are anywhere near mature enough to relate to him, and he's so small. Last night he told me he had invited you to be his date for senior prom and, well, I just thought I better meet you. Then if I felt it was at all inappropriate, I could put a stop to it. I hope you're not offended."

"I understand," Grace said. "You're a good mother. I like talking to Elvis; he's been helping me figure out some really hard stuff that's going on in my life. He's so smart."

"The thing is it's easy to forget he's only twelve," Ms. Johnson said. "I find myself doing it all the time, and then something like this happens ..."

"Would you like me to stop calling him?"

"No. I don't know. Maybe," she said. "I think he has a crush on you and I just don't want him to get hurt."

"I don't think of him as a boyfriend," Grace said. "That would be creepy."

"I'm glad to hear that," Ms. Johnson said. "I just don't know if this prom thing is a good idea."

"I'm not excited about going to prom," Grace said, "but I was honored he asked me. I wouldn't let anything happen to him."

"It's so hard to know what to do," Ms. Johnson said. "I went to prom when I was in high school, and if this is going to be anything like mine was, a twelve-year-old boy has no business being there. But if I tell him no, it's like I'm cheating him out of that prom experience. His life has already been so far from normal, you know?"

"Have you told him what you're worried about?"

"We talk about everything," Ms. Johnson said. "He insists he can handle this but what empirical evidence does he have on which to base his assertion? I say none. He gave me the statistics: for instance, the number of teenagers involved in traffic accidents on prom night in Pine County over the past twenty years; he says if I drive him there and pick him up he won't be in any danger."

"But you're worried about his feelings getting hurt," Grace said.

"Exactly," Ms. Johnson said, pointing at Grace. "Exactly."

They sat in silent contemplation for a few moments.

"Well, it was nice meeting you," Ms. Johnson said and stood up.

She stuck out her hand, and Grace shook it.

"It was nice meeting you, too," Grace said. "Let me know what you want me to do."

"You seem like a sensible person, Grace Branduff," Ms. Johnson said. "I'm so relieved, you just don't know. I lay awake last night imagining the worst. I'm glad I came."

Grace pictured a few of her contemporaries and could imagine as well. Ms. Johnson waved before she drove away.

Grace picked up the rolled-up copy of the *Rose Hill Sentinel* that Tommy had left on the porch early that morning, took it back inside and dropped it on the kitchen counter. As she dried her hair, the warm air of the blow dryer felt so good she blew some air up her shirt. No matter how accessible heat and hot water were, Grace was sure she would never take either for granted. The combination of the warmth and Kay's cheerful house, filled with bright morning sunlight, made Grace feel something she rarely did: hopeful.

She looked in the mirror and said, "Happy birthday."

Tommy was eating cereal at the breakfast bar in Ed's house. He still had on his pajamas but didn't seem embarrassed about it.

"Where's Ed?" Grace asked.

"His big story on the Rodefeffers and the mayor came out today," Tommy said. "He was up all night laying it out, and the printer had to do a rush job early this morning. He's at the office meeting with somebody from the governor's office."

Tommy offered Grace a copy of the newspaper. She took it in the living room and spread it out on the coffee table. Tommy picked up his cereal bowl and joined her.

"Mayor's special interest schemes revealed," was the headline. The story made up the whole front page and was continued inside. There were pictures of the documents Grace had confiscated as well as photos of the mayor, Knox, and Trick Rodefeffer. Ed had also illustrated the articles with photos of the wind farm turbines, the proposed site of Eldridge Point, and a photo of Congressman Green with all three men at the ribbon cutting for the new condo development. The article stated that when contacted for a comment late last night all three men denied any wrongdoing and Congressman Green's office stated that they would look into it.

The phone rang until the voicemail picked up.

"The governor's office called first," Tommy said. "Then the county prosecutor and the FBI called. Our phone's been real busy. He told me to quit answering it."

"It says the source was someone close to the alleged conspirators," Grace said.

"Well, you were under the pool table when they were standing around talking about it," Tommy said. "You don't get much closer than that."

"Do you think they'll figure out it was me?"

"Naw," Tommy said. "They didn't even know you were there."

"Can the FBI make Ed tell it was me?" Grace said.

"They could haul him into court and try to make him," Tommy said. "But Ed would go to jail before he'd reveal a source. He's, like, super ethical that way."

"I don't want Ed to go to jail," Grace said.

"Don't worry," Tommy said. "The only people going to jail over this are Stuart, Trick, and Knox; maybe even Congressman Green."

303

"I guess I didn't think about what would happen," Grace said. "I feel kind of bad now."

"Don't," Tommy said. "You did the right thing. Otherwise, the bad guys would get away with everything. You don't want that."

Grace was thinking about Kay, that she would be blindsided by the news at church this morning.

"I gotta go," she said.

"Hold up," Tommy said. "Wait for me to get dressed."

When Tommy and Grace arrived back at Kay's house, she was sitting in the living room reading the paper. Her face was pale.

"Are you okay?" Grace asked her.

"It's just so overwhelming to see it in black and white," Kay said. "They will all think I did this, you know."

"Oh, no," Grace said. "I didn't think of that."

"I probably had access to all these documents at one time or another," she said. "It would have been so easy for me to make copies."

"What will they do to you?" Tommy said.

"Nothing that could be traced back to them," Kay said.

"There's a bunch of people wanting to talk to Ed," Tommy said. "They'll probably want to talk to you, too."

"Oh dear," Kay said. "I wonder if I should say anything."

"Call Sean," Grace said. "He'll know what to do."

After Kay called Sean, she went through the newspaper article again, reading parts of it out loud.

"I knew about some of this," Kay said. "They might claim I was part of the conspiracy."

"But could they prove it?" Tommy said.

"Sean told me not to answer anyone's questions until he gets here," she replied. "I guess he was coming over anyway for Mother's Day lunch."

"I forgot all about that," Grace said. "I'm supposed to be helping Maggie, Hannah, and Claire."

"I'll go with you," Tommy said.

"You all go on," Kay said. "Have a fun time."

The look on Kay's face was two parts worried and one part sad.

As they ran down the sidewalk, Grace said, "I feel bad about leaving her here by herself."

Tommy said, "We could ask Maggie to invite her. She probably doesn't have any plans today."

"I should have done something for her," Grace said. "She may not be my mother, but she's my foster mother."

"We still have to go water the plants in the greenhouse," he said. "We can get her some flowers then."

"I forgot about that, too," Grace said. "Life's gotten so complicated."

Down at the greenhouse, after they watered everything, Grace and Tommy loaded up the red wagon with vases full of flowers and pulled it up Pine Mountain Road to Fitzpatrick's Bakery. Inside, Maggie, Hannah, and Claire were spreading white tablecloths over a line of small tables pushed together.

"Beautiful!" Claire said when she saw the flowers.

"Sammy will be so glad to see you," Hannah said. "He asks me every day when Grace is coming out to the farm to play. Sam's going to bring him down later. He was up late last night scaring the bejeezus out of some teenagers who were looking for the infamous pot field we're supposed to have on our farm."

"I heard Ava's house got toilet-papered last night," Claire said to Hannah. "You know anything about that?"

"I had forgotten how fun that is," Hannah said. "We should really do that more often."

"I'll start a list," Maggie said. "I think Mamie's next."

"You helped her?" Claire asked Maggie.

"I may have supplied the rolls, and I may have thrown one or two," Maggie said, "but I'm blaming it all on Hannah if Scott asks me about it."

"Why didn't you call me?" Claire asked. "I feel left out."

"You didn't want to have anything to do with our plans for Ava, remember?" Hannah said. "'Leave me out of it,' you said."

"How are you?" Maggie asked Grace.

"I'm okay," Grace said. "Would it be alright with you if I invite Kay?"

"Of course," Maggie said. "We'd love to have her here."

After asking Bonnie for permission, she used the bakery phone to call and invite Kay.

"I'm meeting with Sean right now," Kay said. "I'm going to have a press conference in front of my house at noon."

"Are you scared?" Grace asked her.

"Terrified," Kay said.

"You'll do great," Grace said.

"I appreciate you thinking of me," Kay said. "Thank Maggie for me."

Tommy and Grace placed a vase of flowers in the middle of every small table and put the leftover vases on the counter.

Ava Fitzpatrick arrived with Charlotte, plus her red-headed little brothers: Timmy, who was nine, and Little Fitz, who was six. Little Fitz ran to Grace and hugged her.

"Why don't you come over anymore?" he said. "Are you mad at us?"

"No, silly," Grace said. "I've just been real busy."

Charlotte was focused on her cell phone, and Timmy ran off to hang out with Tommy. Little Fitz soon followed.

"Hello, Miss Grace," Ava said, with a chilly smile. "I didn't know you'd be joining us today. I thought this was going to be just for the family."

Grace immediately felt that she was not welcome, that she was a charity case on be-nice-to-orphans' day. No one else seemed to have heard what Ava said; they were too busy arranging the huge feast that was to be served. Grace continued laying out the silverware and napkins, feeling sorry for herself.

"It was a huge mess," she heard Ava tell Claire, who somehow kept a straight face. "Luckily a few of the men in my neighborhood offered to clean it up. I wish parents would keep better track of their children and what they get up to."

Hannah and Maggie were laughing behind Ava's back and making faces at Claire, who ignored them.

Delia arrived with more baskets of food covered with dish towels, and Bonnie rushed to help her through the door. Afterward, Bonnie clapped her hands and said, "May I have your attention, please."

"Mom," Maggie said.

"You shush," Bonnie said. "It gives me great pleasure to announce that after years of stringing the poor little fella along, my stubborn, ignorant daughter Mary Margaret has finally agreed to marry Scott Gordon."

There was applause and cheering while Maggie's face turned bright red.

"I already knew," Hannah told Grace. "She told me first."

Bonnie received as many if not more congratulations than Maggie.

"When will the wedding be?" Delia asked.

"The sooner, the better," Bonnie said.

"We haven't decided," Maggie said.

Grace waited until everyone else had congratulated Maggie before she approached her.

"I bet he's happy," Grace said.

"He is," Maggie said. "I don't know why I waited so long."

"He loves you so much," Grace said. "That must be nice."

"It is," Maggie said. "I can hardly stand it."

"You are so funny," Grace said.

"She's contrary," Bonnie said. "She doesn't deserve him."

"Thanks, Mom," Maggie said.

"Miss Grace," Bonnie said. "You are now an honorary member of this family. You make sure to sit by me; I'll see that you get enough to eat."

Delia hugged Grace and looked at the table settings Grace had already placed.

"Not like that, honey," Delia said and moved the fork to the opposite side of the plate.

Grace went back and fixed all the other place settings she had done incorrectly. She felt like such a loser; she didn't even know how to set the table properly. Her face burned with embarrassment. She glanced up and saw Ava looking at her with one eyebrow raised and an expression of contempt on her face. She quickly changed it to a bright, fake smile, but Grace looked away.

Maggie's brother, Patrick, and Hannah's father, Curtis, helped Maggie's father in through the front entrance; he was seated in a wheelchair. He was pale and mopping sweat from his brow with a handkerchief even though it was chilly outside. Grace watched Patrick pour some coffee into a mug and then spike it with whiskey from a flask before taking it to his father, who looked up at his son in gratitude as he grasped the mug with both hands. He took a big drink and seemed to relax.

Maggie's father's wheelchair was at the end of the table, and when Grace placed the silverware before him, he leaned back and looked at her with mock surprise. There was kind humor in his face that extended to his sad eyes.

"And who are you?" he asked her. "You're not a Fitzpatrick, are you?"

Grace smiled and shook her head.

"I thought maybe I lost track of one," he said. "They're all the time springing new ones on me when I least expect it."

Maggie introduced Grace to her father, and he shook her hand. His hand was trembling and clammy. He said Grace should call him "Fitz."

"I knew your grandfather," Fitz said. "His father had a horse that used to graze in the field across from your house. Every evening after supper that old horse would come over to our house and whinny at the back gate until my mother took it something to eat. She'd give him a carrot or a sugar cube or some cornbread, and then he'd go on back home. It was the darndest thing."

Grace had never heard this story; had never heard any stories about her great-grandparents. She wished he'd tell her more, but she was too shy to ask.

"The Rodefeffers built your house," Fitz said. "When they moved up to Morning Glory Circle, Gustav sold the house to his plant manager, your great-grandfather. Your great-grandparents lived there until their youngest son Edgar died; his mother couldn't bear to live there anymore afterward, so they moved to a smaller house on Lotus Avenue. The big house sat empty then until your grandfather married your grandmother."

"Edgar?" Grace said. "Grandpa's little brother was named Edgar?"

"Edgar Branduff," Fitz said. "He was the apple of his mother's eye. My mother said Jacob's face was always puckered up like a hen's butt, but little Edgar was as cute as a speckled pup."

"How did he die?"

"Scarlet Fever, I believe," Fitz said. "Or maybe it was influenza."

Grace thought of her great-grandmother, having to raise her grandfather, who wasn't her son and then losing her own son so young. She wondered if her great-grandmother Branduff ever loved her grandfather, even though he was adopted. Grace thought about Edgar the ghost. He disappeared when Grandpa yelled or when visitors came. It was no wonder he was shy, and she never felt afraid of him. He was just a little boy; a little boy who missed his mother.

Ed came in through the front door of the bakery and said, "Turn on the TV; Kay's having a press conference."

Patrick turned on the small, old-fashioned box TV that sat on the side counter, and turned it so everyone could see. They all gathered to watch, except Charlotte, who was sulking and texting on her phone.

Kay had her chin up and a determined look on her face. Dressed in the suit she wore to church, she was standing on her front porch with the "Spring has Sprung" flag flapping in the wind next to her. Sean was also there, standing behind her, near the front door. He wore a business suit and looked as handsome as usual. When Kay spoke, her voice was strong and confident.

"Thank you for coming," she said. "Just like all of you, I read the *Rose Hill Sentinel* this morning with great interest and great surprise. I was not the source for this information nor will I speculate on who was. I also cannot comment on the veracity of what was reported except to say that I have known Ed Harrison, the editor of the *Rose Hill Sentinel*, for his entire life, and I have never once doubted his integrity or honesty.

"I will cooperate in any investigation that may follow these allegations, and in response to every question I am asked by the proper authorities, I will tell the truth, no matter what the consequences to those involved.

"As you all know, I am running for mayor of Rose Hill. Those of you who know me well know that I will not tolerate the kind of shenanigans that are outlined in today's paper. I will not condone this kind of behavior, participate in it, nor turn a blind eye just because it's convenient or politically advantageous.

"In every moment we have the opportunity to do the right thing. Even if in the past we've done the easy thing or have gone along just to get along. Right now the people of Rose Hill have the opportunity to make a change and do things differently. We may not succeed, but at least we will know in our hearts that we did what we thought was right when it was important."

Reporters erupted, and Sean stepped forward to say they were not going to answer any questions that might impede the subsequent investigation. Bonnie turned off the television, and everyone in the bakery started talking.

Grace went to Ed.

"Is Kay going to get in trouble?" she asked him.

"No," he said, shaking his head. "They'll give her immunity to get her testimony and use what she gives them to indict the bunch of them. Don't you worry about Kay; she'll be just fine. This is going to be just the housecleaning Rose Hill needs before Kay becomes mayor."

"Do you think anyone would be mad if I left?" Grace said.

"No," Ed said. "You go on home."

Grace smiled, thinking about having a real home to go to.

She went to Maggie and said, "I feel like I want to be home with Kay; do you mind?"

"No, of course not," Maggie said. "You know, Grace, Scott and I just want you to be safe and happy. We're okay with you choosing Kay."

"You guys would be great parents," Grace said, "but maybe you should practice being married awhile first."

Maggie laughed and said, "No doubt."

"I can tell your mom loves you," Grace said, "even if she doesn't say it."

"I know," Maggie said. "We're just both too stubborn to be nice to each other."

"I never knew what having a good mother was like," Grace said. "My mother didn't know how to love anybody.

311

My grandmother loved me, but she was too afraid of my grandfather to stand up for me. I think a good mother feels love for you, but will also do anything to help you, to protect you, to make sure you're safe; even if she has to go to jail to do it."

Maggie and Grace both looked over at Tommy, who was entertaining Timmy and Little Fitz.

"I'm sorry you didn't have that," Maggie said.

"I'm luckier than a lot of people," Grace said. "I have several moms now. I went from having nobody to having all of you."

Maggie's eyes filled with tears as Grace hugged her, long and hard.

"Happy Mother's Day, Maggie," she said. "I love you guys."

"The urge to pinch you is so strong," Maggie said. "You just don't know."

"I know," Grace said and held out her arm. "I don't mind."

Maggie pinched her, but just lightly.

As Grace left the Rose and Thorn, she ran into Sean outside on the sidewalk.

"Hey, Grace Branduff," he said. "How's my favorite client?"

"I saw you on TV," Grace said. "You looked good."

"That's half the battle," Sean said. "I can speak gibberish but if I look good then maybe they won't pick apart what I say."

"You think Kay's going to be all right?"

"She'll be fine," Sean said. "She's an intelligent woman who isn't afraid to stand up for what's right. Plus she has a great attorney."

"Do you think I'll be able to stay with her?"

"After what Mamie did, and with Knox and Trick in so much trouble, I don't think any court in this county would award them custody."

"When will we know?"

"I filed for an emergency custody hearing to be held on Tuesday," he said. "Judge Feinman will be on the bench, so what's that suggest to you?"

"A box from the bakery will be delivered to his house on Monday night," Grace said.

"You're one smart cookie," Sean said. "You already understand how things get done in this town. Later today I'd like to sit down with you and draw up a will that cuts out those bloodthirsty Rodefeffers. We also need to talk about what's in your trust. After lunch be alright?"

"I'll be at home," Grace said. "At Kay's."

As Grace walked up to Rose Hill Avenue, she saw a Greyhound bus pulling out of the Dairy Chef parking lot. The lone passenger who had disembarked looked familiar to her. She was petite, with long blonde hair pulled back into a ponytail. She had on a jean jacket and carried a backpack. Grace crossed the street in the middle of the block to get a closer look.

"Grace?" the woman said, her face breaking into a huge smile punctuated by dimples.

"Hey!" Grace said, now realizing that this was Tommy's mother. She hadn't seen her in three years, but she hadn't changed much. Her skin was pale, her hair a darker blonde, and there were a few more lines under her green eyes, but she was still very pretty.

Tommy's mother gripped Grace in a tight hug and squeezed her so hard it took Grace's breath away.

"Oh, Grace," his mother said. "It's so good to see you, baby girl. How in the world have you been?"

"I'm fine. Tommy's going to be so excited to see you," Grace said. "Melissa? Is that right?"

"That's right," his mother said, as a worried frown passed over her face like the shadow from a cloud. It was there and gone in an instant.

Melissa held Grace out to look at her.

"You're so grown up," she said. "I hardly recognized you. Where's Tommy?"

"They're at the bakery," Grace said, "for Mother's Day dinner."

"They moved that dinner down there from the Thorn so I could come," Melissa said. "While I'm on probation I can't go into bars let alone work in one. Bonnie offered me a full-time job at the bakery and Patrick's going to move home so I can have my trailer back."

"So they knew you were coming today?"

"Patrick knows," Melissa said. "It's gonna be a big surprise to everyone else. A good one, I hope."

"C'mon," Grace said. "I want to be there."

Melissa and Grace walked back to the bakery together.

"I heard your grandpa died," Melissa said. "I was so sorry to hear about that."

"He wasn't very nice to me," Grace said, "but I still miss him."

"Course you do," Melissa said. "I had a rotten husband once, but I was sorry when he died. You just get used to people."

Just before they reached the bakery, Melissa paused and took a deep breath.

"It'll be great," Grace told her. "Tommy loves you."

Melissa smiled and squeezed Grace's hand.

"I hope everyone else is as nice as you," she said.

When Melissa opened the door to the bakery, there was a brief silence.

Then Bonnie cried out, "Oh my Lord, Patrick, look. Our girl's come home."

Tommy reached her first.

"Mom," he said.

"Oh, honey," Melissa said. "Thank you."

Tears fell from both of their eyes as they embraced.

Patrick took them both in his arms and squeezed them until Tommy protested.

Grace looked for Ed and saw that he was smiling, but his eyes were sad. He didn't come forward along with everyone else; he sat back down and watched.

Grace happened to look at Ava and was startled by the hatred she saw on the woman's face as she watched Patrick embrace Tommy and his mother. Ava said something to Charlotte, who rolled her eyes and went back to her phone.

With a determined look on her face, Ava got up and started walking toward the hugging trio. She smoothed her skirt, patted her hair, and arranged a bright smile on her face, but her eyes were full of venom.

Grace was afraid of what Ava was going to do. Something mean. Something that looked nice to everyone else but that Melissa would know meant Ava hated her and was going to make things hard for her. Almost without realizing she was doing it, Grace started forward to intercept her and then noticed Claire's mother Delia was doing the same thing. Delia blocked Ava's path and would not move, even when Ava gave her an irritated look.

"Stop it," Delia said to Ava, in a voice so low that Grace only just caught what she said. "Leave them be."

Ava smiled a tight smile at Delia and then backed away, slightly bowing to the older woman as she did so. Delia turned back toward Grace and took a deep breath that had a "whew" at the end.

Delia winked at Grace, and then said, "Not on my watch."

Everyone gathered around Melissa and Tommy, held on either side of Patrick by his strong arms. Patrick looked so happy.

"Let's eat!" he said.

As Grace passed Tommy on her way out, she grabbed his hand and squeezed it.

"Congratulations," she said.

"I'll call you later," Tommy said.

When Grace got home, Kay was lounging in her chubby armchair, her stocking-clad feet propped up on the coffee table. The newspaper was spread out around her, and she was sipping her tea.

"Hey, kiddo!" she said. "What are you doing here? I thought you were celebrating Mother's Day with the Fitzpatricks."

"I decided I'd rather celebrate it at home, with you," Grace said.

"Not much to celebrate with," Kay said. "There's some leftover vegetable soup in there, but I really need to go to the grocery."

"You stay there," Grace said, as Kay started to get up. "I'll heat it up and call you when it's ready."

"Thank you, Grace," Kay said. "I'll take you up on that because I am plum tuckered out. I will probably be worthless the rest of the day."

There was a knock on the door, and Grace said, "I'll get it. You stay put."

It was Matt Delvecchio, and he was grinning from ear to ear.

"Hi, Matt," Grace said.

"Happy Birthday, Gracie," he said and gestured behind him.

There, parked on the walk leading up to Kay's house was a brand new bright red bicycle with a white and red basket attached to the handlebars.

Grace gasped.

"I can't accept that," she said, although she sure wanted to.

"You need something reliable to ride to work every day, don't you?" Matt said. "That old bike of yours is so worn out it's not worth fixing up. This way you'll have no excuse not to be on time. Think of this as my investment in your future as an IGA employee."

Grace hugged Matt as Kay came to the doorway to see what was going on. She and Matt greeted each other and chatted as Grace tried out the bicycle, riding it up and down the short block in front of the house.

"I love it," she called out. "Kay, look at me!"

"I am looking," Kay said. "You look great."

"I'll take it out for a longer ride after lunch," she said as she came to a stop on the walkway to the front porch. "When can I start at the store?"

"As soon as you want," Matt said. "I mean, as soon as Kay, here, says you can."

"As long as you remember she's going to college in a couple of years," Kay said. "If I have anything to do with it, that is."

"I will gladly work around her school schedule," Matt said.

"I feel awful," Kay said to Grace. "I completely forgot about your birthday."

"Don't worry," Grace said. "This has already been the best birthday I've ever had."

Grace hugged Kay and then Matt and then Kay again. She was crying, but it was just that her heart felt so full there was nowhere for all her feelings to go except out of her eyes as tears.

A little later, seated in the cheerful red booth in the kitchen, Kay and Grace ate hot vegetable soup with crackers crumbled up in it.

"This is even better the second day," Kay said.

"I saw your press conference," Grace said.

"What'd you think?"

"I thought you did a great job," Grace said. "I was proud of you."

"Well, thanks, Grace," Kay said. "It's probably going to get pretty hairy around here for a while. Are you up to it?"

"A smart lady once told me that life is tough and we have to watch out for each other," Grace said. "We're in this together."

"Happy Birthday and Mother's Day," Kay said and clinked Grace's mug with her own. "And thank you, Grace, for making it real."

Scott let himself into his mother's house and closed the door behind him. He'd been putting this off for weeks, but it had to be done. Each time he came, he brought something he needed to complete the job: boxes, packing tape, garbage bags, and black markers. Each time he got as far as the kitchen and then turned around and left.

In the kitchen, there was a large stack of broken down boxes from Maggie's store and a pile of newspapers supplied by Ed. He looked beyond the kitchen, down the hall, to the door to his mom's bedroom, and felt that familiar tightness in his chest, the closing of his throat. He turned to go, feeling not so much defeated as panicked to get away from these feelings. As he reached the front door, the doorbell rang.

He opened it to find Claire, her mother, Delia, and Hannah. Claire carried a bucket with cleaning supplies in it, Delia carried a package of garbage bags, a mop, and a broom, and Hannah carried a six-pack of beer and a bag of chips.

"What are you doing here?" he said.

"We're just going door to door, talking to folks about Jesus," Hannah said. "Do you want a beer?"

"We're here to help," Delia said.

"If you don't mind," Claire said.

"Did you follow me here?" he asked as they filed in.

"We had Dot call us when she saw you arrive," Delia said, pointing across the street to the neighbor who was waving from her front porch.

"I can't make an unsupervised move in this town, can I?" Scott said, waving back.

"No one can," Claire said. "It's easier just to give in to it."

"Are those for me?" he asked Hannah as she popped open a beer and opened the bag of chips.

"Are you kidding?" Hannah said. "This is my snack; go get your own."

He gratefully accepted the beer she offered and sat down at the kitchen table with her.

"You don't have to stay," Delia said as she sat down on the other side of him.

"I can't explain it," he said. "I just can't go down that hall."

"You don't have to explain," Claire said. "We understand."

"Do you want all her clothing to go to the church?" Delia asked.

Scott started to respond, but his throat closed up and his eyes filled with tears.

"This is your area of expertise," Hannah said to Delia. "I just apply food and alcohol."

Hannah patted his hand while Delia put an arm around him.

"It would really help me," Delia said, "if you would go visit with Ian while we do this. He gets so lonely and restless on his own."

Scott nodded and wiped his eyes. He didn't look at anyone as he stood and turned to go. He started to say, 'Thank you,' but found he couldn't, so he squeezed Delia's hand instead. Delia followed him outside onto the front porch.

"Your mother was so proud of you," she said. "You were always so good to her."

Scott nodded and wiped his eyes, but the tears kept falling.

"Ah, honey, come here," Delia said and embraced him. "You did everything you could to help your mother. It was not your fault she died. It just happened. Sometimes these things just happen."

"I should have made her go to the doctor earlier."

"Now you know you couldn't make your mother do a single thing she didn't want to do, don't you?" Delia said. "Some people are just stubborn that way."

"I guess not," Scott said. "I just wish I'd known how bad it was."

"There was no way to know," Delia said. "Now, come on, listen to me. You have got to let it go now. Let your mother rest in peace so you can get on with your life. You're getting married to the woman you love. How long have you been working on that project? Feels like forever to me."

"Me too," he said with a slight smile.

"That mother-in-law-to-be of yours is as prickly as a porcupine, so you just consider me your mother-in-law by proxy. Whenever you get to feeling like you need someone to fuss over you, you just come down to my house, okay?"

"Okay," Scott said.

"You've been like a son to Ian, and it helps me so much that you take him to breakfast every morning," she said. "Let us help you through this. We can't make the pain go away, but we can support you while you go through it."

Scott nodded.

"Alright," Delia said. "Now, you go on down to the house and watch golf with Ian. Then I'll come home in a little bit and make you and Maggie some dinner."

"Thanks, Delia," Scott said. "You did make me feel better."

"That's what we mothers do," Delia said. "It's all part of the service."

As he left the porch, Scott waved at Dot, who lived across the street. She was slowly walking down her front stairs, holding her toddler grandson in one arm and his older sister by her hand. As Scott walked down the street past Sacred Heart Catholic Church, he waved at Sister Mary Margrethe, who was supervising a group of parishioners who were painting the food-bank building. Just ahead, he could see Kay sitting on her front porch steps, watching Grace ride her new bike up and down the block. It seemed as if everywhere he looked there were mothers, those with children and those without, helping others do the right thing, do their best, be kinder, and feel better.

Acknowledgments

This book is about mothers: the ones who give birth to us, but also the people who show up right when we need them and selflessly give of themselves in order to help us.

I have warm and cozy childhood memories of my Mamaw Hattie, mother of nine and grandmother of twenty-five, who fed me hot, sweet tea and gingerbread while we watched her "stories" after school.

My mother, Betsy, has always taken great care of me, even when a younger, more reckless version of myself didn't always appreciate her efforts. For the past several years we were partners in taking care of my father, and for the close friendship we developed as a result, I will always be grateful.

My father was a good person who took care of a lot of families in addition to his own. He loved us, and he knew how much we all loved him.

I am thankful for my sisters Terry Hutchison and Kate McComas, niece Ella Curry, and their families, who cared deeply, generously, and all the way through until the end.

Terry Hutchison and Betsy Grandstaff were also my faithful first readers; Terry especially helped me with the ending of the book. Joan Turner and John Gillispie are good friends and ace proofreaders, and for their assistance, I am deeply grateful.

Thank you to Tamarack: The Best of West Virginia, for selling my paper books in your beautiful building.

And last, but not least, I want to thank the people who buy and read my books. Thank you so much.

If you liked this book, please leave a review on Amazon.com (Thank you!)

For more information go to RoseHillMysteries.com

Made in the USA
San Bernardino, CA
23 March 2019